Scorched

Scorched

The Anderson Brothers Series
The Beginning

MARIE LONG

Scorched

CHAPTER 1

Tacoma, Washington, 1991

CLENCHING THE STEERING WHEEL, I GIVE A SIDELONG LOOK out the driver's-side window at the white, tricked-out '87 CR-X beside me. I don't need to see through its dark-tinted window to know that the driver is Jacob Sutherland, leader of a small crew from Tacoma's Southside called 'the Ninez'— and my nemesis. I thought for sure I'd have to go up against one of their Integras, or maybe a turbocharged RX-7, or that they'd be desperate enough to race one of their sport bikes. Nope. This is something new, and by the looks of it, something serious.

I need to be on my game. I could lose my car tonight.

My crewmate and best friend, Luke Sirocco, walks out in his brown bomber jacket—beer bottle in one hand, powered-off flashlight in the other—and stands on the small concrete barrier between our cars. He flips his baseball cap backwards, points the flashlight at us and gives us both a lopsided smile.

Our engines roar in anticipation of breaking the peaceful September night with our war-drum pipes and tearing up the cracked asphalt of this deserted industrial road with fearsome horsepower. My heart leaps into my throat, sending a nervous twitch to my foot. I tap the gas pedal and give the engine another rev. For as long as I've been at this street racing game, I should be used to this feeling. But the roar of motors and sharp odor of burning gasoline is always like a first high—fear and exhilaration all in one package. Euphoric. Besides, this race is about more than just my gearhead fix. The Ninez thought they could take my car and run us out of our own turf. I had raced Sasha, my '87 300ZX Turbo, against the Ninez before, but this wasn't the Sasha they knew. This is a new and improved monster, and they were about to feel the wrath of her brand-new, five-hundred-horsepower, nitrous-infused, turbo system that took me hours of blood, sweat, and tears to install and dial in for just this moment.

The sound of the crowd—consisting of both of our crews and some nosy teenagers—egging us on becomes distant in my mind. The only thing I can hear at this point is Sasha's low rumbling engine as I keep my eyes on Luke like a hawk.

The flashlight powers on. *Ready.*

I give Sasha's engine another rev.

The flashlight powers on again.

My foot instinctively floors the pedal before my brain has even registered Luke's signal. My tires squeal, churning up white smoke that briefly cuts off my view of the spectators gathered at the starting line. Sasha surges forward with the initial blast of fuel, red-lining through second gear. Adrenaline rushes through my brain, making me feel dizzy and weightless in the moment, sending a brief numbing sensation that spreads through my limbs. Lost in this racing trance, I tighten my death-grip around the cue-ball shifter and crank it to the next gear, and the next... In seconds I have Sasha clawing for her top speed. The world passes by in a blur of streaked lights, and the only focal point is what's left of the 1,320-foot stretch of industrial road before me. I flick my gaze to the rear-view mirror at Jacob behind me, then slightly let off the gas for a moment to give Sasha a chance to recover before unleashing her final trick.

Damn, this is gonna be easier than I thought.

Finish line in sight, I flip a switch beneath the steering wheel, activating the nitrous, and giving Sasha an extra burst of speed. My foot slams the gas as I milk every last bit of energy she's got.

Time to put that bastard in his place...

I'm less than a hundred feet away when a white streak zooms past me as if I'm standing still. Smoke covers my windshield, clouding my vision and sending the pungent odor of exhaust and burned rubber filtering through Sasha's open-air vents. The CR-X crosses the finish line and slows to a stop. Clayton, one of my crewmates who had been waiting at the finish line, waves his arm to the crowd at the starting line, signaling that the race is over. His face is pale, and I can read exactly what he's thinking as I lay on the brakes. I'm thinking the same thing. *What the hell just happened? How did Jacob's shitty CR-X just completely overpower Sasha?*

I pull up next to the CR-X as two of Jacob's guys who had also been waiting at the finish line make their way over. Bryce McConnell—a tall, burly dude who looks like he lives in the gym—and Preston Hartsford—a skinny, preppy guy with a bright-green beeper clipped to the side pocket of his jeans, gather and give each other high-fives in victory.

While their little celebration carries on, Clayton comes up to my car and taps on the driver's-side window.

Rather than rolling down the window, I fling the door open, almost hitting him in the head. Seething, I hop out of the car and glare at Bryce and Preston still standing around the white sports car.

I feel Clayton's hand on my shoulder. "Hey, Adam…"

I shrug his hand off violently and storm over to the two men. In the distance, I can hear the squealing of tires and revved engines as the rest of the crowd, including mine and Jacob's crews, roar up in their cars and on motorcycles.

I can't believe it's actually happening. After all these years—victory after victory—I have to give up Sasha to that prick, Jacob. But a deal is a deal. Time to surrender with the last bit of dignity I have left. I just wish it didn't have to be in front of this large of an audience.

Fuck me.

Before I can reach the CR-X, Preston and Bryce block my path. Preston bows up to me, smiling crookedly. "How'dya like that, loser? Eh?" he jeers, then shoves me in the chest.

"Ooh!" the crowd eggs him on.

Growling, I shove Preston back. He stumbles and grunts. I try to get Bryce out of my way, but I can barely budge him. There's a click from behind me, and then another. Turning my head slightly, I notice the glint of a .38 aimed right at me. I swallow. My heart drops to my gut.

"Yo! What the hell, man?" I say, holding my hands up. For the eight years I've known the Ninez, it never came to this. This wasn't Jacob. This wasn't… *us*. What the hell happened to him to take things this far?

"Gun!" One of the youths in the sea of spectators yells. The crowd quickly thins as people begin to scatter.

The rest of my crew approach, and then stop in their tracks when Preston aims at them.

"Don't fucking move," Preston says, his weapon hand steady.

"What are you doing? This is crazy, man!" Clayton says, his hands up in surrender.

The driver's side door of the CR-X suddenly flings open.

Regaining my composure, I open my mouth, ready to give Jacob a piece of my mind.

And then immediately shut it, forgetting all coherent thought. I blink.

The guy in front of me isn't Jacob.

Hell, it isn't even a guy.

I'm staring at a pair of holey, faded flared jeans that fit snugly around a set of gorgeous, full hips. My gaze draws upward to an exposed set of defined, chestnut-brown abs with a diamond piercing glittering in the belly button. She wears a long-sleeved, plaid-patterned, button-down shirt that's tied and knotted in the front, just above her midsection. The top two shirt buttons strain by their threads to contain her full breasts. She adjusts a white headband in her thick, curly hair, and casts me an icy stare with narrow, dark-brown eyes. But the longer she glares at me, the more contemplative her look becomes.

Holy shit. I swallow. My whole body feels hot. *This woman beat Sasha?* I open my mouth, attempting again to form a clear thought, but no sound comes out. *I've never seen her before. Is she one of Jacob's new recruits?*

She lifts her index finger and casually twirls it at Preston.

Preston lowers the gun and looks down his nose at us.

Noticing how quickly he obeyed her, I wonder if she'd replaced Jacob somehow. *Did something happen to him? Is he...?*

She smirks at my obvious befuddlement. "A deal's a deal. Now hand her over," she says.

I suck in a breath. She has a smooth, honeyed tone to her voice. The kind of tone that could enthrall any man to do her bidding. A dangerous woman. I harden my gaze at her. "Who the hell are you? Where's Jacob?"

"Jacob had some other business to take care of," the girl replies. "But he'll be glad to see Sasha waiting for him when he gets back."

Car doors slam, and hurried footsteps head my way. *Shit.* Mariah, Luke, and Gabriel have arrived, as well as the rest of the Ninez. Things could get out of control if my friends and I aren't careful. Jacob has a crew of nine, compared to just the five of us. A scuffle with guns in the mix never ends well.

"Hey." Clayton comes up beside me and glares at the mysterious girl. "The deal was that Adam was supposed to race *Jacob*. Not his sidepiece."

Her smirk quickly becomes a scowl. "The deal was the *winner* gets the loser's car and owns this strip." She glares at me. "Now give me those keys and get the fuck off my turf."

Clayton looks to me for confirmation, but I don't give him any signal to leave. I look beyond him at the rest of my crew—Luke, Gabriel, and Mariah—standing in the path of the rest of Jacob's guys, but we hadn't prepared for them to come to this race with firepower. *Are these cowards really gonna turn this into a bloodbath?*

"Adam, let's go, man," Clayton mutters in my ear.

White-knuckling my fists, I cast another look at the beautiful, mysterious female driver in front of me. Her face still dark, she shifts to one hip and folds her arms across her chest, creating an even deeper cleavage between her breasts.

My gaze flicks there briefly against my will, then back to her face. Feelings of lust and anger in me clash like two bulls. I grip the keys tight, the metal digging into my palm.

"Hell, no," I growl.

She arches an eyebrow. "What?"

"This ain't your turf, and Sasha for *damn* sure ain't yours. *Jacob* challenged me. *He* set the rules. I never made any fucking agreement with you."

Preston cocks his gun again, then aims it back at me. "We were playing for keeps, asshole."

I purse my lips. "You wanna kill me? Do it. Right now. Take Sasha for all I fucking care. It still won't change the fact that Jacob's too chickenshit to run his own damn race and decided to send a woman to do a man's job."

The woman steps closer to me, her dark-brown eyes raging. "No, you piece of shit. Jacob ain't man enough to do a woman's job… and neither could you, loser."

My throat tightens. *Touché.* I have no response to that. Yeah, I lost. To *her.* But for some reason I don't feel so bad about it now. Being this close to her, I can feel her warmth. My skin crawls with excitement and my mind travels to the places of my deepest fantasies. She smells like sweat, rubber, and gasoline, but beneath all that, I can make out the hint of a sweet, cherry scent.

"Okay, Adam." the woman continues in a cool tone, forcing me to haul my thoughts back to the present. "You wanna make your ass-beating official, then? Fine. Three days. You and me. Fife Airstrip. Nine p.m."

Never backing down from a challenge, I reply, "I'll be there."

"Good." Smirking again, she casually checks her nails. "And if I win, Sasha is mine."

"And *when* I win?"

She thinks for a moment, then her lips curl into a deep smile. "*If* you win, then Bella is rightfully yours." She gestures to the CR-X.

Several gasps come from Jacob's crew. But I just laugh out loud. "I don't want Jacob's shitty-ass car."

"Need I remind you that you just got scorched by Jacob's 'shitty-ass car'?" She laughs. "Besides, after this next race, you'll want her. Maybe even more than Sasha. Believe me."

I snort. "You've got balls wagering Jacob's ride when he ain't even here."

"My win's guaranteed, and I don't need his permission for that. Now, if you don't get the fuck outta here in ten seconds, they won't hesitate to waste your asses."

I look back at the rest of the Ninez, several of whom flash their guns. I can guarantee there are plenty of knives and brass knuckles hidden among them too. They all stare at me and my crew like a pack of hungry wolves. Gritting my teeth, I head back to my car. I only need to give Clayton the briefest of glances and he heads for his car, whistling to his girlfriend Mariah. Gabriel and Luke follow. Like dogs with tails tucked between our legs, my crew and I burn rubber and leave the scene.

Fifteen minutes later, we return home—a run-down 1940's service station that sits along what was once a main road, now a dead-end, that we dubbed 'The Shed.' We'd fixed it up with shabby, secondhand furniture from dumpsters and junkyards, and Luke decorated the walls, ceilings, and even parts of the floor with his infamous, colorful graffiti. I've called this place my "home" for the last eight years.

It's deathly quiet as we sit around the large, open common room. I prop my feet up on an empty wooden fireworks crate, tilt my head against the back of the couch and close my eyes. I run a hand over my face and sigh, my mind replaying tonight's loss on an infinite loop.

"Look, I'm sorry, guys," I finally say, breaking the silence. Opening my eyes, I look back at my friends. "I totally didn't see that shit coming. Don't know who she is or where she came from… Or what the hell they put under that hood."

"You think she might've been running a 396?" Gabriel asks, sitting in a backward-facing steel folding chair. His eyes are glued to his little black beeper as his thumbs fiddle with the tiny buttons.

I shake my head. "Naw, I think she was using avgas."

"Seriously? That shit's expensive as hell."

Clayton, sitting cross-legged on the floor next to the couch, pops open a can of beer. He takes a sip, and then wraps his arm around Mariah. She rests her head on his shoulder with her eyes closed, as though she's trying to block out this conversation.

"Who would've thought Jacob would be chickenshit enough to have his sidepiece race for him?" Clayton says.

I frown. *No, she's too good of a driver to be Jacob's lapdog.* Her skills behind the wheel rival Jacob's. Hell, she's better. *So what's she doing running around with his group? Did Jacob put her up to this or did she want a shot at me?* More questions swarm my mind.

Mariah slams her fists down on the raggedy brown stained carpet. Her eyes shooting open, she glares at each of us, then settles her gaze on me and scowls. "What *I* want to know is, where the hell did they get those guns?"

"And *why* the hell are they bringing guns in the first place?" Clayton added.

11

I swallow a lump in my throat. "I don't know, but Jacob's sunk to a new low with this one."

"Things change, Adam," Mariah says. "People change. They start taking shit way too seriously. It's the way of the world."

The more I think about it, the more I realize that things *have* started to change around here. New crews popping up, new problems, rivalries, claiming turf... but nothing big enough to be settled with bullets—at least that's what I thought. I've tried my damndest to stay away from the person I once was. Maybe my ignorance is starting to get the best of me.

"They're packin' way more than us," Luke says, sitting in the far corner of the room with his face behind his black sketchbook.

I know he isn't just talking about their Glocks. "They've been waiting for tonight to happen."

"Of course they were," Clayton says. "You're the best street racer in this town, Adam. All these years, Jacob's been trying to take your spot *and* your fucking car. Now he's taking things personal."

"Whatever happened to the days when we used to just race for fun?" I say with a sigh.

"Those days are long over, Adam," Gabriel says. "It's a new era. New... business opportunities. People are doing whatever they can to get ahead."

I grunt. 'Business opportunities' that required threatening people with guns? Based on my experience, that usually meant far worse things were involved. "This ain't the way," I finally say.

"Psh. Time to stop living in the past and get with the times," Gabriel retorts.

I miss the days when things were simpler. When we all just enjoyed the thrill of racing.

"We need to arm ourselves," Mariah suggests.

"Don't worry, Rai. I got the hook-up," Gabriel says, then gets up from the chair. "I gotta make some calls to a few friends."

She nods. "Good, 'cause we don't need this shit happening again."

I frown. After the trouble I'd gotten into back in New York City with drugs and gunrunning, I'd gotten clean and sold all my guns, and vowed to never get caught up in that lifestyle again.

I'm over that shit. No more. I can't... I tighten my jaw as I wrestle with my thoughts.

"No... There has to be another way," I say.

Clayton looks at me with an arched eyebrow. "There is no other way, Adam. If this is the way they wanna play, then we gotta step up our game too."

I take a deep breath. *I don't want to do it this way, but...* I glance at each of my crewmembers one by one. A lump forms in the back of my throat. I had no choice back then, and it seems I don't have a choice now. *This is my family. I have to protect them.*

Fuck promises. I've lost so much in my life as it is. I'm not losing them. I won't.

"Ok. Then we step it up." I feel a burning sensation in my chest as I say this. A sensation I hadn't felt in so long. "And Jacob's not runnin' this side of town if we have anything to do with it. We got three days to get it right."

Clayton snorts. "If you seriously think we can dial in Sasha to coming even remotely close to that CR-X in three days, then you're insane. We'll be lucky to find just some of the parts we need in time. Besides, even while we're scrambling to play catch-up, the Ninez'll be adding all sorts of new shit to Bella to scorch us all for good."

"I'mma hit their shitty-ass cars." Luke shuts the sketchbook and looks at us, smirking.

"They'll hang you by the balls if they catch you," Mariah says.

Luke raises his eyebrows. "I ain't a toy. I don't get caught."

"Look," I say, trying to steer the conversation back to the issue at hand. "I know we can do this. Three days is plenty of time to turn Sasha into a beast. Trust me on this. One more race is all we need to get our reputation back and keeping those punks in their place."

I receive silence and skeptical looks in response. Of course, they don't trust me, but I'm no stranger to people I care about and trust not having my back. Back in New York, I got busted running drugs for so-called friends. They all disappeared on me when I needed them the most. I would have been stuck in juvie if my grandma hadn't used a hefty chunk of her savings toward my bail and a miracle hadn't happened in court—the judge dismissed the charges on account of my rights never getting read at the time of my arrest. Not wanting to risk me pressing my luck anymore, Grandma sent me away to Tacoma to live with my grandfather.

I cross my arms and lift my head slightly, eyeing my crew. "So that's the way it's gonna be, huh? Fine. I'll do this shit myself." I get up from the couch and march to the back door leading to the Shed's two-car main bay, where Sasha is parked. If no one is going to help me, then I'll have to help myself. The streets taught me that lesson a long time ago. I'm gonna fight for what I love, and I'm gonna fight to win.

Starting with *her*.

Chapter 2

WHEN I WASN'T OUT RACING INTO THE EARLY HOURS OF the morning, I slaved grueling hours part-time at Donaldson Road Construction Company from sunup to early afternoon, and then repaired and restored old cars at Anderson's Antique Auto—my grandfather's antique car garage—until evening. A daily routine with steady pay. Can't complain.

I admire the gleam coming off the polished chrome bumper of a blue '35 roadster I'd just finished wiping down for the past three hours. It's amazing how much more intricate the older cars are, and how much more of a pain in the ass it is to detail them. But it sure is a lot easier than rebuilding engines from scratch, which Grandpa often tasks me with.

At seventy-six years old, Grandpa is an ace mechanic who knows his way around any car, new or old. When I moved to Tacoma as a young teenager, Grandpa taught me everything he knew. I'd given up the gangster life and became a gearhead. But while Grandpa's love was always antique cars built for show, I was more interested in modern, tricked-out sports cars built for racing.

I give the rag a quick snap, then begin wiping the hood. I frown. Thoughts of last night's race return to the forefront of my mind. I still have to figure out how to best optimize Sasha in three days. We need to keep our turf. New Tacoma's industrial district has some of the best places to race without worrying about cops.

And I need to keep my car.

No doubt that mysterious girl is going to up her game next race too. But I'll be ready.

I smile to myself. I don't know why I'm so intrigued by her. Yeah, she's cute, fly, and knows how to handle her ride. But she's also Jacob's girl, and that's reason enough for me to forget about her. *What the hell does a girl like her see in that insecure motherfucker?*

"Adam," Grandpa's sharp voice shakes me out of my thoughts. "Go easy on that finish, son."

Damn, for an old guy, Grandpa sure gets around stealthily. I wipe the hood in gentle, slower, circular motions. "Sorry," I mutter.

"There's no room for mistakes, especially when it comes to paint. I want this baby looking flawless for the car show on Saturday."

I stare at the reflection of dozens of gleaming gold trophies lined up on a high shelf behind me on the polished hood. In addition to the awards he'd won from the many cars he'd restored, Grandpa had also made a fortune from the many more he'd sold. I bet he's a millionaire right now, even though he had never really talked finances around me. He sure never acts like he has money, though, living in a tiny, two-bedroom house in Fern Hill. I never realized there was such a big market for antique cars, especially among the rich and famous, which made up the majority of his customers. Unfortunately, I was still waiting to meet one of these famous celebrities during my shift.

I snap the rag again and move to one of the front wheel fenders. Like the rest of the car, I'd wiped it down twice already, but it was never good enough for Grandpa. *It's never good enough.* I frown and stare blankly at the rag, wishing I could easily wipe away the shit that happened last night.

Grandpa approaches and crosses his thick arms. I look sideways at him—his aged, bearded face is stony as he glares at me through his thick, horn-rimmed glasses.

I focus my attention on the fender as I wipe in gentle, circular motions, but I can still feel Grandpa's gaze.

"Have you been racing again?"

I stop wiping and clench my jaw. I can never hide anything from him—he always seems to have some kind of weird, freakish sixth sense. *Must be an old man thing.* He'd been on my case about illegal racing when I'd first got into it at sixteen, and it seemed like the older I got, the more he complained.

"For fuck's sake. I'm twenty-four years old," I snap back. "Why do you care what I do in my spare time?"

Grandpa fumes. "Because I don't want to see your damned mugshot on the evening news. You already got a record for reckless driving seven years ago. Not to mention all those drug charges from your little stint in New York."

I roll my eyes and then resume wiping the fender of the roadster. "I'm a hell of a lot better driver now, Grandpa. I don't go places where cops hang out. And I've been done with drugs since I left New York."

"Listen to me, knucklehead! You're one felony away from getting locked up for good. And unlike your naïve grandmother, I ain't puttin' up a single cent of bail for your ass, you hear me?"

"Yeah, sure." Racing was one of the few things he and I didn't see eye to eye on. Obviously, he didn't understand my world and the thrill of underground racing—the heart-pumping suspense of high speeds and high stakes—against other crews, and the law. And he didn't understand what the Wild Aces—my *family*—stood for. Sometimes it felt like I was closer to my racing crew than my own blood.

Grandpa sighs. "Look, son, I ain't gonna be around forever. You better think about what you're gonna do with your life when I'm gone."

"I'm content with what I'm doing now."

"What? Playing race cars with these *kids*? Like you said, you're twenty-four years old. You're a man, Adam. Start acting like one."

I grit my teeth. "You know, maybe that's what keeps me fucking sane, and less stressed after dealing with all the hard-asses like you at work."

"You're too young to be stressed. *I* should be the one who's stressed, trying to keep your damn head on straight."

I stop wiping and grip the rag tight. "Why are we having this conversation? So I race every once in a while. So what? Ain't it better than me slinging drugs or running guns? I thought you'd be glad I'm not back in that life. Nothing I ever do is good enough for you, is it? What the hell do you want from me?"

Grandpa purses his lips and exhales through his nose. "I *want* you to get ahead in life."

Shrugging, I make a face. "The hell's that supposed to mean?"

"Ever thought about starting a business?"

I arch an eyebrow at him.

"A *legal* business."

"Really, Grandpa? Do I look like an entrepreneur to you?"

He snorts. "We're not born entrepreneurs. It takes work. And time."

My time is better spent with Sasha. Before Grandpa hired me, he'd used to run this business by himself, handling both the cars and the paperwork. I still don't know how he'd managed to do both. These days, with me being his only employee, I'm tasked with all the grunt work he used to do.

"That's not for me," I say. "Besides, no one will trust a business run by someone with my track record."

"You'd be surprised, Adam. If you're doing good, honest work, most people won't care."

"Whatever, man. My mistakes are gonna haunt me for the rest of my life."

Grandpa swipes the rag from my hands. "Look. You need to decide what's more important: risking your life every damn night with that street-racing nonsense, or working an honest job, having a family of your own, keeping your nose clean, and not making the same mistakes your parents did."

I tighten my jaw at the mention of my alcoholic, drug-addicted parents who OD'd when my older brother, Michael, and I were young kids. I regretted barely knowing them, but I hated them for abandoning us. Grandpa seems to always know how to hit me where it hurts.

"Drop it, old man," I warn.

He slams the rag down and bows up to me, glaring. "Or else what? All that tough-guy nonsense ain't flyin' with me. You're better than this, Adam."

I clench my fists, a mix of violent emotions surging through me. *"You're better than this,"* Grandpa always says. *What the hell does that even mean?* I exhale a deep sigh. *It's worthless to keep getting worked up over things I can't control.*

"Fuck it," I finally say.

Grandpa shakes his head. "So, 'fuck it'? You know what, I'm tired of arguing with you today. I've got too much work to do. Just go home."

I glance at the vintage-hubcap clock on the wall that reads 2:25, and then look back at Grandpa. "You're letting me off early?"

"Yeah, and don't think you're gettin' paid for the hours you were supposed to work." He points to the door. "Get outta here, boy."

I look at his pointing finger and notice it's shaking slightly. *Damn, I really riled him up this time...*

Too mentally exhausted to argue, I grab my duffel bag out of one of the wall-mounted metal lockers and storm out the front door, not looking back.

I take the bus to my favorite cheap Chinese food place, Dim Sum Noodle House, and grab a bite to eat. I never drove Sasha as a utility vehicle. She was strictly built for racing, and that's all she ever did. Besides, driving a car like Sasha—a flashy, bright-red sports car—around downtown Tacoma or on the highway would be the perfect cop magnet. While I always loved showing her off, there was a time and place for it.

I remain at Dim Sum Noodle House for a few hours, trying to clear my head. Before I know it, it's almost eight o'clock at night. I take the bus back home.

The bus winds through the streets and across the river to the edge of the industrial district of New Tacoma. I get off on the corner of Pacific Highway and 52nd Avenue, and take a shortcut off the main road, following the bank of Wapato Creek north.

It's nine o'clock when I finally arrive at the Shed. Rounding the front of the building, I spot Mariah sitting outside the front door in an old steel beach chair, smoking a joint. Her eyes are fixed toward the entrance to the dead-end road, and the narrow bridge that spans over a small creek and out to Blue Road. I stop a few feet from the front door, and her gaze flicks to me. She exhales a cloud of white smoke and scowls.

I frown. Mariah only smokes when something's seriously bothering her. I can take a few guesses as to what it is.

"Hey," I say with a slight nod.

She takes another drag. "Either your boy Luke really *is* an idiot, or he's the smartest man I know."

I arch an eyebrow at the mention of my best friend. "Why? What's he up to now?"

Her stoic expression suddenly breaks, and she throws her head back and laughs. "He went out to Moonshine Milly's to tag all their cars!"

I widen my eyes. "What!" Luke was a joker, but I didn't think he was really serious about what he said last night. "Damn it, where's Clay and Gabe?"

"They were out all day getting parts and supplies. Should be back soon. They have *no* idea…"

I rub my hands over my face and swear under my breath.

"Man… Luke's got balls, I'll tell you what." She carefully extinguishes the joint in a small glass ashtray with a few others. "He wasn't gonna let anyone stop him. Not even *you*, Adam. He's gonna fuck up every precious thing the Ninez own for humiliating us."

"Look, I'm trying to make things right here, but I don't need to be scraping bodies from the asphalt because of stupid shit like this."

She stands, frowning. "I'd rather die than be clowned by those fuckers." Without another word, she spins on her heel and walks inside the building.

The front door slams behind her and I flinch. I swallow a lump in my throat as I think about her last words. She's giving up too soon. Luke too. But I'm sure as hell not giving up without a fight. My first priority is to find Luke and bring him back, however, by any means necessary. If something happens to him, I won't forgive myself. This is what I get for caring so damn much.

I rush inside and head to my sleeping area in the back room. It was once a large storage space, but with mine and Clayton's construction know-how, we put up plywood walls and curtains to construct our individual, sectioned-off 'rooms.'

I throw on my leather jacket and grab a wad of cash from under my floor mattress. I'm not sure what's going to go down tonight, but I'm not taking any chances. As I'm about to leave my room, I stare at my car keys sitting on a wooden crate—my 'bedside table'—next to the mattress. I hesitate grabbing the keys, knowing the big risk I'm taking with Sasha. *But Luke is my friend, damn it. I have to save him.* If the Ninez are at Moonshine Milly's, then I won't need to worry about cops. That place is so far out in the boondocks it isn't funny.

But, if something *does* go down out there, then there's no help coming. As soon as the Ninez spot Sasha, all hell will break loose. I hope tonight doesn't end with bodies hitting the ground.

After another round of debating with myself, I finally swipe up the keys. I race back outside, hop in my car, and burn rubber out of there.

Chapter 3

MOONSHINE MILLY'S IS A SMALL RUN-DOWN BAR THAT SITS on a long, lonely stretch of country road just outside the city proper. Guys like us consider it neutral territory—meaning, no one actually owns this spot. Certain nights are reserved for certain groups of people, and going there when it isn't your night is just asking for trouble. But that doesn't mean someone isn't always trying to start shit. It's a favorite watering hole for the local bikers too, but they usually leave us gearheads alone unless someone's had a little too much to drink.

Sasha's headlights shine on Moonshine Milly's rotting wooden sign pointing down a narrow dirt road. I turn and ride a little ways until the Old-West-style building comes into view. A few cars parked among a sea of gleaming chrome and leather indicate the place is packed at eleven o'clock on a Thursday night. I park in a grassy spot, away from the other vehicles, positioning myself for an easy getaway. I don't recognize any of the cars as belonging to the Ninez, and I wonder if I'm too late. Then again, the bikers don't take too kindly to our hogging up the front parking lot with our sports cars during Bike Night, so I assume the Ninez are probably parked in the back.

I stare at the glove compartment long and hard, then slowly reach a shaky hand toward it. I moisten my lips and take a deep breath. *Am I really about to do this again?* I tug the handle and the compartment drops open, revealing a .45 pistol. Gabriel had come through and hooked our entire crew up. Can't say I was thrilled. It's crazy how the past tends to rear its ugly head over and over again, no matter how many times I try to escape it.

As long I have to protect my family, I'll never escape these nightmares...

I grab the pistol and tuck it into my jacket. I really hope it stays there.

I get out of my car. Laughter, loud voices, and the screaming electric guitars and lyrics of AC/DC filter out from the partially open door.

I don't see Luke's truck anywhere. *Is he already gone?* I sure hope so. *I need to know for sure.*

I approach the bar's entrance. Two bikers in patch-covered leather vests walk out, laughing obnoxiously with beer bottles in their hands. As I brush past them, they give me the side-eye then continue toward the parking area.

A thick cloud of cigarette smoke envelops me as I enter the bar. The bikers and their hang-arounds have completely taken over the bar, the lone pool table in the corner, and the pinball machine. A few of them dance drunkenly around with drinks in their hands near a faux-vintage CD jukebox blasting *Back in Black*.

The only spot not overrun with the greying, leather-clad crowd, is a big round table of younger-looking people in the back. They remain concentrated at this table, knowing not to push their luck on Bike Night.

I immediately spot Jacob among the group, sprawled out in his chair as he tips back a beer. The rest of his crew talk and laugh, and don't appear to pay any attention to the rest of the bar. Luke's not lurking nearby, for which I'm glad, but it still leaves me a little worried. Jacob's mystery girl is nowhere around, either.

I do an about-face, ready to leave. My body stops mid-turn as I notice a woman in high-waisted, studded-denim shorts and a matching jacket coming out of the women's bathroom down a small hallway. A pair of fishnet stockings cover her long legs. As she exits the hallway, Preston staggers out from the shadows behind her and follows, attempting to cop a feel of her ass, but she dodges out of his reach.

"Fuck off, Preston." She glares back at her drunken comrade before making her way back to the younger crowd. She goes to Jacob's side and says something in his ear, but he just shakes his head and casts his hand up at her dismissively. Frowning, she storms away from the table and leans up against the wall with her arms crossed. The rest of the guys at the table laugh at her, and she shoots them an annoyed look, then scowls around the rest of the bar. Her gaze sweeps in my direction, and I quickly turn my head. *Time to go.*

I head for the exit. As I reach for the door, it suddenly swings open. I dodge out of the way, the edge of the door just barely missing my face as a pair of rough-looking men barge in. They cut their eyes at me in passing, and I stiffen, holding my ground. Without a word they shove by me, my built, six-foot-six height not seeming to intimidate them. Once they're inside, I notice the black-widow-spider patches on the backs of their jacket. My heart starts to pound. *Damn. One-Percenters.* Anybody from the streets knows to never fuck with them—Jacob's crew better be on their best behavior.

Outside, I round the back of the building, hugging the wall and staying out of the orange glare of the nearby security light that illuminates the rear parking lot. A dimmer floodlight posted at the back corner of the building provides ample light to the area. I recognize most of the cars parked here as belonging to Jacob's crew, and one of them is completely covered in graffiti. Colorful obscenities like 'FUCK THE NINEZ' and cartoon images of dicks decorate every inch of what I assume—judging by the body style—was once a pure white CR-X. On the hood is a damn-near perfect caricature of Jacob bent over with his pants down, while one of his crewmates gives it to him from behind. The words 'SUCK IT, NINEZ!' is scrawled across the windshield in artistic, spray-painted bubble letters.

Yep, Luke's been here, all right.

I hear faint clacking nearby behind a white GT-R that's parked the furthest away from the others. I glance over my shoulder to make sure I'm alone and follow the sound. There's a hiss that stops abruptly as I approach. Either Luke is finished with his masterpiece, or we're not alone out here. I duck behind one of the nearer cars, then move quietly to the back of the GT-R, crouched as low as I possibly can. Shadows move from the other side. Still kneeling, I plaster myself against the bumper and slowly peer around the corner...

...and right into the barrel of a gun.

Holy fuck. My heart leaps into my throat. I stare at the barrel a moment, then up to its holder—Luke.

The lower half of his face is covered with a black bandanna, making him look like one of those old-fashioned bank robbers. Luke stares back at me with widened, dumbfounded eyes. "You scared the shit outta me, bro!" he says, just above a whisper as he lowers his gun. "I thought you were one of Jacob's guys."

Glaring, I backhand him upside the head. "Idiot! What the hell are you thinking?"

Rubbing the side of his head, Luke glares back at me like he's going to retaliate.

I lift my chin—and my fist—welcoming the challenge. But when I give my biceps a firm flex as a warning, Luke does the sensible thing and backs down. He peeks around the front bumper of the car, and resumes spray-painting his current masterpiece—the word 'NINEZ' with dicks coming out from the ends of the letters—on the passenger-side door. "I'm doing what I should've done a long time ago. I'm sendin' 'em all a message. Jacob's such a pussy, sending his girlfriend out to do his dirty work. I ain't about to be fucked with by a coward who's too scared to race."

I grit my teeth. "They're gonna kill us all for this. You're not helping right now. We need to be back at the Shed getting Sasha dialed in for the next race."

Luke scoffs. "Seriously, bro? There *is* no next race. Don't you get it?"

"I agreed to race Jacob's girl this time. Not him."

"And you really think she's gonna keep her word? Tonight was about humiliation, nothin' else."

I think about his question. "Actually, yeah. I *do* think she'll keep her word." I don't know why, but there's something genuine about her that Jacob lacks. Ambition, perhaps? A competitive edge? Desire? A true love and appreciation for the race? "She still wants Sasha and our turf, doesn't she?"

He shakes his spray can. "Whatever, man. Don't let the T&A fool you. If she's with Jacob, then she's just as slimy as his ass is."

I frown. "C'mon, man. Let's get out of here before they catch us." I place my hand on his shoulder.

He violently shrugs my hand off. "I told you before. I don't get caught."

"I'm not leaving you out here, shithead. Come on!"

He ignores me and continues spraying the door. I flare my nostrils in frustration and snatch the can from him. Some excess paint drips down from the lettering.

"Shit! Now look what you did. You ruined my work!" Luke says.

"Luke, you better get your ass out of here. Right now." I suddenly hear several familiar voices coming from the bar's entrance. I peer around the corner of the GT-R's bumper at the group of shadows near the corner of the building. My heart pounds. "Shit, they're close. We gotta hide."

Cursing under his breath, Luke snatches the spray can back from me and quickly stores it in his backpack with the others. He unhooks his skateboard from its straps on the pack and tucks it under his arm.

Using the shadows, I scramble toward the opposite side of the building and press my back flat against the wall. Luke follows.

I stare dumbfounded in the dim light at Luke's grungy skateboard, riddled with his graffiti art and stickers of half-naked anime girls, and logos of some of his favorite rock bands. "Don't tell me you actually came all the way out here on that thing." I whisper.

"Hell yeah, bro. I'm not gonna bring Tess out on a job like this, you crazy? Might as well be wearing a neon sign."

I shake my head at the absurdity of it all. *Traveling for miles up hills and on dirt roads on a fucking skateboard...* Then again, Luke *is* from Southern California, and he's got some odd little quirks.

Peering out from our hiding spot, I watch the Ninez approach their cars. Jacob halts in front of his graffiti-ridden CR-X, and his cigarette drops from his lips.

"What the fuck!" Jacob exclaims.

Bryce, standing before the white GT-R, yells a long string of curses. "I'm gonna kill that son of a bitch!"

"I bet it's those Wild Aces, man," another one of Jacob's guys whom I don't recognize says.

"No shit, Sherlock…" Preston manages to drunkenly reply.

Luke, suppressing a snicker, nudges me in the arm. But I don't find it all too funny that the Ninez are going to be out for our blood after this.

Jacob gives his comrade a dumbfounded look. "Why would they be that stupid to fuck with us after what we did to them?"

"You mean, after what *Cassandra* did to them," Preston interjects.

"That bitch didn't do, shit, Pres. First of all, it was *my* car." Jacob scoffs, and some of the other guys laugh. "She's just lucky she has too nice of an ass and pair of titties for me to be mad at her for wagering my car in the next race."

"Yeah, 'cause she sure as hell ain't never gonna beat Sasha in this shitty piece of junk." Bryce kicks the back tire of an old, rusted '75 Nova parked next to Jacob's car, prompting more laughter from the guys.

I narrow my eyes. Jacob's an idiot to not realize just how great of a racer she is—better than him, even. But his words don't matter. Only cowards speak behind people's backs, and Jacob is the biggest coward I know.

And I find it hard to believe that someone like Cassandra drives an unmodified jalopy like that. *Cassandra… So that's her name. It's beautiful… like her.*

"Where is she, anyway?" Jacob's youngest-looking member asks. He looks like he's fresh out of high school. Most likely a new recruit.

"Trying to make back the money she lost in a pool game." Preston smirks. "When's she gonna learn not to ask for what her pretty ass can't handle?"

Jacob scowls. "Fuck her. I'm more worried about my damn car. I want the Wild Aces found—dead or alive."

"Preferably dead," Bryce says, rubbing his hand over the spray-painted expletives on his passenger-side door.

The Ninez finally get in their cars and leave, with Jacob having to drive with his head leaned out the driver's side window on account of the giant graffiti dick spanning the entire windshield.

When the group leaves, Luke steps out of the hiding spot, a satisfied smile on his face. "See ya back at the Shed, man."

I blink. "I could just drive us both back, you know."

"Thanks, but no thanks." With his skateboard tucked under his arm, he winks and leaves.

I curse under my breath, giving up on trying to change his mind. I look back at the beat-up Nova, which is untouched by Luke, and wonder if that girl—*Cassandra*—really is still in the bar. *Her crew would just up and leave her like that at Milly's of all places?* Figures. Jacob's a shitty leader, and an even shittier excuse for a man. *I should go and make sure she's okay.* She'll probably want to kick my ass once she sees me. Honestly? I don't think I'd mind that one bit if she tried. She'd pissed me off so much last night, but she'd also earned my respect. What kind of a man would I be for not checking up on her?

I brave the rowdy crowd once more as I enter the hazy bar and make my way toward the pool table in the back. Cassandra is leaned over the table with her back to me, giving me a wonderfully clear view of her perfect, round ass. A few other guys gathered nearby have their gazes focused in the same direction. Cassandra sinks the last striped ball in a side pocket, then ends the game by sinking the eight-ball in a corner one. With a look of relief on her face, she leans the cue stick against the side of the table and swipes up a wad of cash sitting on the edge. Some of the guys whistle and cheer her victory as she pockets the money.

I twist my mouth to a smile. *Damn, she's even got the bikers liking her.* That's not an easy feat.

As she starts to walk off, one of the bikers puts his hand on her shoulder, stopping her. "C'mon, baby. You're winnin.' You'll get your money back in no time. Don't stop now."

She turns her head, gives him a humorless smile, and slides free from his grip. "Nice try, but no. I'm tired. It was fun, though."

He grins back, forcefully. "I *really* think you should keep playing." He turns to the other gathered bikers. "Right, guys?" The crowd responds with cheers and taunts.

Cassandra keeps walking. "Sorry, gotta go. My crew's waiting on me outside."

One of the guys steps in front of her, blocking her path. The black widow spider patch on his back sends my heart pounding again. *Fuck.*

"You ain't with them punks with the flashy cars, are you?" he asks in a deep voice.

She holds her head up high and hardens her gaze. "Yeah, that's right. And what's it to you? We didn't cause any trouble here tonight."

"This ain't your night, sweetie," the One-Percenter says. "That means you were playin' only under our good graces. And not lettin' my friend here try to win back some cash, well… that'd just be rude. And we don't take too kindly to that." He slips his hand in his back pocket, where I notice the distinct outline of a switchblade.

I widen my eyes. "Whoa, man! Wait!" I step in between the man and Cassandra, not knowing why the hell I'm signing my own death warrant.

The man glares at me. His thick arms flex. "Who the fuck are you?"

I surrender both hands in the air. "Just passing through, man. Not here to start any trouble. Just let the girl go on her way, all right?"

The biker looks down his nose at me. "She your bitch? She took two hundred bucks from my brothers. What're we gonna do about that, huh?"

I swallow a lump in my throat, my mind racing with anger and fear. With one hand still up, I slowly reach in my jacket, my fingers briefly gliding over the butt of my gun. Thankfully my senses reel in my impulsive urges, as I'm outnumbered thirty to one, and I find the wad of cash instead. As soon as I pull it out, he swipes it from my hand.

He quickly counts it and flashes a crooked smile. "This'll do nicely." He shoves past me and Cassandra, handing the money to one of his biker brothers, and they resume playing pool. The crowd of spectators dissipates, the music starts up again, and the bar returns to its normal rowdy state.

Cassandra's dumbfounded look turns to annoyance. Her lip curls, and she pushes me aside as she makes her way to the exit. I watch her a moment, then follow. She marches toward the back of the building and stops. Looking around, she balls her fists and then storms over to her car.

"They left about fifteen minutes ago," I say, loud enough for her to hear.

She grabs the handle of the driver's side door, then looks over her shoulder at me. "What do you want? If you're looking for a 'thank you,' piss off. I could have handled that myself."

I slowly approach and stop a few feet from her. "I wanna know why your crew abandoned you."

She rolls her eyes. "They didn't abandon me. Probably had something important to take care of. Whatever."

"And they'd leave behind their best driver?" I raise my eyebrows.

She purses her lips. "What's it to you?"

I shrug. "Just an observation. Bad leadership on Jacob's part. Then again, he's always been a self-centered douche."

She fights down a smile and lets out a soft chuckle. "Whatever you think he is, you're wrong. I'm his number one."

"Oh? And how do you figure that?"

"He let *me* drive his car in that race, for one." She thumbs herself proudly in the chest. "*No one* touches his ride."

It's my turn to laugh. "Really? You think one race will make you his number one?"

She narrows her eyes and flings the door open. "Yes, and it has. Now, fuck off, Adam. You got two days left."

I approach the door before she has a chance to close it and hold it open. "You think Jacob's gonna let you drive his car again? I know he'll dial in that CR-X as hard as he can. But I'm gonna be ready for it."

She snorts a laugh. "You think you'll be racing against his shitty-ass car again? I've got my own set of wheels." She pats the side of the door.

"You sure you wanna race Sasha with this thing?" The sheer absurdity of it makes me almost burst out laughing, but somehow, I manage to hold it in, and it comes out as a small snicker instead. It's amusing, and yet, I respect the hell out of her for even attempting to put such a beater up against Sasha. *She's got a bigger set of balls than Jacob does...*

Her face hardens. "She'll be more than ready to take on Sasha. When I'm done dialing her in, she's gonna scorch all you cocky motherfuckers. And I'll be taking Sasha off your hands—might be nice for spare parts." She tugs at the door.

Damn, she's serious. I let go of the door, and she slams it shut. She starts the car and rolls the window down, looking me up and down briefly before moistening her lips. "Thanks for bailing me out back there."

My gaze lingers a little too long on her luscious lips. What I wouldn't give to kiss them right now, taste her, and find out if she kisses as good as she races. But she's obviously keen on Jacob—the guy who abandoned her in the middle of no-where. "No problem."

She rolls the window back up and revs the engine. For a junky-looking thing, the Nova has a motor that roars aggres-sively, loud and deep—music to my ears. Sounds like she's running some serious horsepower. She drives off, her back tires kicking up clouds of dust that obstruct my view of the dirt road leading out of Moonshine Milly's. By the time it settles, she's already long gone.

Chapter 4

After that weird encounter at Moonshine Milly's I get some serious hunger pangs. I head back into town, and to the nearest Out the Box joint to grab a quick, late-night meal. It's well after midnight when I return to the Shed. Only one light is on. Clayton's car is in his usual spot in Bay Two, while Luke's, Gabriel's, and Mariah's vehicles are out front. I park Sasha in her designated spot in Bay One and hop out. I notice three different-sized boxes propped against the wall, but I'm too whipped to wonder what's inside them. Entering the common room through the side door, I find Gabriel fiddling with the rabbit ears on our small television while Luke sits on the couch with his nose in his black sketchbook. His skateboard is leaned up against the side of the couch.

"Holy shit, Luke. How the hell did you get back before me?" I ask.

"Skills," Luke replies, keeping his eyes trained on his sketchbook.

Gabriel looks toward me and does a double take. "Damn. You made it back in one piece."

"Told you he would," Luke says.

"So what the hell happened? And don't go silent on me either like that one." Gabriel says, cocking a thumb at Luke.

I shake my head. "Not now, Gabe. I'm too damn tired to get into it. The important part is Luke's not full of holes."

He rolls his eyes. "After me and Clay got back from Dave's, Rai told us where you and Luke went. I would've gone out to help, but Clay told me to stay here."

"Clay made the right call," I say with a firm nod.

Gabriel frowns. "I seriously freaked out, man. The last thing I need to hear is you guys got wasted by One Percenters."

"It's all good now." I pause and look around. "Where *is* Clay, anyway?"

Gabriel makes a sour face. "In the back room with Mariah. I'm tired as hell, and they've been at it all night."

I roll my eyes. The main downside of having rooms sectioned off by thin plywood is that I could hear every damn thing. Including Clayton and Mariah's fucking. Clayton, the lucky bastard, was the only one of us able to pick up and keep a girl—who was just as much as a gearhead as he was, no less. I've had my share of women, but for most of them this wasn't a lifestyle, just some night-time diversion and excitement. And when that excitement was constant, most tended to burn out, or bolt when the danger got too real. Not Mariah, though… or Cassandra.

"Good news, though," Gabriel continues. "Clay and I got something cool from Dave today. He gave us one hell of a deal."

I raise my eyebrows. "How much of a 'deal'?"

"As in, we didn't clean out the community pot this time." Gabriel crosses his arms and puffs out his chest. "You should be proud of us."

"That depends. You get anything good?"

He grins. "Take a look in the bay and see for yourself."

Curiosity overcomes my sleepiness as I head out to the garage. I assume the three unmarked boxes against the wall are the ones Gabriel was referring to. I sift through the endless packing popcorn inside a long, slightly heavy box, and pull out a bubble-wrapped steel muffler attached to a curved, three-inch-wide pipe. My jaw drops, recognizing the top-of-the-line quality of a Q&R-brand Cat Back dual exhaust system. I'd been eyeing this baby for months, but Dave, our go-to underground dealer for parts, was never able to get his hands on one. Until now.

My cheeks hurt from grinning so wide. The other two boxes contain a new air filter and a body kit. "Hell yeah!" I yell loud enough for my friends to hear me.

"You're welcome!" Gabriel yells back.

Even though I have to go to work tomorrow, sleep is the last thing on my mind. I crank Sasha up on four jack stands, retrieve the dolly hanging on the wall, and get to work on the exhaust system install. My mind wanders as I roll underneath the car and begin unscrewing nuts and bolts, and un-hinging pipes. I wonder what kind of mods Cassandra is going to put on that Nova. I would be a fool to think I have this race in the bag. With a good set of tires and a new intake and ignition system, Cassandra could easily give my 300ZX a run for my money.

I bet she's somewhere rolled up under her Nova right now, just like I am with Sasha, while the rest of Jacob's crew are probably still scrubbing graffiti off their cars. A woman who not only looks sexy but isn't afraid to get a little oil on her hands or dirt under her nails is fucking orgasmic. God, and the way she looked tonight in those denim shorts and fishnet stockings. So deliciously hot. Those legs… long and lean.

I smile, my hands going on autopilot as I'm swept up in the memory of her tonight.

And her ass was amazing, too. So big and round and tight. I *love* a woman with a tight ass.

My smile widens.

And those tits. So fucking big and full and perky… That jacket she wore tonight stretched so much, it looked like it was ready to rip. *Sweet Jesus.*

She's perfect.

She's Jacob's girl.

I still don't know what she sees in that douchebag, and I wonder what it will take for her to look my way. She's a new face in the Ninez, and a rare one—I can't remember the last time Jacob recruited a woman into his crew. But she makes him and the other drivers look like amateurs…

Two hours and a couple of blistered fingers later, I'm done. I start Sasha up and rev the engine a bit, relishing her full, healthy sound. With a job well done, if not entirely in good time, I shut her off and head back inside. All of the lights are off, but the television is still on, tuned to some old sci-fi movie—one I've most likely seen at some point. I'm a sucker for these old, cheesy flicks.

Hearing Luke and Gabriel's light snoring coming from the couch, I turn off the television. I take a quick shower in the Shed's only bathroom, and head to my room for what little sleep I can manage, but it's hard to find. Cassandra knows her shit. I can only wonder what sort of surprise she'll have in store for me at the airstrip...

CHAPTER 5

Work is light at Donaldson Construction, and the boss lets me off thirty minutes early. It's Friday, which means payday—my favorite day of the month. When I arrive at Grandpa's shop, I find him in the office on the phone with a client, his hand at his forehead. He doesn't seem to notice me, so I check the mail basket for anything with my name on it. Just junk. Tossing it away, I head straight for the garage to get started on today's work. Some new parts have come in, which I begin sorting through and setting aside to be used in the engine rebuilding project that I've been working on for Grandpa the past week.

An hour passes and I hear Grandpa finally come out of his office. I look up from the stripped-down engine on the workbench and he's standing in the doorway, an exhausted look on his face.

I furrow my brow. "What's up?"

Frowning, he points his thumb over his shoulder. "Elouise is on the phone."

I swallow a lump in my throat at the mention of my sister-in-law. Even though she's four years older than me, she might as well be the little sister I never had. About two years after I'd moved to Tacoma and started working for Grandpa, she'd started calling his shop, wanting to talk to me, asking me for advice and comfort when she needed it. I can't say I was all too thrilled at first, since she's married to my hothead brother, and I can only imagine what *he* thinks about the conversations Elouise and I have. Michael tends to take everything personally, as if the whole world is out to get him. Part of me is glad that he and I live on opposite ends of the country because we can never carry on a civil conversation for more than a minute.

I abandon the stripped engine with a sigh and walk past Grandpa to the office. I pick up the telephone receiver from the desk. "Hello?"

"Adam?"

Smiling at the sound of her soft, yet concerned voice, I plop down in the desk chair and twirl the coiled telephone cord between my fingers. "Hey. How are you?"

She sighs. "I'm okay. Michael's not. He got fired from his job yesterday."

I blink. "What?"

"The company's cutting back, hiring people for less pay. Michael is beyond upset, and I'm worried about him."

"Is he looking for another job?"

"I told him to do that, that we can find something else, but I don't think he's listening to me. He went out drinking last night and didn't come back until almost three in the morning."

"Sounds like Michael, but… well what do you want *me* to do?" I ask, already regretting what she might say.

She pauses. "Maybe talk to him? I know you two don't see eye-to-eye, but I'm hoping there's a chance you can talk some sense into him."

"Pfft. If he won't listen to you, then there's no way in hell he'll listen to me."

"Please, Adam. I don't want the boys to see their father act like this."

I chew my bottom lip. Being concerned all the time for my sister-in-law also meant being concerned for my three nephews: Dominick, Kevin, and Michael Jr. With the family living all the way across the country, I'd only had the occasional phone call to talk to them, and mailed photos of the boys to see them, since their birth. Still—whether it was my bond with Elouise, or worry about Michael, or maybe even something in myself—I cared a lot about the boys. Sighing, I lean my elbow on the desk and bury my face in my palm. "Fine. Let me talk to him."

There's rustling on the other end, and the sound of two muffled voices speaking in sharp tones. Finally, someone comes to the phone. "Hello," Michael's cold voice hums through the receiver.

I make a sour face. "Hey, man. Just seeing if everything's all right with you and the family."

"No. Everything's *not* all right. But I'm sure she already filled you in on that."

I note the slightly cynical way he says that, and my blood begins to boil. "What the hell's that supposed to mean?"

"It means you need to mind your own fucking business."

I roll my tongue in my cheek for a moment, trying to keep my cool before replying. "It *is* my business, where my sister-in-law and nephews are concerned."

"Fuck off." He hangs up.

I tighten my grip around the receiver at the buzzing sound of the ended call and slam it back on the cradle. I knew that wasn't going to go over well. Minutes later, the phone rings again. Grandpa hasn't returned to his office, so I push my frustrations aside and do my best to answer it in a professional tone, "Good afternoon, Anderson Antique Auto. Adam speaking."

"Hey, Adam. I'm so sorry about that," Elouise says.

I frown. "I told you he wouldn't listen to me."

"I don't know what to do. He stormed out of the apartment again. Hopefully he's gone to the unemployment office this time and not the bar." It was Elouise's turn to be cynical, apparently.

"He's drinking already?" I check the clock on the wall, realizing it's only six o'clock in New York City.

"I wouldn't put it past him. I don't want him to give up, Adam. If he can't find work here, then, maybe…"

The line goes silent a moment, and I wonder if we've been cut off. "Maybe…?"

"Maybe we should consider moving," she finally says.

I exhale. Moving is an option, but I doubt Michael would be too keen on that. "Have you talked to him about it?"

"No, not yet. But the idea has been floating around in my head. Rent is going up around here faster than you can blink. And I'm kind of tired of the big-city life. I need a change of pace. I want a house with a yard and all that, y'know? And I think the boys would like the change. I'm just not sure how to approach Michael about it without upsetting him even more."

I shudder at a disturbing thought. "Why? He hasn't been hitting you or the kids, has he?"

"No, absolutely not. He's never been physical with us. Michael's a lot of things, but he's definitely not *that*. I just worry about him giving up so easily. The boys are seeing this, and I don't want them to think any less of their father."

"Well, you'll just have to continue being strong for them in the meantime."

"I'm trying." She pauses again. "Maybe we can move out to Washington near you."

Oh, God. I certainly don't mind Elouise and the kids, but being so close to my stubborn brother is the last thing I need, or want. "Ehh…"

"You'll get to finally see the boys, at least."

The hopeful thought tugs at my heart. I never really cared about kids until I saw the first photos of my nephews when they were born. Having kids of my own has never really been on my radar, either, living the life I live. "Yeah, that'd be nice."

We talk a little while longer and hang up. She'd sounded a little better after I assured her everything would work out. I'm not sure what that would even mean. I'm no counselor, and my little pep-talk probably doesn't mean shit. But Elouise seems to take almost everything I say as gold. All that matters is that she stays strong for those kids.

I return to the garage and find Grandpa at the workbench, adjusting some engine valves with a torque wrench. He stops working and looks up at me. "Elouise all right?" he asks.

I shrug and take the wrench from him. "She's fine," I say, hoping he won't ask any more about it.

He frowns, then shakes his head. "Why that dear, sweet woman ever married someone like your brother, I'll never know," he says, returning to the office.

Ditto. As I continue torquing bolts, I can't help but think about Cassandra and her affinity for Jacob. He's just another dime-a-dozen asshole, like my brother. How could any girl find someone like that attractive?

Or am *I* the one with the problem?

Five o'clock rolls around, and I clock out with my second paycheck of the day in tow. Grandpa had left earlier to take care of some things with his business consultant, and I was tasked with locking up the shop. I head over to Dim Sum Noodle House down the street for a cheap, but filling, two-dollar beef lo mein dinner. Most of the tables are occupied with city workers and small families, but I find an empty ta-ble in the back. A small radio posted on a shelf in the corner is tuned to a baseball game. I absently watch the crowd while my mind wanders back to tomorrow's race.

With only twenty-four hours left to get Sasha dialed in, I plan on pulling an all-nighter. Clayton and Gabriel had promised to look for a good deal on a new set of tires after they got off work, while Mariah and Luke went to see Dave about getting their hands on some avgas. I'm glad they final-ly came around and are working with me to win this race—it wasn't just Sasha on the line, but *our* turf and *our* pride as well. Sometimes we didn't see eye-to-eye on things, but in the end, the Wild Aces were family, and we weren't about to let the Ninez rub our family name in the dirt. I just hope it will all be worth it in the end.

I tip back my head, chugging the last contents of my soda. My ears are suddenly drawn to a radio commercial for Henge Masonry and Construction, a company in Tukwila that Donaldson Construction has occasionally done joint work with. It sounds like the company is currently expand-ing, looking to fill a bunch of roles with higher-than-average pay. I widen my eyes at the mention of the base pay, which is twice as much as I'm making at Donaldson. I resist the temp-tation of submitting an application myself. I doubt Henge would ever give me a flexible schedule like Donaldson does, and I'd probably end up having to quit my job at Grandpa's shop too. But I don't think I could ever do that. I've been working for him for so long, I've fallen into a routine that would be hard to change. Not to mention, he pays me for working on cars, which I love. And maybe most importantly, he's also blood. I couldn't leave him high-and-dry like that.

Besides all that, I don't know the first thing about masonry.

But I *do* have a now-unemployed older brother who's been a block-mason for over ten years. I'm sure he'd get a job with them, no problem.

Just what Elouise was looking for.

I grit my teeth. *I don't owe Michael shit.* Not with the way he's treated me. He doesn't give a damn about anything I'd say, anyway.

But then I think about the opportunity to see my nephews in person for the first time ever. *Helping Michael will help Elouise and the boys,* I try to reason with myself. *Why should they all suffer on account of my stubbornness?*

I fish for a pen from my backpack and jot down Henge Masonry and Construction's telephone number on an unused napkin. *I guess I'll do my good deed for the day.*

Chapter 6

$\mathbf{M}$Y CREW AND I DRIVE TO THE OLD AIRSTRIP IN FIFE around eight thirty Saturday night. I'd only gotten a few hours of sleep early that morning—I was up and awake at the crack of dawn to do some last-minute modifications on Sasha. My heart pounds furiously at a sudden rush of anxiety as I turn off Highway 509 and follow the Puyallup River along the endless, narrow stretch of road. I ride a half-mile and veer off on a dirt path, half-hidden by trees and under-brush. Dozens of sets of headlights in the distance denote the makeshift raceway ahead.

Fife Airstrip is a racing spot owned by another crew in town, the Burn Dawgs. They're a cool bunch, letting anyone and everyone race on their turf, so long as nobody starts shit. And Sasha, of course, is always welcome.

The airstrip used to be a small private airfield back in the late '30s. In time, the only standing structure—a giant block-

and-steel tunnel hangar—had deteriorated to a hauntingly empty ruin overgrown with grass and trees on its roof, and most of the concrete runway had crumbled and become lush with weeds between the cracks of the pavement. But a half-mile's-worth of landing strip had been miraculously untouched by time, or at least untouched enough, and that was where the crews raced. The area, which ran parallel to a seldom-used railroad line, was mostly surrounded by large shade trees, giving us plenty of privacy from the law.

We arrive to a sea of cars parked in and around the large hangar, with others already racing on the main strip. The headlights of some of the idle-running cars provide the place with ample light.

Damn, looks like every crew in Washington is out here. I guess they're all wondering if I'm going to lose Sasha tonight.

I drive toward the heart of the action while the rest of my crew park together in an empty spot that's strategically near the only way in and out of the place in case shit goes south. Heads turn as Sasha makes her grand entrance, and oglers scramble out of her path. Much of the crowd is made up of pimple-faced teens and barely-legal adults. I look for the Ninez's cars, and discover them parked near the hangar, all of them gleaming with new paint jobs. Cassandra's Nova is parked off to the side of the airstrip's starting line. There's new royal blue paint, new wheels, and a high-rise manifold attached to the hood—and that's only the visible mods. I can only imagine what she's done to that engine.

I park a little ways away from her car and get out. A group of teens nearby are rocking out to a Metallica song playing from a boombox, while a couple of young skater guys are engaged in a game of hacky sack. I flick my gaze to the starting line, where a crowd is gathered watching a Trans Am and GTO prepare to burn rubber. A guy in a blue Burn Dawgs jacket, standing in the middle of the strip, a few feet in front of the cars, flicks on a flashlight. The cars surge forward in a cloud of smoke. The surrounding crowd cheers. I stuff my hands in my pockets and idly watch as my crew approaches, then disperses among the crowd. They're blending in to keep an eye on things, ready to intervene in case the Ninez decide to do something stupid. Unlike last time, we're all armed, as much as I hate it. But I can't trust what Jacob's crew might do tonight.

"Hey…"

I pause and look over my shoulder, spotting Clayton.

He steps a little closer to me and continues just loud enough for me to hear, "I meant to tell you earlier… When we get back home, I gotta talk to you about something."

"'Bout what?" I wrinkle my brow.

He smiles. "My new job."

"You got a job? Finally? With your track record?"

"I know, right? Well, I've had it for a couple weeks now. It's easy as hell with amazing pay. They're looking for some new guys who know how to drive, and I thought you might be interested. Anyway, we'll talk later."

I nod. "Sure thing. I'm happy for you, man."

"Thanks, man. Back to work, I guess." He leaves and disappears among a huddle of people who surround and ogle at a tricked-out yellow Camaro with its hood raised.

My sexy rival emerges from the crowd, decked out in a brown leather jacket, jeans, and black boots. *Cassandra.* I drink up the sight of her swaying hips as she walks toward me with a confident swagger. My eyes travel up to the un-zipped jacket, revealing a stretchy red top with a neckline that plunges just enough to tease some of her ample cleavage. I smile, enjoying the eye candy until she stops in front of me and crosses her arms.

"Hey! Up here, asshole," she says.

Caught. I drag my eyes away from her tits, and to the an-noyed, but slightly amused expression on her face. *Damn, she's cute.* "'Sup," I greet with a tip of my head.

"'Bout time you showed up."

I chuckle. "Unlike Jacob, I don't back down from a chal-lenge."

Her amused expression grows, and she uncrosses her arms. "You sound so sure of yourself."

I nod toward her parked car. "You rebuilt that 396?"

She raises her eyebrows, then snorts. "396? Fuck that. She's got a 454 now. Big Block. Q&R heads, rods, and pis-tons."

I widen my eyes slightly, and I can't help but grin. "You like Q&R?"

"Fuck yeah. I trust no other brand."

A woman after my own heart.

"Be ready to give up Sasha at the finish line," she contin-ues. "'Cause you're about to get scorched. No *technicalities* to save you this time."

I don't respond and simply watch her return to the crowd with that same confident swagger in her step. As I stare at her incredible ass, lost in thoughts of what I'd like to do with it, reality suddenly hits me. *Holy shit.* She's modded the hell out of that Nova. She could very well beat me this time around with that much ammunition under her hood. What other surprises did she have in there?

Someone slaps me on the shoulder. "Let's do this, man," Clayton's voice says in my ear.

"Yeah," I say, then look sideways at him. "Hey, if I lose tonight… you're gonna be the Wild Aces' new leader, okay? Without Sasha, I'm back to being a car-less scrub." *A loser.* I'd never be able to show my face around here again. I've got too much pride to just let that hang over my head. To see it in everyone's eyes when I walk by.

Clayton drops his hand from my shoulder and stares at me—or perhaps through me. "You got nothin' to worry about, man." He looks shocked, but his firm voice sounds reassuring. *Maybe even a little excited?* I don't think he has any idea what Cassandra's packing.

I don't respond.

Sudden cheers and whistles signal another race about to begin. Two lowrider pickup trucks—both decked out with sick paint jobs—rumble with anticipation at the starting line, but I'm too edged on adrenaline and nervousness to focus on them.

Off to the side, among the cluster of people and parked vehicles, Preston and Jacob stand together smoking cigarettes. Cassandra approaches them and stands next to Jacob.

Her face is stony as she says something to him, then turns to leave. The continuous roar of the motors, mixed with the chanting, rowdy crowd doesn't draw my attention away from their exchange.

I scowl. *What are they planning now?*

Jacob stomps out his finished cigarette on the ground, grabs Cassandra's arm and spins her around so they're looking eye to eye. His nose wrinkles as he speaks to her. Judging by Cassandra's scowl—and rigid body—it's nothing good. She retaliates by shoving him in the chest and pointing a finger in his face as she shouts something at him. Preston tenses and bows up to Cassandra, but Jacob stops him with a hand to his chest and a shake of his head. Cassandra storms off to her car, and Jacob lights another cigarette like nothing happened.

I step my foot forward, then stop myself. *What the hell am I doing? That's their business, not mine.*

Moments later, someone I don't recognize approaches Jacob—a little shorter in height, athletic build—wearing a red padded jacket and a matching red bandanna. Jacob exhales a stream of smoke through his nose and begins talking to the guy. Jacob's lips move, then stop, and the side of his mouth gives a nervous, twitchy smile. The red-clad stranger doesn't seem to respond. Jacob's eyes not so subtly dart around, focusing on everything else but Red Bandanna Guy. Preston, his face the same as Jacob's, stands next to them, anxiously tapping his fingers on the biceps of his crossed arms.

The high-pitched whines of small engines slice through the night air. I turn to the sounds and watch as two sport bikes perform burnouts at the starting line. Clouds of thick white smoke billow from beneath their back tires and envelop the surrounding cheering crowd, eventually passing over me. My eyes water and my vision blurs as I wave off the rubber fumes, and, as the smoke dissipates, I feel a presence beside me. I look to my right, where a man dressed in red, just like the mysterious guy who confronted Jacob, is admiring Sasha. He's taller than the guy who talked to Jacob, a little stockier, and he stands there with his arms crossed, studying the car with a stern expression on his face.

He finally looks at me and tips his head, covered by a red bandanna. "What's up, man."

I return the gesture, feeling a hint of wariness in my gut. *I've seen his type before.* "'Sup."

He slowly walks around the car, staring as though he were examining a pure diamond. "Damn, Jacob wasn't kidding about Sasha. She's beautiful."

I feel my throat tighten. "You know Jacob?"

Mr. Red stops and smirks. "I know *of* him."

"Funny, I thought I saw one of your guys talking to him earlier."

His expression doesn't change. "Yeah, my crew's new in town, and Jacob is—shall we say—giving us a little tour."

"Oh, well welcome to the neighborhood," I say bitterly.

"Thanks." He turns his attention back to Sasha. "So how much you want for her?"

I blink. *The fuck?* "She's not for sale."

He laughs. "I've got fifteen grand waiting right now. We got a deal?"

My left eye twitches. I've never even seen that much money before in my life. But all the money in the world isn't enough for me to part with Sasha. "Maybe you didn't hear me the first time. She's *not* for sale."

He runs his finger down the front of her hood, leaving behind a tiny, smeared line of dirt, too small for an average person to notice. "Very, very nice paint," he says, as if ignoring me. "How 'bout twenty-five grand? Cash. Deal?"

My jaw drops. *Did he just...* I storm over to the guy and shove him back away from the car. "Don't touch my fucking car again, asshole, or you'll need that money for the hospital!"

Mr. Red stares daggers at me, and he bows up in retaliation. But that shit doesn't faze me. At six foot six, I tower over the guy a good three inches at least.

I bow up to him as well. "What?" I taunt.

The sounds of a chain clink behind me.

"Problems?" Someone comes between us, giving us space. It's Martin, a member of the Burn Dawgs. A giant red-and-yellow patch of his crew's symbol—a fiery Cerberus—is emblazoned on the back of his black leather jacket. Apollo, a large, full-grown Rottweiler and one of the Burn Dawgs' mascots, sits beside him on a chain leash.

Mr. Red looks from Martin to Apollo, and then holds his hands up in surrender. "Nope. No problems at all, man. Just amping up the competition, y'know."

"Bullshit," I spit.

"We'll talk later, Adam." Mr. Red laughs and walks off, joining the rest of the crowd at the starting line, where another race is about to begin.

How the hell did he know my— I growl and buff off the dirt with my shirt sleeve. *Of course. Jacob probably blabbed my whole life story to him.* "Who the hell is that guy?" I ask Martin.

Martin shrugs. "Drew, I think he said. He's the leader of a crew called the Red Ravens. They're new in town, from Portland."

"Drew wants to buy Sasha for twenty-five grand. Cash," I say, checking and double-checking the spot for the slightest speck of dirt.

Martin whistles. "No shit? You gonna do it?"

I rip my attention from the hood to Martin and glare. "*Hell* no!"

"Yeah, that's what I thought you'd say. Everyone wants a piece of her."

"Then they need to build their own and leave my shit alone. You better keep an eye on those guys. The fact that they're hanging around Jacob can't be a good sign." The entire encounter reminds me of my days in New York and roughing it up with cocky bastards like Drew. They were wannabe gangsters, and a few of them even had some ties with the Mob. I'd gotten out of that life just in time.

"Yeah, I know. We got it handled. Now, what about you, man?" Martin smiles and pats me on the shoulder. "Ready to give us a show?"

I push my anger aside and think about the upcoming race. "Always." I bend and give Apollo a good scratch behind the ear. The dog sniffs me a moment, and then his body relaxes as he wags his tail, happy for the attention. Aside from the rest of the Burn Dawgs crew, I've been the only outsider Apollo tolerates.

"Damn, he still likes you," Martin says.

"That's 'cause he knows what's up." I stop petting the dog, and he slobbers my hand with his tongue. I remember when Martin's crew first found Apollo and his brother Cronos abandoned as puppies three years ago. Both dogs had taken a liking to me back then, just as they do now, and I still haven't figured out why.

"This race is gonna be somethin' tonight," Martin says. "You got balls wagerin' Sasha. I'm pullin' for you, though." He nudges me in the arm with his elbow. "Ain't nobody can ride 'er the way you do."

I chuckle. "Thanks, man."

The familiar roar of a 454 motor riles my heartbeat. Cassandra pulls up beside me in her Nova. She rolls down the driver's side window, and smirks. "You might as well hand those keys over to me right now, Adam."

I snort. "You gotta earn 'em, baby."

Her mouth turns to a frown. "Don't worry. I will." She cranks the window back up and drives up to the starting line.

I hop in my car and take my place beside her. In the distance, the Ninez's cars head toward the finish line. Moments later, my crew's vehicles follow. I exhale, trusting that my family has things under control while I concentrate on the race.

The race. I cut my gaze to the guy in front of us, wearing the black Burn Dawgs jacket and holding the flashlight. Taking a deep breath, I stretch my fingers over the steering wheel and slowly curl them around the top.

I got this. Nobody's taking my baby away tonight.

"Don't fail me now, girl," I mutter, drawing one hand down to the gear shift.

Chapter 7

Time suddenly stops. Adrenaline sends blood rushing to my ears, drowning out the cheers of the crowd around me. Darkness shades my periphery, and all I can see is the line of small white dots in the distance from headlights, which outline the end of the 1320-foot stretch of road ahead. My future in the racing scene—my car, my crew, my credibility… my passion—is waiting for me at the end.

Last chance. Do or die.

My heart leaps into my tight throat. Sweat slicks my palms, and I white-knuckle the wheel with one hand and the cue-ball shifter with the other.

The Burn Dawgs flagger shines the flashlight.

My foot instinctively floors the pedal. Sasha's engine roars and her tires squeal, kicking up clouds of white smoke. I keep my focus straight ahead as I crank the shifter to fifth gear as Sasha pushes for top speed. The roar of the Nova's 454 looming so close tempts me to look and see how much Cassandra's hanging on—or gaining.

Not now. Gotta stay focused.

The swarm of lights at the finish line rapidly draws nearer, individual sets of headlights becoming more and more distinct.

The chrome glint of a high-rise manifold slides into my periphery as it slowly creeps ahead. I've squeezed nearly everything I can out of Sasha, and Cassandra's right on my heels. My breath hitches.

No! No no no no!

I can't believe it. Sasha's met her match. What the hell kind of mods did Cassandra make? But I can't give up. Not now. I'll be damned if Jacob or that Red Raven clown get their hands on *my* car.

"C'mon, baby…" I mutter.

The Nova roars louder, and I can see Cassandra through its passenger-side window. I've only got one move left—nitrous. Last time, I had flipped the switch too early, sure that 'Jacob' was already buried. But Cassandra wasn't playing with me now. This had to be perfect. *Is she waiting for me to pull the trigger?* I try to make sense of the distance and timing in my mind, but nerves and adrenaline shatter anything coherent. This would have to be all instinct.

Five hundred feet left. *No.*

There wouldn't be time to let Sasha breathe before punching it at this point, and now a new concern floats into my consciousness—would she even hold together all the way to the finish?

Four hundred feet. *Not yet.*

Three hundred feet. *Now!* I flip on the nitrous switch and give Sasha her second wind. The engine screams with its newfound energy, sending me blazing toward the finish line and thrown back in my seat. Sasha shakes and rattles, her body pushed to the absolute limits, but Cassandra's still just inches behind me *Did she activate her nitrous at the same time?* I instinctually press the pedal down even harder, trying to bust it through the floor, but she's got nothing more left to give.

Sasha chokes, and a loud *pop* erupts from her hood…

Almost there.

…And she crosses the finish line, winning by a nose.

I come to a screeching halt and exhale. I release my hands from the wheel and shifter, and they begin to shake uncontrollably. My heart still pounds as the fast and furious high slowly winds down.

Cheers and whistles surround me. Among the rowdy crowd, which is a mix of various crews and unaffiliated kids, is the Wild Aces, celebrating my victory. I take a deep breath and slowly get out the car. People jump and whoop at my victory, and the cheering gets louder.

"Holy shit, man! That was the best race I've ever seen!" someone says.

"That was close! You got her ass, though!" another says.

Nearby, secured on a chain leash that's tied to the hitch of a parked pickup truck is Apollo's identical brother and the Burn Dawgs' other mascot, Cronos. He gives an enthusiastic bark my way and wags his tail.

Cassandra, who's parked about thirty feet away, gets out of her car. She leans against the door, crosses her arms, and glares in my direction. A mix of frustration, sadness, and disbelief mar her beautiful brown eyes.

Moments later, Jacob appears from the crowd and storms over to her. "Bitch, can't you do *anything* right?" he yells.

Cassandra balls her fists. "Fuck you! I did a whole hell of a lot better than your cowardly ass would've done!"

Some curious young spectators leave the victory crowd and gather around the shouting match. The Wild Aces can't help but follow to watch the show. The rest of the Ninez shove their way through the mob to stand with their leader inside the circle. Cronos' barks grow deeper. This shit's going south fast. It's déjà vu. Jacob's liable to hurt someone out here. Maybe Cassandra. I can't let that happen. It wasn't her fault that Jacob is a shitty leader. My fingers twitch, ready to withdraw the hidden, holstered .45 from my jacket's inner pocket. I pray to God it doesn't come to that.

"You owe me more than you fucking know!" Jacob yells in her face.

Cassandra responds by slugging him in the mouth so hard that Jacob stumbles backward.

"Oooh!" the spectators holler, then close my only vantage point with their huddled bodies.

Aw hell. I rush to the crowd and push my way through, just in time to see Jacob regain his composure.

"I don't owe you shit, so don't act like you own me, asshole!" Cassandra warns, pointing to him.

Bryce and Preston position themselves around Cassandra in such a way that she would have nowhere to run.

A Burn Dawgs member squeezes his way to the center and tips his head at Jacob, then at Cassandra. Jacob clenches his fists, about to confront the guy, but when he realizes just how taller and brawnier he is, he pales and unclenches his fists.

"Problems?" the guy warns, his voice as deep and foreboding as Cronos' bellows. I know the guy. Goes by Francis—funny name for a guy like him, but he's the Burn Dawgs' enforcer. If anyone fucks with him—*especially* his name—he'd turn their face into a punching bag.

Francis addresses the rest of the crowd. "Nothin' t'see here. Leave." He points toward the starting line. "Another race is about to start." It seems that's all he has to say for the circle to quickly disperse.

Francis tips his head at me. "'Ey. You takin' her ride or what?"

I look from the brick wall of a man to Cassandra, who gives me a cold stare. "Naw, man," I reply.

Cassandra looks back at me as I say this, scowls, and heads for her car.

"Fine, whatever," Francis says. He brushes past me and slaps me on the shoulder. "Good race, by the way."

After he leaves, I look back at Jacob, who's now confronted by a Red Ravens member. There's an exchange of words and Jacob stiffens. The rest of the Ninez gather around their cowardly leader—everyone except Cassandra, who stands next to the open door of her Nova and watches from a distance.

The air grows tenser. The pounding in my chest returns and becomes uncontrollably faster—so fast, I can hear it over the voices of the crowd. Even though my crew and I are carrying, it wouldn't do any good if Drew and Jacob's crews teamed up on us. I may not be able to save Cassandra if she can't let go of Jacob.

My crew is heading toward their cars, about to leave the scene, so I do the same. Whatever happens here isn't my problem.

I hope Cassandra hauls ass on Jacob. It's the least she could do for all the times Jacob's mistreated her.

I grab the door handle and look over my shoulder at the crowd once more, just in time to see Jacob throw a punch at the Red Raven's face. A brawl ensues. From out of the crowd, three more guys in red appear carrying a bat, knife, and bare-handed brute strength enter the fray with the other Ninez members. Francis and more Burn Dawgs members rush back to intervene.

My street senses are screaming at me that it's time to go. *Now.* I open Sasha's driver-side door.

"Uh-uh."

That voice. Drew. I freeze and feel something sharp press against my lower kidney. Looking sideways toward the voice, I notice the splotch of red cloth wrapped around the man's head, and another tied around his upper forearm.

Swallowing, I slowly hold my hands up in surrender. "Whoa, man, what're you doing? I'm not with the Ninez."

Drew presses the sharp object a little firmer, making my body flinch. Any harder, and he'll be puncturing skin, for sure. "Jacob didn't follow through on the deal he promised us, so I'm here to collect."

I blink. "What deal?"

"I paid a shit-ton to get this car, and Jacob promised he'd get it to us tonight. Well, he might've fucked up, but the car is here, and that's all that matters."

I grit my teeth. "How many times do I have to tell you? Sasha's *not* for sale!"

He chuckles. "Yeah. She's not. She belongs to the Red Ravens now."

"Fuck that. Whatever deal you made with Jacob is your own damn problem. Not mine."

"Oh, it's *definitely* your problem now. See, I tried to be nice. Offer you some cash… Then you threaten to send *me* to the hospital? You don't know who the hell you're messing with. Sasha's mine, and like I tell my bitches, I don't take 'no' for an answer."

My left eye twitches. I never thought I'd hear someone who sounds worse than Jacob. I need to put some distance between myself and that knife if I've got any chance of leaving here without a few new holes. An idea flashes through my mind—maybe the only shot I've got. Just hope it works. "Fine. Take the damn car," I say, keeping my hands up.

"Gimme the keys."

"Get 'em yourself." I make a small head gesture to my left pants pocket.

Scowling, Drew moves to fish for the keys. I feel the knife ease off from my skin while Drew's briefly distracted. It's just enough of an opportunity to turn this situation back into my favor. As Drew yanks the keys from my pocket, I jerk my body forward slightly and spin toward his weapon hand, grabbing it with my left, while I follow through with a punch to his jaw with my right. His body hits the side of my car, the impact taking his breath. He drops the keys and the knife, and I kick them both away.

I grab him by the collar, but he returns the favor, headbutting me hard, and I'm seeing stars for a moment. I'm suddenly slammed to the ground from behind. Drew pins me there and wraps his arms around my neck in a rear choke.

"I'm gonna break your fuckin' neck!" he says through gritted teeth as he squeezes his forearms harder.

I grunt and attempt to push him off me, but he has me good. I peg his husky build at least two hundred and fifty pounds of pure muscle. With him on top, budging him is going to be challenging.

The sound of a chain breaking cuts through the noise, and Cronos' rabid barking gets closer. I manage to catch a dark shape racing toward us from my fading periphery. Headlights soon reflect the dog's glowing eyes, and he pounces on Drew and clamps down on his leg with powerful jaws. Drew screams and attempts to kick the dog off, but Cronos is solid. His hold on me loosens. I punch Drew hard in the chin, sending his head snapping back, and I roll out from under him. Drew crumples to the ground as Cronos mauls him.

I stand, grab my discarded keys, and hop in my car. "Thanks, boy," I tell Cronos.

A pang of several gunshots fire, the sound triggering screams among the crowd of spectators, and they scatter in a frightened panic. Some flee on foot, others drive off. The sea of chaos gridlocks the only way out of here.

"Shit!" I yell. I grab my .45 from my jacket and look out the windows for the shooter. A pit starts growing in my stomach. I catch sight of Cassandra's Nova—three distinct bullet holes riddle the windshield, but thankfully, Cassandra isn't inside. I try to make her out among the fleeing crowd, but she's nowhere to be found. A few Red Ravens and Burn Dawg members—including Francis—lay on the ground, not moving.

Two more shots ring out, followed by a large bang and the shattering of glass behind me. I look out the driver's side mirror at a green MR2 Turbo crumpled into one side of the Nova. The driver lolls forward, his forehead resting on the steering wheel. Two bullet holes pepper the spiderweb designs of the windshield's broken glass.

I maneuver through the gridlock, dodging vehicles and people. My headlights shine on a group of people who push and shove and trample a woman to the ground just as a car zooms past. Sasha's headlights shine on the brown leather jacket of the fallen woman, and my breath hitches.

She's not moving.

Fuck! I slam my feet on the brakes. I feel the tires lose their grip on the crumbly ground, and my entire body lurches forward, only to be immediately detained by the seat belt.

I look around at the sea of escaping cars and people and pray that the Red Ravens aren't on my tail. Looking back at Cassandra, I clench my jaw. Whether she's alive or dead, I can't just leave her here. I scramble out of my car, run to her body and carry her in my arms. An incoming car rushes toward us as I reach Sasha. I press myself flat against Sasha's hood, with Cassandra sandwiched between me. The car zooms past. My heart skips a beat as the wind from the car's uncomfortable closeness sends the hair on my arms standing on end. I check to make sure it's clear for the moment, and I hurry and set Cassandra in the passenger's seat. I jump back in the driver's seat and haul ass out of there.

Chapter 8

My gaze bounces repeatedly between my front and rear-view mirrors for trailing headlights as I zoom farther and farther away from Fife Airstrip. My heart's still pumping and the sweat from my palms makes the steering wheel slippery. I tighten my grip, trying to keep steady on the road. With my crew already gone ahead of me back to the Shed, I still have one little problem in the passenger's seat. But I can't go back to the city just yet. Not when the Red Ravens and Ninez might still be around.

Instead, I detour east to Edgewood, about four miles away from the airstrip. I pull into a gas station along the highway and park on the side of the building, near a pay phone. I shut off the car and look beside me. Cassandra still rests in the same position I set her in. Frowning, I flip on the interior lights. She suddenly mutters something I can't understand, and I blink.

"Cassandra?" I call in a soft, concerned voice. The overhead dome light shines on the side of her bruised face. Her left eye is slightly puffy. I run my hand along her hair and feel a small lump at the back of her head. Cringing, I pull away. That probably explains her loopiness. I look at the rest of her and spot a pair of bloody knuckles.

"Cassandra!" I say again, but she doesn't reply. I'm not sure if she can hear me. I place my hand on her cheek and feel warmth. I notice the faint rise and fall of her chest. I exhale a long, slow breath of relief. Thank God she's still alive.

I should let the rest of my crew know I won't be home anytime soon.

I get out the car and hustle to the nearest pay phone, call Gabriel's beeper, then hang up. Waiting by the phone, I frequently glance back to the road to make sure no one had been following. The pay phone soon rings. "Hello?"

"Adam! Where the hell are you?" Gabriel asks. I can hear the panic in his voice even through the bad-receiver static.

"I'm alive," I reply calmly. "I didn't want to take the chance that those Red Raven guys might still be tailing me, so I'm laying low in Edgewood for now."

"Edgewood? What the fuck, man?"

"Look, I gotta take care of some things, then I'll head home, okay? Just let everyone know I'm fine."

He sighs. "Yeah, whatever. Do what you gotta do."

"Clay's in charge for now, understand?"

"Yeah."

I hang up on him and head inside the gas station's convenience store to buy a box of bandages, some antiseptic, and a bottle of Coke. Before leaving, I also grab a wad of napkins from the food station. Back at the car, I check on Cassandra. She's still out, her head leaned to one side. She occasionally mumbles gibberish. I squeeze some antiseptic on a napkin, then gently take one of her hands in mine and carefully dab the napkin over the wounds on her knuckles. Her slender hands aren't smooth and silky like ordinary girls'. Her short, unmanicured nails have a little oil and dirt underneath them. There's a certain beauty about her hands that gives me goosebumps. They're the hands of a hard-working woman who knows how to mod the hell out of a 454.

As I wrap a bandage around the wounds, the muscles in her forearm suddenly twitch, and I pause. Her closed eyelids flutter, and the side of her mouth twitches. She stirs, slowly opening her eyes, and looks at me groggily. She pushes on the seat trying to sit up and lets out a small groan of pain, gingerly feeling for the knot in the back of her head.

"Who… Where…" she mutters.

"Hey," I say in a calm, reassuring voice. "It's okay. Don't try to move too much. Do you remember the last thing that happened?"

She focuses on me with narrowed eyes. "Adam… You…"

Well, at least she remembers me.

"Yeah… look. There was trouble back at Fife Airstrip. We'll be lucky if this shit doesn't make the local news tomorrow. I found you lying on the ground, probably about to get trampled or run over. Do you want to go to a hospital?"

She hisses and sneers. "Fuck no."

"Okay, then. So, what the hell happened back there?"

She averts her gaze.

"Do you remember anything?" I persist.

There's a long pause, and she still doesn't look at me. "I got caught up in this huge fight and some motherfucker hit me from behind."

I exhale deeply through my nose. "Well, looks like you did some work on him," I say, indicating her bloody knuckles.

"Someone shot up my car too. Ugh. I need to go back and—"

"No, it's a bloodbath back there. It was a real shitshow. I saw bodies hit the ground. There's no point in going back."

She grits her teeth. "Did Jacob make it out?"

Seriously? Jacob's shitted on her more times than I can count in the short time I've known her, and she's still concerned about him. "I dunno. He wasn't around when I found you, so I'm guessing he and the rest of your crew abandoned you—again."

She frowns. "That motherfucker…"

"What do you see in that guy, anyway?"

"That's none of your business."

I snort. "Whatever. You're too strong of a woman for him. I've known Jacob long enough to know that he's a pussy when shit gets tough. He lets other people do his dirty work, like he's been doing with you, racing me for Sasha."

She scowls. "You don't know shit about my relationship with Jacob, so don't act like you do."

I shake my head, then grab the Coke bottle and pry off the metal cap with my car key. "I don't know what the hell kind of *relationship* you two have. Definitely not one I could understand." The cap pops off and I offer her the bottle. "Want some?"

She looks at it a moment, then takes it and presses the cold bottle to the side of her head.

I sigh, watching her. Jacob sure as hell wouldn't be by her side like this. Does she really find some sort of security with him? "You know, it really sucks to watch you get abused by that asshole who walks like a man."

She glares. "What's it to you? You think I'm fucking him or something?"

"It's not that hard to tell when you hang around him the way you do."

"It's not what it looks like. I'm trying to be his number one."

I arch an eyebrow. "You know he's gonna make you fuck him before he even considers making you his number one, right?"

"In his dreams. He'll see he ain't shit without me when he tries to rely on his scrubs. He'll be the one begging me."

I snicker. If it's one thing I know about Jacob is that he never begs. Ever. Especially to a woman. I put my key in the ignition, but don't start up the car just yet. "Well, if I were in your shoes, I'd rather be a car-less scrub than Jacob's number one. But hey, you're a grown woman. Do whatever you want."

She watches me in silence.

Nothing? I hadn't expected that as a response. *Maybe she's actually reconsidering.* "Uh, yeah, so… you want me to drop you off somewhere, or…"

"Yeah. Take me back to Fife."

I blink, my hand sliding off the key-lodged ignition. *My ears must be deceiving me.* "Did you not hear what I said earlier?"

"I gotta get my car back."

Nope. They're not. "You're serious? The Red Ravens are probably still there. I wouldn't go back there for a while."

"Hell no. I worked too hard to get my car dialed in. That's my last bit of dignity." She removes the cold bottle from the bump on her head and takes a long swig.

I can't believe this. She wants to risk her life for that fucking Nova. Hell, I guess I'd do the same, too, if it were Sasha.

My God. She's amazing.

She wrinkles her nose. "What are you smiling about?"

"Jacob's such an idiot, abandoning a girl like you."

She continues looking at me oddly.

I start up my car. Cassandra lets out a deep sigh and closes her eyes.

"You sure you're okay?" I ask her.

"I'm fine. Just drive," she mutters.

Without another word, I leave the gas station and head down the street, back to Fife.

"So who are these Red Raven guys, anyway?" I ask, glancing sideways at Cassandra.

She puts the Coke bottle to her lips and chugs the rest of the bottle's contents. "No idea. Apparently, Jacob knows 'em. Guess he pissed 'em off pretty bad."

"Yeah, he has a knack for doing that."

Another pause. "Why are you doing this?"

"What?"

"Helping me."

I fall silent. *Because I like you,* I want to say, but then realize how cheesy that sounds. "'Cause no one ever helped me when I was in deep shit."

"What about your crew? Your family?"

"My crew's got my back. My family, not so much. They live on the other side of the country, anyway."

"Where're you from?"

"Originally? The Bronx, New York. These days? Tacoma Eastside."

She raises her eyebrows, seemingly impressed. "So, you're a street punk like me. Well, you should know not to meddle in another crew's affairs, then."

"Yeah, I know. But you're too good of a driver for me to just ignore. The best I've seen in a really long time." I pause and look at her carefully, then dare to say, "And you're hot as hell."

Her lips twist to a coy smile and she laughs it off.

Yeah, I know that look. She knows she's hot.

Still smiling, she crosses her arms. "I'm not fucking you because you helped me out, Adam."

I look at her in surprise, then laugh. "Whoa, what? I never asked you to. But it sounds to me like the thought is on your mind."

She laughs again. "No, I'm just setting the record straight before you get any bright ideas."

"Mmhmm."

The expression on her face softens a little, and I notice a side of her I hadn't seen before. A more vulnerable side. She looks comfortable, safe. She has a sense of humor beneath that rigid, grungy, street façade. I'm sure she's not this way around Jacob. *If she'd just let me get to know her…*

We ride the rest of the way in silence. The roads are dark, and when we return to the airstrip, we discover it empty with garbage strewn all over the ground. We drive down the stretch of the eerily desolate airfield. The headlights reflect the tiny dots of bullet casings on the ground around where the big fight broke out. I even spot Cronos' broken chain leash.

No bodies, though, thank God. The crews must've gotten their people out—hopefully some of them made it.

The headlights finally shine on the Nova—or what's left of it.

The car has been stripped down to a bare body and shattered, bullet-riddled windows. The tires, raised manifold, and every other visible modification are gone.

The green MR2 Turbo that had crashed into the Nova has been moved to the side. The driver's body is gone.

Damn, everyone cleaned up quick.

Cassandra gasps and gets out of my car. She limps to the Nova, staring at it for a moment while swaying on shaky legs, and then balls her hands into tight fists. I get out the car and stand beside her. Her eyes are glittering like she's about to cry, but no tears fall. I lower my head and stay quiet. She hugs herself and rocks back and forth slowly.

"They took… *every*thing from me," she whispers.

My frown deepens as I look back at the empty husk of the Nova. A small, torn piece of red cloth is stuck to a shard of the shattered windshield. I swipe the cloth and examine it. It's thin to the touch, and there's a paisley design on it—the same kind of design that's commonly seen on bandannas. *The Red Ravens did this?* Gritting my teeth, I show her the cloth.

She takes one look and frowns. "I can't believe this shit."

"I'm sorry," is all I can say.

She spins on her heel and heads back to my car, getting in the passenger side. I follow her and climb into the driver's seat, but don't start up the car just yet. "You… want me to take you somewhere?"

She stares blankly at the dashboard and mutters, "Anywhere but here."

I scratch the stubble on my jaw while I think. "I'll take you back to the city, and Jacob can—"

"No. Fuck Jacob. Fuck the Ninez."

I blink several times. *Whoa…*

"I have no car. I have nothing now. Because of his bullshit I'm a scrub. You know how long it took me to get this far? All my hard-earned money and the tireless fucking work I put into that car. All the respect I'd earned from my crew and everyone else—*everything* I've worked hard for—gone in a night."

You damn sure have my *respect.* "You're too good for them. They couldn't handle you on your worst day."

She finally raises her gaze to me, then purses her lips, looking thoughtful about something. "I'll make a deal with you."

I raise my eyebrows with piqued interest. "I'm listening."

She chews her bottom lip, as though she's already regretting what she's about to say. "I'll help you take out the Red Ravens. Put the Wild Aces on the map. You guys will rule Tacoma."

"You'll help me and my crew? What about the Ninez?"

"What *about* them?" She shakes her head. "I can't keep doing this. All my blood, sweat, and tears—all of my *dignity*—has been stripped away by a bunch of motherfuckers that Jacob decided to piss off. What's to say he won't do the same to the next rival crew that rolls into town? His fuck-up made me lose *every*thing."

"So you're done with the Ninez—completely?" I ask.

She opens her mouth to reply, closes it quickly, and looks thoughtful for a moment. "Y-Yeah…"

"You don't sound too sure of yourself."

She averts her gaze. "I don't know, all right? I just know I haven't been this pissed at so many people before in my life."

Her offer sounds tempting, but I know when something sounds too good to be true. "Okay. So if you help me, what do *you* get in return?"

Her gaze turns ice-cold. "I get to be your number one."

CHAPTER 9

THE TRIP BACK TO THE CITY IS QUIET. I REMAIN FOCUSED ON the road while Cassandra's words replay over and over in my head. *"I get to be your number one."* But Clayton has been my number one since the Wild Aces formed eight years ago. I can't just replace him for an outsider and expect the rest of my crew to be cool with that. *Especially* when Clayton would be replaced by somebody from a rival crew. Hell, I don't even know why I'm even considering it. Clayton is family—and family comes first above all else. But Cassandra… she's a girl who's lost her family. She at least deserves a second chance. Right now, I need to take her someplace safe and think this through. There's only one safe place I know, but how am I going to explain all this to the rest of my crew?

I can't leave her alone. I won't. I've no doubt she can take care of herself, but she's been abandoned too many times. Shitted on by people she trusted. I can see the pain all over her face—she needs someone with her now. *She deserves so much more.*

I look over to the passenger's seat at Cassandra, who's staring out the window. "Hey."

She turns her head.

"Can I trust you?"

She arches an eyebrow. "I dunno. Can you?"

"I'm serious. If you're really, truly done with Jacob, then…" I pause, as I feel my stomach clench. "I'll take you back to the Wild Aces HQ."

"Hmm…" She crosses her arms, looking thoughtful.

"So?" I give her a more careful glance, then haul my gaze back to the road. "Can I trust you?"

She sighs. "Listen, just let me out right here. I can—"

"I *want* to trust you. I want to trust that you're not going to run back to Jacob."

Her eyes narrow. "Why the hell would I do that?"

"I'm not saying you would, but I have to be careful. For my crew's sake. It's not the first time I've been betrayed by people I've cared about."

Her expression softens again, and I can once again see the pain in her eyes as if I'd triggered something. She turns her head and stares out the passenger window again. "Jacob was the one who betrayed *me*. Honestly, Adam? I really don't have any beef with you—well, other than the fact that you beat me."

Out of the corner of my eye I notice her look back at me and smile.

It's almost three o'clock Sunday morning when Cassandra and I arrive at the Shed. Everyone's home, and a few lights are still on inside.

"Is this a… gas station?" Cassandra asks.

"It was, once upon a time," I say, pulling into my designated spot in the open bay door. "We gutted it and turned it into a livable place."

"Nice."

I shut off the car and look over to her. "I'm trusting you, Cassandra. Don't make me regret it."

She glares. "Is that a threat?"

"No," I say quickly. "But I know the rest of my crew ain't gonna be cool with this."

"And why should you give a fuck? You're their leader."

"Yeah, but they're also my family. Practically the only family I've got left."

She falls silent, leans her head against the headrest and looks straight ahead, deep in thought. "Look, if it's gonna be too much of a problem, then I'll just leave. I'll find my own place to stay."

I swallow. "You shouldn't be alone right now." *I don't want you to be alone, not anymore.*

"I can take care of myself. And I damn sure don't care about being alone."

"Yeah, I know." I sigh. "I want you to stay here. Maybe one of these days you'll be a Wild Ace too."

She snorts. "You trying to solicit me?"

I let out a chuckle. "Naw. But... if you *want* to join, then..."

She gives me a pathetic look. "I was only kidding, Adam."

Damn. I feel about two inches tall, but that's okay. I'm not mad at her. I somehow don't feel inclined to ever be mad at her. "All right, well... let's go inside."

"Whatever."

We head inside through the side door. Everyone's in the common room. Clayton and Mariah lay together on the couch staring bleary-eyed at the television. Gabriel is sprawled out on the floor next to the couch, his eyes closed and head bobbing from whatever's playing in his headphones. Luke sits alone on the other side of the room with his nose in his sketchbook, his hand scribbling away.

Clayton is the first to notice me, and he springs up from the couch. "Adam!" He approaches in three strides. "Jesus Christ, man, you—" He pauses, looks beyond me, and his face goes rigid. He takes a step back. "What the fuck is *she* doing here?"

The others stop what they're doing and look toward us. Then, they get up and approach.

I hold my arm out in front of Cassandra to keep them from getting any closer to her. "Back off. It's not what you think. She's done with Jacob."

Clayton's mouth drops open. "You serious right now? Is that what this bitch told you? And you *believe* her?"

"Don't call her that," I warn.

"Hey, man, fuck you!" Cassandra barks at Clayton. She shoves my arm out the way and stands beside me, her head held high.

I clench my jaw. "Look, I know this is complicated, but I need you guys to trust me right now."

"We trust *you*," Luke says. "Not *her*."

Gabriel lets the headphones, which still blare with music, hang around his neck as his gaze bounces from me to Cassandra. He focuses on me and sneers. "Her crew pulled guns on us. Could have killed us. They've made our lives a living hell. Now you want us to *trust* her?"

I purse my lips, unsure of how to answer.

"I can't believe this," Mariah says, shaking her head. "Inviting her into our home. She's just gonna run and tell that bastard the first chance she gets."

"I'm not telling him shit!" Cassandra protests, balling her fists.

Mariah confronts her and points a finger in her face. "You shut the hell up!"

"Or what?" Cassandra bows up to her.

My eyes widened, I come between the two women. "Whoa! Stop!" I wait for the two to back off before continuing. "Look, *I* brought Cassandra here. It was *my* choice. She's *my* responsibility, not yours. Whatever happens, it's on me."

An awkward silence fills the room as my friends exchange glances. Finally, Clayton crosses his arms and lets out an annoyed snort. "Wow."

"What?" I say.

He shakes his head. "I never would've thought that you of all people would let pussy come between your family."

Cassandra fumes.

I blink. "I told you it's not what it looks like!"

"Ain't it?" Clayton says. "You've never messed with girls from different crews before. Why's she different?"

I take a deep breath, trying to keep my cool. "You were there when she knocked the shit out of Jacob in front of everyone. You know how he is about his ego. No other girl would've gotten away with that shit. Besides all that, she's a damned good driver and her crew abandoned her when she needed them the most."

Clayton goes silent, then scowls. "I still don't trust her," he says, prodding me in the chest for emphasis. "She betrays us, and it's *your* ass." He turns and marches toward the sleeping area.

I don't budge or reply. He has every right to be upset, and I'm too damn tired to fight with him right now.

Gabriel follows Clayton without another word, his head down while he fiddles with his beeper. I furrow my brow at him, wondering who the hell is calling him this time of morning.

"How could you, man?" Luke mutters to me, then storms out the front door shaking his head.

Mariah glares at Cassandra and me, then shakes her head. "You've done some crazy shit before, Adam, but I think this tops them all. I'm seriously questioning your leadership right now."

I sigh. "I understand."

"No, I don't think you do." Heading for the front door, she mutters, "I need a smoke."

Cassandra and I are alone, with only the television providing a low buzz.

"Fuck this," Cassandra says, marching to the side door that leads to the garage. "Your friends are dicks."

I reach out and touch the back of her arm, then slide my hand down to her wrist, feeling the smooth warmth of her skin. "Wait."

She stops and glares over her shoulder at me, ripping her arm away. "Get your hands off me."

"Don't go."

"I'm obviously not wanted here."

"*I* want you here. Give the rest of them time. Earn their trust."

She shakes her head. "I don't have to prove anything to anyone, or kiss ass just to earn someone's trust. I've done that almost all my life, and I'm sick of it."

"Just be yourself. You don't need to kiss anyone's ass."

"I have to fix my life now that Jacob's destroyed it. And I'm not going to do it with your idiot friends harassing me."

"They won't harass you. And if they do, I'll take care of it." I step closer and lower my voice, speaking a little more reassuring. "Jacob can take away your car, but he can't take away your skill or your spirit. I'll help you get another car. We'll build something way better than your Nova."

She snorts. "'We'? Where'd this 'we' come from?"

I roll my eyes and smile. "Okay, *you* will. Now will you stay, please?"

She looks at me thoughtfully, then sighs and gives a faint nod. "Fine. But the moment they start shit with me again, I'm done."

"Fair enough." I motion to the couch. "You tired?"

She gives a puff of laughter. "Yeah… I think I could sleep for days. Tonight was crazy. But what I could *really* use right now is a shower. I stink."

"Heh. Yeah, me too." I point to the closed door near the sleeping area. "Bathroom's through there. I'll see if I can find you some extra clothes."

She smiles briefly, then gets up and heads to the bathroom. "Thanks."

While she's gone, I go to my room and search through my drawers for the smallest-sized sweatpants and T-shirts I own. Mariah and Cassandra were almost the same size, but Hell would have to freeze over before she would ever let Cassandra borrow some of her clothes. I retrieve an extra pair of sweatpants and a tank for myself and head for the exit.

As I walk past the closed curtain of Clayton and Mariah's room, Clayton suddenly slides the curtain open and growls, "Where is she?"

I look back at him. "Taking a shower."

"You're making a mistake, bringing that bitch here."

My left eye twitches. "I told you not to call her that."

He laughs. "Now I *know* you're fucking her."

I tighten my grip on the bundle of clothes. "I respect her more than that."

"*Respect*? She has no respect for us. Why should we kiss her ass?"

"I'm not asking you to kiss her ass. I'm asking you to hear her out. Give her a chance to prove herself. You can't deny what she did to Jacob out there was pretty ballsy."

Clayton looks thoughtful for a moment, then grins. "Heh. That look on Jacob's face was priceless."

"What if she's really telling the truth and is no longer with the Ninez? What if she proves herself enough to you guys and joins our crew?"

Clayton raises his eyebrows. "She wants to join?"

I shrug. "Well, she didn't really say that, but if she ever did, then the Ninez would be fucked. She's too good of a racer. She'd scorch them all every time. Maybe the Ninez would finally admit defeat and even help us run that new crew, the Red Ravens, out of town. Then Tacoma would be ours again. We can go back to the way things were. Before all the violence and guns and just have fun and do what we all loved to do."

"Quit dreaming, Adam. Those days are over. Don't you see that? Even the most mellow crews have gotten with the times. No one's just racing for the hell of it anymore." His face hardens. "Which is also why I think it's too risky having Cassandra around. Not only do we have the Ninez to worry about, but now the Red Ravens. They might be after her too."

"They're not, trust me."

"Look, I know I'm your number one and all, but even *I'm* starting to have doubts. About you. About all of us. We're all we've got. We don't need outsiders breaking us apart and destroying what we've got going here."

I look at him carefully and narrow my eyes. "You're scared."

His whole body stiffens when I say that. "Of her? Fuck no."

"But you're still scared."

He purses his lips and exhales exasperatingly through his nose. "That was crazy what happened earlier. Those Red Ravens are bad news, man. They didn't come here to race. They wanna take over and who the hell knows what else."

"Yeah…" I frown, staring at the now-wrinkled clothes in my hand—I'd been clenching them the whole time. I'd noticed some of the cars the Red Ravens drove looked too flashy to be used for actual racing. Hell, one of them even had a god-awful spoiler attached to the back. Even the most ignorant scrub knows that's a major no-no. "Well, we're not letting that happen. Those guys are on *our* turf now."

"Hmm." Clayton looks at me dubiously, then yanks the curtain closed. As I leave the room, I hear the curtain slide open again. "Hey, by the way, about what I mentioned before…"

I stop and look over my shoulder.

"My new job." Clayton's head peers out again, grinning. "I'm a delivery driver. They're still hiring too. I can put a good word in for all you guys. I'm tellin' ya, man. The pay is beyond awesome. We'll all be set for life and never have to worry about finances again. You can quit your two jobs and actually enjoy life for a change."

I arch an eyebrow. "As a delivery driver?"

"Damn right. Best job I've ever had."

His response leaves a funny feeling in my gut. I'd love to be able to quit my labor-intensive jobs and do something much easier with higher pay. But even I know that everything 'easy' tends to have some strings attached. Dangerous strings. Out of the five of us only Mariah and I were able to secure decent-paying jobs, in spite of our criminal records. Our combined incomes were enough to cover the basic upkeep and contribute to the community pot. Still, I wonder how Clayton managed to land a high-paying job. *What the hell is he delivering?* "I'll get back to you on that."

As I pass the closed bathroom door, I don't hear the shower on, so I knock. "Hey, it's me."

Moments later, Cassandra opens the door a crack, a puff of steam escaping. A towel, which I realize is mine, is wrapped around her body. "Yeah?" she says.

I swallow, my mind going blank. It takes everything I have to keep my eyes from drifting away from her face. I suddenly remember the clothes I'm holding and present them to her. "Uh, here are some clean clothes. Sorry, they might be a little big."

She smiles slightly, opens the door a little more, and takes the T-shirt and sweatpants. "Thanks." She looks at me with a spark of mischief in her eyes, as if she knows just how much I'm struggling to keep my composure, and then shuts the door.

I stand in front of the closed door a few moments longer, then exhale a long breath. The image of her naked body wrapped in my towel burns through my mind.

Sweet Mother of God... A chill runs through me, the sensation waking up my manhood. I take another breath and finally step away from the door. I return to the common room and set up a pillow and a blanket on the couch for Cassandra—letting her sleep in my room would just be confirmation of everything my crew was thinking right now. I'd rather not have her sleep out here alone, though, so I lay a sheet and pillow on the floor for me to stretch out. The thin-carpeted floor is just as hard as the concrete beneath it, and definitely doesn't make for a comfortable place to sleep, but it would be a pain in the ass to drag my heavy mattress out my room.

As I finish setting things up, Mariah storms in through the front door, muttering something to herself about work and four hours of sleep. She glares at me and says nothing. A strong whiff of weed follows her as she walks past. I look back to the door, waiting for Luke to enter, but he doesn't follow.

"Where's Luke?" I ask Mariah.

"Said he had to air out some steam," she says in a cold tone, then disappears into the sleeping area.

I sigh. That can only mean he went to the big railyard at the New Tacoma industrial park to paint up some of the boxcars. He'll probably end up sleeping out there too. He'll come back.

The bathroom door opens just as Mariah leaves, and Cassandra tiptoes out wearing one of my old T-shirts and sweatpants, which fits loosely around her hips and legs. The bandages on her hands are off, the small scrapes and bruises remaining. She stops before me, scowling. "I *thought* I heard her. Thank God she's gone."

I furrow my brow. "Who? Mariah?"

"Yeah. I really don't want to get into it with her. Seriously. I'm not in the mood for a fight right now."

"Well, you don't have to worry about that. She's probably all cuddled up with Clay now."

She makes a face.

"You can sleep here." I point to the couch.

Her expression softens and she walks past me to the couch. Her fresh scent mixed with my soap plays with my senses. I inhale a little deeper and smile to myself, etching her scent in my mind.

"You don't have to do all this," she says. "I would've been fine sleeping on the floor."

I shake my head. "Naw, you had a rough night. It's the least I can do."

I leave her to get settled while I go to the bathroom to shower. The image of Cassandra repeatedly crosses my mind while I wash up. I think about her beautiful, naked body pressed against mine in the shower and smile. The thought sends a surge of emotion to my dick. I exhale and stand there, willing down my erection while the warm water pelts my back. I shouldn't keep thinking about her like that. But I'm a fool to convince myself that she's the enemy. I've never obsessed this much over a woman before. Maybe there could be something more between us.

But how does she feel about me?

I step out of the shower and dry off. The towel still carries a trace of her scent, and my mind wanders again. This time, it's to a fantasy of me taking Cassandra over the hood of my car and making passionate love to her. I grunt, feeling myself harden again, and quickly shake myself from the fantasy. *Damn, I'm a horny wreck.*

After getting dressed, I leave the bathroom and return to the common room. Cassandra's lying on the couch, staring heavy-eyed at a muted, snowy, nature documentary on television. She notices me and her eyes open a little wider.

I smile at her, then situate myself on the spot I set up on the floor.

"Don't you have a bed?" she mumbles.

I lie on my back and pull the sheet about halfway over me. "Yeah, sort of. But I'd rather sleep out here for now." *Damn, this floor is hard.*

"You look uncomfortable."

"Eh, I've slept in worse places."

She looks toward the television again, this time a little more contemplative. Several minutes pass. "Why don't you… sleep up here…" she finally says.

I turn away from the cheetah chasing a gazelle and look at Cassandra with slightly widened eyes. *Is she serious?* God, I hope she is. "Well, I…"

"Oh, c'mon, I don't stink… anymore." Amusement returns to her eyes again.

I sit up on my elbows. "You never did."

A small smile hints at her lips. It seems like an open invitation, all right.

"Are you sure?" I continue. "I mean… I really don't have a problem with sleeping here."

She rolls her eyes. "Oh, for fuck's sake, Adam. Just get your ass up here."

She doesn't have to tell me again. I get up and join her on the couch, settling behind her. She lays in a fetal position beneath the blanket, her back against me. I carefully lay my arm across her body, anticipating her pushing it away. Instead, her body relaxes, and so does mine. Her ass presses against my dick, and I'm right back to where I was in the shower.

"Damn, sorry…" I mutter, bunching some of the blanket between us.

"Can't fault you for being a man," she says.

Does that mean she liked it? The flashing light from the television winks off her smile, which becomes more apparent. I hadn't realized just how beautiful her smile really is.

"I don't want you to get the wrong idea about me," I say.

"You're cute, Adam, but don't go out of your way to impress me."

She thinks I'm cute? "I'm just being myself. I actually treat women with respect."

She turns her head slightly toward me. "Haven't you heard? Chivalry is dead."

I frown. "You might think so. But not all men are assholes."

"I'll be the judge of that." She turns her head back to the television. "Thank you for helping me."

I smile. What I wouldn't do to kiss her right now. "Don't worry about it. I'm just glad you're okay."

She plays with a loose thread on the blanket. "I guess I owe you now."

My smile fades. "Naw, I'm not Jacob. You don't owe me anything."

"Nothing's for free, Adam."

I exhale through my nose. "Why do you think that?"

"That's just the way life is. I thought you were from the streets?"

"I am. But believe it or not, genuine kindness does exist in this fucked-up world."

"Yeah, well, I guess I'm not lucky like you." She nestles herself against me and closes her eyes.

Even through the thick layer of blanket, I can still feel her amazing ass rubbing against me. I grunt from the strain in my rock-hard manhood. "It's not luck. Maybe one day you'll see that not everyone is like Jacob."

She doesn't respond, so I assume the conversation is officially over. I shut off the television with the remote and lie there with my arm around her, careful not to let my hand accidentally settle someplace off-limits. I inhale the scent of her hair and close my eyes, smiling. The room's silence and Cassandra's light breathing soothes my mind. It's hard to imagine only several hours ago, she almost died. *We* almost died. My feelings and concern for her became apparent the moment I discovered her alone and helpless. I saw myself in her moment of weakness. Now, I can't get this girl out of my mind. She's rekindled a flame in me that had been burnt out for years. Flames of compassion. Fear.

Love.

Damn, I'm in trouble.

CHAPTER 10

It seems like I've only closed my eyes for a moment before I'm awake again. My mind is still racing with last night's craziness. I should have known that sleep was the last thing I'd be able to do, even though my body was physically exhausted. Now, I'm wide awake, staring up at the ceiling, where sunlight streaks through small slits in the closed blinds.

Taking a deep breath, I slide my hand beside me. I blink. *Something's missing.* I look over and Cassandra's gone.

Did she really leave? I roll off the couch and check the other rooms. Luke's truck is gone, and the rest of my crew has left too. The faint sounds of Gabriel's beeper go off outside, and hurried footsteps approach the front door. Gabriel rushes inside and to the telephone next to the mini-fridge. He doesn't seem to notice me—or maybe he's just ignoring me.

Leaving him to his business, I head to the garage. As I approach the side door, I hear the muffled thumping of bass beats playing. Curious, I open the door. One of my Public Enemy tapes blares from the big boombox sitting atop the rolling tool cabinet. At the opposite end of the garage, I spot Cassandra's beautiful ass moving in time to the beat of *Welcome to the Terrordome* as she leans over the open engine compartment of my car.

I swallow, my emotions torn by the mix of lust and annoyance. I shut off the boombox and approach her. She looks over to me when I'm halfway across the room, and smiles crookedly, a hint of mischief in her dark brown eyes.

"What are you doing under there?" I ask, a suspicious edge to my tone.

"Just seeing what you're packing," she replies.

I stand beside her and cross my arms. "Why? So you can find a way to finally beat me?" I'd meant to sound playful, but when her smile falls and the mischief in her eyes turns to a hard glare, I realize she didn't take it that way.

"No, asshole," she snaps.

I hold my hands up in surrender. "All right. Sorry. I just get a bit defensive when people are searching around under Sasha's hood."

"Right." She starts for the side door in a huff.

I hold my arm out, stopping her. "I never said *you* weren't allowed to touch Sasha."

She shoves my arm aside, not looking at me. "I've seen all I needed to see. You're not running a Flo-XL like I thought."

I raise my eyebrows. "What's that?"

"It's Q&R's newest racing injection system. Top-of-the-line."

I laugh. "Nice sales pitch. You sure you're not one of their reps?"

Her face brightens slightly when I say that. "Man, I wish."

And I thought *I* kept up closely with Q&R news. If I can get my hands on a Flo-XL, Sasha would be truly unstoppable. *I wonder if Dave would have luck finding one for me?*

"It's got a six-thousand-dollar price tag on it, though," she adds, as if she can hear my thoughts.

I deflate. *Well, there goes that idea.* As much as I love Q&R, even I have my budget limits. "No way in hell I can afford that right now."

"Shame. Would've loved to see the way she runs after *that* upgrade."

"You'll have to wait a while. I already installed a pretty new exhaust system."

"Wait about six months when the new Q&R catalog drops, and Sasha will be considered obsolete."

I shrug. I knew the deal. Mods were never permanent in the underground racing world. New products came out all the time and it was a never-ending hamster wheel of always being on top of the game.

Cassandra reaches the door and puts her hand on the knob. She looks back at me over her shoulder. "I need to get some new clothes." She pauses and adds under her breath, frowning, "But I don't get paid for another week…"

"Where do you work?"

"Eh, I flip burgers part-time at Out the Box, Monday through Friday."

Everything she's owned—including her cash—is most likely with Jacob, and there's no way in hell he'll give any of it back to her. Not without a fight. But after what happened last night, it doesn't seem worth the trouble. Things can easily be replaced, as I'd learned long ago.

I rub the stubble along my jaw. Mariah would kill me if I went through her clothes without her permission. "Okay. Give me a sec and we'll go into town so you can get some clothes. My treat."

Her frown deepens. She looks thoughtful about something, then exhales through her nose. "Look. Let's get one thing straight. I don't accept free handouts. How about I help you mod your car as payment for the clothes?"

I rub the back of my head. I don't want anything from her, but her insistence tells me that she's probably never had anyone do anything for her out of their own goodness. How many times had she been used? Abused? Betrayed? Her reluctance was pathological. "Okay, sure," I say absently.

Back inside, I slip out of my sleeping shorts and T-shirt and into a less-wrinkled shirt and pants. Gabriel's still yapping away on the telephone. I don't bother telling him where I'm going. Not like he'd care right now, anyway.

I hold the front door open for Cassandra as she exits, then I join her outside. I take my usual shortcut down the path in the wooded area behind the Shed.

"Wait, really? We're gonna walk all the way to town?" Cassandra asks when we're halfway along.

"No, we're taking the bus. Sasha needs a break after last night. Besides, I don't like driving her during the day."

"Huh. Jacob doesn't like taking his ride out in the day, either," I hear her mutter.

I frown. *Damn, he's on her mind again.* I'm not sure if that comment was meant for my ears, but I turn around anyway and confront her. "Hey, Jacob and I might have some similarities car-wise, but I promise you, we are *very* different people."

She crosses her arms. "Didn't you guys used to be friends?"

I let out an empty laugh. "Yeah, maybe back when we all used to race for fun. But he's become like the rest of these punks and takes things personal. He lost my respect and he'll never have it again."

"Huh. He's sure burned a lot of bridges."

"You don't know the half of it." I turn back around and continue walking.

We finally emerge from the woods and cross 12th street to the nearest bus stop on Pacific Highway. We get off at a stop further into the city, to one of the thrift stores I frequent with a bargain outlet next door. By two o'clock in the afternoon, Cassandra has scored fifty dollars'-worth of clothes and personal items. I haul the heavy bags for her—I could use the workout, anyway.

Back on the bus, Cassandra thumbs through the Auto section of today's newspaper that she'd found discarded on a bench at the bus stop. I stuff the rest of the newspaper in one of the clothes bags. They'd be useful for catching oil spills.

My body jostles as the bus continues through town. I rest my head against the back wall and gaze out the window at the passing buildings. The bus stops to let a passenger off, and I realize we're a few blocks from Grandpa's shop. *I wonder how Grandpa did at the auto show yesterday...*

"Hey." Cassandra lightly elbows me, taking me out of my thoughts. "Did you know that Q&R is developing a new fuel system stabilizer that's supposed to revolutionize racing fuel performance?"

I chuckle. "There you go again."

She smiles crookedly. "What?"

"That salesman talk. You sure you're not working for them?"

She laughs. "I swear I'm not working for them. If I were, I sure as hell wouldn't be here on this bus with you."

"Fair enough. So, what's this new product all about?"

"It's supposed to be better than using avgas. Cleaner, too. And way cheaper." She points to a newspaper column.

"Wow. I'll have to keep an eye on that." I lean over to peek at the article. I'm close enough to catch a whiff of her scent again. A hint of my soap still lingers on her, and memories of seeing her wrapped in my towel last night return. I glace at the shirt she wears—one of my shirts—and notice faint outlines of her perky nipples.

I take a slow, deep breath, staving off the sensation in my pants. Then I focus on the article again. "Man, Q&R is so ahead of its time. I just wish some of their parts weren't so damn expensive."

"You get what you pay for," she says. "I wouldn't have it any other way. I always try to tell that to these scrubs who install cheap knockoffs in their cars, but they don't wanna listen."

I laugh. "You know, you really would make a great Q&R sales rep."

My suggestion brings a twinkle to her eye. "That'd be fucking awesome. But they're way too elite. They won't hire a bum like me."

I disagree, but it's useless arguing with her.

Back at the Shed, I notice Clayton's car parked in the garage. The boombox blasts the grungy guitar riffs of Alice in Chains. A pair of legs pokes out from underneath the car and Mariah is working under the hood.

Cassandra notices the pair as well and frowns. Speeding up her walk, she passes me and goes to the side door.

I'm halfway behind her when Clayton rolls out on a wooden dolly from under the front of the car and fishes through a nearby toolbox. He stops and looks over to us, casts a brief glare at Cassandra, then tips his head at me. "'Sup."

I reluctantly halt. "Hey," I say to Clayton, returning the nod. Another blast of heavy metal blares through the speakers, making me cringe. I march over to the boombox and turn the volume down—*way* down.

Mariah pulls herself out from under the hood and looks over to me. "What the hell?"

"I don't feel like yelling over that," I say, then gesture to the car. "You got another race, Clay?"

He stands and flashes me a coy smile. "You could say that."

I furrow my brow. "What does that mean?"

Clayton casts another glare at Cassandra, then gestures with his head for me to step outside so he can talk to me alone.

I frown and give Cassandra an apologetic look as I hand her the bags of clothes. She heads inside without a word. As soon as Clayton and I are away from the garage, Mariah turns the radio on full blast again and goes back to tinkering under the hood.

"I couldn't decide whether or not I was gonna bring this up to you," Clayton begins, "but the money is too good, man…"

"What money?" I ask.

He reaches in his back pocket and pulls out a thick wad of twenty-dollar-bills wrapped with a rubber band. My eyes widen. There's got to be over a thousand dollars' worth in that stack.

"This was after one night of making deliveries. Easy shit."

"Holy—"

Clayton returns the money in his pocket. "There's more where that came from. I told you, man. We're set for life. You can quit your jobs, easy!"

"You earned all that making deliveries?" My throat tightens. The last time I saw that much money in one place was back in New York City where I'd gotten wrapped up with the wrong people—doing the wrong things.

"Yup," Clayton confirms. "I get paid for every delivery. The more deliveries I make, the more I get paid. Simple."

I swallow again, the lump in my throat making it harder to breathe. I've heard those words before. The feeling of déjà vu hits me hard. *Please don't be what I think it is...* "W... What *kind* of deliveries?" I ask, already regretting it.

Clayton shrugs. "Packages. Like I said, easy shit."

I exhale slowly, my suspicions confirming. "The rest of the guys doing this too?"

"Gabe started a few days ago. Rai will be in on it, too, as soon as she wraps things up with her current job. I didn't get a chance to talk to Luke yet, though."

I'm relieved that Luke at least hasn't gotten caught up with this. Still, I can't believe what I'm hearing right now. "Who's your employer?"

"I don't have just one employer. But the people who hire me are looking for the fastest drivers to get shit done. I've heard about other drivers getting paid extra for faster deliveries. You'd make a killing with Sasha."

"Other drivers?"

"Yeah, a couple other guys from some of the other crews around here are in on it. The operation seems new, but I've heard rumors that they're spreading all up and down the West Coast."

No. I can't get caught up in that shit again. But Clayton's starting to sound convincing with all that money he flashed in my face. I could easily afford every Q&R upgrade ever made, if the cash flow is as good as he says it is.

But is it worth it?

"I dunno, man," I say. "That's a lot of work on Sasha. She's not made to go long distances like that."

Clayton waves his hand dismissively. "I could set you up with some local deliveries. Whenever a client needs a package delivered, they call Gabe, and we take care of the rest."

"Where do you get these packages from, anyway?"

"Eh, it varies. But they mostly come from clients who're small manufacturers too. We just help... disperse their product."

"And no one's ever gotten caught?"

"Some drivers have, but the law's never been able to trace it back to the main operation. I've heard this shit's been going on since '79. Heard some rumors there's some cartel in Central America behind it, but nobody's certain." Clayton slaps me on the shoulder. "I'm tellin' ya, man. This is it. This is our big break."

I swallow a bad taste in my mouth. The more he talks, the more it lingers. *Is this what we've become? A bunch of drug runners?* I don't want to go along with this, but how the hell do I explain that to him? The fact that Clayton is telling me this means he still trusts me, despite my past. Despite everything, including Cassandra. I can't betray him. I won't, but... "I don't know if I wanna do this again."

"It ain't nothing like all that shit from New York that you told me about. This is way different. Trust me."

I take a deep breath. Yeah, sure, I trust my family. But what Clayton is asking me to do—to open that dangerous door again—I'm not sure I'm ready to commit. "I need some time to think about it. I'll get back to you."

Clayton shrugs. "Fair enough. When Luke gets back, I'll talk to him about it and see if he's on board."

I shake my head. "No, I'll talk to him."

"I got this job, not you. I'll tell him."

"No," I say a little firmer.

He makes a face, then puts his hands up in surrender. "Right, whatever, man." He turns, about to head back toward the garage, then stops and hardens his gaze at me. "Oh, by the way. Cassandra don't need to know about this."

I swallow at the mention of her name.

He steps up to me and scowls. "She *can't* know."

I tighten my jaw. Keeping this secret from a girl I like would tear me up. And yet, I can't betray the trust of my number one or this whole crew's gonna fall apart. *Damn it, why does this have to be so complicated?*

I stare at Clayton, not sure how to respond.

"Her pussy's not worth our friendship."

Growling, I shove him backwards in the chest. He stumbles. "She's got *nothing* to do with us, man," I say through clenched teeth.

He balls his hands into tight fists like he's going to lash out, but I bow up to him like a bull. Finally, he concedes and sulks back to the garage, shaking his head.

CHAPTER 11

Tᴴɪs ᴡᴇᴇᴋᴇɴᴅ ʜᴀs ʙᴇᴇɴ ᴏɴᴇ ʜᴇʟʟ ᴏf ᴀ ʀᴏʟʟᴇʀᴄᴏᴀsᴛᴇʀ, and part of me is still dreading work tomorrow. At seven o'clock Sunday evening, I'm in the garage tuning-up Sasha. The boombox is switched to a radio station Cassandra picked, and the upbeat music of Michael Jackson's *Smooth Criminal* plays. Cassandra swivels back and forth on a stool with her nose in the newspaper's Classifieds section, looking for her next project car to replace the Nova.

With Clayton, Mariah, and Gabriel having left in a hurry a half an hour ago—to do some more 'deliveries,' no doubt— and Luke gone to see what new mods Dave got in, it's just me and Cassandra here alone. And it's strangely relaxing.

I tighten the oil drain plug and roll out from under my car. With the wooden dolly hung on the wall, I return to my work under the hood, checking the rest of Sasha's fluids and connections.

"Holy shit," Cassandra suddenly says.

I stop fiddling with a wire and look over my shoulder. "What's up?"

Cassandra slides off the stool and approaches me in a few quick strides. "Someone's selling a '69 Hemi Barracuda for five grand!"

I blink several times. "That *has* to be a printing mistake."

"Nope!" She points to the ad with her red pen. Sure enough, the price is right there in fine print.

I shake my head in disbelief. The holy grail of muscle cars being sold for mere pennies for its worth? "That's crazy. There must be some sort of catch. Maybe it's a junk car that's not worth salvaging."

"Who cares? It's a Hemi 'Cuda! I *need* to check on that." She pauses, glances back at the article, and scowls. "But the ad says to call between nine and five on weekdays…"

I smile and wipe my oil-and-dirt-smeared hands on a towel sitting on the tool bench. "You can wait till tomorrow, right?"

"Yeah, I guess I have no choice," she replies with a sigh.

"And you have five grand in your pocket, right?"

She rolls her eyes. "Not exactly, but damn it, if it's salvageable… I'll take out a loan if I have to. I may never get an opportunity like this again."

I scratch the back of my head. I admire her determination, but I would hate to see her drowning in debt over this. "Well, if you're meant to have it, then you'll have it."

"No. If I want it, I'll take it." She crosses her arms, cocks a hip, and gives me an amused look.

I return the amused look, the double entendre not lost on me. My mind drifts a moment to the thought of me taking *her*—over the hood of my car. The mere thought sends a shockwave to my groin, and I exhale slowly. God, I've been so horny lately.

She lifts an eyebrow. "What are you smiling about now?"

I haul my thoughts back to the present, and quickly turn away from her. "Nothing," I mutter, shutting the hood. I leave my hands splayed there and stare idly at the cherry paint. I see an image of Cassandra there, grinding her beautiful ass against my groin... *Damn, I need to get my mind off her.*

It *would* be nice to get that 'Cuda and work on it as a side project. The sky would be the limit for all the mods that can be done to it. Cassandra obviously loved her muscle cars.

"You done tuning 'er up already?" Cassandra asks.

I shake off my thoughts and nod. "Uh, yeah, I just need to check the struts on the rear axle, but I'll do that later."

"I'll check them for you," she says, heading to the back of the car.

"No." I gently grab the back of her arm, stopping her. She tenses but doesn't pull away. "I got it." I slowly release her arm. "Hey, you wanna go inside and watch a movie or something?"

She snorts out a chuckle. "Okay. What's with you? Seriously?"

Can she really see right through my bullshit? "I told you. Nothing."

"Did anyone ever tell you that you're a terrible liar?"

I take a deep breath, trying to gather my thoughts and stave off the sensation in my pants. *What would she think if I really told her how I feel?*

She crosses her arms, looking at me expectantly.

I swallow and will my eyes to look into hers. Then I close the gap between us. "In case no one's ever told you, you're an amazing woman."

She blinks.

"Strong, determined, smart, beautiful... you've got the whole package, and I like that." I gently uncross her arms and take her hands in mine. "So... I'm wondering what it would take for someone like you to give someone like me a chance?"

Her body tenses again, but I keep my gentle hold. She's been hurt by others, but I want her to know she's safe with me.

Her gaze falters, shifting slightly downward to my lips. The tension in her body slowly eases. "Don't be an ass like Jacob," she mutters.

I grin. "That all?" I reach up and caress the side of her face. Some stray dirt from my fingers smudges her cheek, but I don't care. She's even more beautiful with that little imperfection. I lean my face closer to hers. The heat from her skin electrifies my own.

"For now," she murmurs, and meets me halfway.

Our lips touch for the first time, and a heavenly feeling sweeps over me. I can hear and feel her heartbeat pounding as fast as my own. I deepen the kiss, savoring her delicious natural taste. I trail my hands down her arms and over her hips. Groaning, I pull her into me, and she inadvertently presses into my hard dick. A small moan barely escapes her. Breaking the kiss, I pull back, giving us space from the heat of our bodies. "Damn..."

She smiles crookedly in response. "What?"

Her question makes my mind spin. Her taste still lingering, I lick my lips as I try to make sense of her simple question. *So she liked it...* "Ah... nothing..."

"That's a whole lotta 'nothing.'" With an impish smile, she draws close to me again and slides her hand to my groin.

My eyelids snap shut, and another groan escapes me at her touch. *Holy shit.*

She gives my rock-hard dick a good squeeze through my sweatpants, and all sensible thoughts leave my mind. Her lips are on mine again, and I helplessly concede to her demand. *Damn, she kisses so good.* I run my hands along her hips, then up and under her shirt. She breaks the kiss, and I pause. She looks down at her shirt a moment, then steps back and pulls it off. I take a moment to adore her ample treasures confined in a black lace bra underneath. I stare at her tits, hypnotized by their size and perkiness.

God, I want her so bad...

She approaches me again and walks me backward until I'm pressed up against the driver's side door. Her hands on my shoulders, she eases me to the cold, concrete floor. I slide down and sit, looking up at her curiously, my heart fluttering with anxious beats.

Wait... she's supposed to be pinned against the hood, dammit...

She straddles my lap and presses her lips against mine with greedy fervor. Moaning, I answer earnestly, wrapping my arms around her.

I kiss down her neck, and her body relaxes in my arms. She seems to trust me in this moment, embracing her vulnerability. While I work my tongue down her sternum, my hands draw up behind her to the hooks of her bra. As the last hook is undone, her ample chest is put on full display. I pull back and admire her as she lets the bra fall down her arms and tosses it to the side.

Oh, fuck. I'm done.

"Like what you see?" she whispers.

I smile broadly. "*Hell* yes." I cup both handfuls of her breasts and squeeze them greedily. She exhales and whimpers, then draws her fingers down my chest, to my abs. I watch her expression change rapidly between arousal and satisfaction as I fondle her breasts and rub her nipples with my thumbs. They become as hard as pebbles, and I take one of them into my mouth. My dick presses against her thigh while I suck hard, my fantasies of this moment becoming real. This can't possibly be a dream. She feels too good, and tastes even better.

"Damn, your mouth is amazing," she says breathily.

"Mmm..." My tongue draws circles around her areola until it gets puffy.

She exhales a ragged breath and wraps her arms around my neck, her fingers digging into the back of my shoulder blades. "God, I am so sensitive there, I can't take it anymore."

I moan in response and make a mental note of her sensitive spot. I tease her other nipple with my tongue while my hand draws further down over her firm abdomen until, finally, my fingers graze along the top of her denim shorts. Her breath hitches, and I test my luck, undoing the button.

She exhales, and I feel the warmth of her hand over mine. She squeezes it and I give her nipple one last lick before drawing away and looking up at her, curious, but ready.

"Not so fast," she says, appearing to have regained her composure. "That don't come free."

I grin at her challenge. "Of course it doesn't. So what's the price?"

"Among other things, keeping your promise of making me your number one."

My grin falters slightly. I hadn't promised her that, and I'm not sure I ever could at this point. "I'm working on that, but… you're my number one in other ways," I attempt. "You're the first woman to ever steal my heart."

She chuckles. "Nice try, but you know what I'm talking about."

"I can't do that to Clay right now. But that doesn't mean I won't still help you make your name."

She stabs me in the chest with her finger. "Figure out something. If I'm going to be part of this crew, I'm not going to be some scrub or side bitch. You guys are one of the most elite crews in Tacoma—I want my position to mean something. Besides, I can drive a whole hell of a lot better than Clay any day."

"I know." I admit. "But Clay's a good friend. He's had my back for forever and he knows how to get shit done when things get tough. And he knows a lot of people."

"I can do all that too. And it's not like I don't know a lot of people either."

I frown. "Look, give me some time to figure something out, okay?" I lean in for another kiss, hoping she'd finally drop the issue.

To my relief, she accepts the kiss and mutters against my lips, "Mmm… fine…"

I reach down and cup her ass in my hands. I give her cheeks a firm squeeze while we indulge in a deep, passionate kiss. I inhale her natural scent and my mind goes wild.

"I know you're horny as fuck," I mutter my thoughts aloud, drawing one hand around to her front and grazing my fingers between her legs. Even through the thick denim, I can feel a wet spot. *Yep. I was right.*

She twitches, and a small moan escapes her. I trace my fingers along her waistband, teasing her a little, then slowly ease my hand down inside her pants. Her panties are soaked. I guide my kiss from her lips to her jawline, and then down her neck. My hand finds its way beneath her panties, and I tease her hot pussy with my fingers.

"*Nnngh…*" She sinks her teeth into her bottom lip.

I massage her clit, my fingers becoming coated in her nectar. Moaning, she squirms, but I hold her steady. I plunge two fingers into her, and her entire body shivers. My kisses return to her lips, and I savor her addicting taste once more.

I massage her folds with my palm and another rush of her hot wetness covers my hand. *Did she cum already?*

She breaks the kiss, then grabs my arm. "Fuck, I can't take anymore. You're too good with your hands."

I smirk. "Of course I am. You've seen me drive."

She lets out a hollow laugh, then looks at me with dark eyes. "You've seen me drive too."

Knowing that look, I watch her curiously.

She pulls my hand out from her pants. As tempted as I am to taste her nectar off my fingers, I don't move, enthralled by whatever she's scheming.

She lowers my sweatpants and briefs just enough to release my dick, which stands ramrod straight. Biting my bottom lip in anticipation, I inhale through my nose, trying to keep my composure.

"Like what you see?" I mutter her own question back.

She looks from my dick to my face, then back to my dick again, as if she's having an epiphany. "Oh my god…"

"What?" I ask with a slight fear that she actually *doesn't* like what she sees.

"No wonder Jacob's got beef with you. You're fucking huge!"

I can't help but laugh, relief easing my fears. "Well, I promise you he's never seen this, so I'm pretty sure his beef with me is just because he's a first-class asshole."

Not replying, she locks her gaze on my dick. She takes it in her hand and gives it a gentle stroke.

I lean the back of my head against the door and scrape my fingers against the concrete floor, trying to grab something—anything. I'm at her mercy.

I watch her occupied hand. "Whatcha gonna do with all that?" I ask, my voice cracking.

Her crooked smile returns. "Oh, you have jokes now. Don't think I know what I'm doing?"

I grin slightly. "I never said that."

"Your face says it all. Watch." She leans her face close to mine, planting a teasing kiss on my lips, then pulls away slowly. Her face grows darker, a hint of mischief flashing in her eyes.

Then she lowers her head to my groin.

All I can feel at that moment is the warmth of her mouth on my dick. Electric pangs of pleasure shoot through every inch of my body. Mouth open, I try to breathe steadily, but my breath falters every time her lips slide up and down my shaft. I can feel the back of her throat. One hand clamps the base of my dick, while the other slithers under my T-shirt and up my abs. I reach for her with shaky hands and bury my fingers in her hair.

Damn, she's good.

She sucks and slurps, and all I can do is groan in satisfaction. I've been horny all day; it won't be long before she manages to unleash all my pent-up energy.

Her head bobs faster. She sucks harder. My fingers dig across her scalp. "Cass... I... I'm—"

My dick still in her mouth, she gazes readily up at me. That look alone sends me over the edge—my mental dam breaks. I shudder, and a pang of numbing pleasure surges from my brain all the way to my groin. My hot seed fills her mouth, but she doesn't seem fazed. In fact, the liquid disappears down her throat.

Damn...

"Mmm... Not bad," she says, then licks the remnants from my shaft clean. She runs her thumb across her lips and licks that too.

Oh hell. She keeps doing that, and I'll be ready for round two. I pant the more I watch her. I'm still riding this sexual high, and it seems like she's just getting started.

"God, Cassandra..." I whisper between breaths. She continues licking me with that amazing, soothing tongue.

"You're some kind of man," she mutters, looking at me.

"And you're one hell of a woman," I reply without hesitation.

She smiles and stands, getting dressed again. I remain seated with my pants still down, watching her. It's only after she goes inside to clean up that I finally stir from my spot. My mind is still reeling from what just happened, and I think about what we talked about earlier—her desire to be my number one.

Was that even supposed to happen?

This seemed like more than a negotiation. Maybe there could be something more between us.

God, I hope so.

CHAPTER 12

M**ONDAY MORNING, I'M UP BEFORE ANYONE ELSE IN THE** Shed. I've been so used to routinely getting up at four thirty on weekday mornings I haven't needed an alarm in ages. I click on the shade-less lamp sitting on a wooden crate next to the couch. Cassandra stirs next to me, muttering something in her sleep. It's the second night I've slept with her on the couch, and I'm starting to wonder if we shouldn't just sleep out in my room together now.

I watch her sleeping form and smile. I can't get what happened in the garage last night out of my mind. Was that even *supposed* to happen? I probably shouldn't be getting caught up in a girl like this, but my feelings for her are too strong. *Dammit.* I've never been attracted to a girl like this, it was strange—and dangerous. *Maybe it's because we both understand each other.*

I shower, shave, and get dressed and ready to head out to my first job at Donaldson Construction. Before heading out the door, I scribble a note to Cassandra, letting her know both places I work and how to get there in case she wants to stop by. I leave the note on the crate where she's sure to see it when she wakes up.

After several hours at Donaldson's, I clock out at and head to Grandpa's shop. He's in the garage on a ladder, placing a shiny new gold trophy on the shelf with the rest.

"Hey, Grandpa," I say. As I come closer, I realize just how much bigger the trophy is than the others. "Wow, that thing is huge!"

Grandpa looks over his shoulder at me and grins. "Damn right it is. Best Overall in Show. Plus, a five-thousand-dollar check. Everyone was especially impressed with the paint job." He waggles his finger at me. "'Told you, boy. Paint is everything."

"Yeah, yeah." I smile. It's always good to see Grandpa in high spirits whenever one of his babies takes home a prize. Pretty soon, he's going to need another shelf.

Grandpa climbs down the ladder and gestures with his head toward a purple vintage 1940s hot rod sitting on a lowered suspension platform, glimmering in the sunlight filtering through the windows. "Remember that engine you were rebuilding? Well, this is the car that it needs to be put in. 'Needs to be done by the end of the day."

"Sure thing." I glance at the almost-finished engine on the workbench.

Grandpa pauses and looks at me a moment, then furrows his brow. "You're carrying yourself a little differently today. You give any thought about what I said the other day?"

I *have* felt in a pretty damn good mood with Cassandra on my mind all day, but I didn't think I was carrying myself differently. Grandpa can't possibly know what I'm thinking, can he? "Uh… not really. I got more important things to worry about than running a business, man."

He frowns. "Like what? Better not be that damn street racing again…"

I don't reply.

Sighing, he shakes his head disappointingly. "You got so much going for yourself, and you're gonna piss it all away on nonsense!" He points his finger at me like a scolding parent. I notice his whole hand shake slightly.

"Calm down, Grandpa. You're shaking," I say.

Grandpa quickly lowers his hand and places it in his other. "I—I *am* calm. It's just… just nerves, is all. Now go take care of that engine." He storms off to the office without another word. The door slams behind him, causing the trophies on the shelf to vibrate.

I stare at the closed door curiously. *What was that all about?* Grandpa's been on my case way more than usual, it seems. Why is he so hell-bent on entrusting his business to a hoodlum like me?

I sigh, the thought already making my head hurt. I get to work on the engine, trying to block out Grandpa's words. I try thinking about last night, and the way Cassandra claimed me with her mouth. It was totally unexpected, but fucking sexy as hell.

How can I make this work between us?

My thoughts drift to that Hemi Barracuda from the newspaper she was determined to buy. I wonder how she made out with that? I doubt she'd be able to afford it, and who knows if she'd manage to get a loan. Maybe I can get it for her instead, as a surprise. *Didn't Grandpa get a five-thousand-dollar check?* I grin. He might be more willing to part with it if he knew that it was going toward such a rare gem.

"Adam," Grandpa's voice shakes me out of my thoughts. A quick glance at the clock reveals nearly two hours have passed. The engine rebuild is finished, and all I need to do is install it in the hot rod.

I look over my shoulder at Grandpa standing in the office doorway. "Yeah?"

His face grows somber. "Elouise is on the phone."

His look makes me nervous, and I immediately think of the worst-case scenario—something has happened to her or the kids. I abandon the workbench, scramble into the office, and pick up the telephone receiver. "Hello?" I say in a hurry.

"Hey, Adam." Her voice is calm, not distressed, which makes me relax just a little.

"Hey. Is everything okay?"

"Yeah, everything's fine. Um… Michael wants to talk to you."

I blink. *Did I hear that correctly?* "What?"

"He wants to talk to you," she repeats.

My mouth goes dry. After that last conversation we had, I have a feeling whatever he has to say won't be good. But hell, Michael is actually taking the initiative for a change and wants to talk to *me*, so maybe things will be different. I exhale the breath I had been inadvertently holding. "O—kay…"

"Hold on," she says, and I hear rustling, followed by their muffled voices for a moment.

Michael comes to the phone. "Hey."

I still can't believe what I'm hearing. His voice isn't cold or angry. It's actually *pleasant*, a tone I can't remember hearing from him in what seemed like years. I'll take any positive from him that I can get. "Uh, hi."

"I just wanna say thanks for what you did."

I blink again. No, this can't be my brother. I can't remember the last time he's ever thanked me for *anything*. I was always the delinquent, the bad influence. And now he's *thanking me?* "Are you okay, man?"

"I'm fine. Elouise passed along a phone number she said you gave her the other day. To that masonry company in Tukwila."

It takes a moment for me to remember. Friday night after leaving Dim Sum Noodle House, I'd called Elouise from a phone booth on the corner and gave her the number to Henge Masonry. I'd figured she'd give Michael the number, but I didn't think he'd actually give them a call, especially since the number came from me. Anything associated with me was like poison to him. Boy, am I wrong now. "Oh, that. No problem, man. So, you called them?"

"Not only did I call them, they interviewed and hired me on the spot," Michael says. "They're even gonna pay to relocate us to Renton."

"Wow," I say, genuinely surprised. "That's almost unheard of. You must have made an impression for them to do that."

"You're telling me. Looks like I'll be headed out your way soon. I can't believe all this is happening."

I smile. It's the first time in a long time I've smiled while talking to my brother. "Hey, that's really great, man. I'm happy for you. So does this mean I'll finally be able to meet my nephews?" Renton wasn't far from Tacoma. Maybe a twenty, or thirty-minute drive.

"Sure. With the amount of work the company is talking about, looks like our move to Renton is gonna be permanent."

"You tell Grandpa, yet?"

I hear a small growl in response. Just like that, his demeanor changes. "Hell no, I ain't telling that old man shit. He never wanted me to get ahead. And telling him this will probably make him hate me even more. Fuck him."

I sense something different in his anger with Grandpa, something that runs even deeper than what he's telling me now, but I don't bother pressing my brother any more about it. "So... when are you moving?" I ask, steering the topic back on track.

"Six months, they said, I should be all moved in and starting the new job. It's going to be one hell of a move, though, getting in touch with real estate agents and all that. But I think it's going to be worth it in the end. Hell, I'm even gonna have to get a driver's license before I leave."

"Eh, you'll be fine," I say. "Driving's not so bad." I'd almost forgotten Michael never had a driver's license. For most people living in New York City, owning a car was pretty useless, not to mention stressful. "This is a big step in your life, man. For the whole family. You gonna miss New York?"

"Nah, but I think the boys will since they've got friends here and all that. But whatever. They'll make new friends. We have to go where the opportunity is."

"I hear that. Well, can't wait to see you and the family." *Damn. Did I just say that out loud?* It's too late for me to take back those words. But I do want to see Michael, even if he is an ass sometimes—well, *most* of the time.

The line is silent, as he doesn't reply. He was never one to get all sappy and shit.

I clear my throat and continue. "So, uh, I guess if you need anything, you know how to reach me."

"Uh-huh…"

We end the call on that awkward note. Michael sounds sure of himself about this job, and I *do* hope it's a permanent one—for the family. Elouise is a damn good woman to stay at his side through all of this. I admire her the most. I guess good things like Elouise can happen to even the biggest assholes.

But even as certain as Michael sounded on the telephone, I could still sense a hint of doubt in his voice, like he's already anticipating something bad happening with the job. I guess I would be paranoid, too, if a job offered all those incentives just like that. It *does* sound too good to be true, but at this point, Michael isn't really in a position to push his luck.

I leave the office and find Grandpa at the workbench, wrestling with the chains on the engine hoist—the "cherry picker" as it's informally called. His hands are shaking again as he tries to secure the chains to the V8 engine, and he curses under his breath.

"Hey, I got it," I say, stepping beside him and securing the chains.

He scowls. "Damn it, boy, I'm not old and broke-down."

"Whatever, man. You don't even have a steady hand," I mutter, rolling my eyes.

"It's just some minor arthritis," he shoots back.

Minor my ass. "I thought you said before it was just nerves?"

"Does it matter? I can still hoist a damn engine."

I shake my head and don't budge from my spot. Grandpa reluctantly concedes, slumping his shoulders with a sigh.

"Is Elouise okay? She didn't say much to me," he says.

"She's fine," I reply. The engine secured, I crank up the hoist. "Hey, why don't you hold the engine steady while I steer?" I ask Grandpa, who wrings his hands and looks around like he's anxious to do something.

"Yeah." He nods and gets to it.

I exhale and push the four-hundred-plus-pound hoist and engine toward the hot rod. Grandpa holds the engine steady while he walks with me. When the engine hovers over the open hood of the car, Grandpa moves out of the way, and I take it from there.

"Can I ask you a question?" I ask, not looking at him while I crank the hoist down.

"You just did," Grandpa answers in an amused tone.

I smile and let out an airy snort. "I'm serious, man."

"Shoot."

I measure the engine's distance and adjust the hoist. "What's up with you and Michael?"

He pauses. "What makes you ask?"

I look over to him. "I've always asked, but you never give me a straight answer. Maybe this time I might get lucky."

He crosses his arms. "I've got nothing worthwhile to say about your brother."

"Come on, Grandpa. I think it's about time you tell me what the hell's going on between you two."

"Why do you want to know so bad, huh? You think you're gonna change something?"

"I never said I wanted to change anything. But I've been kept in the dark about this for so long, I think at this point I have a right to know, at least, damn it."

He exhales through his nose and averts his gaze. "To put it mildly, I don't trust Michael."

I roll my eyes. "Well, yeah, I kinda figured that much already. But why the beef for all these years?"

"Your naïve grandmother spoiled him to no end. According to her, Michael was 'traumatized' over your parents' deaths, which gave her the excuse to give Michael extra pampering. She thought that all would 'fix' him, or some such nonsense, make him the ideal son that everyone could love, but she just ended up making him a spoiled, entitled son of a bitch.

"He turned out just like your father—only cared about himself. Michael cleaned out her bank account *twice*—blew it all away on parties, booze, and whatever else he wanted. Of course, your grandmother simply turned a blind eye."

"Maybe she didn't know," I say.

Grandpa arches a skeptical eyebrow. "Oh, she knew, all right. After *endless* back-and-forth telephone conversations, I finally got it through her thick skull to stop pissing her money away on Michael. Then, of course, he tried to weasel more money out of her, and she finally put her foot down. He got mad she cut him off and blames me for getting involved. He and I haven't talked since."

I blink. "All this over money?"

"No, all this over taking advantage of weaker people! *Especially* when the people are your own family! It's the one thing I can't stand. It's the same thing your parents did."

I raise my eyebrows. "They tried to take money from you and Grandma too?"

Grandpa nods curtly. "I fell for it once. After I found out I was helping to fund their drug habits, I never fell for it again. Your grandmother, unfortunately, wasn't so bright."

I frown. I barely knew my parents, only that they were junkies who died way too young. Even still, it was hard to hear that my father would take advantage of his own parents like that.

"Michael is treading down that same path," Grandpa continues. "And I will *not* get involved with anything that snake touches."

"So, what'll happen when you and Grandma die?" I ask. "If Michael's as bad as you say he is, then no doubt he'll try and get as much money out of you as he can."

Grandpa smiles darkly. "I don't know about your grandmother, but he ain't gettin' a penny from me whether I'm alive or dead. I made that clear a long time ago, and it's been legally bound since."

"Whoa, you mean you left him out of your will?"

"Damn right, I did. He ain't pissing away my hard-earned money. He don't give a damn about this business, either. He'd sooner see this place burned to the ground for the insurance money if it were up to him."

So that's *why he wants to give this business to me so badly...* He's put a lot of pressure on me, like he's expecting me to run it just like him, or better. He wants me to keep this business afloat, but what if I can't? What if I make too many wrong decisions and end up pissing money away? It'd be no better than if it were in Michael's hands. I don't think I'll ever be able to live up to Grandpa's expectations.

"What about Elouise and the kids?" I ask, curious about the rest of Grandpa's estate plan.

"Oh, they're well taken care of. I have an attorney involved to ensure my money is dispersed accordingly and kept far out of your brother's reach." Grandpa's brow pinches. "Why the hell are we still talking about this?"

I open my mouth, about to tell him about Michael's move out here, but I reconsider. Maybe it's for the best that I don't tell him. Save him the stress. *But what about Elouise? My nephews?* It wouldn't be fair to Grandpa to keep this a secret.

I finish installing the engine, and the customer comes by a short while later to pick up his car. When we're alone again, I join Grandpa in the office. *I guess it's time...*

"Hey," I begin. "I have something I need to tell you..."

Chapter 13

I stare blankly at my half-eaten Kung Pao Chicken as I run my hands over my face, then drag my fingers across my hair. Tonight has sucked so far, and the only hope of it getting a little better is if Cassandra ends up accepting my invitation to join me at Dim Sum Noodle House. But the fact that she'd gotten off work over an hour ago and still isn't here is a clear indication that she decided not to.

It's all good. I'm no stranger to rejection, especially from women.

Maybe she ended up getting that 'Cuda, after all. That must be why she's so late, I keep trying to convince myself. But the more I try, the more doubtful I feel.

But what if she didn't get it?

I still want to try and get the car for her, if she hadn't already. I know I can. But that kind of money ain't pocket change. Grandpa stormed out in a sour mood after I told him the news about Michael, just like I knew he would. I didn't even bother asking him about the five-grand check he got. And I only have fifteen hundred dollars in the bank—I couldn't just drop a third of it like that...

Maybe it's just not meant to be.

Someone slides in across from me into my booth. The aroma of french fries fills my nose, and I look up. My heart pounds.

"Y-You came!" I say with raised eyebrows.

Cassandra smiles crookedly and removes the nametag from her Out the Box red-and-white-striped shirt. "Yeah, sorry about that. One of the guys was late for his shift, so I had to cover." She glances at my barely touched food. "Not hungry much?"

"Not today, I guess. You want something?"

She looks toward the overhead menu by the cashier's counter. "Mmm... I think it's a lo mein night." She begins sliding out of the booth, but I stop her.

"Stay. I got it," I insist, getting up.

She rolls her eyes. "Fine. But I got the next one, understand?"

"Yeah, sure," I say, but I make a mental note to beat her to it again next time. And the next. Smiling, I head to the front counter to order. When I return, Cassandra is engrossed in the discarded Classifieds section of today's newspaper that she'd probably swiped off one of the vacant tables.

"So, did you get a chance to see that Hemi?" I ask.

Her face lights up and she sets the paper down. "I did, and it's the most fucking amazing thing I've ever seen. All it needs is a little TLC, and it'll be as good as new."

"That's great! So, when are you going to pick it up?"

Her expression dulls. "Never. I wasn't able to get that loan... But at least I got to actually see the car in person. Even touch it! I'll probably won't get that opportunity ever again."

"Never say never," I say reassuringly, but she returns a dubious look.

I'll find a way to get her that car if it's the last thing I do.

Back at the Shed later that night, I find Clayton in the garage fine-tuning his silver '83 Celica GT-S. Alone with Clayton at last, what I'm about to do finally hits me, and my throat tightens. Asking Grandpa was pretty much a no-go now, and I didn't have any other options to earn more money legally.

I lean against the side of Clayton's car, my arms crossed, and I look sideways at him. He's bent over with his head poked under the hood.

"I've thought about it." I pause and take a deep breath. "I'll do it."

Clayton stops tinkering a moment, then his head turns in my direction. "You'll do it?"

"Yeah..." I give him a slight nod, hoping he catches my drift.

Grinning, he straightens and turns to me fully. "That's awesome, man! I know it was a hard decision for you, but c'mon man… the possibilities!"

"Uh-uh." I shake my head and hold one finger up. "I'm only doing this under *one* condition."

His smile quickly fades. "Why am I not surprised?"

"I'm only gonna do just enough jobs to make five grand."

"Five grand? That all?" Clayton asks with raised eyebrows.

I nod. "That's all. How long do I have to do this shit?"

"You can make that and more in one night if you hustle hard enough. Maybe about four deliveries' worth, depending on the locations."

"For the record, I don't like this. At all. I'm only doing it 'cause I need some quick cash. This is the only time I'm doing this shit."

Clayton snorts. "Yeah, yeah. That's what they all say—until they see how much bread they're raking in every night."

"I'm serious, man." Because I *do* know what it's like to rake in a lot of bread every night. And it always ends badly. Hopefully just one night of this shit won't be too rough. The problems usually arose when it became a habit.

"So, is there any work tonight?" I ask Clayton.

"Probably. Gabe hasn't gotten any messages yet. Some nights are booming. Others, not so much. In the meantime, Rai, Gabe, and I are gonna head over to a meet-up tonight."

"And Luke?"

He shrugs. "He'd rather go doodle. I don't fuckin' know."

"Right. So where's this meet-up?"

"The old warehouses over on Adams Street, just across the tracks. Liberation's supposed to show."

I roll my eyes. Liberation was a crew mostly made up of barely-legal kids who loved showing off their latest and greatest mods they bought with daddies' money. Everyone was always envious of them, but not me. They always talked trash about Q&R, even though they would never dare say that shit to my face—they knew I was a Q&R brand loyalist. They might've talked a big game about their mods but were too chickenshit to race me. I usually just left them alone with their stupid thinking and subpar brands.

"Seriously, Clay? Why are you even gonna bother with those kids?"

"'Cause rumor has it one of them managed to get their hands on LeatherRock's newest suspension kit. It's not even in stores yet. Hell, Dave doesn't even have any! I'm gonna race that kid for it."

I don't know much about LeatherRock parts these days since I discovered Q&R, except that they're cheaper-priced, and even cheaper made. But despite it all, LeatherRock has a hugely loyal following, including Clayton. I've tried over and over to convince him to switch to Q&R, but it was like talking to a brick wall.

"A waste of time," I mutter.

"I'm sure you'd do the same thing if it were a Q&R suspension kit."

"Not really. I'd be happy to know that the kid knows quality when he sees it. Why would I want to take that away from him?"

Clayton snorts out a laugh.

"So," I try to steer the conversation back to the original subject. "We have to wait for your... *employer* to call for us to make deliveries?"

"Yeah, they tell us where to pick up the packages. Though... I still have a bit of overstock from the last run.

I blink. "*Overstock?* You mean you didn't deliver everything? Are you fucking crazy, man?"

"I did deliver everything, but the guys I delivered to only gave me money for two cases, not four. I wasn't about to fuck over the boss."

"Who's your boss?"

Clayton shrugs. "No idea. Never met him. He's some guy Gabe talks to on the phone that tells him the pick-up and drop-off locations."

"So you got... overstock... in your car right *now?*"

"Yeah, the boss wants it delivered on the next run. I hope it's soon, man. I hate having that shit in my car, y'know?"

I give him a blank stare then push off the car. I swipe his keys which were sitting in the ignition, march around to the trunk and open it. A paper grocery bag containing two tightly packed, Saran wrapped bricks greet me. I simply stare at the drugs in silence, memories of my days as a young thug in New York City coming to the forefront. I clench my jaw.

God, I don't want to do this again. Why the hell do I have to do this again? I hiss. *Because I'm doing it for* her, *dammit.*

"Yo, Adam. You there?" Clayton suddenly says.

I'm dragged back to the present and try to gather my thoughts. I shut the trunk, not wanting to see that shit anymore. "Yeah. Look. I want to work hard tonight so I can earn my cash and get this over with for good."

"I'm sure you'll get lots of work. But hey, man. Don't be takin' all our jobs away."

"Believe me, Clay, you don't have to worry about that. After I get my five grand, I'm done."

"Right."

I head to the side door. Putting my hand on the knob, I look back to Clayton over my shoulder. "Tell Gabe to call me as soon as he gets something, all right?"

"Yep."

I leave Clayton to his work and head inside. Mariah and Gabriel are on the couch watching television, Luke is off in his little corner of the room drawing something in his black sketchbook, and Cassandra sits opposite of him with her nose in the Auto section of today's newspaper.

As soon as Mariah sees me, she springs up from the couch. "Damn, it's about time you two are finally done out there. You guys ready to go or what?"

I shake my head. "I'm not going."

Cassandra gazes up from the newspaper and at me.

Mariah blinks. "Not going? What the hell?"

"He's pussy-whipped, Rai," Gabriel mutters, not taking his eyes off the television.

I clench my fists but keep my cool. "Naw, I just don't feel like wasting gas on a bunch of kids."

"They're not just kids," Mariah says. "They're kids with a top-of-the-line suspension kit. And we're gonna get our hands on it."

"Right. Well you go play around with them. I've got some business of my own to take care of."

"I'm sure you do." Gabriel smirks. "Just don't forget clean up after yourself."

I growl. "Fuck off, man."

He finally looks at me with a little hesitation in his eyes, probably realizing that he crossed the line.

Mariah blows a raspberry. "Whatever. Gabe, I'll meet you and Clay down there." She swipes her keys from the hook hanging on the wall by the kitchenette and heads for the front door. She glances back at Luke, "You coming or doodling?"

Luke says nothing and remains focused on his sketchbook, his hand moving steadily.

Mariah rolls her eyes and leaves, slamming the door behind her.

Gabriel hops up from the couch and starts for the bedroom when his beeper suddenly goes off. He checks it a moment, grins, and heads to the side door leading to the garage. "Yo, Clay! It's them!" he yells out the door. He steps out into the garage and shuts the door behind him. Staring at the closed door, I wonder if 'them' is a new delivery job.

I look back toward Cassandra, who has her nose in the newspaper again. If Clayton *does* have a new job for me, how the hell am I going to make the deliveries with Cassandra around? I hate having to lie to her about anything, but she doesn't need to know what I'm doing. This is all for her, anyway. *It's all to surprise her. Yeah.*

The side door opens again, and Clayton and Gabriel come through. Gabriel gives me a sour look as he passes, and Clayton slaps his hand on my shoulder and guides me toward the bedroom.

"Tonight," Clayton says in a low tone.

I arch an eyebrow. "Tonight?"

He nods. "Down in Waller. They need it delivered by 10:30." He hands me a slip of paper. "The first address is the pick-up. Second address is the drop-off."

I take the paper and unfold it with my fingers. The address is less than fifteen minutes away from here. "So how many deliveries am I making?" I ask Clayton.

"Just one. Three bricks. Two-grand payoff."

My eyes widen. "Holy fucking shit."

"Right?" Clayton grins.

"How pure is this stuff?"

"I think I heard someone say it was around eighty-nine percent. It's good shit, man."

"Wait… two grand for *three bricks* of heroin *that* pure? That can't be right. Last I checked, the street price for a single *gram* was close to three Benjamins, easy."

Clayton smirks. "That price ain't for the bricks, man. It's the delivery fee. And our commission."

I blink. *Whoa…*

The pay is incredible, but I can't go overboard with this. I'd already sworn I wouldn't get caught up in that world again. *Yet here I am.*

I'm only doing it for her.

I hate the fact that I have to take Sasha out on this run. I'm gambling with fate. If a cop stops me, I'm done—and with my record, for good.

I sigh. "All right. I'll take care of it."

"Cool. Now excuse me while I go get me a brand-spanking-new suspension kit."

We do our special handshake, and Clayton leaves with Gabriel.

"Luke," I call, when it's just the three of us left. "I need to take care of something with Dave real quick. Think you can keep Cassandra company while I'm gone?"

Both Luke and Cassandra look up at me.

I scratch the back of my head. "Uh, I won't be long," I add.

"You want Luke to babysit me?" Cassandra says flatly.

"You want me to babysit her?" Luke says at almost the exact same time, pointing his thumb over to her.

I roll my eyes. "No, but I'll never hear the end of it from Clay and the others if they come back and Cassandra's here alone. They still don't trust her."

Luke raises an eyebrow. "And what makes you think *I* do?"

I give him a look. "Come on, man. You're my best friend. I would think that you of all people would have my back and trust me when I say that she's good people."

"Uh… you realize I'm sitting right here, right?" Cassandra interjects.

"Yeah," I say to her. "And I want you to see that I'm not bullshitting you about what I said before. I trust you and I'm willing to give you a chance."

She frowns slightly and returns to her newspaper. "Do whatever you gotta do. I ain't goin' nowhere."

I look to Luke for confirmation. "You'll do this for me, right?"

Sighing, he resumes his doodling. "Yeah, sure, whatever."

I exhale a small sigh of relief, then head for the garage. "Thanks, I'll be back."

Chapter 14

I WHITE-KNUCKLE THE STEERING WHEEL AS I TURN DOWN A dark, potholed road in Waller's sparse unkempt countryside. This place is as boondock-country as hell—all the more reason I want to drop off the shit and get the fuck out of here. My high beams are barely enough help to navigate through this pitch-black area, and I'm forced to drive slow.

I'm doing this for her, I keep telling myself. I think I may seriously be in love. I would've never delved back into this dangerous world otherwise.

My heart pounds as I reach a cul-de-sac, where a shoddy mobile home sits—the only residence for miles on this barren road. Parked out front are several dressed-up cars and a few sport bikes. A small group of people are gathered around the cars. I note their distinctive yellow colors and a foreboding logo of a piranha on the back of one of their vests. I have a sinking feeling in my gut.

A gang hideout. I must be at the right place. These guys aren't a crew I recognize, and I sure as hell don't want to know who they are.

I park next to a rusted mailbox along the curb and hop out of the car without turning off the engine. All chatter stops—and all eyes turn to me—as I walk around to the trunk. I glance toward the group and casually swipe my thumb across the bridge of my nose, sending a silent message of who I am and why I'm here.

One of the guys leaves his group and approaches. His dark eyes scan me up and down, and he smiles smugly.

"Well, shit. If it ain't prettyboy," he says.

I arch an eyebrow. "You know me?"

"Who doesn't know you now, after you scorched Jacob's bitch in that race at Fife?"

I wrinkle my nose. "Oh, you saw that, huh…"

"Fuck yeah. You spanked her ass." His gaze shifts to the trunk of my car. "Anyway… onto business?"

"You got the money?" I say flatly.

"You got my shit?" He raises his eyebrows at me.

I make a sour face and open the trunk, revealing a paper grocery bag containing the stash.

He peeks into the bag, grins, then pulls out a wad of rubber-banded bills. "It's all there," he says, tossing the cash to me.

I catch the money, flip through the bills to make sure it's all accounted for, and then stuff it in my jacket pocket. "Pleasure doing business."

The guy takes the bag out of the trunk and carries it into the mobile home. The rest of his yellow-clad friends follow.

I shut the trunk, hop back into the driver's seat, and haul ass out of there—all the while unable to stop thinking about how easy this job was.

Too easy...

I was making a steady four figures a night back in NYC. Life was good, until it wasn't. That was the thing with these jobs: it only took one night to change everything. *I shouldn't be doing this anymore...* Grandpa has such high hopes for me. At least, more hope than Michael.

And here I am tempting fate yet again. *But it'll only be until I get to 5k...*

Fuck. The things I do for love.

Finally making it back home, I park Sasha in the garage and then rush through the side door. Cassandra's sitting in front of the television, alone on the floor amid dozens of newspaper and magazine clippings. But Luke is gone, along with his skateboard.

Damn It, Luke! I exhale. "Cass..."

She pauses cutting something out from an auto magazine, acknowledges me briefly, then resumes cutting. "That was fast."

I rub the back of my head. "Yeah, uh, Dave didn't get any new parts in. You here alone?"

She arches an eyebrow. "I'm a big girl, Adam. I can stay home alone."

"You know what I mean."

"Luke left in a hurry. Something about some 'perfect mural' he's got, and he's gonna show some asshole who's been painting over his pieces." She shrugs. "Honestly, I have no idea what that all means."

I swear under my breath. "Oh for fuck's sake. Must be another stupid graffiti war he's gotten himself into. Last time I tried to help him, I almost fell off the roof of a building chasing his ass. This time, he's on his own."

"Seriously, Adam. You need to stop acting like a damn parent with these guys. They're adults. They make their own decisions. They don't need your constant supervision."

"Someone needs to keep order around here. If things were up to Luke or Clay, we'd be screwed. Besides, these guys are my family. They're all I've got."

Her face softens. "You've got a big heart. I'm starting to get the family-man vibes from you. Y'know. Wife, kids, dog, white picket fence…"

I snort, and then plop down on the couch. "You got me all wrong, babe. A man like me doesn't deserve all that. The only kids in my life right now are my three nephews… and sometimes Luke."

"I thought you said these guys were your only family?"

"They are, because they're the only ones I'm closes to and spend the most time with. More than my own blood relatives. I have a grandfather that I constantly butt heads with, a grandmother who's pretty much disowned me, a brother that hates me, and three nephews that I haven't seen since they were born."

Her expression dulls. Her gaze flicks back to the newspaper and she continues cutting. "My mom and I were never close. She always expected me to be this perfect daughter who could do no wrong, and I did plenty of it. And dad never liked me, because I wasn't the son he always wanted. He tried to teach me football and all the other stereotypical things that simple-minded fathers try to teach their sons. He did get me interested in cars, though." She stops and smiles a moment, then continues. "But the older I got, the more he had to accept me for who I was. Which he never could, of course. He just… gave up on me.

"I had a little sister once too. She got killed by a drunk driver. Never got a chance to meet her. She was supposed to be born that night. Mom survived, but… My parents separated when that happened, and I haven't seen them since."

All the wind is suddenly knocked out of me. "Holy shit. I'm so sorry…"

She frowns. "It is what it is. I've found closure. She's in a much better place than this hellhole."

The subject stings, and I try to steer the conversation elsewhere. I glimpse the auto magazine she's cutting from. "What are you doing?"

"Planning out the mods I'm gonna get for my new ride. I hope I can still get the Hemi, but it's not looking like it."

"Did you check on it again today?"

"Yup, and it's still there. There's still hope." Her half-hearted smile suggests she doesn't quite believe that.

I grin and remember the wad of cash in my pocket. I'd only need one more good job to make her dream a reality. I hop up from the couch, pick up the wall phone by the kitchenette, and dial Gabriel's beeper. I hope he'll have some more jobs tonight. If not, I'll have to try again tomorrow. If they were as easy as the last one, I'd have the money in no time.

As I hang up the phone, I watch Cassandra in the main room as she busily cuts out pictures of engines and Q&R products. She's determined.

I'm going to get that money for her, if it's the last thing I do.

CHAPTER 15

IT'S TUESDAY NIGHT, AND I'M ON THE ROAD AGAIN, THIS time, headed down to Summit. It's a bit of a longer drive, but it'll be the last job I'd need to pull. Seeing Cassandra's excited face once I get her that Hemi will make all of this worthwhile.

I hated having to lie to her again, saying I was going to see Dave, but it was the only way to keep her from suspecting anything.

Clayton had more 'overstock' in his trunk—seven bricks—and our employer wanted us to deliver five of them. While I kept Cassandra distracted inside the house, Clayton transferred the goods from his trunk to mine.

Riding into another shady area of town makes the hair on the back of my neck stand on end. *Just deliver and leave. No conflict...*

Following the last set of written instructions, I turn down a dead-end road. A small, shoddy-looking wooden house with plywood-covered windows sits at the end of the road. Six dressed-up sports cars, including a flashy red '88 Fiero with a giant spoiler, and a mud-covered pickup truck sit outside the house. No one's outside this time, which means I'll have to take the packages up to the door—and away from Sasha, preventing a quick getaway if I needed to make one.

Sighing, I park along the curb, positioning Sasha so that I can floor it back out to the main road, if necessary, then get out. I look around the eerily quiet, pitch-blackness of the area, and I shiver. I've been out of the drug-running game for so long, I never thought I'd feel scared like this again.

I retrieve the paper bag from my trunk and trudge to the front stoop of the house. A dim, yellowish light pours out from under the rickety front door, and slivers of light peek out from between the cracks of the plywood boards on the windows.

I knock once. The light from one of the windows winks out briefly, then a shadow moves near the door.

"What's your number?" Asks a muffled, familiar-sounding male voice.

I furrow my brow a moment, trying to discern the voice. I know I've heard it before, heard it recently even, but I can't quite pinpoint it.

I unfold the list of instructions from my pocket and read the final note at the bottom: "Seven, seven, five, zero, two." I have no idea what it all means. The order number, maybe? Password?

Several locks and latches click and slide, and the door creaks open.

My eyes widen.

Red Bandanna Guy—*Drew*—the leader of the Red Ravens crew stands in the doorway. Half of his face is bruised and bandaged from Cronos' vicious mauling last Saturday. With one hand behind his back, I know he's concealing something.

Oh, fuck me.

"You! Motherfucker!" Drew grits his teeth. "How the hell did you find me?"

I hold back the urge to reach into my jacket, grab my own gun, and blast this guy away for what he and his crew did to me and everyone else that night at Fife. But any sudden movements now would be my last—there was no way I could get a shot off before Drew while his hand was already on his gun. I need to keep him focused on business and not all that shit the other night. *Just deliver and leave. No conflict...*

I need this money, and I'm not going to let this asshole come between me and Cassandra's happiness.

"Look, man, whatever happened in Fife never happened. Cool? I don't know nothin,'" I say.

"You good, Drew?" another man calls from inside the house. I don't recognize the voice.

"All good," Drew replies to the unknown voice, keeping his gaze fixed on me. Moments later, he draws his attention over my shoulder and smiles smugly. "I see you brought Sasha," he says to me.

I frown. "Yeah, 'cause I'm runnin' tonight. She still ain't for sale, so don't ask."

"I can always just take her now. In fact, maybe I will."

"Here's your shit," I say, holding out the paper grocery bag in my right hand and hoping I can steer the topic away from Sasha and keep things moving.

He glances at the bag. "All of it?"

"Yup. Now, pay up."

He reaches for something concealed behind the door, produces a thick white envelope secured with duct tape, and tosses it to me.

I fumble with the envelope then catch it, tear it open, and briefly skim the bills. *Three grand. It's all there.*

There's a click.

My heart pounds as I clench the envelope. I slowly draw my eyes up, and I'm suddenly staring down the barrel of a .45.

"W-What the hell, man?" I say, not dropping my hands.

"Stay," he orders, then swipes the bag from me.

Tightness clenches the back of my throat. I can feel the tension rising in the air. There are more Red Ravens in that house, and they were pretty much guaranteed to be armed as well. No chance I could shoot my way out of this if it came to that. *Stay cool...*

Drew secures his concealed weapon in the back of his waistband and then checks inside the bag. His brow furrows. "There's supposed to be five. Where's the fifth?"

I arch an eyebrow. "What are you talking about? There are five bricks in there."

Scowling, Drew whips out his gun again and aims it at me. He shoves the bag into my chest. "Count 'em."

I swallow once then exhale. I peek inside the bag and count the bricks. *One. Two. Three. Four... No, that can't be right.* "M-Maybe one of them fell out in my trunk. Lemme check," I say.

He grits his teeth. "I don't think so, motherfucker. I think you're try'na steal from me."

My heart races. "I didn't steal your shit."

"You callin' me a liar?" He presses the steel barrel of the gun to my forehead.

My breath hitches.

"Yo, Drew? What's going on?" another voice calls from inside the house.

I look to the gun, then notice shadows appearing behind Drew. Looks like the rest of his friends are on their way, and I can't stick around to find out what they have in store for me. *This is going south way too fast.* There's only one way to escape, and I've only got a fifty-fifty chance of pulling it off.

I train my eyes on Drew's hand, and his index finger that's poised steadily over the trigger. I offer the bag back to him. "Here, take 'em. I'll figure out what happened to the fifth. We'll get this straightened out."

He grabs the bag with his free arm, and the movement puts some welcome space between his gun and my head. His gaze swivels to the contents. *Now or never.* In a flash, I lean to one side, then swoop in and cup my hand over the gun's slider.

He fires.

My ears ring, and a sharp pain soars through the palm of my hand as the slider railroads across my bare skin. Drew and I wrestle with the gun. I kick his legs out from under him, and he falls. Swiping the gun from his hand, I pick him up and press the gun against his temple. Drew pants, then slowly raises his hands in surrender. I glare at his friends, all clad in Red Raven colors, crowding at the door with their weapons drawn.

"Tell your boys to put 'em down, or I'll blow your fucking brains out," I warn.

Drew hesitates, then gives his friends a subtle nod. His friends comply and drop their weapons on the ground.

"Now," I continue. "I'm gonna get in my car, and I'm gonna leave. You fuckers better not follow me, or else."

Drew seethes. "You'll pay for this. No one steals from me and gets away with it. No one fucks with the Red Ravens."

"For the last time, I didn't steal from you." I slowly back away from the house, keeping the gun aimed at the group and Drew held in front of me. Finally, I reach Sasha and throw Drew to the ground. I hop in as quickly as I can, tear out of there, and don't look back.

I can't do this anymore.

I can barely drive straight as the anxiety from my brush with Drew and his boys keeps my hands shaking on the steering wheel. Was all of this really worth it? I did all of this for a girl. I've *never* done shit like this because of a girl. I cared about Cassandra way more than I should. She's going to be the death of me if I keep this up.

All this over a damned Hemi.

My entire body is spent. I'd earned five grand from two jobs in two days. No wonder I was caught up in this line of work for so long. What teenaged hoodlum wouldn't be tempted to do it?

But this isn't me anymore. The feeling was no longer a thrill, it was a nightmare.

I return home and discover Clayton and the others are back too. Clayton must've won that race, because a set of bright red coilovers sits on the workbench beside his car. I shake my head at the cheap-looking parts. Why some people insisted on modding their ride with subpar parts from a subpar company like LeatherRock, I'll never know.

Clayton... I think about tonight's ordeal with the Red Ravens. Those bricks were accounted for when Clayton transferred them to my car—or were they? With his car locked, I wouldn't get an answer tonight. But I plan on finding out soon enough.

My eyelids droop. I glance at the wall clock, which reads 3:30. *Damn.* I'll only get two hours of sleep before I have to get up again for work. But nothing in the world, it seemed, would stop me from making Cassandra happy. *Am I falling in love with her?*

I trudge out of the garage and into the common room. It's dark and quiet, and I hear Gabriel's light snoring in the back room. My eyes adjusted to the darkness, I noticed a lump of a blanket on the couch, slowly rising and falling. Smiling, I tiptoe over to the couch. I peer at the faint, dark outline of Cassandra's peacefully sleeping face. I wonder if she's mad at me for leaving earlier. I'll make it up to her, though.

Tomorrow, she'll have that Hemi.

CHAPTER 16

I WAS A ZOMBIE AT DONALDSON'S LATER THAT WEDNESDAY morning. My hands worked autonomously, while I mused over last night's ordeal. Clayton was already gone to who-the-hell-knows where before I'd awoke. Maybe he knew he'd fucked up this job. Either way, we were going to have words.

My thoughts shifted to the Hemi and how Cassandra would react when I gifted it to her. I hope that Hemi wasn't sold yet, or everything I'd done the last couple nights was for nothing. I planned on haggling the seller to three grand instead of the five he was asking. That way, I could put the remaining money toward repairs and detailing. If there was one thing I'd learned from my grandfather besides fixing cars, was how to wheel and deal. The day dragged on slower than molasses.

After clocking out of my first job, I head over to Anderson Antique Auto. Grandpa's in the main office with a customer, closing out a sale.

"…Appreciate your business. Have a great day," Grandpa says, nodding to the suited man who heads out the door. "What's wrong with you, boy?" he asks me when he returns to his desk, plopping down in the chair.

I sigh and approach the desk. "I need to step out for a bit to get something important. Shouldn't take too long."

He furrows his brow. "You can do whatever the hell you want, but you ain't getting paid for work you don't do."

"I know." I grin from ear to ear.

"What's going on? And what are you smiling about?"

I take a deep breath and try to calm my nerves. "So, there's this girl. Fucking amazing. Knows her way around cars like the back of her hand. She's been eyeing this Hemi Barracuda in the Classifieds that she's been wanting to mod—uh, *restore*. Well, I want to get it for her today and surprise her, and…"

Grandpa's eyebrows rise. "Now I've heard everything. You've found yourself a lady, eh? And one who's car-crazy?" He laughs. "Well, son of a bitch. It's about damn time."

I look at him, shocked. "Y-You're cool with it?"

"Son, if a lady will keep you from doing stupid shit like street racing, then you're damn right I'm 'cool' with it.'"

I swallow a lump in my throat. Of course, I'm not going to tell him that she races too. "Yeah…"

"So, this Hemi is in good condition?"

"Eh, it needs a lot of work. She wants to gut the whole thing and start from scratch."

A small smile parts his lips, and he chuckles. "Hot damn. I might need to meet this lady. Maybe hire her here and get some decent help for a change."

I wave my hand dismissively. "Nah, she's more into muscle cars, not these old roadsters."

"Hmph. These aren't 'old roadsters.' They're timeless classics."

I blow a raspberry. "Only in your world, Grandpa."

"All right, Adam. Do whatever you have to do and get back here. I got another engine rebuild waiting for you in Bay One."

I groan. "Ugh, another one?"

Grandpa's eyes twinkle in amusement. "Them's the breaks, kid."

It's almost seven-thirty at night when I return to the Shed. *I got it. I fucking got it!* I can't stop smiling. I got the Hemi for a steal after I'd managed to haggle the price down two thousand dollars cheaper. Afterwards, I'd gotten the car towed to Grandpa's shop. He was impressed beyond words—maybe even a little jealous—and he was even more eager to meet Cassandra.

As I pull into the garage, I'm met with the sounds of loud, angry voices coming from inside. Frowning, I hop out of my car and head toward the commotion in the common room.

"Don't tell *me* how to build my fucking car!" Clayton barks as I open the door.

I barge inside and the heated conversation halts. I glance at Clayton, Luke, and Cassandra and scowl. "What the hell's going on here?" I demand.

"Can't you see they're having a friendly conversation?" Luke answers sarcastically.

Cassandra, who's still wearing her Out the Box uniform, glares back at me then stabs her thumb at Clayton. "Your boy Clay has got some serious anger issues."

"She keeps saying I ain't using the right fuel filter," Clayton says. "What the fuck does she know? It's *my* car!"

"You're the one using LeatherRock," Cassandra says to Clayton. "The shittiest brand on the market. That trash is definitely not made for racing. You'll be lucky to get a week out of it before it starts leaking gasoline."

"Hey, this is brand new, and I got one hell of a deal for it," Clayton retorts.

She snorts. "LeatherRock's so shitty, they can't even give parts away."

"Fuck you. I ain't like your bitch, Jacob. Don't tell me how to build my damned car."

With her fist cocked back, she lunges at him. "What the hell did you say?"

"Whoa!" I come between them and hold my arms up to block her incoming blow. It lands solid on my bicep, frogging it. I grunt at the blow, and for a moment, my arm goes dead. Damn, she's got some power behind that punch.

Cassandra narrows her eyes at me. She doesn't seem the least bit sorry for hitting me.

"That's enough, you guys," My gaze bounces between Clayton and Cassandra, and then settles on Clayton. "Honestly, Clay, I hate to tell you this, but she's right. LeatherRock is the worst. I've easily scorched everyone who was running LeatherRock mods. Cass knows her parts like nobody's business. You should listen to her, man. She knows what she's talking about. Just saying."

Clayton growls. "What the hell are you siding with *her* for? She sucking your dick now or something? That it? Huh?"

Anger boils my blood. "Listen, asshole. She's here whether you like it or not. She's my responsibility."

"I'm *no one's* responsibility," Cassandra breaks in, glaring at all of us. "Whatever, I don't give two shits what you people do." She spins on her heel and heads out the front door.

I fight back the urge to follow her, but my issue with Clayton is more important.

Clayton sneers. "Aren't you gonna go after her?"

"Not till we talk." I glance at Luke. "Alone."

Luke rolls his eyes, grabs his sketchbook, and heads to his bedroom. "Whatever."

"What do you want, Adam? I got shit to do." Clay says once we're alone.

"It's about yesterday's drop." I cross my arms. "Did you count those bricks before you put 'em in my trunk?"

His brow furrows a moment. "Yeah. Four. Why?"

I shake my head. "It was supposed to be five. And you won't guess who that drop belonged to—Drew. The Red Ravens."

His eyes widen. "Oh, shit. I must've looked at the wrong order. I was wondering why I still had extra in my trunk…"

"Your mistake nearly got me killed. Now I got the Red-fucking-Ravens on my ass because they think I stole their shit!"

He holds up his hands reassuringly. "Don't worry, man. I'll take care of it."

"How? They're out for blood."

"I'll take care of it, I swear. There's a race happening tonight at the old railyard in Auburn. I'm going out there. Drew's guys will probably be out there too. I'll give them their missing shit and be done with it. Easy."

I purse my lips, my mind drifting back to New York. It was never that easy, not in this business. But at this point, I didn't have much of a choice but to go along with his plan. "All right, Clay. But for your sake, you better not fuck up again."

"Don't worry. I got this."

I turn and head outside to find Cassandra. She's leaned up against the wall by the door with her arms crossed, staring straight ahead at the darkness of the woods beyond.

"Cass…" I murmur, gently reaching out and touching her arm.

She starts, whirls around, and slugs me in the jaw with her fist. My head whips to the side and I taste blood. *Damn, that smarts.* I put my hand over my mouth. "You didn't have to do that," I mumble.

"That's for keeping that asshole, Clay, as your number one," she spits.

I frown. "Really? Is that what you're upset about?"

"No." She narrows her eyes and folds her arms back across her chest. "Where were you last night?"

"I told you. I was out at Dave's."

"Until three o'clock in the fucking morning?"

"Why do I need to explain to you where I've been?"

"You think I'm stupid?" Her eyes get glassy.

I think for a moment. *Does she think I'm sleeping around?* As I study her carefully, noting the fear and concern in her eyes, I realize there's something else bothering her.

I gently grab both of her arms and look her straight in the eyes. "Hey. What's going on? Talk to me," I say in a soft voice.

She opens her mouth to reply when the sound of Clayton's car starting up cuts through the common room, sending my attention over my shoulder. His tires squeal as he violently backs out of Bay Two and kicks up dirt as he flies out of the yard and onto the main road.

Moments later, the front door swings open and Luke storms out, wearing his backpack and carrying his skateboard under his arm.

I furrow my brow at him. "Where the hell are *you* going?"

"Out to find the motherfucker that painted over my mural."

I roll my eyes. "Luke, man, let it go."

"You don't understand. This is war."

"And you're going to skateboard all over town looking for him?"

"I know where he is. And I'm not gonna waste gas going five miles. Later." He heads toward the woods and disappears into the darkness.

Sighing, I turn back to Cassandra. She glares back at me.

"You're a shitty leader, Adam," she says. "Can't even keep your own crew under control. You know what? Fuck being your number one. I don't think I want it anymore."

Is she serious? Have I fucked up that bad? "They're only acting like this because I'm fighting for you. I want them to trust you. They just need time."

"You just don't get it, do you? They'll never trust me, Adam. All I'll ever be to them is Jacob's whore."

"Well, you and I know that's not true. You're too good for Jacob. Too smart. And a hell of a better driver than him. That shit is too intimidating to him."

She half smiles, and then averts her gaze. "Thanks… but that doesn't change the fact that I'm not wanted here. And to be honest, I don't want to be here anymore. Especially not with these people you call friends."

The stress and tension between my crew and Cassandra, my family drama, and last night's near-death experience has begun eating away at my soul. I'm juggling so many things at once, trying to keep everything balanced, and there's no one to share the burden with. I can't tell Cassandra about the deliveries and nearly dying or ease her fears about me disappearing until three in the morning without more lies. And

Clay just thinks everything will be cool with Drew and the Red Ravens... I hope he's right. And it doesn't look like there's much I can say to the rest of the crew at this point about everything with Cassandra. The more I press, the more it will just confirm what they've been thinking the whole time. And God help me if I tell any of this to Grandpa. The harder I try, the more shit breaks.

What the fuck have I been doing all this time? Grandpa was right. I needed to get my head on straight and stop playing Russian Roulette with my life.

I take Cassandra's hand. "Come here."

I don't feel her pull away as I lead her around to the open garage where Sasha is parked. I roll the bay door down so we're alone in here—just me and Cassandra. I let go of her hand and stare at her intently. "Listen. I need to tell you something."

Arching an eyebrow, she steps back and crosses her arms, watching me attentively.

Pursing my lips, I exhale through my nose. "I'm thinking about giving all this up."

Her other eyebrow raises. "Giving what up?"

"Racing," I reply, a bad taste filling my mouth at the thought. "Back in the day, we used to do this shit for fun. But now, everyone's out for blood. The guns, the drugs... hell, I *met you* at gunpoint... It ain't fun no more."

Her jaw drops. "Wait. You're done racing? *You?*"

I nod. "I can't keep doing this. I've been doing some soul-searching ever since what happened at the airstrip."

The surprise in her eyes dims. Maybe she was remembering too. "That was scary, yeah… So, if you're done racing, what are you gonna do? Just hang around and go to work? Do you want that white-picket fence after all?" Her eyes drift down as she says this, and eventually flick toward my car. "And what about Sasha?"

So many questions. I have no idea what I'd do next if I called it quits. Racing has been my outlet—my *sanity*—for so long. I look at Sasha sadly and run my hand over her shiny red paint. "I dunno. We've made some good memories."

"She won't be worth shit to you if you're getting out of the racing scene. She was made to race, not sit around or go on joyrides around town."

"I know that." I frown. "You want her?"

She blinks. "*Me?*" She pauses, then shakes her head. "I only raced you for it for Jacob, because he wanted it. But now, I don't give a shit. She runs nice, but she's not my style."

I quirk a smile. "Yeah, I figured. You're into muscle cars, anyway."

She smiles back. "Damn straight."

"Speaking of…" I casually steer the conversation. "Any word on that Hemi?"

Her face turns dark and rigid, as though I'd said something offensive. "It's been sold. Can you fucking believe it? My dream project car sold to some scrub who will probably ruin it with a stupid-ass spoiler and shit."

I look at her with mock sympathy. "Damn, sorry to hear that.

"Yeah… I suppose I can't be too upset. It was a well-sought-after car for an amazing price. I'm amazed it wasn't scooped up faster…" She says with a sigh.

"Well, on the bright side, my grandfather wants to meet you."

She blinks several times. "Your grandfather?"

"Yeah, he owns Anderson Antique Auto over on Sixth Avenue. I told him about you, and, well… he's intrigued."

"You told your grandfather about me?" She wrinkles her nose. "Why would you do that?"

My heart leaps up to my throat. "Because… I… I *really* like you."

Her eyes widen slightly, and she uncrosses her arms.

I clench my jaw. *I can't believe I said that, for fuck's sake.* "I respect you, Cass. And my grandfather is the biggest gearhead I know. He's always looking for someone to talk cars with. Will you at least come by the shop and say hi?"

One corner of her lips tugs upward as she attempts to fight down a smile. "Okay. I'll humor him." She pauses and looks me in the eyes. "I kinda like you, too…"

I stare back at her, my smile broadening. "Yeah?"

She gives a faint nod, then her smile quickly disappears. She draws away from me and hugs herself. "Damn it…"

"What?" I ask, cocking my head to the side.

"I… I can't get distracted. Not by you, not by anyone."

What does she mean by that? I wonder. "What about the other night?"

She shakes her head. "It should've never happened."

My heart sinks. "You regret it?"

She says silent.

I hang my head and sigh. Maybe that shouldn't have happened. But one thing led to another. If she regrets it, then what does that mean for us?

"Cass…" I murmur, stepping closer.

"No." She puts her hand up, stopping me.

I freeze.

"I don't regret it…" she continues. "But I have to stay focused if I'm ever gonna land this new job at Q&R."

For a moment, I think my ears are deceiving me. "Wait… *What?*"

Her smile returns. "I heard Q&R is hiring for an entry-level sales rep position at their Bellevue headquarters. But even though it's entry-level, they're still looking for all this required education and work experience bullshit.

"So, I figured to get around that, I can show them a good, dialed-in muscle car enhanced with Q&R parts. Then, maybe they might look past the education and experience shit and hire someone like me." The excitement in her eyes quickly leaves, and her smile fades. "But now, since the Hemi was sold, my plan went right out the window."

I rubbed my chin in thought. So, *that's* what she's been up to all this time. I figured all those times I saw her perusing the Classifieds, she was looking for a new car, but apparently, she was also looking for a new job too. And I couldn't be happier for her. Working at Q&R is a dream come true for her, and one day, I know she'll be living that dream. She'd be perfect for them.

And she'll have her Hemi too. Man, this is going to be the best surprise for her ever.

"That's great news," I say. "Wow, a chance to work at Q&R headquarters? You'd be an amazing sales rep there."

She shakes her head. "Without that Hemi, I don't have a chance now. I don't have any kind of academic degree that they're asking for, and I don't have five years of work experience."

I arch an eyebrow. "Five years for an *entry-level* job? What kind of backwards shit is that?"

She shrugs.

"I'll find you another Hemi."

"You don't just *find* another Hemi Barracuda. A good, workable one is rarer than a diamond. I may never find another perfect one like that in my lifetime."

"Then, I'll search every junkyard and classified ad for one. We can make this happen."

Her smile grows. "You're sweet, Adam. You really are."

Smiling sheepishly, I step closer to her. "I just want to see you happy. Trust me, you're worth it."

"Adam…" Her gaze draws away from me again.

"And just so you know, I don't regret the other night. You're one hell of a woman. I hope you know that."

A hint of red flushes her cheeks.

I inch my face closer to hers, unable to resist the urge to kiss her. "Don't worry about being distracted. You're the most focused woman I know. But sometimes, you just need to listen to that little voice."

She lets out an airy chuckle, and her head slowly turns to me. "What little voice?"

I gently run the pad of my index finger down her soft lips, then lean in and plant a loving kiss on her lips. "The same one that spoke to you the other night," I murmur.

She exhales. Her eyelids flutter. "Oh… Yeah, that little voice is gonna get me in trouble." She returns a small kiss to my lips, then gently pulls away. "I got another idea."

Damn, that tease. "What's up?"

"Let's go check out that circus in Auburn."

"You mean the race?" I make a face. "Ugh. I really don't want to."

"I know you don't. That's why we should check it out. I want to laugh in Clay's face when he ends up losing to a scrub."

If that had come from anyone else, I would've jumped to Clayton's defense by default. It's definitely what I should've done for family. But Cassandra's presence has me seeing some things differently. And lately, I've been feeling my friendship with him slowly tearing away. We were family because we didn't have anyone else, but now? People change. The race scene used to be about the adrenaline rush and having a good time. That's what it used to be about for Clayton too. But now with the drugs and guns moving in, I was looking for a way out, and he was diving in deeper. The thought is unnerving, and I try to change the subject. "Eh, okay. You think Jacob will be there too?"

She shrugs. "Probably. But I'm not there to see Jacob. Fuck him. At least he doesn't use LeatherRock in his car."

I grin and pull out my keys from my pocket. "You should've let that argument with Clay go, by the way. He's as loyal to that brand as you are with Q&R."

She grimaces. "I was *trying* to tell him about the faulty suspension system before he started being an ass and yelling over me."

"What?"

"LeatherRock issued a mandatory recall on the suspensions because the coilover reservoir leaks and can explode. There was a big article in the Auto section in last week's newspaper. I was trying to say something, and then he started arguing, so I started arguing, and then…"

"Oh shit," I mutter. Clayton barely read the paper, unless it was the Classifieds section, and even then, only when he was looking for certain parts.

"Exactly. And your boy Clay's racing in that ticking time bomb. Who knows? Maybe we'll see some fireworks tonight."

I frown. As pissed as I am at him, I'm also genuinely concerned for my friend. I dread venturing out there and running into Drew and the rest of the Red Ravens, though.

But Clay is in trouble…

I hop in Sasha, jam the key in the ignition, and gesture to Cassandra with a tilt of my head. "C'mon. We have to stop him."

CHAPTER 17

It's a packed Wednesday night at the abandoned railyard in Auburn. People of all ages, dressed in the finest colors of their crew are everywhere, racing and showing off their rides. It's like one huge not-so-legal car show. Normally, I'd be shitting my pants with the opportunity to show Sasha off to most of these newbie scrubs, but tonight, I'm not feeling it. Not when there's so many things on my mind. And that near-death experience with the Red Ravens the other night was the cherry on top of my shitty mood.

This feels like a nightmare. My friends doubt me because of the choices I've made. I'll lose them at this rate. A rival crew wants my head. And on top of that, I'm starting to go backwards, doing things that I swore I'd leave behind in the past.

I find a place to park in the sea of cars, but strategically close enough to the exit to make a quick getaway. Cassandra perks up in the passenger's seat and cranes her neck to scan the thick crowd.

"This place is bumpin' tonight," she says, hopping out of the car.

I get out as well, carefully scanning the area for the Red Ravens, but can't spot any from here. *No doubt, those bastards are probably somewhere nearby...* A group of teenagers spot me and approach, fawning over Sasha.

"Yo! Over here! Look at this one!" one of the teens yells to his friends.

The younger crowd multiplies, forming a circle around me and my car. I glance beyond the crowd at Cassandra, who walks off toward another crowd watching the live races.

I lock my car and swipe away a stray speck of dirt from her hood. "Look, but don't touch, or I'll crush your fingers. Got it?" I warn, sliding my key into my jacket pocket. "And believe me, I'll know who touched her." It's an empty threat—I'm above beating up a kid—but my demeanor is intimidating enough to convince their gullible minds.

"N-No, man, we won't touch!" one of the teens stammers, turning pale.

The crowd parts as I stride past, making my way to the racing strip. I pass by numerous tricked-out cars with their hoods up, showing off their mods. I can tell at a glimpse that all but two of them are using LeatherRock. If I were a newbie, I might find the sight orgasmic. But seeing all those cheap, sub-par parts is like a punch to the gut. This whole damn place is nothing but one big gathering for LeatherRock cocksuckers.

Yeah, I really *don't want to be here.*

Shoving my hands in my pockets, I spot Cassandra among the sea of spectators, checking out the goods under the open hood of a lime green MR2 Turbo. A group of guys standing nearby shoot wolfish glances at her. Then, one of them dares to approach her.

Frowning, I take my hands out of my pockets and start walking over to them. The guy puts his hand on her shoulder and brings his face close to her ear, saying something to her. Cassandra shrugs off his hand, turns and looks at him coolly. Then she blows him off by giving him the finger, and shoves past him.

I halt a moment and crack a smile. The man slumps his shoulders and dejectedly watches her leave. Meanwhile, his group of friends point and laugh at him.

Cassandra walks in my direction, her head held high as if she doesn't notice me. As she's about to walk past me, I reach out and hook my arm around her waist, stopping her.

"Hey," I say.

She tenses a moment and then relaxes, the flustered, red tint on her face disappearing. "Oh, hey, sorry. I got distracted. I know we're supposed to find Clay."

"What were you looking for before?"

She rubs the back of her head. "Eh, I was kinda hoping I might see the Hemi out here. I wanna know who bought it. Maybe I can make some kind of deal with them."

I fight down a smile. "I doubt any of these kids are interested in a Hemi."

"You never know."

"Oh, I know. Trust me, ain't no one packing anything worthwhile under these hoods. They wouldn't know quality if it hit 'em."

She grins. "You're right. Okay, let's go find Clay—for real this time." She takes my hand in hers and tugs me along through the crowd. I happily let her take the lead.

I stare at our clasped hands and smile. Her hand is rough and warm and feels so good in mine. I think about that amazing night her hands were all over my body… *my dick…*

"Let's do this, Clay."

My revelry is shattered when I catch Mariah's voice nearby. Cassandra leads on through the thick crowd until we discover a mixed group of teenagers and adults gathered around Clayton's car. He leans against its side with his arms crossed, watching the group of ogling youths.

Mariah stands next to Clayton, her arm hooked with his. Gabriel is pacing back and forth with his head down, fiddling with his beeper.

Cassandra and I push through to the center of the crowd.

Clayton spots me and Cassandra, and nods.

"Yo, Clay," I say, reluctantly letting go of Cassandra's hand. "You race yet?"

"Not yet." Clayton stabs his thumb toward another group of people nearby gathered around a black Integra. "See my competition over there? This guy just got a sweet new supercharger I've been wanting to get my hands on for a while. If I ever got my Sylvie here dialed in with that, she'd give Sasha a run for her money."

I snort. "Man, it's still LeatherRock. It's garbage—you can't trust their shit."

Clayton shakes his head. "Whatever. Watch me scorch this guy and tell me if LeatherRock is still garbage."

"Garbage beating garbage... It don't matter. Seriously, though, you shouldn't race. You need to take a good look at your mods."

"My mods are fine, Adam. Now get off my back about it."

"No," Cassandra breaks in. "You *really* shouldn't be racing. There's a recall on that suspension you put in. A fucking big one."

"Fuck that. There ain't nothing wrong with my mods." Clayton sneers at Cassandra. "You just don't want me to race at all. That's what it really is, isn't it?"

"Yes!" she says. "Didn't you hear what we just said? Those coilovers are dangerous!"

Mariah groans. "I thought this conversation was over back at the Shed? I didn't come all the way out here to hear the brand-loyalty dick wars again."

Clayton kisses Mariah's forehead. "Don't worry, babe. That shit's done." He shoots me and Cassandra an icy glare, then he hops into the driver's seat. "Time to race. Get outta the way."

I sigh and watch him start the car as the crowd breaks. Clayton beckons me over.

Curious, I approach the driver's side window.

I looked for Drew when we got out here, but I didn't see him or any of the Red Ravens," Clayton says. "All bullshit aside, I don't want to see you get hurt. We're family. I promise, I'll make it right and get 'em off your back for good."

I nod. "Thanks, man… And hey, I'm serious—I don't want to see you get hurt either—don't race tonight. Please."

His nostrils flare. "I'll be fine." He rolls the window up.

Sighing, I back away from the car and return to Cassandra.

"What was that all about?" she asks.

I wave my hand dismissively. "He, uh, just wanted to gloat some more about his superior LeatherRock mods."

She rolls her eyes. "Pfft. Let the embarrassment begin. Hopefully *just* embarrassment…"

There was no convincing Clayton out of racing. I can only hope and pray that he really doesn't have a defective suspension installed.

A Nirvana song blares from a portable radio sitting on the roof of a nearby car. Teens and young adults headbang to the song, a few of them dancing wildly while holding up bottles of beer. Beyond the crowd of partying kids is a group of familiar looking adults huddling around a white CR-X.

I nod toward the group and ask Cassandra, "Is that Jacob?"

She squints. "That's his car, all right. But who are those guys?"

It takes me a moment to remember where I've seen the guys in yellow before. I'd made a delivery for one of them a few nights ago, and they were hanging around Fife Airstrip that night too. *But who are they?* "You think Jacob lost a race?"

Cassandra smirks. "Oh, I fuckin' hope so. Let's go see."

We approach the group of five dressed in yellow padded vests and ripped blue jeans. They stand in a circle in front of Jacob's car, watching a confrontation between Jacob and one of their yellow-vested comrades.

I quicken my steps, walking ahead of Cassandra and make my way over to the huddle. I can feel the tension in the air, and sense a fight is about to break out. Occasional raised voices begin to draw a small crowd.

The man squaring off with Jacob is tall, and built, with a white lollipop stick poking out the corner of his mouth. He glares menacingly at Jacob, who, for a moment, cowers, pale-faced, like he's about to shit his pants. Jacob composes himself quickly, stands a little straighter and holds his head high. But the headlights from a nearby car reflects beads of sweat from his face, betraying his courageous expression.

The Ninez stand outside the circle. Bryce breaks through the crowd and makes his way toward Jacob. One of the yellow-clad thugs steps in his way and rests his hand over a small bulge in his jacket pocket. Bryce reaches down to the bulge at the side of his waistband, and Mr. Yellow slowly shakes his head. Bryce concedes, his hand falling away from his side, and he helplessly watches his leader.

Jacob's yellow-vested aggressor pulls the lollipop from his mouth. His solid frame makes Jacob look like a scrawny kid.

"Don't tell me *you're* the man to beat around here." Lollipop Guy's menacing glare suddenly turns to amusement.

Jacob moistens his lips, then opens his mouth, but no sound comes out.

Damn, is Jacob actually scared of this goofy-looking guy? Who are they, anyway? I look at the leader's yellow-vested companions. One of them with a white Mohawk blows a pink bubble with his gum while he looks on, amused.

"What's going on?" Cassandra mutters beside me. She cranes her neck, trying to see beyond the crowd

I shake my head at her. "You wouldn't believe me if I told you."

"Try me."

I squeeze my body between two spectators, creating a small opening for her to slip through, then return my attention to the stand-off.

A slight bit of color returns to Jacob's face, and he lifts his head. "Y-Yeah, that's right. I'm number one here. the Ninez rule New Tacoma."

I crack a smile. *Oh, the irony.*

Lollipop Guy laughs and stabs his thumb at Jacob as he says to his yellow-vested friends, "This bitch! Leader of the Ninez!"

The rest of the yellow-clad gang laugh in response. Some of the other spectators break out in laughter too.

Cassandra nudges me. "Now *this* is what I call entertainment. Aren't you glad we came here after all?"

I grin. It *is* nice to see Jacob get humiliated for a change after the hell he and his crew had put us through. But strangely, as I continue watching him get shit on and ridiculed, I get a niggling feeling in my gut. These guys in yellow are new on the scene. What's their angle? Did they just like to race, or did it have something to do with the bricks I delivered? Heavy dealers moving into the scene probably wasn't a good thing, regardless.

And I'm the one running drugs for them…

"You drift?" Lollipop Guy asks Jacob.

Jacob shakes his head. "Nah."

He lifts an eyebrow. "Are you fucking kidding me? With that CR-X? The way it's been modded, it's a perfect drifting machine."

"Yeah, well, she's made to drag, not drift."

Lollipop Guy blows a raspberry. "Dragging's for pussies."

I perk up at that. Years ago, when Jacob and I first met, he was all about drifting. Pretty damned good at it too. So good, in fact, he was top dog for a while. He tried to get me into drifting, but I quickly learned it wasn't my thing. I got him into dragging, though, and he's been hooked on it ever since. We'd stopped talking about drifting ever since that day.

"What are you doing out here?" Jacob asks Lollipop Guy.

"My crew runs these parts. We're teaching these kids what it *really* means to race." Lollipop Guy cracks a smile. "Then we'll expand to New Tacoma and beyond."

Jacob bristles. "You're not taking my turf. Not on my watch."

Cassandra lets out an airy chuckle, then mutters to me, "Jacob's a little too late to start growing a pair."

Smiling, I muter back, "I still don't know what you ever saw in him."

"You've made more mistakes than I have, Adam."

Touché.

Lollipop Guy looks thoughtful for a moment as he idly twirls the candy on the tip of his tongue. "To claim a place like New Tacoma means you gotta know how to drag *and* drift, cause it's Eden out there. Race me, and let's see how the mighty 'Number One in New Tacoma' holds up to Liz." He gestures toward an immaculate, tricked-out cherry-red '87 Supra parked nearby.

A wave of *oohs* and *ahhs* sweep over the crowd.

Damn, that car looks sweet. I've heard how powerful the Supras were at drifting. Jacob's gonna have his hands full with his CR-X.

"I ain't driftin.'" Jacob shakes his head.

"What's wrong, chickenshit? Afraid to get smoked?" Lollipop Guy jeers.

Jacob opens his mouth.

"This pussy seriously ain't the ruler of New Tacoma, is he?" Lollipop Guy scans the rest of the crowd. "Who's the *real* top dog around here?" His gaze briefly stops on me, and then moves onto the next person.

My throat tightens. Anxiety rises in my chest. If this were dragging, I would've gladly stepped forward and put this cocky son of a bitch in his place. But drifting? I was as helpless as a fish out of water, and the thought drives me insane.

"*Challenge! Challenge! Challenge!*" the crowd chants.

Jacob grits his teeth. He tilts his head a little higher and clears his throat. "Okay… Okay, fine. I accept."

Another wave of cheers and whistles erupts form the crowd.

"Sweet," Lollipop Guy says. "Friday night. Eleven p.m. Industrial Park. Get ready to be smoked."

"If I win, you and your bitches stay off my turf," Jacob says.

Lollipop Guy smirks. "And if *I* win, your CR-X is mine."

Jacob's face pales.

"Oh man, this is priceless. Look at that sorry son of a bitch! The karma, it's beautiful," Cassandra says to me, grinning from ear to ear.

I have to admit, it is refreshing watching Jacob get put in his place, but this still bothers me. Jacob hasn't drifted in years, and I think he's getting in way over his head with this race. *Am I actually worried about Jacob?* I may have lost all respect for the guy, but Jacob and I had history. We'd been here since the beginning in Tacoma and, despite the bullshit between us, we knew how things worked in the scene. I couldn't stomach a crew of outsiders like those guys in yellow taking over my town.

A hush falls over the crowd as all eyes turn expectantly to Jacob. He takes a deep breath and then nods once. "Challenge accepted."

The spectators cheer and shout, some waving beer bottles in the air, before eventually dispersing. Lollipop Guy returns to his yellow-clad friends, while Jacob trudges back to his crew like a wounded dog.

Smirking, I beckon Cassandra with a tilt of my head. "C'mon, Cass. Let's go see an old friend."

She snorts. "Why? I have nothing to say to him."

"I'll do all the talking. Not like he can say or do shit to me now."

"I'm just fine right here."

I shrug. "Suit yourself." I leave her alone and approach the Ninez. Preston is the first to spot me, pinning me with a glare.

"Adam! Fuck."

I give them all a casual wave. "Nice to see you fine folks too."

Bryce reaches into his waistband like he's about to pull out a weapon, but Jacob smacks his hand against his friend's chest, stopping him.

"Are you fucking crazy, man?" Jacob exclaims. "Don't go pulling your shit out like that with those guys around." Jacob's eyes swivel back to the guys in yellow walking away in the distance.

Scowling, Bryce reluctantly removes his empty hand from his waistband.

Jacob grits his teeth. "What are you doing here, Adam?"

"Same reason why you're here. I came to watch some races. Damn, I thought you were a pussy before, but holy shit… Who was that guy?"

Jacob purses his lips. His nostrils flare. He seems to be at mental odds with himself and I can practically smell his fear. I've never seen Jacob act like this before. "His name is Kaine, leader of a drift crew called Oculus X from Lakewood."

I lift an eyebrow. "And… you're actually *scared* of them?"

"Hell yeah. And you should be too."

I snort out a laugh. "First of all, I've never even heard of them. And second, I ain't scared of a grown-ass man who dresses like a banana and probably sucks on a lollipop better than he sucks tits."

Preston starts to bark out a laugh, but Jacob's glower cuts him short. Preston clears his throat and crosses his arms, trying futilely to fight off an amused smile.

"Yeah, well, be glad you don't know them, Adam," Jacob says. "They like to fuck with anyone who looks important."

"So why were they fucking with *you*, then?"

Bryce snorts. Jacob shoots another glare and Bryce casually averts his attention elsewhere, though I can still tell he's smiling.

Jacob turns back to me. "Look, man, I'm serious."

"So am I."

He balls his fists. "Are you done now? I'm fucking screwed right now, and all you want to do is make fucking jokes."

I cross my arms, smiling in victory that I'd managed to dog him enough to make him concede. "Why'd you agree to race him, then?"

"Because Oculus X doesn't take 'no' for an answer."

"But you don't drift anymore."

Jacob shakes his head. "Doesn't matter. If I lose, they take Bella. If I don't race, they'll still take Bella. At least this way I've got a shot."

"Damn, that's harsh. So I take it you knew these guys back when you used to drift?"

"Yeah, but they never knew me, despite my reputation in the drifting scene. These guys are in the business of running crews off and taking turf, no matter who they are."

"Funny, all this sounds vaguely familiar."

Jacob sighs. "All right, man. Damn. You don't get it, do you?'

"Hey man, this is your problem, not mine. You're number one in New Tacoma, after all."

He averts his gaze. "Yeah... Look, Oculus X needs to be dealt with before they come rolling in on our turf. We need to stop them."

"Who's 'we'?"

Jacob rolls his eyes. "Look, I'm calling a temporary truce until those guys are dealt with."

"A truce?" I raise my eyebrows. Damn, he must be desperate.

"Yeah, man. I'm telling you, they're bad news. Nobody's rides will be safe with them around."

I glance at Sasha parked in the distance. "Yeah? Well, I'd like to see those bastards try and take Sasha."

Jacob laughs. "It's only a matter of time before they start gunning for Sasha. Their crew is growing fast. If we don't protect our turf, we're all done for."

"Oh, so now when your ass is in trouble, we're suddenly friends now? After all the shit you put me and my crew through? After the way you treated Cassandra?"

His nose wrinkles. "What does *she* have to do with anything?"

"She has a lot to do with it."

"That bitch betrayed me."

"You abandoned her."

Jacob scowls and averts his gaze. "If you're talking about that night in Fife, I didn't abandon her. It was every fucking man for himself. She's street smart, she knew the play, and she knew how to get home. And now she's gone for good, and I don't give a fuck anymore."

I narrow my eyes at him. "And that's why you don't deserve her."

"What the hell does *that* mean?"

Before I have a chance to respond, Cassandra approaches me from behind. Standing beside me, she takes my hand in hers. She looks up at me, and then casts Jacob a disgusted look.

"Hey, Adam. You missed Clay's race while you were busy talking with this garbage." she says to me, not taking her eyes off Jacob and his crew.

Relishing the warmth of Cassandra's hand, I give it a gentle squeeze. Then I turn my attention back to Jacob. I can tell the wheels are turning in his head, as his gaze falters to our clasped hands. Then, his face darkens.

"So that's where you've run off to, huh, Cass?" Jacob says in a tone tinged with pain.

Cassandra narrows her eyes at him. "Yeah, away from the likes of your sorry ass."

A small smile creeps over my lips. I let go of her hand and wrap my arm around her waist, underlining our current relationship for him.

Jacob's eyes turn dull. "Oh, so it's like that?"

"Yeah, it's like that," Cassandra retorts, holding her head high.

I turn away from Jacob and his crew and begin heading toward the racing strip with her.

"C'mon, Adam!" Jacob calls. "You can't seriously leave me to deal with Oculus X alone. You think they'll stop after me? They'll come after you next!"

Ignoring him, I continue to the crowd. When Cassandra and I are far enough away from him, I unhook my arm from her waist.

"Are you done fucking with him now?" she asks.

I crack a smile and nod. "Yeah. Can you believe he wants a truce?" She raises her eyebrows in surprise, and I tell her about the conversation and Oculus X.

She laughs out loud. "You didn't believe me when I told you that Jacob is a pussy? He's scared of his own shadow."

"Honestly, though? I've never seen him this scared shit-less before. Maybe he's onto something with them. You know anything about Oculus X?"

"Only that they're drifters." She shrugs. "His history with them goes longer than I've known him. Of course, he's never told me about them, but I don't care to keep up with the drifters, anyway. But Jacob's fucked big time if he thinks he can go up against a Supra. Especially when he doesn't know the first thing about drifting."

"Well, he knows about drifting. He was pretty good at it too, he just hasn't done it in a long while." There *is* something else about Oculus X that bothers me. I can't shake the feeling that they really do mean to take over New Tacoma. A thought suddenly strikes me—one of those annoying ideas springing from my damned conscience. *Maybe I* should *help Jacob win. But how?* Sighing in exasperation, I rub my hand over my face.

"What's up with you?" Cassandra asks, jarring me out of my thoughts.

I shake my head dismissively. "Nothing. Did Clay win?"

"Yeah. Apparently, he had the lesser of the shitty intake systems. No fireworks, though, thankfully. You ready to split, or are you going to go play patty cake with Jacob some more?"

I quirk a smile. "Nah, I'm good to leave the poor bastard to his own problems. Let's go."

CHAPTER 18

"HEY, LET'S NOT GO BACK TO THE SHED YET," CASSANDRA says from the passenger's seat once we're back on the main highway, headed southwest back to Tacoma.

"Okay. Where to?" I ask, not taking my eyes off the road.

"How about…"

She directs me off the highway near Fife Heights to a back road that winds through a thick forest. Lights from the very few houses this far out dot the landscape in the distance. I turn down a narrow dirt road and head right to a dead end. My headlights shine on a set of guardrails, and I slow to a halt. Beyond the guardrails is a steep ridge that overlooks a massive farmland valley caressed by moonlight.

I look sideways at Cassandra. "Where are we?"

Cassandra smiles. "Just an overlook point. Found it on accident before I met Jacob. I liked coming out here to think."

Smiling, I shut off the engine and turn off the headlights. Darkness consumes the car's interior, which soon becomes softly illuminated by the moon's dim glow. "We all need thinking spots. Mine is a certain Chinese restaurant."

She chuckles, then nestles herself comfortably in her seat. "You know, ever since I left Jacob and his crew, I feel like I have a whole new perspective on my life."

"I'm glad you were smart enough to get away from him. He would have kept you tied down with his bullshit."

"It's not the first mistake I've made in my life. Won't be the last, either."

I frown at that. "Hey, you're still going to meet my grandfather, tomorrow, right?" I ask, trying to lighten the mood.

She raises her eyebrows. "I said I would, didn't I? Why are you so worried about that, anyway?"

"Because it would mean a lot to me." *And I can't wait to surprise you with your new Hemi.*

"When I make a promise, I follow through."

"Unlike a certain cowardly douchebag we know."

She laughs. "I am so over Jacob."

I look at her carefully. "So, where does that leave us?"

She looks back at me, then bites her bottom lip. "Us?"

"Yeah…" My gaze briefly drifts down to her lips, then back to her eyes, twinkling in the moonlight filtering into the car. "Whatever this is between us," I continue.

"What do you think it is?" she asks.

"I'm not sure what to *think*. But I *know* I need a woman like you in my life."

One corner of her lip tugs upward. "Oh, really?"

I stare at her lips again, yearning to taste them. Slowly, I lean across the center console and plant a kiss on her lips—gently, at first—then when I feel her reciprocate, I deepen it. I caress her cheek with the back of my hand as she rests her hand on my arm. I want to get closer to her, but the damn console is in the way. Finally, she pulls back from the kiss.

"Let's stay out here for a while," she whispers, her eyes hooded.

"Sure," I whisper back, staring longingly at her lips.

She smiles playfully and gets out the car. Standing before the guardrail and crossing her arms, she stares out at the dark valley below. I sweep behind her and wrap my arms around her waist, slowly pulling her to me. Her body tenses a moment, then relaxes. We're alone out here on this ridge—it's so quiet, so peaceful. I look out into the valley. Tiny dots of moonlight twinkle and waver off the surface of a small lake.

"I can see why this is your thinking spot," I say.

"Yeah. There's nobody around but you and nature. Kinda takes your mind off shit for a while."

I gently kiss the side of her neck and murmur, "There's only one thing my mind is focused on right now."

She sighs and leans her neck to the side, exposing it a little more, her body relaxing in my hands. I deepen the kiss and smooth my hands along the contours of her hips. Her body shivers.

I spin her around and stare at the dim outline of her face. I cup the sides of her face with my hands and indulge in another deep kiss.

She moans against my mouth as she feverously returns the kiss. Her arms wrap around my waist, and she splays her hands over my ass. Her body presses into mine, and my dick becomes instantly hard from the contact, wanting more.

God, her touch is magic. Her taste is addicting.

She breaks the kiss briefly and whispers in my ear, "Fuck me tonight."

My heart pounds. That's one of the sexiest things I've heard uttered from her sweet mouth. "I think I can manage that," I say with a smirk. I fish around my back pocket for my wallet and pull out a foil packet.

She puts her hand over mine and shakes her head. "I wanna feel you raw."

I blink. "I don't want to get you pregnant."

"I had my period recently. You don't have to worry about that."

I hesitantly return the packet to my wallet. She knows her body, so who am I to argue? Besides, I can only imagine how amazing she must feel raw.

"Okay," I say, my smile returning. I back away from the guardrail until I bump into Sasha. Returning my lips to Cassandra's, I spin her around and pin her against the warm hood while I indulge in her sweet taste. Her hands skillfully unzip my jacket and tug it off, then travel beneath my shirt. Goosebumps prickle every spot on my bare skin that she touches.

She begins lifting my shirt. I pull back briefly to give her more room to work with and suck in a breath. The fabric lifts over my head and is tossed away in the dirt with my jacket, the cool night air penetrating my skin.

I run my hands beneath her shirt, and fish for the clasps of her bra. Smiling crookedly, she wriggles out of both garments, and tosses them atop my discarded shirt. I stare at the dim outline of her full breasts, then run my hands over them, my fingers trekking across her raised, hardened nipples. As the cool air hits her skin, they feel like stone.

She lets out a small moan, and squirms. I grope a handful of one breast and enclose my mouth around the other. I use my thumb to flick and play with one nipple while I swirl my tongue around the other. Moaning louder, Cassandra squirms again, then splays her hands across my back, driving her nails into my skin.

I grunt, the pain causing me to squeeze and suck her tits harder. My dick steels.

"Please…" she utters.

I release her nipple from my mouth with a wet pop as I lift up and undo my pants. My dick slips out, stiff, erect, and beaded with a dollop of precum.

Biting her bottom lip in anticipation, she undoes the single button on her jeans. I finish it by lowering the zipper and slipping them down, along with her white panties.

I spin her around and push her forward, forcing her to lean over and brace herself on the hood.

Sweet déjà vu. My fantasy come to life.

"More…" she whispers.

Moistening my lips, I grab her hips with both hands, teasing her ass and soaked pussy with my dick.

Moaning, she grinds her ass against me. I hiss as the overwhelming sensation of her eagerness over my pulsating member sends electric pangs through my body. Steadying her hips, I thrust into her pussy hard and fast. She cries out, her entire body jerking in response to my throbbing intrusion. My breaths become ragged. I lean over her, driving my hips against her ass, pounding in and out of her. Harder. Faster. She moans louder.

"Oh, fuck yes. You feel so good inside me," she says between breaths.

Grunting, I drive into her deeper, finally reaching her core.

"*Mmm*... You're gonna make me cum..."

Good. My dick pulsates in her. I'm so close to letting go. I tighten my grip around her hips and give her another powerful thrust. Her walls constrict, and I can feel her on the verge of release. I steel myself to hold out for her, just a little while longer.

"I'm gonna make you cum so fucking hard," I growl, kissing and nibbling her earlobe.

Another shiver ripples through her body. I feed on her need. When I sense her at the height of her breaking point, I pull out, then thrust right back into her, faster than her walls can hold me this time, and land deep into her core.

She screams. Heat from her released passion suddenly consumes my dick. Her body continues trembling. With a loud groan, I respond earnestly, pumping hard into her, filling up her womb with all of my pent-up energy. I continue thrusting into her until I'm spent. I collapse onto her back, lightly slicked with sweat. Panting, we ride out the sexual high.

"Don't pull out," she whispers.

I relax, nestling my dick into her. It gives little occasional pules. She feels incredible. I'm so wrapped up in her.

"I've never had a man make me cum like that," she continues.

I smirk. "You've never been with a man who can make you cum." My hands leave her hips and travel back up to her breasts. I grope two handfuls of her soft, well-endowed goodness.

Her breath hitches and her body jerks again. "Ugh. You keep doing that, I might cum again."

"Yeah?" I give her breasts a gentle squeeze. "Then cum," I whisper in her ear.

"Uhhh… stop. I can't take it anymore…" she groans. "I'm numb…"

"Yeah. You're right. It's late. I still gotta go to work, y'know." I give her a final tease and twist her nipples between my fingers. Her pussy suddenly squeezes my dick.

Wow, her tits are sensitive as fuck…

She grunts in response. "Next time…"

I chuckle and finally pull out of her. I get myself situated and zip up my pants.

She awkwardly turns around and slides to the ground on wobbly legs. "I don't think I can walk."

I put my shirt and jacket back on. "I'll carry you." I pick up her clothes and hand them to her.

After she finishes getting dressed, I effortlessly pick her up and carry her to the passenger's seat. I hop in and start up the car. The illuminated radio clock reads 3:55 a.m.

Holy shit! I'll be lucky if I only get an hour's worth of sleep in before I have to get up to go to work. Grandpa would have my ass if he ever caught me sleeping on the job. But what just happened would be well worth the scolding.

I head back to the Shed in double-time. Thankfully, at this hour, there's barely any traffic on the interstate. Not long after entering Tacoma, I jump at the wailing sounds of a fire-truck's siren. Red flashing lights zoom past me moments later. Not realizing I'd had an emergency vehicle behind me, I look in my rear-view mirror and see several bright headlights behind me. The hint of blue lights flashes atop one of the sets of lights. *Shit!* My heart pounds, and I pull off to the shoulder.

"Why are we stopping?" Cassandra asks, looking around curiously.

"Cops," I say in a choked voice. The worst-case scenarios fly through my mind. I'm gonna get pulled for not moving over, and then when they find out who I am they'll pull my record. Maybe there was something on one of those that came back into the light, and now they have a warrant for my arrest. Or maybe one of those Oculus X guys got caught and snitched about the heroin. I clench the steering wheel tight and exhale through my nose, trying to beat down the irrational paranoia creeping through my mind. *I never should have gotten back into this...*

"What are you scared of?" Cassandra asks.

"I'm not exactly an innocent man," I reply, not taking my eyes off the approaching lights.

"You a wanted criminal or something?"

"Ehh… I got into some trouble when I was a teenager, and that shit's been haunting me since."

"You're, what—twenty-five? That was years ago."

"That doesn't matter in the eyes of the law. And I'm twenty-four."

The headlights suddenly zoom past in a streaming blur of blinking red-and-blue police lights. They disappear down the road.

I exhale and relax my grip on the steering wheel. *Thank you, God.*

"See? Nothing to be worried about," Cassandra assures.

I half-smile at her and continue along the highway. As I turn down the dirt road leading to the Shed, I spot an orange glow flickering from beyond the trees. I draw closer and spot the familiar flashing lights of the emergency vehicles from earlier. My heart's pounding out of my chest again as we draw closer to home.

Cassandra straightens in her seat. "What's going on?"

"I… I don't know." I turn around the bend, and a mass of emergency vehicles are swarming the area.

Then, I see it.

The Shed.

All of it.

Engulfed in flames.

Chapter 19

I SCRAMBLE OUT OF MY CAR AND STARE AT THE BURNING ruin that was once the Shed—my home. My eyes are wide, and my mouth hangs open as I helplessly watch the fiery destruction. The rest of the world is dead to me. Mariah and Gabriel's cars sit in their usual spots out front, completely engulfed in flames. Firefighters scramble about, dousing the Shed and the car fires with their hoses. Luke's truck is the only one untouched, but it's parked further back than usual from the others.

Paramedics wheel a covered stretcher into an ambulance. The white sheet covering the stretcher flips up slightly, revealing a mess of red and char in the shape of a hand and arm, the fingers curled and locked.

I gasp. *No...*

"Holy shit," Cassandra says.

I barely hear her. My chest hurts and my breathing falters. My legs shake, and I fall to my knees. *Clay... Mariah... Gabe... Luke...*

"Adam." Cassandra kneels and embraces me tight.

My eyes sting from tears that threaten to fall. "This... This can't be happening..."

"You have to pull it together, okay?" she says, her voice quivering. "They might not have been in there... We'll find some answers."

My throat tightens. *Answers.* The answers seem to be in that body bag.

Cassandra suddenly gasps. "Hey, isn't that Luke?"

For a moment, I think my ears deceive me. Cassandra breaks the embrace and grabs my attention with her stare. "It's him, Adam!" She points to a policeman and paramedic talking with Luke, who's sitting down on a hollow log, rocking back and forth. He hugs his skateboard.

I suck in a breath. A bout of relief spreads through me like a wave. *Luke is alive!* Maybe that means the others are too. Maybe someone else was under that sheet. Maybe someone was trying to break into our place.

I leave Cassandra's side and rush over to Luke.

Pushing past the first responders, I say in a panic, "Luke! Are you okay, man?"

A uniformed cop grabs my arms and blocks my path, but I fight back. "Let go of me!" I bark, squirming violently.

The cop keeps a firm grip on my arm. "Hey! You need to calm down!"

After a moment I finally relent and relax, but my heart is still pounding.

Luke stares up at me, his face pale, his eyes wider than saucers. There's a dark charcoal mark smeared across the bottom of his cheek and across his forehead.

"Luke…" I mutter. Cassandra comes up behind me and takes my hand, but her touch does little to ease my nerves.

"The paramedic is still conducting a medical assessment over here," the cop continues. "I'm going to have to ask you to keep back." He finally lets go of me, and then assesses both Cassandra and me. "Do you either of you need medical assistance?"

"No," I say quickly.

Cassandra shakes her head.

"Were you in the area when the explosion happened?" the cop asks.

I blink. *Explosion?* I look from the cop, to Luke, then back to the cop. "No, sir, I wasn't. But I live here with Luke and three of my other friends. Where are the rest of them?" I crane my neck, trying to spot Clayton, Gabriel, and Mariah in the midst of all the commotion.

The cop's face turns pale. "I'm sorry, but there were no survivors in that building." He nods toward the house, where the firefighters continue dousing the remaining flames.

My vision wavers. *No survivors… That means those bodies were…* I watch several of the ambulances rush out of the area in a wail of sirens and flashing lights.

"The firefighters found three bodies—there was nothing we could do for them," the cop continues somberly.

I swallow a lump in my throat. My ears ring. The world around me becomes smaller. Everything is starting to sound farther and farther away. *None of this is real...*

"I know this all is a lot to take in right now, but I'm going to need you to come down to the station for questioning," the cop continues.

No... I can't... I swallow and look to Cassandra worriedly. She gives my hand a reassuring squeeze and nods. I exhale a heavy sigh and reply, "Y-Yes, sir."

"It shouldn't take long. When we're finished, someone will drop you off wherever you wish."

Cassandra, Luke, and I reluctantly climb into one of the patrol cars and head southside to the station. It's deathly silent in the car, save for the occasional staticky voices cutting through from the police radio. I never thought I'd find myself sitting in one of these cars again. And now, this time, I'd have to face my past alongside my best friend and this woman, whom I think I'm starting to fall in love.

As I'd feared, my record was pulled up, and I was drilled with more questions than Cassandra or Luke. Cassandra gave simple straight answers and was quickly dismissed. Luke's clever thinking, despite his long rap sheet of vandalism misdemeanors, earned him an interrogation lasting less than five minutes. I, on the other hand, was questioned for almost an hour about my prior history. Despite it all, I'd answered the questions as honestly and respectfully as I could, avoiding any mention of street racing or my new—and very brief—side hustle. When the cops were finally done with us, we were brought back to the Shed—or what was left of it.

Climbing out of the patrol car, I stare at the remains of my home for what might be the final time, barricaded with yellow police tape. Once the three of us are out, the patrol car drives off, leaving the three of us standing around in silence. My exhausted mind swarms with thoughts.

"Please tell me that cop was wrong," I mutter, then look to Luke. "Please tell me Clay, Rai, and Gabe didn't get back from Auburn yet. Please tell me they all walked to get food or something and left their cars here."

Luke swallows, then turns his head and closes his eyes. His whole body trembles.

Damn. I look back at the smoldering ruins of our home, and the ashen frame of Clay's car, which sits where the garage once was.

"Is it really just us?" I ask Luke again, turning back to him.

Luke cups his hand over his eyes. A single tear streams from beneath. "Y-Yeah, man," he says in a choked-up voice. Then he quickly wipes his face.

"There's nothing else we can do here," Cassandra says. "The longer we stay here, the more it hurts."

Pursing my lips, I struggle with the torrent of thoughts and memories swarming my mind. All the memories we had made here, and all of the turmoil of the last few weeks with Cassandra entering the picture, whipped through my consciousness. And Clay had seemed like he wanted to set things right between us before... It was all too much to process right now. Finally, I nod in agreement. Luke still looks badly torn. "Let's go," I say to him.

Luke takes a deep breath, then looks at me, scowling. "Go where? This was our home."

"We'll find a new place to call home," I reply. "We'll rebuild, like we've always done when shit happens."

He slowly shakes his head. "No, man. Not this time. I'm out."

I blink. "What?"

"We can't rebuild from this! Our crew's gone. It'll never be the same again. I'm done, man. I'm just... I'm just done."

"Luke." I place my hand on his shoulder. "We're like brothers, man. We're all we've got. Are you seriously going to leave at a time like this?"

He sighs and wriggles my hand off his shoulder. "Yeah. I think I need to."

"You sure about that?" Cassandra asks. "People like us have to stick together."

"No." Luke shakes his head. "We don't. Every time I look at you, I'm just going to see them. I just... I can't right now. Not right now."

I open my mouth to reply, then close it, giving up. He's as stubborn as Clayton was. But as Luke's best friend, I have to respect his wishes if he wants space. But it still hurts.

"Fine, if that's the way you want it."

"That's the way it is. See you around." Luke turns and heads to his truck. I watch as he tears out of the area, his mud tires kicking up clumps of grass and dirt.

And just like that, my best friend is gone.

Cassandra and I return to Sasha. I start the engine, but don't touch the gear shift.

"So where are we going?" Cassandra asks.

My eyes shift to the dashboard clock that reads 6:44 a.m. I sigh. "I don't know. I guess… I guess I might as well head to work." My body is numb. I really don't know what to do. I had lost four friends today, and it was all too much to handle. Maybe this would help me stay sane, at least for a little while, until I could actually process what had happened this morning. There's no fucking way I could right now. I put the car in gear and head out. My eyes are heavy, and my mind is a muddled mess. I know there's no way I'll be able to effectively do my job.

We're halfway to Donaldson's when Cassandra breaks the silence. "I'm sure you know what caused that explosion."

I glance sideways at her.

"I told him. Damn it, I *told* him! He didn't believe me when I said that shit he put under his hood was a ticking time bomb. I just didn't think… *that…* would happen."

"Clay is a proud man," I say. "…But he didn't deserve that." *Was. Was a proud man.*

"Nobody did. Think of all those kids back at Auburn putting LeatherRock on a pedestal like it was the holy grail. How many more victims will that shitty brand make?"

"We could sue them, right?"

She laughs out loud. "With what money?"

Ugh. She has a point there.

"Besides, LeatherRock has been sued more times than you can count and the company has miraculously won every single case. Don't ask how."

"Follow the money." I scowl. "Well, we can't stay silent about this. I can at least write a complaint letter to them, right?"

"Not sure what good that'll do. If they're constantly winning lawsuits, they probably don't give a shit about a bunch of complaint letters."

"Three people died tonight!"

"More than that have died since the company started up." Cassandra shakes her head. "Trust me, Adam. I've been researching them longer than you think. It's a losing battle."

"So, there's no hope for any kind of justice for my friends?"

"Not that way. But it's not impossible to seek justice for this. It's gonna take a little more work, and a lot more influence." She gives me a reassuring smile. "Don't worry, Adam. That shitty-ass company is going to get what's coming to them, mark my words."

I sigh. My hands are tied with this, and all I can do is trust that Cassandra will be able to handle things. As much as she knows about Q&R, she knows even more about their competitors, which is more than I can say for myself.

I turn into the rear parking lot of the main office of Donaldson's Construction. Less than two minutes to punch in. I shut off the engine and look at Cassandra. "What are you going to do in the meantime?"

She leans her head against the headrest. "I'm tired as hell. Mind if I sleep in here for a while? I don't have to go into work till two today."

"Yeah, sure. Man, what's happened, I don't think I'll be able to think straight, much less do my job."

"Me neither." She reclines the seat back and closes her eyes. "But we gotta just keep moving forward."

"I miss my friends."

She opens her eyes. "As much as they were douchebags to me, I never would've wished anything terrible like this to happen to them. I'm sorry about all this, Adam. I really am. I'll help you find closure... somehow."

I smile at her, noting the genuine sincerity in her voice. "Thanks..." My eyelids droop, and I shake myself awake. "See you later." I climb out of the car and drag my feet toward the office like a mindless zombie.

The day dragged on slower than a snail's pace. I'd nodded off more times than I can count. The construction materials would become the burnt-out skeleton of the Shed, the tarps would become the white sheet on the stretcher. *That arm...* Finally, after botching-up three concrete mixtures in a row I was called to the boss' office.

The leather chair before Mr. Donaldson's desk is soft and comfortable, and it conforms to my exhausted body. I force my eyelids open, trying to stay awake while the boss drones on about something regarding my work performance. My brain is so scattered. I pretend to look interested.

I just want this day to finally be over so I can sleep… and forget.

"…and mistakes cost me money—lots of it," Mr. Donaldson continues. "You think I'm made of money?"

I put my hand over my mouth, suppressing a yawn. "Yes, sir…" I mutter, struggling to keep my eyes open.

Mr. Donaldson arches an eyebrow. "Did you even hear a thing I just said?"

I perk up. "Uh…" I blink my eyes open wide and stare at his fuming, beet-red face. *Oh, shit.*

"You know what. Why don't you take yourself a little extended vacation?" He asks in a tone that sounds more like a demand than a suggestion. "I'll let you know when I'll need you again."

My brain jolts awake. *Wait. Extended vacation? He doesn't mean…* "Are—Are you firing me, sir?"

"If you haven't gotten a pink slip in the mail, then no."

A small sigh of relief escapes my lips. It's good to know I still have a job, and it's generous of Mr. Donaldson to let me take some time off. *I told him I had a death in the family, right? Didn't I? I think I did…* Still, I can't shake off a strange feeling in my gut. "Uh… is this a paid vacation?" I ask.

He looks at me dumbfounded, then laughs out loud. "You're hilarious, Adam."

That strange feeling in my gut rises to my throat, causing it to tighten with dread. "Sir, I need to work. I need the money. Is there anything I can do?"

"I pay you to work, not sleep. And I don't need half-awake workers on the job botching things up and making things dangerous. Go home."

"When will you need me again?"

He gives me a stern look. "I'll call you."

Frowning, I stand. I sense in his tone of voice that it might be a long while before I'm contacted. I need to find another job, fast. Or convince Grandpa to pay me more. Returning to my car, I discover Cassandra still fast asleep in the passenger's seat. I smile at her peaceful, relaxed face. I quietly open the door and climb into the driver's seat, but as soon as I start the engine, Cassandra awakens.

She glances at the dashboard clock, which reads 10:32 a.m. "Mmm. Back already?" she asks me groggily.

I sigh at the time. Then I avert my gaze out toward the front door of the office. "My boss is giving me an 'extended vacation' for sleeping on the job."

"Damn, I'm sorry."

I shake my head dismissively. "I'll figure something out. For now... I don't know. I guess I'll head over to my grandfather's shop."

She gives me a reassuring smile. "Well, since I'd promised I'd meet your grandfather, it seems like now would be a perfect time to follow through with that."

I do my best to force a smile for her, then put the car in gear and drive off to Grandpa's shop. The visions returned with a vengeance along the way. *Clay... Mariah... Gabe... Luke...* This was quickly becoming one of the worst days of my life, but I could at least brighten it for Cassandra when she sees the surprise waiting for her at the garage. When we arrive, to my surprise, the shop is still closed.

"Anderson Antique Auto? This is it?" Cassandra asks, looking up at the large marquee sign above the building.

"Yup." I drive around to the back of the building and park in the small alley. "Weird that Grandpa's not here yet. The shop's supposed to open at nine."

"I hope he's okay," Cassandra says worriedly.

"Yeah. I'm sure he is. He probably just got held up in traffic or something," I answer, though the thought of something happening to Grandpa after everything else that's gone on today has my stomach in knots. "Luckily, I have a key." In a daze, I grab today's mail and newspaper from the mailbox by the front door, then unlock the shop and flip over the *Sorry, We're Closed* sign to *Yes, We're Open*. Entering the stuffy office, I spot the answering machine on the desk blinking like crazy.

"Make yourself comfortable. I just need to do a bit of admin work, then I'll show you around the place." I plop down in the swivel chair at the desk and replay the messages—all from customers—on the machine. Looks like I have my work cut out for me for the rest of the day. I just hope I can keep my eyes open. I barely listen to the messages while my mind wanders again. *Clay... Mariah... Gabe... Where's Grandpa?*

The answering machine beeps, shocking me from my thoughts. *How many messages did I miss?* I look over to Cassandra, who's relaxed in a chair with her nose in today's Auto section of the newspaper. Seeing her smiling face might add some silver-lining to the day. I get up from the desk and tiptoe out the side door to the main garage. A baby-blue '56 Cadillac convertible sits in Bay One with its hood up. Next to the car, its engine sits on a red, wheeled stand.

Meanwhile, in Bay Two, Cassandra's Hemi remains, all ready for her to work her magic.

I return to Cassandra and lower the front of the paper with my finger. "Hey, I have something to show you."

She lifts her gaze. "What?"

Smiling, I take the paper from her and set it on the desk. Then, I grab her hand and lead her to the garage. "Close your eyes."

She pouts, then shuts her eyes. I lead her to Bay Two and position her in front of the Hemi.

"Open your eyes," I say.

She does, and simply stares in silence. Then, a crease appears at her brow. She slowly walks around the car, studying it curiously. Suddenly, her eyes widen, and her face lights up brighter than a child's on Christmas Day. "Ho-ly shit! This is the same Hemi from the ad!"

I grin. "It is."

Her jaw drops. "Y-You mean, you... You...?"

"Yup. She's all yours."

She covers her mouth with her hand and looks back at the car. "Seriously, Adam? You really got this for me?"

I nod.

"But it was a five-thousand-dollar car!"

"Actually, I managed to negotiate it down to three. But yeah, I got it for you. I want to see you smile."

Her face softens. She throws herself into my arms and hugs me tight. "Adam. You didn't have to do this. Thank you."

I plant a deep kiss on her lips. "I know I didn't, but I wanted to. I like you. A lot." *And I think I might be falling in love with you.*

She returns the kiss. "I like you a lot too."

Her sweet taste takes some of the pain of the morning away. I continue kissing her, indulging in the momentary reprieve of *her*. "I... I better let you have your fun with your new project. I have my own work to do."

Beaming, she pulls away from me and lifts the hood of the Hemi. I wheel a rolling toolbox over to her.

"This baby's only going to be running the best mods when I'm done," Cassandra says. "I found some fantastic deals on Q&R parts in the Autoland insert in today's paper."

"Great. We can head over there later, if you want," I say, grabbing a spare toolbox and getting to work on the engine rebuild. "How's the Q&R job looking, anyway?"

She blows a raspberry. "Terrible. They prefer someone with college papers over someone with actual hands-on experience and know-how."

"Don't give up. They *have* to hire someone who's enthusiastic about the brand. And I've never met another person more enthusiastic about them than you."

She undoes a few screws and sets them on a nearby workbench. The shop falls silent, and I'm tempted to turn on a portable radio as background noise. I've always hated working in complete silence, and right now that silence would be filled with all the crushing memories of today.

"Soo… are we seriously going to be living out of your car now?" Cassandra asks, approaching me.

I pause in mid-removal of the timing chain cover and look to her. I didn't want to have to ask Grandpa for as big a favor as staying at his house for a while, but it looks like I might not have a choice. "I'll figure something out." The spark of happiness I'd felt for a moment when I surprised Cassandra quickly dissolves as her question brings back memories of this morning.

My friends.

I scowl. This is fucked up—me and Cassandra shouldn't feel happy while Clayton, Mariah, and Gabriel lie on some metal slab, and Luke abandoned us.

The muffled jingling sounds of the bell at the front door jolt me out of my thoughts. I set down my socket wrench. "Stay here," I say to Cassandra, heading to the side door. I discover Grandpa in the main office. *Thank God he's all right.* He wears a tired expression his face as if he'd had a long night. "Hey, Grandpa."

He jumps and places his hand to his chest. His face pales a moment, then he relaxes. "Holy shit, boy, what are you trying to do, give me a heart attack?"

I smile apologetically. "Sorry. What happened to you? It's almost eleven o'clock."

"Ah…" He averts his gaze a moment then waves his hand dismissively. "Stupid accident on the interstate, that's all."

"That's what I figured."

"And what are you doing here this early?"

I rub the back of my head. "Uh, well… Donaldson put me on an extended break."

"What the hell did you do now, boy?"

"I uh… I fell asleep on the job because I was up all night dealing with a disaster."

Grandpa blinks. "What?"

I sigh. "We need to talk, man."

I tell him everything that happened last night at the Shed. I lose track of time. After having to relive every detail of that experience again, my brain is numb.

When I finish, Grandpa sits back in his chair, takes off his glasses, and looks at me somberly. "I'm sorry, son. I really am."

"Nothing you could've done, man. But yeah, now, I guess I'm homeless…"

"No, you're not. I'll let you stay at my place as long as you need until you can get back on your feet."

I pause. "Just me?"

He raises his eyebrows. "Was there someone else?"

"Ah, well… there's this girl…"

His surprised expression morphs into amusement. "Is there? Well, she can come, too, if she's decent enough."

I blink in surprise. "You'd let me bring a girl in your house?"

"Like I said, if she's decent, then she's welcome."

"She knows more about Q&R than I do."

His eyebrows shoot up again. "She tinkers? Even better. Wait. Is this the girl you bought that Hemi for?"

I nod with a smile. "Yeah. She's in the garage working on it right now."

"Excellent. I want to meet this amazing woman that's swept my grandson off his feet."

Beaming, Grandpa steps from around the desk and heads for the side door. He reaches for the knob, and his hand suddenly gives a violent, uncontrollable shake. He yanks it away, hissing and cursing under his breath.

Noticing this, I furrow my brow at him. "You okay?"

"I'm fine, son, just another damned cramp in my hand. Too much paperwork, I guess," Grandpa mutters, discreetly rubbing his hand. "Get the door for me, will you?"

As I do, I can't help but hear a hint of fear in Grandpa's casual response.

Chapter 20

One month later...

Grandpa lives in a small, two-bedroom house in Fern Hill. It's amazing that he's allowed me and Cassandra to stay here with him. I was nervous when I'd first introduced him to Cassandra last month, but he'd taken an instant liking to her, with all her mechanic knowledge.

It was nice to finally sleep in an actual bed for a change instead of a couch or a grungy floor mattress like I'd been used to back at the Shed too. But memories of that fateful night still stung, even after a month.

That pain in my heart will never go away.

I'd been working more hours at Grandpa's shop while I hopelessly waited for the call from Donaldson's Construction. But as the days and weeks had gone by, I became more and more certain that I would never get that call.

While I'd gotten used to my new working routine, I was also looking for another place to stay. Meanwhile, Cassandra had continued her job at Out the Box while keeping up with the latest news from Q&R and continuing to submit her résumé to more positions at the company. I'd never seen a woman so determined. I'd wished her dream would finally come true.

Cassandra still had the drive to check out the local races, while I'd preferred to stay away. Hell, I couldn't remember the last time I'd raced. I hadn't even gotten Sasha over eighty miles an hour in a long time, which was never good for a racing machine like her. I had already been thinking of getting out of the racing game back then, and now I couldn't stomach the idea of going out to my crew's old hangout spots when they were gone.

Cassandra, however, seemed to have her own way of dealing with pain—ways I could never understand.

It's Saturday afternoon, and I'm still lying in bed. Grandpa is doing extra paperwork at his shop like the workaholic that he is. Thank God he lets me work just the normal weekday hours.

Cassandra comes into the bedroom, eating a ham sandwich. She holds the folded Auto section of today's newspaper in her other hand.

She'd just gotten back from work an hour ago. Unlike me, she works odd shifts and fills in for people a lot. The sad look on her face after work had become a near-daily occurrence—she's clearly fed up with her current job, and I don't blame her.

"How the hell are you still sleeping?" she asks with an arched eyebrow.

I sit up and sigh. "I wasn't sleeping. Just thinking about some things. Hey, where's my sandwich?"

"Go make your own." She smiles mischievously, then takes a hefty bite.

I laugh. "Yeah, yeah."

She approaches my bedside and slaps the folded paper on my lap. "Look at that."

I look at the red-circled article about Q&R's new super-charged engine. I could only imagine the kind of beast Sasha would be with an engine like that—*if* I was racing. But when I'd stopped all that cold turkey, I'd also lost the drive. "Cool." I hand the paper back to her.

She blinks. "'Cool'? This is the engine of the decade! Its technology is way ahead of its time. They've outdone themselves. This is just what I need to finally get ol' Trish dialed in."

I grin at her choice of a nickname for the Hemi. She'd been working on the car ever since the day I'd first surprised her with it at the shop. Over the past month, little by little, she'd slowly replaced its old parts with newer, Q&R-branded ones.

"You gonna try and race her?" I ask Cassandra.

She nods curtly. "Sure am. I haven't been out there in weeks, and I've been kinda curious about what's going on. Besides, it'll give me a chance to try and dissuade more misguided youths to stay away from LeatherRock."

She's pretty much on a crusade to get people to stay away from LeatherRock. News of the fire at the Shed had spread a few days after it had happened. Police reports had said the fire was caused by an explosion which originated from the garage—right where Clayton's car was parked. There were traces of gasoline on the ground and all over the burnt out coilovers Cassandra had warned Clayton about. All the evidence was there and pointed right to LeatherRock's shitty, faulty products, spawning yet another wave of lawsuits.

Cassandra and I were not among the ones doing the suing. We were too poor for that. However, there were thousands of others who had reported the gas leak from the coilover reservoir, enough to take legal action against the company. But it seemed like there was a whole lot of back and forth, and not enough action. It would've been nice if the lawsuit got resolved quickly and put LeatherRock out of business.

But only time will tell.

The weekend goes by way too fast, and before I know it, it's Monday again, and time to go back to the auto shop. Settling into this new life away from the fast and furious racing scene is like a breath of fresh air. I can learn to get used to this.

I polish the fender skirts of a client's lime-green '40 hot rod coupe that's scheduled to be picked up by the end of the day. I had a hell of a time restoring the engine on this baby.

"Put some elbow grease into it, boy. This is for an important client," Grandpa's voice barks. His voice is so close, I jump.

I stop wiping and look up.

He swipes the rag from my hands and wipes the fender skirt in swift, yet firm, circular motions. "I don't pay you to pussyfoot around," he continues, the muscles in his arm tensing as he works.

I frown. He's been more irritable lately. Probably because Cassandra and I still hadn't moved out. It's already been well over a month. I hadn't intended to stay at his house for this long, but it's been hard to find a decent, affordable place to live around here. And it didn't help that I had a criminal record. I've been seriously making a real effort to find a place, and I hope Grandpa knows that.

Does he think I'm just sitting on my ass all day mooching off his generosity?

Grandpa cringes, tiny beads of sweat forming along his wrinkled brow. He stops wiping and passes the rag back to me. "Like that…" he says with a soft pant.

Is he winded from that little bit of waxing? I tilt my head curiously. "Are you okay?"

He scowls. "Boy, don't ask me that again. I'm fine! Now finish waxing before Mr. Faulkner gets here."

"Mr. Faulkner?" I gasp. "As in *the* Mr. Demetri Faulkner?" I widen my eyes at the thought of this car belonging to the lead of the hit television police drama series, *Crime & Law: L.A. Unit.*

Grandpa snorts. "Like I'm gonna tell you. Now, get to work." He points with a shaky finger.

Before I can say anything more, Grandpa turns and heads back into the office, slamming the door behind him.

An hour later, the car is polished to a shine, and I park it out front. The client comes right on time, and to my disappointment, it's not Demetri Faulkner, just another random old bald guy who happens to have a lot of money to burn. Grandpa always teased me with stories of all the famous people who'd brought their cars to the shop. I wonder if it's all bullshit sometimes, but Grandpa *did* know a lot of people, so I wouldn't be surprised if some of those stories were probably true. For as long as I'd worked for Grandpa, I'd hoped to meet at least one celebrity, but it looked like that was never going to happen.

At closing time, I lock up the garage and return to the main office. Grandpa sits at his desk, doing the usual paperwork. He doesn't acknowledge me as I come in. I rummage through today's mail, which sits in a basket at the edge of the desk. I search for my name among the piles of envelopes, magazines, postcards, and junk, and notice a single envelope addressed to me from Donaldson Construction.

My heart pounds. *Finally. My vacation's over. I can work more, make more money to afford a place...* I tear open the envelope.

Inside is a termination letter—literally typed on stiff, pink-colored paper.

My eyes glaze over as I read to the end. I slump my shoulders and sigh. My vacation's over, all right.

"What's wrong, son?" Grandpa asks, not looking up from his writing.

I toss the letter in a small wastebasket by the desk and head for the door. "Donaldson fired me," I mutter.

"What?" Papers rustle behind me. It sounds like Grandpa snatched the letter from the basket. "Get back here."

I stop, but don't turn around. "I thought everything was cool over there—he just needed time to cool off or whatever. I mean, besides that one incident last month after the fire, I did a damn good job every day I was there. I worked hard—harder than most of those other guys there. But I guess Mr. Donaldson is one of those one-and-done assholes… Doesn't matter how much good you bring to the company."

"From the looks of this letter, it sounds like the company is downsizing. You're probably not the only one they laid off."

"Don't try and make me feel better, Grandpa. This was probably the plan ever since he put me on that 'temporary vacation' last month."

"Adam, come here."

I roll my eyes, turn around and trudge back to the desk. "Don't worry, man. I'll look for another job first thing tomor—"

"Damn it, shut up!" Grandpa glares. "Don't look for another job. I'll put you on as a full-time employee."

I blink. "What? A-Are you sure? But—"

Grandpa holds up his hand, and I fall silent. "Adam, let me tell you something. Anderson Antique Auto is almost a seven-figure business. When I'm dead and gone, I want this company to stay in the family and continue to thrive. And I want *you* to be in charge. This business will provide for you, Elouise, and the kids."

Me? Inherit this business? Grandpa really is serious about me taking over the family business. *But am I really ready?*

I purse my lips, realizing he hadn't mentioned Michael among his list of beneficiaries, and I have no doubt of the reason. But even so, Michael is still family, and neglecting him was pretty cold-hearted, even for Grandpa. But bringing up the subject of Michael right now is probably not a good idea.

"But this place is more than just putting engines together and wiping fenders—I don't know a *thing* about all that paperwork and shit you do."

"I'll teach you. First, you need to learn how to read and write up different types of orders, invoices, and receipts. I'll keep showing you a little more each day." He checks his watch. "Not today, though. I need to meet someone in a half-hour." He sets the documents he was looking through in a paper tray, gets up from his desk, and heads to the door.

When we're outside, Grandpa takes out his key and fumbles with it, struggling to insert it into the lock. He holds his shaking hand, but still keeps missing the lock, muttering under his breath.

"Here." I gently push Grandpa aside and lock the door.

He scowls. "I could've done that myself."

I roll my eyes. "We'd have been here all night by the time you locked it."

He grumbles and looks away, not responding.

"Seriously, man, what's wrong with you? I've never seen you this cranky before. Did a recent deal go sour or something?"

His nostrils flare. "I'm fine. It's nothing. Just… age. Don't worry, you'll be feeling it soon enough when you're as old as me."

I snort out a chuckle. "I got a whole lifetime before I'm as old as you, man." I watch Grandpa head to his car, parked along the curb. I purse my lips. "Hey, should you be driving with your hand hurting? You want a ride?"

"I told you I'm fine!" Grandpa snaps.

I raise my hands up in surrender. "All right, fine. Geez." I watch him drive off until he's out of sight, and then I hop in my car and ride to the Chinese restaurant for some fried rice.

Around seven o'clock, after a filling dinner, I head over to Out the Box to pick up Cassandra. She's been working as much as she can at Grandpa's shop getting her Hemi restored, installing new parts and fixing up old ones. She's almost finished, and the car is looking sweet. I'm so proud of her doing all this herself.

Fifteen minutes later, Cassandra finally exits the restaurant and climbs into the passenger seat.

"Hey," I greet with a smile.

She looks back at me, her face sickly green. "Hey…"

"What's wrong?"

She grimaces. "Ugh, that's the last time I eat a greasy bacon double cheeseburger for lunch."

"Hey, at least you get free food working here."

"Yeah, but 'free' apparently comes with a price." She cups her hand over her mouth and burps. "Excuse me."

I arch my eyebrow. "You gonna be okay?"

"I'll be fine," she assures, and then pauses. "Let's go to the industrial park tonight."

"What?" I hadn't stepped foot in the Wild Aces' old stomping grounds since that night I lost to her—the night we met. It was bad enough that I'd still went out with her to check out the races around other parts of town and beyond, but this is the first time she's wanted to go back to the heart of where it all began. What she was asking was to return to a past that I want so desperately to forget.

"No… I can't. Not there. Too many memories," I murmur.

She looks at me carefully. "Honestly, Adam? The only way you're going to find closure is to face these demons head on. The more you run, the more it hurts."

"That may work for you, but not me. I don't want to go back to the place where the Wild Aces started—where we used to hang out and race all the time. When it was for the thrill of it. For fun. We made too many good memories there. They're gone now, and those good memories went with them."

"The memories will always be there, Adam. It's *you* that's avoiding them." She reaches over and gently places her hand over mine. "Trust me. We'll go there and have fun, like you and your friends did. That's one legacy I'd like to keep around too."

I look at our hands a moment, relishing her warmth encompassing mine, and I smile. *Carry on the legacy...* But that smile is short-lived when another thought strikes me. "Jacob and his crew have probably moved in on that place..."

Her expression falls. "Yeah, Jacob probably has. But maybe now that he hasn't had you to worry about lately, he's calmed the fuck down. Let's go have a look. We don't have to stay out there for long."

I look at her carefully. "Do you *really* want to go out there for old time's sake, or to see what Jacob's doing?"

She shakes her head. "Look, I told you I'm over him. And if he's there, I'll happily point and laugh at him *and* his shitty car, knowing I can scorch him and his crew with Trish once she's dialed in."

I smile slightly at that, knowing that's exactly something she would say to him. "Okay," I finally concede. "We'll go. Just for a little while."

Chapter 21

I DRIVE WITH CASSANDRA LOUNGING IN THE PASSENGER'S seat next to me. We take the back roads to the industrial park like I used to all that time ago. It's a longer drive, but it keeps us under the cops' radar. We ride in silence, and by eight o'clock, we arrive at the industrial park located in the eastern part of New Tacoma. There's already a crowd despite the early hour, a mix of teenagers and adults. A few races are underway.

I park the car away from the crowd, close to the park's entrance. As I get out the car, a strange feeling wells up in my gut. Something is wrong, but I'm not sure what it is. *It must be the memories.* I made a lot of good ones here with my crew—I can still envision where we used to park almost every night, despite the sea of cars and people. All of our cars would be parked in a neat row, showing off new paint, or some fancy new mod…

My eyes burn. *I miss you guys. So much...*

"Hey!" Cassandra calls.

Her voice jolts me from my thoughts. She waves at me, and then makes her way toward the crowd.

I frown. I know they weren't exactly close, but has she really gotten over their deaths so quickly? Or does she just know how to deal with this kind of shit? It's like her mind and emotions are made of steel. Or maybe a woman like her has seen so much death in her life that she's become numb to it.

I can't imagine how that must feel...

Shoving my hands in my pockets, I slowly make my way toward the crowd. As I draw nearer to a race in progress, I notice something strange. These aren't normal drag races. In fact, they don't look like drag races at all. The entire area has been converted into a massive, makeshift racetrack with sets of cones spread throughout. Two dressed-up cars zoom by, expertly sliding around sharp corners in a smoky cloud of squealing tires.

I clench my jaw. *Drifters...*

I search the spectators. I don't recognize any of the faces here. Hell, everything about this place feels foreign, even myself, here and now. I feel like such an outcast, like I don't belong. The sounds of the roaring engines and the smell of exhaust and burned rubber don't seem to trigger my competitive urge. Instead, they're just white noise.

I discover Cassandra away from the main crowd, exchanging words with the only group I recognize—Jacob and the Ninez.

Jacob still has that same hint of fear in his eyes. His lackeys, Preston and Bryce, still accompany him like the mindless cronies they are. Jacob has picked up four more recruits I don't recognize too. They all look to be about my age or slightly younger. I pity them following a coward like Jacob around.

I walk up to the group, and Jacob stops talking. His gaze swivels from Cassandra to me.

"Oh, look who's back from the dead." He sneers.

I fold my arms across my chest and narrow my eyes. "After what happened to my friends? Seriously? I should kick your fucking ass for saying that shit."

Jacob purses his lips. "Look, man. I'm sorry about what happened to them. Really."

"Just drop it."

He opens his mouth, looking like he wants to say more but then decides better of it, and glances back at the ongoing drifting race for a moment. "I'm surprised to see you out here." He looks back at me.

"Yeah, well… you know. Just wanted to check things out."

"What's up with all this, anyway?" Cassandra breaks in. "You drifting again now?"

Jacob sneers. "Hell no. I've got nothing to do with this shit. It's Oculus X. They've taken over now. Thanks for the help, Adam."

"*What*?" Then I remember the confrontation that night in Auburn. "All that shit was on you, Jacob. I wasn't gonna fight your battles."

"You have the fastest ride this side of Tacoma," Jacob says. "I ain't afraid to admit it. You were the only one who would've stood a chance against Kaine in a drag race. Could have taken him in a drift too." He pauses and shakes his head somberly. "That crew came in and took names. As well as our cars."

My jaw drops. "They took your cars?"

"Might as well have. Bastards stripped our cars of all our good shit. Thousands of dollars', and months—years—of sweat, worth. None of us can race like we used to. Not when those guys are running the scene." He stabs his thumb over his shoulder at two cars drifting through the cone-lined track.

Cassandra rolls her eyes. "Well duh, *your* car was never built for drifting."

Jacob sneers at her then looks back at me. "Oculus X ran all the old crews out of town—the Burn Dawgs, the Black Keys, the Chefs…"

I feel the wind get knocked out of me as I listen to Jacob rap out all the crews we used to race. I don't know why I feel pissed about this. I'd sworn off racing, cold turkey. But I can't deny all the fun times I'd had racing some of those guys, and the friends and allies I'd made in the end.

"These fuckers took all of our spots and used them for drifting," Jacob says. "They set the rules around here. If anyone gets caught dragging, they get a painful lesson." He nods over his shoulder at Bryce.

I look at Bryce, now noticing the faint dark outline around his right eye. My jaw drops. "Holy shit. You got beat up for dragging?"

Bryce frowns and scratches the back of his head. "I didn't think they would actually do it."

"Yeah. Next time you'll listen to me, idiot," Jacob says.

Damn. "This ain't the way things are supposed to go down here. No wonder the other crews left."

Jacob shakes his head. "This ain't fun no more, man. I hate to say it, but… I miss the good ol' days when we'd fuck around and pit our shit against each other."

I smile slightly, but it's short-lived. "Those days are long gone. I'm done racing."

"I'm not," Jacob mutters, scowling.

"Then you deal with this shit on your own," I say, and then turn to leave.

"Why did you *really* come here, Adam? Huh?"

I halt mid-step and look over my shoulder at Jacob's question.

"Was it to gloat again?" he continues. "You made your point, all right? Were you looking for an apology? Fine. I'm sorry. For everything. There. Happy now?"

Are my ears deceiving me? I spin back around and face Jacob fully.

Jacob waves his hand dismissively. "You know what, fuck it. Go back to hiding. You're right. I'll deal with this shit myself." He storms off with his friends and disappears into the crowd of spectators.

I exhale a breath I've been inadvertently holding. Jacob is genuinely concerned. *Scared.* This Oculus X crew sounds like more trouble than I thought.

"Damn, I never thought in a million years I'd see the day Jacob would be that desperate," Cassandra says.

I shake my head at her. "He's hurting, Cass."

She lifts her nose in the air. "Good. Now he knows how it feels."

My retort is on the tip of my tongue, but I refrain. She's right. He'd hurt her and my friends, and now he's paying the price. But there had to be a limit in this lesson if he was ever going to turn from his old ways. Perhaps this was it.

I can't stand to see this place be taken over by a bunch of bastards who weren't in it for the race—for the thrill, the fun. The one way to run Oculus X out of town was to race them and win. It seems to be the only way. But the only ones who tried like Jacob apparently had failed. Unlike Jacob, though, I know my limits. Sasha was never built for drifting, and I'll be damned if I fight their fight.

We return to my car while I'm lost in thought. Cassandra walks ahead and jumps into the passenger's seat. As I reach the driver's door, five sets of headlights quickly approach. The lights shine on me, and I wait a moment before opening the door in order to let the group of cars pass.

The fancy sports cars slow to a stop several feet away from Sasha, and I tense. There's something familiar about the group of cars, especially the bright red '88 Fiero with the ridiculous-looking spoiler.

I blink. *It can't be...*

Someone gets out of the Fiero—a man wearing a red bandanna. The last person I'd hoped to see.

Drew... Oh, shit...

He takes one look at me and sneers. "You!"

I swallow the lump in my throat. *Of course, I left my gun back at Grandpa's house.*

The rest of the Red Ravens get out of their gaudy sports cars and converge around their leader. I notice Cassandra slowly get out of the car and look my way.

No! Damn it, stay in the car! I want to yell at her, but it's too late.

I put my hands up in surrender. "Look, man, I'm just leaving. No trouble, all right?"

Drew marches over to me. Gritting his teeth, he looks me up and down. "First you steal from me, and now you're all up on my turf?"

"*Your* turf? This belongs to Oculus X."

The fury on Drew's face morphs to amusement, highlighting the faint scar on his face. "Yeah, we have an agreement. What's theirs is ours."

I blink. *Holy fucking shit. Oculus X and the Red Ravens are allies?* Things have just gone from bad to worse.

"And what's mine... is *mine*." Drew's scowl returns. "Like the shit you stole from me. I told you this wasn't the last time you would see the Red Ravens. No one steals from me and gets away with it."

"For the last time, I didn't steal your shit," I say, trying to remain calm. "I gave you everything I had."

Drew shakes his head. "No, you didn't give me *everything*." He looks over to Sasha, then spots Cassandra. "Mm… does that bitch come with the car, too?"

I grit my teeth. "If you touch her…"

"The car or the girl?" Drew laughs.

I shoot a glimpse at his group of friends, who burst out laughing as well. I have only one chance, and I seize it. I ball my fist and clock Drew so hard in the jaw his head snaps back, and his entire body follows, crashing to the ground.

The laughter stops, and the Red Ravens reach into their jackets.

A gunshot goes off, one that's not from any of them. The crew ducks low or plasters themselves on the ground. I'm about to follow suit when I notice Cassandra out of the corner of my eye taking aim. My breath hitches and I look over to her.

"Get in!" She says to me, keeping the gun aimed at the group.

I jump in the driver's seat while Cassandra slowly enters the other side of the car, never taking the gun off the grounded Ravens. I crank the engine, slam my foot on the gas, and burn rubber out of there.

"Holy shit, Cass!" I finally say as we peel out onto the backroads back to the city. "Where'd you get that?"

"It's your gun," she says. In almost a single motion, she drops the magazine out, expels the round from the chamber, and activates the safety. Then she sticks the gun in the glove compartment.

"You brought my gun?"

"You're welcome," she says flatly. "I wanted to come out here tonight, so I figured it might be a good idea to bring it along just in case."

"Yeah…" I take a few more deep breaths. I'm sure I've shaved about ten years off my life from that encounter.

"But enough about me. Let's talk about you," she says, her tone growing cold. "What the hell was that back there?"

I repeatedly tighten and loosen my grip on the steering wheel, trying to ease my shaky hands. I should have scoped the place out for the Red Ravens when we first showed up. And now they were siding with Oculus X? Now it won't be just Drew and his people coming after me for that fucked-up drug run.

How much longer will I have to keep running like this? I'm not afraid of a bastard like Drew, but I'm not in the mood for a fight against two entire crews on my own, either.

"I don't know, Cass," I finally reply, not taking my eyes off the road.

"Well, those Red Ravens sure acted like they knew you very well. Is there something you're not telling me?"

I swallow. There's been so much I've told her, but I didn't think she needed to know all of that business. "Probably from all that shit that went down at Fife. Drew—the guy I hit—tried to buy Sasha off me, and I said 'no.' Apparently, he's decided Sasha belongs to him anyway."

She growls. "Those motherfuckers were the ones who stripped my car."

"They're just a bunch of drifter scrubs, and Jacob's scared shitless of them."

"They've taken over this place, Adam." She crosses her arms. "Doesn't that concern you in the least bit?"

It really does, but I'm not sure how to answer her without getting myself involved again. I stay silent.

Her expression hardens. "You know you could help run these nobodies out of town easily, but instead, you'd rather go on with this fantasy about you being done racing. Meanwhile, everyone you used to run with suffers. People looked up to you, Adam. You might have had enemies, but they respected you, first and foremost. Stop being so damned selfish. You might've given up racing, but I haven't, and a lot of others, too."

My throat tightens. *Am I really being selfish, not wanting to get involved?* While it's true that I probably still have the most powerful ride in this town, how much longer am I expected to keep playing this dangerous game when Grandpa wants to invest so much in me? Invest virtually the *entire family's inheritance* on me?

I think long and hard as I turn down the street to Grandpa's house. There's only one thing I can do, and I didn't like it one bit.

I pull up along the curb in front of Grandpa's house. Shutting off the car, I decide to finish the conversation out here. "You know anything about drifting?" I ask Cassandra.

She wrinkles her nose at me as if I'd said a dirty word. "Only that you need a good-ass rear-wheel drive." Her eyes slowly widen. "You're going to learn how to drift?"

"I'm not, but Jacob is."

She blows a raspberry. "The idiot can't even drag."

"He used to be a damned good drifter back in the day. But he quit all that and got into dragging instead. If he wants this turf back, he'll have to play—and beat them—by their rules. He'll have to own up to being a fucking leader if he wants any chance of running them out of town."

"And how is he going to do that? His car isn't equipped to drift."

"Yeah, I'm gonna work on that."

She blinks. "You're going to… *help* him?"

I nod curtly. "Only to help everyone else who's had to put up with Oculus X's bullshit. Besides, if Jacob *does* win, he'll owe me big time. And I'll make sure he never bothers us again."

The corner of her mouth twitches as she fights a smile. "You know, that's the craziest idea yet. Only you would want to help someone like Jacob, after all the things he's done. You really do have a big heart, Adam. A big, brave heart."

I return a small smile. "I just don't want to let anyone down."

She leans over the center console and plants a small kiss on my cheek. "Fuck what anyone thinks. You do what you feel is right."

My smile grows. "This feels right. I'd rather Jacob be in charge than those other guys. At least he and I have history. And he knows what this thing used to be—a fun, competitive adrenaline rush."

Cassandra nods.

"And you'll never have to worry about him giving you shit again," I continue, placing my hand over hers. "You're my girl, now."

"Does that mean I'm your number one?" She raises her eyebrows.

"You've always been my number one."

Her face softens, and she leans over again and presses her lips into mine in a deep, loving kiss. I eagerly accept her advance, devouring her lips and enjoying her sweet taste. She breaks the kiss and exhales slowly. "I think... I'm falling for you..."

My heart flutters. I couldn't have heard more sweeter words. "Me, too, Cass," I whisper.

Our lips crash again. Heat rises from my body. I want this woman so bad right now.

Then, I feel her hands press against my chest and gently push me back, breaking the kiss once more. "Mmm... I can't get fucked tonight. I need to be focused to do some research," she says.

Damn tease... "Research?" I arch a curious eyebrow.

"Yeah, I'll need to figure out what all goes into building a good drift car, and which Q&R parts are the best to use."

I beam. "You... want to help me... help Jacob?"

"I'm helping you help Jacob, so he'll owe me too. When this car is done, he'll owe me more than he fucking knows." She smirks.

I feel a great weight lift off me, knowing that she'll support me every step of the way. "We're gonna make a great team."

She smiles, then purses her lips in thought. "Jacob won't part with that CR-X easily. And he'll most certainly *not* want to rebuild it into a drifting machine."

"I don't blame him." I cringe at the thought of Sasha getting transformed into a drifter. She'd probably be damned good at it, but I could never insult all those long hours of dialing her in to be the perfect drag racer. "I'll look in the classifieds for our new tinkering project."

"Good idea. Jacob will shit his pants when he sees this beast."

I grin. With her on my team, we can't lose.

Chapter 22

My first week as an official full-time employee at Anderson Antique Auto had gone without a hitch. Grandpa has been teaching me how to fill out bills of sale, read ledgers, and all the other dull, complicated work that goes into running a business. In the midst of all that, I'd still been working on clients' cars. Those were the times I'd wish Grandpa would hire help, because I just couldn't keep up with the workload by myself. Grandpa must've had the most patient customers, though. There'd never been a single complaint about the long wait times that it took for me to finish these jobs.

No wonder Grandpa was loaded. He didn't seem to have much overhead, especially with me being the only employee on his payroll. All his penny-pinching and business know-how was paying off in the end.

Sometimes I wondered how he managed to run this shop all by himself before I came along. *He was a lot younger then, though, and probably a lot more spry.*

But despite all my time there and Grandpa showing me the ropes, my mind had been focused on everything but the business. Aside from the apartment-hunting—which remained a bust, yet again, thanks to that fucking criminal record—I was on a mission to learn how to build the perfect drift car for Jacob. I'd collected every Auto and Classified Ads section out of the local newspapers, bought the latest auto and racing magazines, and even consulted Dave, my supplier. Cassandra and I had gleaned everything we could about part recommendations.

Geez. I never thought in a million years I'd be doing Jacob a big favor like this. I kept reminding myself that this wasn't for Jacob, though. Order had to be restored, and Oculus X and the Red Ravens needed to be ran out of town for good.

More than that, though, I had to do it for Clayton, Mariah, and Gabriel. I owed it to them to make things right again.

Maybe this will finally give me the closure I need...

Friday night, I'm lounging on the couch at Grandpa's house, watching some old, black-and-white sci-fi movie on television. I don't know why I've always found these cheesy, less-than-B-movie-quality flicks so entertaining. But tonight, I can't concentrate on the giant moth-monster terrorizing the world, because the insistent ticking of typewriter keys coming from the kitchen table keeps me alert. Thankfully, Grandpa sleeps like a log, and with his bedroom door shut, the noise wouldn't bother him.

I finally look over to Cassandra sitting at the dinette and staring pensively at a piece of paper lodged in Grandpa's old Remington typewriter. A cup of peppermint tea sits next to it, tiny wisps of steam rising in unique patterns. She'd been drinking it nonstop since this afternoon to ease the sickness in her stomach. I guess she ate something that didn't agree with her, again.

"C'mon, how long does it take to type a résumé" I groan, shoving one of the couch cushions over my face.

Cassandra stops typing. "I'm at a disadvantage without a college degree, so I have to make a good first-impression and get this résumé as professional as possible. I mean, for fuck's sake, Adam, this is Q&R we're talking about here, not some random mom-and-pop parts store. Or fucking LeatherRock," she finishes under her breath.

I slide the cushion from my face. I can't be mad at her. She's been trying so hard for months to land her dream job at Q&R. Recently, a new sales consultant job had opened up at the company. That job entailed traveling the country— even the world—selling Q&R products.

But as excited as she is for the job, I dread the thought not seeing her for long periods of time. Long-distance relationships almost never worked.

I think—no, I *know*—I love her. I've never been so sure about anything else.

But Cassandra is determined. And she's as stubborn as Grandpa when it comes to sticking to a goal.

"How much can you possibly put on that résumé?" I ask. "You're not mentioning street racing, are you?"

"Of course not. But I need to mention *something* about my extensive knowledge of their products." She pauses and taps her chin. "What if I say something like, 'recommended specific Q&R products to be used in the modification and enhancement of various show vehicles, and directly per-formed many of these installations.'"

I furrow my brow. "Show vehicles?"

"Absolutely. After all, I *did* turn my old Nova from a junkyard whore into a racing beast."

"But it was built for racing, not for some auto show."

"Doesn't matter. That car turned heads—even yours—so therefore it counts as a show vehicle."

I roll my eyes and smile, not arguing with her on that. "All right." I get up from the couch and approach her chair, then wrap my arms around her from behind. "Why don't you take a break?" I murmur in her ear. "You've been at this for most of the night."

Her body tenses a moment, then she relaxes. She looks over her shoulder with hooded eyes. "I... I can't. I have to get this done tonight so I can mail it first thing tomorrow."

Frowning slightly, I lift up from her. "Don't burn yourself out over this, Cass," I say. "Besides we're going to have a long day tomorrow visiting the junkyards."

She sips her tea. "Have you finally decided on the project car?"

"Yup. Now we just have to find it for the right price."

Cassandra and I are up early Saturday morning and driving around to every junkyard in town, looking for the one car I'd finally narrowed down from five choices. I couldn't wait to get this done and over with so I could quit the racing scene for good. Once things there were back to normal again, maybe I'd be able to move on from that life and start my new one. The more I think about the opportunities of running the shop on my own, the more I seem to want it too. Fulfilling Grandpa's wishes and taking over his shop would be good, honest work, and I wouldn't have to give up my passion of building cars.

"You know, with all the trouble we've gone through looking for this one car, you could've just let Jacob drive Sasha," Cassandra says.

I turn onto the interstate heading south to Lakewood. "When Hell freezes over."

"Seriously, Adam. When was the last time you really let her breathe? These little joyrides around town ain't doing her any favors."

I'm tempted to floor it while I'm on this long stretch of road, when I spot a highway patrol car parked under an overpass. "I might not be racing her, but I'm not ready to give her up."

She huffs, turns her head, and stares out the passenger's window. "She needs to breathe, Adam."

We pull up to Silly Sam's Pick-n-Pull junkyard and scour the sea of old, rusted, and mutilated cars. One of the salesmen, a stocky guy wearing a blue, oil-smeared baseball cap, follows me and Cassandra a small distance away, his sharp eyes on us like a hungry wolf stalking its prey. I have just one mission, and one car to find. Cassandra and I walk for almost an hour through this massive auto graveyard, while the curious salesman continues stalking us.

Then, I finally see it.

"There." I point toward a mountain of scrap metal and crushed cars, where a wheel-less Datsun 280Z rests beneath it. The body is covered in sun-faded and oxidized light-blue paint. Judging by the body style, the car looks to be from the mid-seventies. Virtually everything under the hood, including its engine and fittings, has been stripped away, and the interior is littered with leaves and stray metal parts.

Cassandra grimaces. "Even for a twenty-something year-old car, time hasn't been kind."

"Cosmetics are an easy fix," I explain. "The body is the perfect size we need for when we update its undercarriage and suspension system. Not only that, it would be a super cheap buy. Two-fifty, max." I look over my shoulder at the stalking salesman. He catches my eye and, with a big smile, rushes over to me.

He tips his baseball cap in greetings and stuffs his thumbs though the belt loops of his tight jeans. "What can I do you for, folks?" he asks in a jolly voice.

I nod to the Datsun. "I'll give you two fifty for that."

Stroking his short, light-brown beard, the man acknowledges me amusingly. "Two fifty? Kid, it might need a little sprucin' up, but that there is a solid quality body if you ever saw one, yessir."

I narrow my eyes. "First of all, I'm not a kid. And second, don't pull that sleazy car-salesman crap on me."

He stiffens. "Nothing on this lot's worth less than five hundred."

"Five hundred?" Cassandra scoffs. "Fuck that. C'mon, Adam. Let's go somewhere else." She beckons me with a tilt of her head.

But I'm not ready to leave. Not when the perfect car is sitting there waiting for me.

Time for Plan B.

Grandpa is a master at wheeling and dealing—it's why he was so damn rich. Over the years he'd taught me a thing or two. Now is my chance to see if I could make some of it work. I pull out a wad of bills from my pocket and count them conspicuously. "Too bad, really. That car's been stripped of all its good shit, it'll be a hard sell. But if you don't want to part with it, then, whatever." I turn and head toward the entrance, casting Cassandra a subtle wink.

Moments later, footsteps rush toward me from behind. I stop and turn around. The salesman is hunched over, panting.

"Okay, kid—uh, sir. Three fifty. That's as low as I'll go."

I look down my nose at him. "Two forty-five for calling me 'kid' again, and we got a deal." I thumb through the bills in my hand like a flipbook. "I just came from the bank. I'm ready to buy *to-day*."

The salesman looks at me with exasperation, his face flushed. Then his shoulders slump, and he lets out a sigh of defeat. "Fine. Deal. You got an hour to get it off this lot."

Grinning, I hand him the cash. *That was almost too easy. No wonder Grandpa's so good at it.* "Trust me, it'll be gone in a flash."

I'd called one of Grandpa's trusted contacts and got the Datsun towed back to the house by Saturday night. Business at the shop was booming more than usual, and Grandpa didn't want me cluttering it with non-work-related stuff. Cassandra and I had made room for the junk car in the backyard and hoisted it up on four jack stands.

When I'd finally gotten a good, thorough look at the heap of sun-faded metal, I could tell that this was going to be a *long* project. We needed to find parts—lots and *lots* of parts. This project was going to take me and Cassandra weeks to finish, possibly months, and a lot depended on how fast we'd be able to get those parts.

After dinner, Cassandra and I sit at the kitchen table making our giant list.

"Think it's about time we told Jacob what we're up to?" I ask, idly paging through last month's Q&R parts catalog.

Cassandra runs her finger along a column in the Classified Ads section of today's paper. "Guess so," she says, not looking up. "This would be a good time for him to start learning how to drift again."

"With what car?"

She rubs her chin. "Y'know, Preston's Corolla might work. He's got the tires for it, at least. Not sure about his rear-wheel drive, though. Honestly, I've never seen Preston drag race, even while I was a part of the crew. I wonder if that son of a bitch has been secretly drifting instead?"

I shrug. "Who knows? Preston is a follower, just like Jacob's other stooge, Bryce."

She chuckles. "Well, then I say we oughta bug Preston for his car. If the Ninez want their turf back, then he'll have to make some sacrifices."

The idea sounds good enough, but will they be on board? *There's only one way to find out.* I set aside the catalog. "Let's go pay the Ninez a visit."

Cassandra continues scanning the Classified Ads. "You go. I'm tired from all that driving around today."

I raise my eyebrows. "Too tired to take jabs at Jacob and his friends?"

"Yes." She covers her mouth, suppressing a yawn. "Go on. I'll stay here and keep looking for parts."

I shake my head, not bothering to try and convince her otherwise. "Just have to figure out where he and his crew might be tonight."

"I doubt they're doing any racing around here. Tonight's Bike Night at Moonshine Milly's, though. They might be hanging out there."

"Worth a shot. Thanks." I leave her to her searching and head out the door.

As Cassandra expected, I discover the Ninez's cars parked together in their usual spots away from the scores of motorcycles that take up Moonshine Milly's lot. I head inside the bar where the music of Mötley Crüe blares from the CD jukebox, and a group of middle-aged and older bikers take to the floor, dancing and laughing while mugs of beer slosh in their hands. I scan the crowd, careful not to make eye contact with any of the bikers, and eventually spot Jacob and his crew sitting alone at one of the back tables.

A few empty mugs and beer bottles litter the tabletop. Preston fiddles with his bright-red beeper, while Bryce sits back in his chair and watches the crowd with his arms crossed, his burly frame making him look like some kind of dressed-down bodyguard. Meanwhile, Jacob watches the crowd with a look of disgust, his hand clenching around the neck of his beer bottle. The rest of his younger crew are gathered at the pool table watching a heated game between two drunk bikers.

I wade through the crowd of bikers and join the Ninez at the back of the bar. "'Sup," I greet, giving the group a brief salute.

The three guys straighten in their chairs with a start, then Jacob looks me up and down and sneers. "What the hell are you doing here?"

"Looking for you, obviously." I pull up an empty chair, straddle it backwards, and sit.

"If you've come to gloat again, then get the fuck away from me," Jacob warns.

I shake my head. "Nope. We need to talk. Cass and I figured out a way to run Oculus X and the Red Ravens out of town for good."

A look of shock crosses Jacob, Preston, and Bryce's faces, followed quickly by suspicion. Despite the misgivings painting their faces, they lean in earnestly, and I explain the plan.

"Wait…" Jacob says when I finish. "You want *me* to drift? Are you fucking crazy?"

"You're the only one of us who can do it well," I say.

"And you want *me* to let him use *my* car so he can practice?" Preston adds with widened eyes.

I nod. "Yeah. It's only temporary until Cass and I get this project done."

Jacob blinks. "Project? You mean… Y-You're…"

"Yeah, we're building you a drifting machine."

"I… I can't believe it." He beams. "That's fucking amazing. I can't believe you guys are building me a car."

"We're not doing it out of the kindness of our hearts," I say. "We're doing it because assholes like Oculus X and the Red Ravens don't belong here."

"True that." Jacob nods. "Okay, I'm in."

Preston blinks. "Wait. Don't I have a say in any of this?"

Jacob frowns at his crewmate. "If you don't want another blackeye for doing what you love, then you'll lend me your car, damn it."

Preston scowls, averting his gaze. Then, he looks back at me and exhales a deep sigh. "Fine…"

"Great." Grinning, I slap Preston playfully on the back. Then, I turn back to Jacob. "You need to be at the top of your game, man. It's going to take us a while to finish the car, so, you'll have plenty of time to practice."

Jacob nods. "Yeah, I get it. Don't worry, I'll be ready. Those fuckers won't know what hit 'em."

I smirk. "I'm betting on it."

CHAPTER 23

I CAN'T BELIEVE IT.

In four weeks, Cassandra and I had managed to turn that old shell of a Datsun into a *mean* drifting machine. With Dave's help, we'd scored some amazing deals on near-top-of-the-line-level Q&R parts. And we'd hired one of Grandpa's paint specialist contacts to add a new coat of sleek, shiny royal-blue paint that made the car look as good as new. Next to Sasha, this was the project I was most proud of, turning rags to riches.

"I'm kind of jealous," Cassandra says, admiring the car that sits proudly on display in the backyard under the chilly late-Saturday-afternoon sun. "I can't believe we're gonna give this sweet-ass car to Jacob. As if that asshole deserves it after all the hours of blood, sweat, and tears we'd put into it."

"Yeah, he's a lucky bastard," I say, wrinkling my nose slightly. "But remember, he's gonna owe us big time." I wrap my arm around her waist and pull her close. I plant a kiss on her neck, tasting the saltiness of her sweat.

She half-smiles. "You still think he's good enough to drive it?"

"Yeah. Some things you just don't forget, no matter how hard you try. Besides, everyone's counting on him." My heart pounds with a small feeling of doubt and anxiety as I say those words. I'd tried to forget my criminal past, but old habits were hard to kill. Jacob was never that great with his drag-racing skills, as hard as he'd tried to convince everyone otherwise, but he was a hell of a drifter once. *And he's only delaying the inevitable if he tries to back out now.*

Cassandra sighs. "Guess it's time to deliver this baby, huh?"

"Guess so."

Cassandra drives her Hemi, and I follow her in the Datsun to the Ninez's hideout down on the southside of Tacoma. This car feels so strange, so foreign, compared to Sasha. The handling is slightly stiffer, and I can feel a different kind of power.

Jacob better have his shit together and bring out this car's full potential.

We turn down a gravel road off 38th street, and drive until we reach a dead end. A tiny, run-down mobile home that looks like it's seen better days is nestled among a cluster of trees and overgrowth. At first glance, the place appears to be abandoned. But then I notice Jacob, Bryce, and Preston's cars parked in the back, along with a couple of sport bikes and a Jeep.

The last time I'd visited the Ninez headquarters was two years ago, back when Jacob and I were friends and allies, and not adversaries. It feels weird being out here again.

I park the Datsun beside Jacob's CR-X and get out. I stare at the mobile home while I reminisce, and suck in a breath.

Cassandra joins me, her Hemi parked near the road. "Never thought I'd be back here again."

"Ditto." I smile reassuringly, sliding my arm around her waist. "You gonna be okay?"

"I'll be fine. We came here for one thing, and one thing only—let's get it over with."

I walk up the rickety, rotted wooden steps and knock on the door. The curtains in one of the windows rustle. Moments later, the front door swings open and Bryce appears, his large frame taking up the width of the doorway. Crossing his arms, he glares at us.

"Special delivery for Jacob," I say, making a small head gesture behind me.

Bryce's eyes go wide, and he slowly uncrosses his arms. "Holy—!" He whistles over his shoulder. "Hey, Jake! Get out here, man! You gotta see this!"

While the rest of the crew gathers, Cassandra and I return to the Datsun and wait.

Moments later, Jacob and the rest of the Ninez pour out the front door.

Standing firm, Cassandra lifts her chin and eyes the group coolly as they approach.

Jacob stands before us. He flicks an icy stare at Cassandra then trains his gaze on me. For a moment, he and I lock eyes.

He nods once, conveying a silent message of thanks. At least Jacob knows what's up.

"We did our part, now you do yours," I say, stepping aside and popping the hood.

Jacob scrutinizes the car. His cold expression quickly brightens. "H-Holy shit…"

The rest of the crew surrounds the car, ogling every detail while they chat with each other excitedly.

Cassandra and I stand off to the side and watch in silence. Cassandra's face remains bitter. I know how she feels, putting all this effort in for someone who never gave a damn about her. After working with her on this project, I'd made a promise to myself that I was going to be a hundred times the man that Jacob ever was. Cassandra is my number one, and she deserves that much.

Jacob finally looks back at me, openmouthed. "Holy fucking shit, Adam! You built this?"

"*We* built it," Cassandra corrects, her face taut. "Ninety-eight-percent Q&R parts under that hood. Full turbo kit. A guaranteed winner."

Jacob's eyes widen. "The T48 turbo?"

"Nah, the T42," I say. "Two steps below Q&R's latest, but still a damn good system."

Jacob hops in the driver's seat. I push my way past the rest of the crew and stand next to the open door.

"Oh man. This feels so sweet. Brings back memories," Jacob says, running his hands along the steering wheel.

"Good. That means you'll know how to drive it, right?"

"Yeah… Yeah, it feels good…"

I snicker. "Admit it, man. You miss drifting."

"A little… Fuck. Okay. I miss it a lot. I never thought I'd feel the bug again."

"Well, keep that bug around so you can put Oculus X and the Red Ravens in their place."

"With this beast? Hell yeah. They'll all get smoked." Jacob flexes his fingers around the steering wheel. "Let's see how she rides."

"*She's* going to need a name." I crack a smile.

Jacob looks thoughtful as he runs his finger along the dashboard. "She looks and feels like a Lucia."

I give him a thumbs up. "I like it."

Cassandra approaches us. She narrows her eyes at Jacob. "You're welcome," she says flatly.

Jacob rubs the back of his head. "Yeah… Thanks, Cass. I can't believe you did this for me…"

She snorts. "I didn't do it for *you*, asshole. I just happen to hate Oculus X and the Red Ravens more."

He frowns and stares blankly at the steering wheel.

"Hey, c'mon," I break in, trying to change the subject. "I want to see Lucia in action. Any place around here where we can test her out?"

Jacob perks up. "Y-Yeah. We can play around in the big public utilities parking lot not far from here."

I hop in Cassandra's car, and we follow Jacob and the rest of his crew down a narrow dirt road winding through a thick forest. Finally, we emerge in a massive empty parking lot behind the city's public utilities building, which is closed on the weekends. Scores of tire tracks and burned rubber lines mar the asphalt.

We all park in a group and get out of our vehicles, except for Jacob.

"Is this one of your secret drifting spots?" I ask Jacob, gesturing to the tire tracks. There's no way these tracks were from drag racing.

Jacob nods. "One of the few places left they haven't discovered."

"Good. And we're going to keep it that way. Now, let's see what you got."

For over three hours, Cassandra, the Ninez crew, and I watched Jacob take to the asphalt, handling the Datsun 280Z like a pro. He didn't miss a beat. He'd picked his winning techniques back up as easily as riding a bike. I'd never seen him handle a car with such speed, finesse, and style—even back when he drifted full time. He did it so effortlessly, it was like watching a dance. Jacob was a natural-born drifter as much as he'd tried to deny it.

It's eight o'clock by the time we finally leave the parking lot. Five minutes later, we're back at the Ninez's hideout.

I chat with Jacob outside the house while the rest of his crew is inside. Jacob can't stop smiling. Today has fired him up. That fear in his eyes when Oculus X or the Red Ravens were mentioned is missing, and he seems eager to take them on.

"It's in the bag," Jacob says, giving me a thumbs up.

I grin. "It better be, 'cause that car cost a shit-ton to dial in. I better get my return on investment."

"Don't worry, man. You will."

I look over my shoulder at Cassandra, who sits alone in her Hemi wearing an exhausted look on her face. It's been a long day for her—long and stressful, being around her old crew. I admire her strength. It doesn't help that she'd spent all those long hours with me getting the Datsun dialed in. I'm sure all that lack of sleep is now catching up with her.

I turn back to Jacob. "So, when are you going to challenge them?"

"Tomorrow night at the industrial park," he replies. "It's gonna be a nice little surprise for 'em, so they won't have a chance to prepare." Jacob nods curtly. "I'm going to contact all our old crews tonight and tell them to come watch the slaughter. I'll have my A-game ready for those bastards."

"You better."

Jacob's determined expression softens. "Hey, man. Thanks for this. Seriously. I still can't believe you two built that car for me."

I purse my lips. "This wasn't just for you. All of us want those bastards out of town. And fortunately—or unfortunately—you're the only one of us who can do it." I harden my gaze. "Just remember, though. You owe us big time."

He nods timidly. "I know, I know. Just say the word. You and Cass just saved this community—this town—by building Lucia."

"It's not saved until you win," I say, shaking my head.

A small smile creeps over his lips. The he sticks out his hand.

I stare at it warily.

"For old time's sake?" he suggests.

I look back at his hand. Then, quirking a smile, I shake it. We do our special handshake that we hadn't done in so long—before this rift between us happened.

"See you tomorrow night, then." I turn to leave.

"Hey."

I pause and look over my shoulder.

"Tell Cass I really am sorry…"

I frown. I'm not sure if he's intending to try and win her back, but from what I've seen any chance he did have with her was D.O.A. a long time ago. What could Jacob possibly offer that I couldn't, anyway?

I hop in the passenger's seat and shut the door. Cassandra awakens with a start. She looks at me, her face slightly pale.

"You okay?" I ask her.

"Yeah. I wasn't feeling good, so I tried to take a nap."

"What's wrong?"

She shakes her head dismissively. "Eh… the curse of being a woman every month, that's all." She tosses her car keys at me. "Mind if you drove this time?"

I catch the keys. Damn, her pain must be excruciating for her to not want to drive her beloved Hemi. "An opportunity to drive your sweet-ass Hemi? Hell yeah."

She gets out of the car and curls up in the backseat without a response.

The curse of being a woman, indeed, I muse as we head back to Grandpa's house. I hate her monthly curse as much as she does, because it usually meant she'd be off limits for a while.

Lord help me, I'm going to be a horny wreck…

Chapter 24

The next night couldn't come fast enough.

Cassandra and I drive up to the industrial park for the second time since the drift crews had taken over. The second time since I decided to quit the racing scene. The second time since the fire. Hopefully we'll be watching Jacob's victory race, and I can walk away from all this with a clear conscience.

But it feels different being here this time, and my heart can't stop pounding.

It's a packed house tonight. I recognize a lot of the vehicles from the old crews like the Burn Dawgs, the Chefs, and even the punks with the tricked-out sport bikes, the Scorpion Posse. It looks like Jacob managed to convince them all to show up. I wonder how he did it? He wasn't very well liked in the community to start with, but after he'd lost the turf to the drifters, he became a full-blown pariah for most of these guys.

It's cool that everyone is giving him a second chance to redeem himself, because this is the only chance he has. Maybe the only chance *they* had to get their turf back too. As if he didn't have enough pressure.

This industrial park has a rear parking lot as massive as the front. But unlike the straightaways of the front lot, the rear one is curved, separated with concrete parking bars and partitions, making it the perfect drifter's paradise. It's no wonder Oculus X had claimed this place as their own.

The cacophony of squealing tires, revving engines, and a rowdy, screaming crowd rip through the air. Nearby, a gorgeous lime-green IROC-Z Camaro performs endless donuts and burnouts before a pumped-up audience.

Near the large crowd, Jacob is gathered with the rest of his crew, as well as some of the members of the old drag crews. Francis, the Burn Dawgs' enforcer, oversees the gathering with one of his arms folded across his chest in a sling, his weight on a cane held in his other hand. It was good to see him alive after what went down at Fife. David of the Killa Speedz crew exchanges some words with Sutter and Raymond, two of the Burn Dawgs' younger members, who each hold an excited Cronos and Apollo by their leashes. Nate of the Chefs has a dubious look on his face as he chats with Preston.

"This is so weird," Cassandra mutters to me as we near the gathering. "I mean, *nobody* likes Jacob. Now the crews are breaking bread with him?"

It's kind of cool to see everyone together like this again, despite the circumstances. I guess they all agreed on a 'temporary truce' with Jacob, as well. "They know what's at stake," I say to Cassandra. "Jacob better show out tonight."

Jacob looks up from his conversation, spots me and Cassandra, and waves us over.

We approach the group. The Burn Dawgs, Chefs, and Killa Speedz members all greet me happily, but keep their distance from Cassandra. During all the meet-and-greets, she stays silent. The last time they saw her, she was Jacob's girl. I'm sure she knows that too. I've missed these guys, and hopefully in time, they'll warm up to Cassandra too. But there's still a lot of wounds that need healing after everything Jacob had done, and the rest of his crew were guilty by association.

"They accepted the challenge… Man, look at this crowd," Jacob says to me.

"Just focus on the race," I say. "You know what you gotta do, right?"

Jacob nods. "Yeah, win. We're doing Bait and Switch. I fucking hate it. I guarantee those assholes are gonna make me the bait. Lucky me."

I raise an eyebrow. "What does all that mean?"

"It's what Oculus X calls their fucked-up version of Cat and Mouse. Basically, Kaine chases my ass, trying to make me lose control. This can end really badly if I'm not careful. They play for keeps."

"How badly?"

"Like, I could spin out of control, flip, crash… anything."

I grit my teeth. "After all the work Cass and I put in that car, you better not put a single scratch on her, got it?"

He swallows and nods. "Y-Yeah, man. I swear, I'll treat this car like gold."

"Good, 'cause we're all counting on you to run these bastards out of town." I pause and look around. "Where are they, anyway?"

"Showing off to their fans." He rolls his eyes. "I just want to get this shit over with."

The lime-green Camaro ends its show, and the ring of spectators parts to allow the car to drive off. Their cheers and whistles echo through the air. A set of headlights from a bright red Supra shine on us from the center of the action before pulling forward into the ring of the crowd. The Supra drifts around in a donut before screeching to a full stop. Over a dozen other cars enter the circle and stop behind the Supra. I recognize one of the cars is Jacob's old CR-X. There're neon-green pinstripes painted across the side and down the hood, and a massive God-awful spoiler attached to the back.

Cassandra snickers. "Holy shit. Is that what I think it is?"

I do a double-take, as if she is reading my mind. "Is that your car?" I ask Jacob.

He slumps his shoulders. "Yeah, man… They took this turf, then they took my car. There were too many of those guys. I couldn't fight them all…"

Wow. These guys really are the top of the food chain around here. Now even *I'm* starting to have my doubts of him being able to save this place. It doesn't matter how many mods a car has—in the end, a car ain't good without a good driver. I really hope these guys aren't stuck in Jacob's head.

The spectators huddle closer to the Supra as Kaine steps out, a white lollipop stick poking out of his mouth like a cigarette. He waves to his fans, then eyes our group and walks our way.

Cronos and Apollo let out deep, angry barks at Kaine. Sutter and Raymond fight with the leashes and eventually calm the dogs down.

Jacob sucks in a breath. "Here we go," he mutters to me.

The other drivers get out of their cars, many of them sporting red. I spot Drew among them and my heart stops.

He's here...

The Red Ravens and Oculus X crews assemble behind Kaine as he stands before us.

Kaine pops his lollipop out of his mouth, his gaze bouncing between everyone in our group. He and I lock eyes a moment, and then he focuses on Jacob.

"Brought your friends to watch you get your ass beat?" Kaine jeers.

I ball my fists, resisting the temptation to clock this guy again, but I stay silent. Tonight, this is Jacob's fight. Taking Kaine down will leave a worse bruise than another haymaker.

"Let's do this," Jacob responds icily.

Kaine chuckles. "You sure?"

"I've never been so sure in my life. Tonight, or bust. For this turf. For this town. Loser never shows their sorry ass around here ever again."

"With what ride?" Kaine smiles crookedly. "You wanted this race, but I still ain't seen no wheels."

With his head held high, Jacob steps away from Kaine and walks over to his 280Z parked nearby. "Right here," he says, patting the hood.

Kaine and the rest of his crews stare blankly, then they all burst out laughing.

"You have *got* to be kidding me," Kaine rumbles. "I thought you were takin' this seriously, bro?"

Jacob flares his nostrils. "Meet me at the starting line and we'll see who's the real joke."

Kaine stops laughing.

"Challenge! Challenge!" the spectators chant as they begin approaching us.

I look around. We're surrounded by people. Nowhere to escape for either of them. This audience wants a show, and they're about to get the biggest one of the year.

"All right, Jacob," Kaine says. "If you're in that much of a hurry to get smoked—maybe we'll take your *new* ride too."

Jacob raises his eyebrows. "Why? Weren't you just laughing at it?"

"Because I wanna watch you *walk* out of this town with your tail between your legs. Don't worry though, I'll make sure it gets turned into a real drifting machine for a member of my crew." He chuckles. "I take care of my people… That CR-X is sweet, by the way," he stabs his thumb over his shoulder at Jacob's old car in the distance. "She's been upgraded."

Jacob's gaze swivels toward his former car. His eyes turn glassy, and he clenches his jaw.

I sigh. I know how much that car had meant to Jacob. To see it desecrated and turned into something completely different must've devastated him.

Jacob opens the driver's side door of the 280Z. "Fuck you, Kaine."

"All right then. You know the game. You're the bait, bitch," Kaine chuckles and turns back to the large crowd. "Watch me smoke this pussy-ass motherfucker!"

The spectators respond with another wave of cheers and shouts. I suddenly notice how much the crowd has grown. The majority of its numbers are made up of the various drift crews that have moved in, including the Red Ravens and Oculus X. Only a few of us originals have shown out for Jacob. Hopefully he can stay focused during the race.

Jacob and Kaine climb into their cars and make their way to the starting line. The crowd follows them closely like a bunch of fleas on a dirty dog.

Cassandra leaves me and follows the crowd. "Here goes nothing, I guess." She looks over her shoulder at me with a nervous smile.

I'm about to follow her when someone slaps me on the back of the shoulder. I flinch, instinctively balling my fist. *Drew and the Red Ravens...* Then I hear Cronos let out a happy bark, and I relax. I spin around and face Sutter. Cronos sits obediently next to him, panting.

"You sure he got this, man?" Sutter asks, giving me a skeptical look.

I snort. "Nope. But he sure as shit better pull something off out there, or it's their show from now on." I kneel and scratch Cronos in his favorite spot on his back, just above his tail, as I nod toward where Oculus X and the Red Ravens have gathered. "Ain't that right, boy?" I say to the dog, watching him pant happily, his bottom half lowering and yielding to my touch, while his excited tail whips back and forth.

"You know those guys aren't gonna play nice," Sutter mutters, leaning in a little closer. "They're probably packing. If they lose, they won't accept it quietly."

I frown. "I'm well aware." I'd kept my gun safely concealed in my jacket, next to the knot that formed in my stomach because I had to carry it—I didn't come unprepared—but if they're smart, they won't start that shit out here. We're not the only ones who came to race tonight. There are plenty of other drifting crews here that have no beef with us and a bunch of young kids. Most of them just wanted to race for fun like we did. They didn't take it as seriously as the Red Ravens and Oculus X. Those two crews are on a serious power trip, and they're a bad influence on the racing community. Our crews claimed turf to make things safe and fun for everyone. These assholes are doing things all wrong.

Would they start a gunfight over this shit? I shake my head. *They'd be showing their true colors in front of everyone. Kaine accepted the challenge. If they got pissy and pulled guns… No, that's stupid. Too stupid…*

…Then again, I've been wrong about a lot of things before.

I sigh. "If it comes down to it," I say to Sutter, "then we do what we gotta do, I guess. If only to stop these guys from killing kids, y'know?" I nod toward a group of teenagers nearby doing some tricks on their skateboards. Juvenile delinquents, all of them—like I once was. Watching the group of kids sends my mind to thoughts of Clay, Mariah, Gabe, and Luke.

Like we all were.

Sutter flicks his gaze at the group, then looks back at me. "*If* it comes down to it, the Burn Dawgs got your back." He joins the rest of the crowd at the starting line. I locate Cassandra in the tumult and stand beside her.

Ear-piercing whistles and cheers erupt from the spectators as the two cars halt at the starting line. An Oculus X member emerges from the crowd and stands behind the cars, his face hidden behind a large video camera resting on his shoulder. A Red Raven stands between the two cars, carrying a red bandanna in each hand.

Suddenly my heart is pounding away, as if I were in the driver's seat. The tension in the air was unbearable. Cassandra wraps her arm around mine as if for balance, anxiousness radiating from her. As nervous as we both seem to be, I can't imagine what Jacob is feeling right now, having so many people depending on him.

The Red Raven flagger raises the bandannas. Both engines roar awake, and rev with raw power. Kaine's people chant his name, while our crews root for Jacob. I stay silent and watch.

The flagger whips the bandanna in the hand next to Jacob toward the ground, then—a second later—the other, letting the 'Bait' get a car-length head start. Tires squeal, and the two cars bolt ahead in a cloud of white exhaust and burned rubber.

I exhale. Every inch of my muscles tighten as the cars near the first curve. Jacob has plowed ahead of Kaine by a few inches, but that lead quickly disappears as they drift around the curve in a series of high-pitched squeals, kicking up another cloud of white, tire-burned smoke. Jacob hugs the curve so tight, I'm waiting for the tell-tale sound of him hitting a parking bar or scraping against the concrete barrier and spinning out. Kaine hugs him as he follows his movement, his car practically sandwiching Jacob's into the barrier.

I clench my jaw. *No, no no no…*

Miraculously, Jacob manages to keep control and squeeze mere inches out of Kaine's trap. The crowd rushes off to the next part of the course to catch a better view of the next set of curves.

"Holy fucking shit. Did you see that?" Cassandra says, wide-eyed.

"Yeah." I shake my head. "Jacob might be in over his head. This shit's real."

She purses her lips, giving me a skeptical look, then follows the crowd.

"Dude! Jacob's smoking him!" someone from the crowd yells, pointing at the trail of white smoke as the two cars drift another curve. I have to hand it to Jacob. His drifting skills are way better than his dragging—this was his element.

Curve by curve, the two cars swing around in semi-unison, like some kind of mesmerizing dance. Kaine inches closer to Jacob with each turn, looking to send him spinning out or worse, but Jacob keeps managing to pull away at the last second. The crowd continues migrating to different sections of the lot to get better views. The Oculus X camera guy doesn't stop filming.

Finally, Kaine and Jacob reach the 1320 section of the lot. The same stretch of asphalt where we used to drag. Finally, familiar ground. *Punch it, now.*

As if my silent thoughts are heard, Jacob's car jolts forward with its second wind. The gap between the two cars widens again. Cassandra takes my hand and squeezes it. I look sideways at her.

"They're not done yet," she says, pointing to two sharp turns that are practically ninety-degrees, thanks to the concrete barricades that line them

I widen my eyes. "Are they really going to run that? That looks *way* too narrow to drift. No way can they make that."

"If Jacob really is this master drifter as you paint him to be, then he can make it."

"I said he was good. I never said he was a master…"

We join the spectators back at the starting area, where we can get a good view of the last half of the race. Just a few feet from the first turn, Jacob's front tires turn hard, stopping on a dime, as the backend skids. His rear tires spin intermittently in short bursts as the car slides between the narrow space, smooth as silk. Lucia's front and back are mere inches away from the concrete barrier, but inexplicably, it doesn't scrape.

Kaine is hot on his tail, following him like a shadow. His car power-slides between the barriers with ease, then straightens and picks up speed on the short straightaway. He quickly catches up with Jacob and the two cars are almost side by side again, Kaine holding back and to the inside to trap him on the turn.

I gasp. The two of them can't make it between that narrow curve at the same time. *C'mon, Jake…*

They reach the curve, Jacob still ahead by a nose. He quickly slides into it. His range going a little wider this time as he oversteers, trying to compensate for Kaine breathing down his side. The back of his car inches closer to the concrete barricade. He swerves, attempting to regain control. Kaine is right next to him now, the sides of their cars nearly touching. Jacob is trapped. The lower quarter panel of Jacob's car side-swipes part of the barricade, sending pieces of metal flying everywhere.

"*Ooh!*" roars from the crowd.

"That doesn't look good," Cassandra mutters.

I ball my fists. "Damn it!"

Kaine sandwiches Jacob's car harder. He takes Jacob's bumper, fishtailing Lucia, but he regains control and squeezes his way around the rest of the curve into a shaky sideways drift. It's a split second, but just enough time to maneuver out of Kaine's trap and onto the homestretch toward the finish line.

Kaine recovers from his attempted PIT maneuver and tries to swerve beside Jacob again as they're less than two hundred meters away from the finish line. Kaine edges closer and closer to Jacob, swooping in for another attempt at sending him crashing off the track. Jacob moves sideways with him. Then, just a few meters from the finish line, Jacob cuts his wheels and drifts sideways.

Kaine's front tires turn hard to avoid Jacob, but he oversteers as he tries to straighten on the track. He fishtails in a cloud of white smoke and screeching tires, sliding off the track and slamming right into a parking bar. The back of his car jolts up from the impact, crumpling the rear axle and sending one of his tires rolling away. *Weren't expecting that, were you asshole?*

Alone, Jacob drifts across the finish line in style.

The crowd goes wild in a mix of cheers and boos. Some of Kaine's people run out to check on their fearless leader and his decommissioned ride. The rest of the crowd surround Jacob's car, chanting in victory.

I beam. *He did it. That son of a bitch really did it!* I turn to Cassandra, but she's already gone off to join the rest of the crowd to congratulate Jacob, and I follow quickly behind. He gets out of his car and raises a fist to his eager audience.

"Holy shit, man! That was sick!" Preston exclaims, slapping Jacob on the back.

"I can't believe you smoked Kaine!" Sutter says.

"We got our spot back, bro!" Matthew, a member of the Chefs says, grabbing Jacob's shoulder.

Jacob grins at the crowd. Then his gaze turns to Cassandra. She nods to him and smiles. She's probably happy for him—she knew what was at stake—but it still surprises me she would give him even that smile. It doesn't matter how many races he wins, he mistreated and abandoned her, and I don't think she'll ever forget that. He doesn't deserve to get her back.

I give myself that reassurance by slowly wrapping my arm around her waist. Her body stiffens for a moment before she turns toward my presence, and then relaxes into me.

Jacob meets my gaze, and his smile slowly fades. The crowd parts as he approaches me. He stands before me and sticks out his hand. "Couldn't have done it without you, man," he says.

I look at his hand and pause before taking it—even after everything that's happened lately, the past still hangs over me and Jacob. "You did your part. I'm just glad it's over."

"You and Cass built this," Jacob says, then his gaze swivels to Cassandra again. "One of you have to head this turf."

Cassandra shakes her head. "Not me."

Jacob raises his eyebrows. "Really? I thought you would've wanted it. It's better than being somebody's number one."

"I have different wants now," she says.

Jacob frowns.

"*You* need to take it," I say to Jacob. "You won, fair and square, and you've got the respect now. Don't lose it again to stupid shit."

Jacob looks at me, surprised. "Seriously, Adam? You're gonna let me have it?"

I nod. "It's yours. Take care of it. Remember, this is for everyone to enjoy and have fun. Don't be a dick like those other guys."

"Deal." Jacob extends his hand again, and we do our old special handshake for the second time in two days. *Weird times.*

A set of car lights approach us and stop. Two Red Raven punks step out, and the crowd instinctually gives us room. They regard Jacob and his audience with a sneer, then their gazes settle on me. "You think you can kick us out that easily?"

I push past Cassandra and step closer to the two Red Ravens, my height easily dwarfing them. My hand pauses at my jacket, ready to draw my gun.

"A deal's a deal, unless you're thinking about settling it some other way," I say.

The Red Ravens appear unintimidated by my presence or response. In fact, one of them smirks and says, "Adam Anderson. You owe us more than you know."

I arch an eyebrow. "What the hell does that mean?"

The two punks slowly back away toward their cars. "It means the tax collector's coming," the other punk says.

Before I could get out another word, they hop back in their cars and drive off.

Chapter 25

WITH JACOB WINNING BACK OUR TURF AND RUNNING those drifters out of town, part of me feels a sense of closure—at least with the racing. Even with all the excitement of tonight, the thrill of the race has all but left me, and I can't bring myself to go back to that life. Not after losing Clayton, Mariah, and Gabriel. Luke running out on me too. I'd lost so much in my life already, being caught up in this game, and I've been one lucky son of a bitch to get out of some bad situations alive. How much more could I tempt fate?

But it wasn't the racing game that had me worried right now. *The tax collector's coming...* Cassandra had asked me again about the Red Ravens, and again I hadn't given her the whole truth. I chalked it all up to Jacob's win adding insult to injury. It's killing me to keep misleading her, but hopefully getting away from the racing scene means getting away from the Red Ravens too. They couldn't collect if they couldn't find me. I can almost bring myself to believe that, but my youth had taught me otherwise.

It's nearing three in the morning. We're halfway to Grandpa's house when Cassandra points ahead to a 24-hour convenience store. "Hey, can you stop there for a hot minute?"

I furrow my brow. "Sure. What's up?"

"I… totally forgot to get yesterday's paper…"

"I doubt they have any now. You know what time it is?"

"They might have some old ones left in the back or something. Q&R was supposed to be making a huge announcement about some new parts getting released, and I don't want to miss it."

I roll my eyes. "Fine." I pull the Hemi into an empty parking space in front of the convenience store, and Cassandra hops out. Minutes later, she returns, carrying a folded newspaper. She sets it on the dashboard, and I pull back out onto the road.

Finally, we pull up along the curb in front of Grandpa's house. I shut off the car and grab the newspaper from the dashboard. Cassandra grabs it too.

"I got it," she says.

I give the paper a little squeeze in protest. I'm about to let go when I feel something rolled up in the paper. It feels like a small box. I look at her carefully. "What do you got in there?" I ask.

She swipes up the paper. "Just some candy."

"Oh. You know, if you wanted some candy, you could have just said so."

She gives me a look and hops out the car quickly, hurrying to the front door. Doesn't she know that I'm the one with the key? She looks anxious about something. I get out of the car and approach her. "Hey, what's wrong?"

"I gotta pee. Can you hurry up and open the door?" She clutches the newspaper close to her chest.

I glance at the paper with skepticism. Why is she being so secretive about some damn candy? Not to mention, if there *was* candy in there, that box would surely get crushed by the way she squeezed that paper. I slowly put the key in the lock and turn the knob, but leave the door closed. I point my thumb over my shoulder at the Hemi. "Hey, you left the passenger door open."

"Huh?" she whips her head around.

While she's caught off guard, I swipe the newspaper, open the door and hurry inside before she can realize what's happened. I rush to our bedroom with long, quiet strides, doing my best to make sure I don't wake Grandpa, and flip on the light. I hear her hurried footsteps approaching as I unfurl the newspaper and a box falls out on the bed.

A pink box that says "One-Step Pregnancy Test."

My eyes widen.

Cassandra's in the room now, out of breath and staring, horrified at my discovery.

I glare back at her and hold the box up. "What the fuck is this?"

Cassandra rips the box from my hands. "Give me that."

"Why are you hiding this from me?"

"It's nothing, all right? I knew you'd act a fool like this."

I blink. "Nothing? You're fucking pregnant!"

"Look, I don't know if I am or not, all right?"

"What do you mean you don't know?"

She chews her bottom lip. "I was supposed to have my period two weeks ago. Still no dice."

I just stare at her. We'd fucked around a bit, but I always wore protection whenever she said she was nearing her period. So, this baby can't possibly be mine, right?

No, damn it. I can't think that. I trust her. I... I love her.

Cassandra leaves me to my thoughts and goes to the bathroom.

I sink down on the edge of my bed and rub my hands over my face. *This can't be happening right now.* I damn sure hope she's not pregnant. I'm a delinquent with a record and a gang out for my head—I'm too fucked-up to be a decent father. Besides, I never had a decent father of my own. How the hell would I even know how to be one myself?

No, I'm not ready. I don't think I'll ever be.

Minutes later, I hear the bathroom door open, and I hop up from the bed. Cassandra enters, looking at me with trepidation. Then she leans up against the doorframe and stares off into space.

"Well? What did the test say?" I ask.

Her gaze flicks to me and she holds up the test. There's a pink plus sign. I stare at the image long and hard, as the world around me gets smaller. *No... It can't be...* "That has to be wrong. We were careful. I used protection. You need to take another test!"

She sighs. "You're the first and only guy I've ever had without protection…"

I open my mouth to reply and stop short, remembering all those sweet, memorable nights she'd taken me raw—especially that unforgettable time we were alone at the lookout, and I fucked her hard over the hood of my car. My dick steels a moment from that fantasy-turned-reality, and then I'm reeled back to the present. *I should have known better…* "I took you raw because I trusted you. You said you knew your body. Did you set me up? Plan this all along?"

She widens her eyes. "*What?* No! And I *do* know my body."

I scowl and shake my head. "Obviously, you don't know it as well as you think."

"Look, I know when I'm close to having my period. I don't know how this could happen, but I swear to you, this was no trick. I would *never* intentionally do that to you…" She hugs herself. Her eyes become a little glassy. "Never…" she whispers.

I can hear the genuine fear in her voice. She really does mean it. I have to believe her. But what happens now?

I swallow a lump in my throat and plop back down on the edge of the bed. "I… I'm not ready for this, Cass. I can't be a father. I'm a bad person. I'm a criminal. I can't put a kid through all of my bullshit. It wouldn't be fair."

She sighs deeply. "I'll… I'll go to a doctor tomorrow and see what can be done to—"

"Whoa…" I give her a serious look. No, I'm not ready to be a father, but I'm not sure it would be cool to just get rid of the baby, either. All I could think about in that moment was the time Grandpa told me that story about my mother. About how she was a prostitute and drug addict and regretted having Michael and me—that our existence ruined her life and that she'd rather be dead. She'd ended up getting her wish, twenty-eight years young, shot up with heroin. "Let's not jump that far yet," I say. Then, I chew my bottom lip. "I mean… unless you really want to—"

Cassandra holds up her hand and shakes her head. "First, I'll go to the doctor and make sure this pregnancy is for real. If it is… then we can decide what to do next."

I don't think I'd closed my eyes for an hour before it was time to get up for work at Grandpa's shop. My mind was racing a hundred miles an hour, from Jacob's big race to the Red Raven's threat to Cassandra's surprise announcement and deciding what to do with my fucked-up life. Of course, the most immediate seemed to be Cassandra's news. What the hell were we going to do? I'd considered calling Elouise, but she was probably too busy preparing for the big move across the country. I hadn't talked to her in a long time, much less my dickhead brother.

Nine a.m. rolls around. I'm busily sweeping up the shop when I hear the office's front door open, and Grandpa shuffles in. Through the glass of the side door leading into the garage, I catch a glimpse of him walk past, and he plops down in his desk chair. I lean the broom against the wall and head through the door to greet him.

Grandpa looks paler than usual. Almost sickly. He's hunched over at his desk, the upper half of his face resting in his palm.

"Grandpa? Are you okay?" I ask.

He slowly looks up at me. "Yeah, son. I'm good. Just had a hard time getting up this morning. Then I had to meet with one of my business partners an hour ago. I'm so damn tired…"

I cringe. "Uh… Sorry if you heard Cassandra and I arguing last night…"

"Huh? No, I didn't hear anything. Slept like a log last night, actually. Today is just gonna be one of those days, I guess."

Concern swirls through my mind. That man always had more energy than me. Maybe his age was finally starting to catch up with him. "When was the last time you saw a doctor? Maybe you should get checked out, man."

He snorts. "Absolutely not. I don't need no stinkin' doctor to tell me there's nothing wrong with me, because I *know* there's nothing wrong with me!"

"Sorry, man. Just worried about you."

"Well, you can stop worrying, because I'm fine." He points to the garage. "Get back to your work, boy. Leave me alone."

As I turn to leave, the phone rings.

"Anderson Antique Auto. James speaking," Grandpa greets.

I halfway shut the door to the office, retrieve the broom, and resume my sweeping. My mind returns to my conversation with Cassandra last night. *I don't know how to be a father, because I never had one.* This kid would suffer because of my ignorance. I can't let that happen. Then again, the only real father figure I knew was Grandpa, and even we'd butted heads more often than not. But I was still grateful to have him in my life. Maybe I could get a few pointers from him if I ever end up stepping out into this dad life.

Maybe I *could* do it. I've done a lot of things I've never done before in my life, and I survived the bumps and bruises. Maybe I could be a better man than my own father was—hell, the bar was pretty low in that regard. It takes a real man to be a dad, after all, and my dad was anything *but* that. Am I going to let myself follow in his footsteps?

Hell, fucking no.

A sudden loud thump comes from the office, snapping me out of my thoughts. My attention snaps to the ajar door. "Grandpa?" I call, but there's no answer.

I drop the broom and approach the door. I can see all sorts of office supplies scattered on the floor in front of the desk. I hurry to the door now and swing it open—Grandpa is slumped over with his head on a pile of papers. The phone's receiver dangles next to the desk by its coiled cord.

"What do you think about that?" a man's voice crackles from the receiver. There's a pause. "You still there, James? Hello? Hello…?"

Furrowing my brow, I rush to Grandpa and nudge him. His body jostles, but he doesn't stir. "Hey, Grandpa. Wake up."

He's silent.

I swallow. My heartbeat pounds a little faster. "G-Grandpa?" I push him back up in the chair, so he's sitting up and looking at me. His eyes are half-open, but it's like he doesn't see or hear me. His face is pale. His skin is clammy and cold.

Panic surges through my body. *No… No…* "Grandpa!" I say again.

Nothing.

I snatch up the phone receiver, end the current call, and dial 9-1-1.

Chapter 26

I PACE ENDLESSLY AROUND THE WAITING AREA OF TACOMA Regional Hospital's emergency room. Some of the other waiting patients occasionally give me an annoying glance as I walk past them, but damn it, I didn't know what else to do. While I'm forced to wait out here twiddling my thumbs, my grandfather is probably in some room with dozens of tubes hooked up to him as if he were some sort of science experiment. He'd always hated doctors.

The front doors to the emergency room slide open, and Cassandra rushes inside, still in her Out the Box uniform and visor hat. Her frantic gaze spots me, and she rushes into my arms. I bury my face in her hair and inhale her scent that lingers under the odor of french fries. I hug her stiffly, too emotionally wrecked.

"Sorry I'm so late," Cassandra huffs. "Apparently, my boss doesn't give two shits if my boyfriend's grandfather is in the hospital."

"It's fine," I say in an absent, choked voice.

"How is he?"

"Your guess is as good as mine. I've been here for three hours, and I haven't heard a damn thing."

She squeezes my hand. "Come on, let's sit down."

I whip my hand away. "No. I don't want to sit down."

Her eyes dull, and she finds a lone, empty seat and sits. I lean against the wall and cross my arms, bouncing my back on-and-off the wall while my gaze remains fixed on the two swinging doors that lead deeper into the emergency room.

Endless seconds—minutes—hours—tick by. Finally, a nurse comes through the doors and looks aimlessly around at the crowd in the waiting room. "Mister Adam Anderson?"

I'm already in front of her in a few short strides before she even has a chance to finish getting my name out. Cassandra stands beside me.

"How is he?" I ask.

The nurse swallows, then she turns and walks back toward the doors. "Come with me, please." She beckons us with a wave of her hand.

I'm on her heels as she leads me out of the waiting room and through the double doors of the emergency room. My skin crawls, feeling the pain and despair that hangs in this area like a dark cloud.

The nurse turns a corner away from the first triage area, stops, and spins around. Her fair, lightly powdered face becomes pale.

"It appears your grandfather had a massive heart attack. We did all we could to try to resuscitate him, but… he didn't make it. I'm so sorry, Mister Anderson."

My eyes widen, and I stare slack-jawed at the nurse. The room around me seems to cave in like I'm being trapped in a small box. *I'm dreaming. I'm having a fucking nightmare right now. Please wake the fuck up, Adam!*

"He's… dead?" Cassandra asks the nurse in a small voice.

The nurse bows her head solemnly. "I'm so sorry."

Dead… I run my hands over my face. *This can't be happening.* "I want to see him."

"Sir, first we need to—"

"Now!"

The nurse swallows and gives a curt nod, then leads us down a long hallway. As I walk with heavy steps, the hallway feels narrower, and the air grows thicker, making it harder for me to breathe. Each step I take echoes a thousand-fold off the floor and walls. We reach room 706, and the nurse steps aside. "He's in here, sir."

I face the doorway, anxiety rippling across my skin. A silhouetted figure moves around in the room, then heads my way. *Grandpa? Maybe they messed up… maybe they got him confused with another patient who passed…* A doctor emerges instead, his face bearing a pained expression. As he brushes past me, he places his hand on my shoulder and sighs.

"I'm sorry," he whispers, his hand sliding off my shoulder as he disappears past my periphery.

Frowning, I step inside. The air is stagnant and rank from medicine and chemicals, and the gripping feeling of death chokes my lungs. I pull back the curtain they had closed around the room, slowly approach his bedside, and halt. Grandpa lays there peacefully, the tubes, needles, and medical sensors from the attempted resuscitation still stuck everywhere in his face and arms. He lays so still—forever resting in peace.

My eyes burn. I can't unsee this moment. Grandpa was the only man in my life who remotely resembled a father. He gave me tough love when my hard-headed ass needed it. And he still cared about me, despite all my fuckups.

And now, he's gone. *Forever.* Ripped from my life when I needed him the most.

I swallow a lump in my throat, trying to hold back the tears, but the feeling comes stronger than ever. The first tear falls, then another. Soon, I'm unable to control them. I collapse at his bedside and cover my face.

A gentle hand touches my shoulder, and I sniffle away more tears. Cassandra embraces me from behind and rests her head on the back of my shoulder. "I'm so sorry, Adam…"

But I don't hear her anymore. My body gets so numb, I can no longer feel her touch. The only thing I can feel is the hospital bed's cold metal railings that I clutch so tightly my knuckles whiten.

I remain at his bedside for a while, sobbing and angry. The more I ask myself '*why?*' the madder I get. I knew something was wrong with him before. I could see it. All the hand tremors, his so-called 'arthritis'—it was all bullshit. He had to have known something was wrong, too, but was too damn stubborn to get checked out. *I told him to go see a doctor... I told him! Damn it, why didn't he listen to me?*

I can't take the sight anymore, and finally lift up from the bedside and regain my composure. I muster the strength to turn away for the last time and leave the room. "Bye, Gramps. Sleep well…" I whisper when I reach the doorway.

I pass by the nurse's station as I make my way to the hospital's exit. The doctor and nurse stand by, watching me with solemn expressions.

"I'm very sorry again, Mister Anderson," the doctor says. "We're just going to need to get some information from you so we can move on to the next step."

I don't reply. I'm not in the mood to talk to anyone right now. *Why didn't he listen...*

Thankfully, Cassandra speaks in my stead, telling them whatever information they need to know. After we're done, we continue to the exit. I drag my feet through the parking garage where we left Sasha. I fumble for my keys in my back pocket and nearly drop them. Damn, I'm so uncoordinated right now.

Cassandra snatches the keys from me, and I start.

"I'll drive this time," she says, a stern look on her face.

I reach for the keys. "No, I'm fine. I got it. Besides, what about your car?"

Cassandra steps away from my reach. "It'll be just fine parked in this garage for a while. I can always come back here later and get it. Right now, I'm worried about you. You're in no condition to drive."

I open my mouth, about to protest further, but I'm suddenly struck with sheer mental exhaustion. She's right. I can't think straight, much less focus on the road. *I can't even grab my keys out of my pocket.* "Fine. Take care of her, please." I slide into the passenger's seat, and the feeling is incredibly strange. I don't think I've ever been Sasha's passenger.

Cassandra smiles reassuringly and hops in the driver's seat. "Trust me, I'll treat her with kid gloves." She starts up the engine. "Now relax. You don't need any more anxiety or stress."

I say nothing, and we drive off. I stare idly out the window at the passing buildings.

"Did you close the shop?" Cassandra asks, breaking the awkward silence that haunts the car's interior.

"Yeah. I wasn't sure how long it was going to take at the hospital. I'm sure there will be a lot of upset messages on the answering machine when we get back."

"Don't worry about the shop. It's not going anywhere." She sighs.

"Yeah," I whisper, not taking my eyes off the passing streaks of city buildings and cars. "I don't even know what to do…" My jumbled mind remembers that she might be pregnant, and I'm desperate to talk about anything else, even for just a moment. "Did you see the doctor today?"

She scowls. "I was going to, when this happened. Don't worry, I will go to the doctor as soon as I can. Right now, helping you is more important than wondering if I'm pregnant or not."

"They're both important," I retort.

She rolls her eyes. "It is, but your situation is much more immediate."

We return to the house. I fiddle with the lock and open the door, struggling against that same incoordination I dealt with before. I can still smell Grandpa's scent all over this place. I can't stay here anymore. Part of me won't feel right continuing to sleep here, knowing Grandpa is gone forever.

I move inside and collapse on the couch, hanging my head in my hands. Cassandra crouches in front me with a solemn expression on her face. "Hey. I know it's overwhelming and surreal, but the doctor said we need to get the ball rolling on some stuff. One step at a time, okay? Your grandfather has a will, right?"

"I think so. Probably. I'm sure it's somewhere in the house."

"Well, we need to find it. It will help us figure out what your grandpa wanted to happen when this… happened." She slowly slides her hands over mine and pulls them from my face. "Don't worry, Adam. You're not doing this alone. I'm here for you."

Cassandra and I spend all afternoon turning the place upside down trying to find that damn will. We finally locate it in a fireproof lockbox sitting on a high shelf in Grandpa's bedroom closet. Cassandra and I sit at the kitchen table and read through the neatly typewritten document.

The document was surprisingly short. Grandpa wanted to be cremated, but there was nothing here about what he wanted done with his ashes. Aside from business deals and the next car competition, the only goals Grandpa had ever mentioned to me was getting to the Techno Classica in Essen, Germany, before he died. Maybe I could make sure he gets there, even if he was showing up a little late. He was giving the business and this house to me and leaving $600,000 to Elouise and my nephews. The rest was to be donated to several charities he had listed. That's it. Neither Grandma, nor Michael, are mentioned anywhere on the will. Grandpa left them nothing.

Cassandra takes the paper. "I'll take care of the cremation arrangements and get in touch with your grandpa's lawyer. Why don't you inform your family?"

I purse my lips. *What family?* "You mean my brother and sister-in-law?"

"And your grandmother? She's still alive, isn't she?"

"Honestly? I haven't talked to her since I left New York City, and I have no idea if she's alive or dead, or if she's even still living in the same place. I don't even think I know her phone number. It doesn't seem like he left anything for her in the will, anyways."

"Even so, you should try to contact her, at least. And definitely let your brother and sister-in-law know." She places her hand over mine and rubs it reassuringly. "I'll take care of the rest." She gets up from the table and heads into our bedroom.

Alone at the kitchen table, I listen to the deathly silence enveloping me. Thank God, Cassandra is here to help me keep my head on straight. After taking a long, slow, deep breath, I stand and approach the wall phone in the kitchen. My hand trembles as I reach for the receiver. It's only right that I tell my family, but what do I say? I'd give anything not to have to make this call.

My mind begins swarming with thoughts again—sadness and anger for my grandfather, fear and nervousness at this phone call. *My nephews will never meet him, never know what type of man he was...* I finally muster the courage to pick up the receiver. It was time to tell Michael. He had no love for Grandpa, and how he reacted might be like throwing gasoline on my emotional fire.

I punch in his number.

"Hello?" Elouise greets.

I exhale at the sound of her sweet, gentle voice. "H-hey, Elouise… is my brother around?"

"No, he went out to get some more boxes for the big move. Is everything okay?"

I swallow again. "No…" I tell her everything.

"Oh, Lord…" Elouise whispers when I finish. "I'm so sorry, Adam. Oh, Lord, I'm so sorry."

"It's one of those things," I say with a sigh. "I guess it was his time to go."

"Have you already made funeral arrangements?"

"No, his will stated that he wanted to be cremated, I don't think he wanted a lavish funeral or anything."

"I see."

I play with the cord of the phone. "Hey, I'm sorry for dropping this news on you like this."

She sighs. "The boys never got to meet their grandfather. Do you want me to tell Michael when he gets back?"

"No, I need to tell him this myself."

"We were going to be heading to Renton in two weeks. Michael is so excited about it. The last thing he needs is bad news, but… he needs to know."

I let out a deep sigh. "Yeah."

We talk a little longer about the upcoming move, trying to lighten the mood a bit, before ending the call. I search through Grandpa's odds and ends in the kitchen junk drawer, trying to find Grandma's number, but I don't find anything. He might have it in the Rolodex at the shop but checking that would have to wait.

Maybe Michael knows about her whereabouts. He was her favorite grandson, after all. I'll leave it up to him to call her. There's no telling when my brother would get around to calling back, so I return to the couch and collapse, all the emotions of the day still wreaking havoc in my mind. *Goodbye, Grandpa.*

By the next day, my physical exhaustion finally catches up with my mental state like two bulls colliding. My mental energy is spent, as if I'd run a marathon. Cassandra had gone out early to finish dealing with the cremation stuff, while I headed downtown to the shop. I keep the shop closed for the rest of the day while I get things in order. I make phone calls to the current clients, explaining the situation. Thankfully, they all understand, and are still willing to do business, which hopefully means that the shop won't take a hard financial hit. As I hang up the phone with the last customer, I look around at the eerily quiet office. I'm sitting in Grandpa's chair. This business—his legacy—is suddenly mine. I soak in that terrifying thought for a while, and then return to the house and go through some more of Grandpa's things—legal documents, sentimental items, and more.

Cassandra still hasn't returned from her errands. I don't know where I'd be right now without her. She'd stepped up when I'd buckled. She really is the perfect woman I need in my life.

She has to be—she could be carrying a child—*my* child.

I'm too rattled to think about the possibilities. I finally take a break and plop down on the couch. I have no idea what time it is, nor do I care. Time has felt like it's passing in a blur these last two days. I rub my temples and wish I can finally get off this emotional rollercoaster. I shut my eyes a moment, then the phone rings. Groaning, I slide off the couch and answer the phone in the kitchen.

"Hello?" I mutter.

"Hey," my brother replies in a cold tone.

I perk up. "Michael? Jesus Christ. It's about time you called."

"Been busy getting ready for the move. What's up?"

I let out a deep sigh, grateful that Elouise respected my wishes and didn't tell him anything about Grandpa's death. For the next several minutes, I spill the whole story to Michael. When I'm done, I'm met with silence on the other end.

Did he hang up? "Hello?"

"I'm still here," Michael says after another long delay. "Did he leave a will?"

Really? That's the first thing on his mind? He sure didn't sound too upset about the news. My skin prickles. "Yeah…"

"And?"

"Six hundred grand to Elouise and the kids."

Another beat of silence. "Six hundred grand? Holy fuck, the old man was loaded."

"It's for her and the kids," I reiterate. "Not you."

He growls on the other end. "Of course not… The old bastard would leave me out of all that money. Fuck him."

I clench my jaw. "Watch your mouth."

"Why? He never gave a shit about me. I'm glad my boys never got to meet that son of a bitch."

I rub my temples, unsure of how to answer him. I knew this would be how he'd take the news, and even still my blood pressure's rising. *Fucking unbelievable.* I take a deep breath, and exhale, trying to calm myself down. I don't want to dig up old bones of the past, nor do I have the energy to do so. I desperately try to change the subject. "You guys still moving out here next month?"

"Yeah. Can't wait to start this new job. Being stuck at home sucks. I need to work."

"Yeah, I feel you."

"So, now that the old man's gone, what about his business?"

I pause. "He gave it to me."

He snorts. "You're selling it, right?"

I'm not sure exactly how much the business is worth, but I'm sure it's not chump change, either. Grandpa put his blood, sweat, and tears into it, and he put his faith in keeping it with the family in me. I'm still not sure I can do it, but I owed it to him to at least try. I couldn't think of selling it. "No, I don't think so."

"What? You're gonna run it? You're not a businessman."

"And you are?" I snap back. "You would've rather him give it to you? This shop was Grandpa's baby. Why the hell would he give it to someone like you?"

He growled. "You know what, fuck this. He's gone. I don't want talk about him or his shit anymore."

"Right. Then I guess that's that."

We end the call, and I can't get my mind off it. *Just like I expected.* How much shitter could this day get?

The phone rings again. *Damn karma.* "Hello?"

"Adam…" Cassandra's voice is solemn.

"Hey, what's up? You get everything taken care of?"

"Yeah… and I stopped by the doctor's office too." She pauses again. "I'm pregnant."

The whole world continues to crash down on me like a raging waterfall. Today has been utter shit, and I feel alone and helpless. I haven't felt like this since I was a young thug back in New York City.

But Grandpa had trusted me. *Only me.* I have to do right by him no matter what. All the times he'd encouraged me to be a better man, I blew him off—he saw more in me than I saw in myself. I'd give anything to have those days back with him again.

My eyes burn as I sort through endless boxes of his belongings. I'm not sure what to do with half of this shit. Sell it, I guess? Michael certainly wouldn't appreciate it. *Grandpa sure had a lot of old model cars.* Maybe I'll give some of this stuff to the boys. The technical manuals might come in handy when they were older.

I hear the front door open, but I don't stop my work. Cassandra enters, a guilty look on her face. I look sideways at her and swallow a lump in my throat. "So, you're pregnant, huh…"

She chews her bottom lip. "Yeah…"

I exhale through my nose. "Right now, I need to focus on one thing at a time."

"Yeah… Yeah, of course." She approaches and looks around at all the boxes, and the mountains of old papers and clothing. "Wow, you got a lot done today, I see."

"Most of it's junk. I don't think I'd even be able to donate it, and the little family I know about probably wouldn't appreciate much of this." Grandpa was a simple man and didn't need a lot to make him happy. After he'd divorced Grandma, he'd never remarried. Most of this stuff is old photos, and odds and ends that only someone like Grandpa would collect—model cars, odd technical books, and other things that I know the rest of the family wouldn't care for.

Cassandra pores over some of the sentimental items and smiles. "You should keep the pictures, at least. Sometimes it's good to have some positive memories to keep you going, y'know?"

"Yeah, I guess…"

She holds up a picture of me and Michael as kids. We were probably no older than three in that photo. "At least you still have family photos," she says solemnly. "I've got nothing."

I frown at the picture, remembering when and where it was taken. Grandma and Grandpa took us to Coney Island that day, and we had the time of our lives.

"Is this you?" She points to the kid on the left.

"Yeah, how did you know?"

She chuckles. "I figured you were always the taller one."

I crack a smile. "Yeah… Michael always gave me shit about that. Okay, we'll keep the pictures, and maybe some of these models and books for my nephews. We'll get rid of the rest." As much as I hate the thought of holding onto old memories, perhaps Cassandra was right that I needed some small nuggets of positive memories to help me through this endless nightmare.

CHAPTER 27

It's been two months since Grandpa's death. I'd gotten the business back up and running again, and, with the help of Grandpa's lawyer and accountant, we'd gotten everything in the will sorted out. As it turned out, Elouise and the kids wouldn't be getting any of that six hundred grand—at least not yet. Apparently, Grandpa was tied up in some litigation with a disgruntled customer, and the money was locked down until the case was settled. Most of it would have to go to legal fees.

Cassandra's pregnancy was starting to get a little obvious, and I still hadn't figured out what I was going to do— whether I could handle this parenting job. I was definitely the father, according to the paternity test, but those fatherly instincts still hadn't kicked in. Would they ever?

My brother and his family had finally made the big move to Renton. I'd wanted to see them as soon as they got to

Washington, but at the time, I was still dealing with the legal mess the business was in and Grandpa's will. Besides that, Michael had preferred I'd wait until they had gotten settled and situated in their new place. I'd understood and respected his wishes. I took that time to get my head right.

My thoughts return to the present as I work on an engine rebuild in the shop bay. The head-bobbing music of Public Enemy plays from the boombox on the shelf, next to the picture of Michael and I at Coney Island, along with a few others from Grandpa's stash. From the corner of my eye, I spot movement in the main office. Cassandra takes a handful of envelopes from an unseen person and smiles. Last month, she'd quit her job at Out the Box and started working full-time at the shop as a bookkeeper, and sometimes helped me with difficult rebuilds on some of the customers' cars. It's nice to have her around more. She was still determined to land her dream job at Q&R, though.

I finish tightening the bolts on a piston rod and return my wrench to the toolbox, then wipe a layer of sweat from my brow. I've been working nonstop all morning, and it was time for a break. I enter the office just as the front door closes behind the mailman walking away. I scan the small pile of envelopes on the desk, casually sorting through them and tossing away the junk mail while sticking the important-looking ones in the plastic mail tray with the others we had yet to get to. I smile at Cassandra, who sits in Grandpa's big desk chair. She tears open an envelope and pulls out a folded piece of paper. As she reads the paper, her eyes widen, and her mouth slowly drops open. When she finishes, she sets the paper down and looks at me, her face pale.

"What?" I furrow my brow.

"It's from Q&R Headquarters. They want me to come in for an interview next Tuesday."

"No shit? That's awesome, Cass! I'm so happy for you. You got this interview in the bag!"

Her smile grows, and she leans over and plants a kiss on my lips. "Thank you."

I close my eyes and savor her kiss. I could never get enough of her taste. I break the kiss briefly and whisper, "I love you."

She exhales slowly and kisses me again, deeper.

While we're busy making out, the phone suddenly rings. I blindly reach over and pick it up and, after giving Cassandra one last deep kiss, I reluctantly pull away. "Anderson Antique Auto. Adam speaking," I say stiffly into the phone.

"Adam, it's Elouise."

I deflate with a smile. "Hey, Elouise. How are you doing?" I look at Cassandra, giving her a silent message that this is an important call.

Taking the hint, Cassandra kisses my cheek and leaves the office, heading into the garage. She examines my current engine project on the workbench.

"We're good," Elouise replies. "Still getting settled. The boys are adjusting well to their new life here too."

"Yeah? That's good," I say.

She chuckles. "They like that we have an actual backyard of our own—they spend most of their time out there roughhousing."

I twirl the telephone cord between my fingers while I keep my eyes on Cassandra.

She picks up a wrench from the toolbox and starts assembling one of the other pistons.

Wow, she knows exactly where I left off. What a woman, I muse. "So, when is my brother going to finally let me come over and see them?" I ask Elouise.

"Well, that's why I'm calling. Michael starts work next Monday, and he was thinking that maybe you can come visit this Saturday. We'll have the house in order by then too. And he wanted to take the boys to see the Space Needle and Pike Place Market. Maybe you could join us?"

I grin. "Saturday's perfect. We can see all those places and more. We'll make it a family outing."

"Yes! I'm hoping it can be. I know the boys will be really excited to finally meet their uncle Adam."

My heart swells with excitement. I can't believe this is actually going to happen—I wasn't sure when I was ever going to get to meet my nephews. "I'll make sure we make the most of every moment." *A family outing...* My gaze drifts to Cassandra working in the garage.

There's a brief pause. "Adam... I, um... I also called to say thank you."

The seriousness in Elouise's voice forces me to break my stare at Cassandra's beautiful ass moving and shaking to whatever new song is playing out there. I straighten in my chair. "For what?"

"Helping Michael get that job has saved our family in more ways than you know. I didn't think we were going to make it after Michael lost his job."

I swallow a lump in my throat. "I did it for you and the kids."

She sighs deeply. "I wish you two would finally come to terms with things."

"You and the kids don't need to be victims of our issues."

"You two are family—brothers. I know you've both have had it rough, but you don't have to let your pasts define your future."

I flare my nostrils. "Have you told Michael that?"

"Yeah…"

"And?"

There's a moment of silence. "It… didn't go well."

"What do you mean by that?"

"I don't want to talk about it…"

I stiffen. "What did he do?"

"Nothing. He did… *nothing*. That's the problem. He wouldn't listen to me."

"Okay." I exhale. "That's pretty much him a nutshell. He doesn't listen." *Why the fuck did you marry him?*

"I'm praying one day he'll come around. You too."

I pause. "Look, I'll make sure Saturday will be the best family outing ever. No fighting, no arguing. Just good, genuine family fun, okay?"

"I'd like that." Her voice sounds cheerier. Hopeful.

As we hang up, I think about her words and wonder if perhaps this family gathering just might be what Michael and I need to mend this rift. Maybe seeing each other face-to-face will have a different outcome than arguing on the phone when we were thousands of miles apart.

I return to the garage. Cassandra is completely engrossed in the stripped-out engine, so I come up from behind and wrap my arms around her. My hands touch the faint bump of her belly, and I'm reminded once more about my other dilemma. I shove those thoughts aside for now and kiss the back of Cassandra's neck. "Like what you see?"

She shivers from my touch. "Yeah. You're doing a good job with this so far." She sets down the wench and looks over her shoulder at me. "Elouise okay?"

"Yeah, she's good. Michael's finally gonna let me to see my nephews this Saturday. Wanna come?"

She spins and faces me. "Why is that even a question? Of course I want to come, you fool."

I look at her skeptically. "I don't want you caught up in our baggage, is all. I'm gonna try and make the best of it. Avoid the drama with Michael and all that, but ...."

"I've been through hell and back, Adam. I can handle baggage. I want to meet your family. I want to be with you no matter what." She moistens her lips. "I love you."

I shiver as her words resonate through my soul. I cup my hands around her cheeks. "I love you too." I lean in and plant a deep, passionate kiss onto her lips.

The Saturday-morning drive up to Renton is quiet. My nerves are shot from the anticipation of finally meeting the rest of my family.

Will my nephews accept me? What am I going to say to Michael? How will Elouise handle this?

I grip the steering wheel and punch it down the interstate, letting Sasha stretch her wings. The landscape passes by in a blur, but I keep my eyes sharp for hidden cops. The speed and the smell of exhaust sends me into a relaxing trance.

"You miss it, don't you?" Cassandra asks from the passenger's seat.

I blink out of the trance as I process her question. I smile. "Sometimes. But I know Jacob's holding things down."

"We should see him again sometime."

I arch an eyebrow at her. "Why?"

"For old times' sake."

I snort. "I'm sure he's doing just fine."

She eyes me coyly. "Aren't you the least bit curious?"

"Nope." *Okay, maybe a little.* Honestly, I'd lost touch with the racing scene and all the old crews after Jacob's win. I've been so wrapped up in Grandpa's business, and life in general.

I shift my gaze at Cassandra's belly. *And the new life growing inside her.*

"Why do you even care about what Jacob's doing, anyway?" I continue. "He'll probably just freak out when he finds out I knocked you up."

Her lips purse. "Yeah. And when are we going to talk about that?"

I exhale a deep sigh. "I don't know…"

She pokes her faint, little bump. "This isn't going to get any smaller…"

"I know." I look sideways at her and can't hide my scowl. She drops the subject, and we drive the rest of the way in silence.

Elouise's directions to the house are pretty straightforward. Ten minutes after hopping off the interstate, we enter a small neighborhood. Toward the bottom of a steep hill, I spot a little blue house with a dark-green, wood-panel-trimmed station wagon parked in the driveway.

"This it?" Cassandra asks, peering out the passenger's window as I park Sasha along the curb.

"Yeah."

"It's beautiful."

"Yeah, that son of a bitch scored big with this house."

We get out of the car and walk a narrow-pebbled walkway that leads up to the shallow steps of the front porch. The ground looks pretty bare—devoid of vegetation except for patchy grass—and could use some good landscaping.

I approach the front door and ring the bell. I can hear the faint pattering of small feet, and children's voices. Then a set of heavy footsteps thump closer. I suck in a breath.

The door opens, and Michael looks back at me with a surprised expression. We were teenagers when we'd last seen each other in person. He's grown into an attractive, clean-cut man. *I'm still taller than him, though.* Despite all the hard labor he does for a living, he has a lean build and a rugged—yet attractive—kind of face that chicks tend to dig. I guess

Elouise had gotten caught up in his good looks and ended up marrying him. It certainly couldn't have been his charm.

"Damn," Michael says, shaking his head slowly as he looks me up and down. "You haven't changed a bit, man."

"Neither have you." I grin. I really want things to work out between us, but my cynical side is already counting the seconds until we start arguing again. "It's… good to see you again."

He pauses. "You too." His gaze swivels to Cassandra.

"Hi, I'm Adam's girlfriend, Cassandra," she says politely, sticking out her hand.

He shakes her hand and raises his eyebrows at me. "Girl-friend, huh?"

I frown at his tone. "Yeah, that's right." I wrap my arm around her waist.

Michael snorts a laugh. "Damn, didn't think you of all people would finally slow down."

I force a smile. "Well, you know. Times change. *People* change."

"Yeah. People… settle." He glances at Cassandra as he says this, then opens the door for us. "Come in."

I catch a whiff of fresh paint as we enter the cozy home. The place is well-furnished in a cedar theme. A plush, dark-blue couch overlooks the large entertainment center set against the living room wall. The TV is on and tuned to some silly cartoon. A six-seater dining table is set next to a kitchen with some state-of-the-art-looking appliances.

"Wow, you did good, man. This is nice," I say, admiring the rest of the place.

"Thanks. I got a good deal on it," Michael says. "A lot of stuff in here was recently renovated, like the kitchen, and one of the bathrooms."

Elouise walks out from one of the back rooms, wearing a white blouse tucked in a pair of white, high-waisted jeans. She still looks as beautiful as I remembered. It's been years, and yet it seems like she hasn't aged a bit. She spots me and her face lights up, full of life.

"Adam!" She rushes to me with open arms, and I hug her tight.

I spot Michael in my periphery, who watches us coldly, and I slowly pull back from the embrace. I look Elouise up and down and grin. "Look at you. I can't believe it."

"It's been way too long." She smiles, and then nods to Cassandra. "Hello. I'm Elouise."

"Cassandra." She nods back.

"She's his girlfriend, can you believe it?" Michael says jokingly, and then disappears down a hall.

His tone crawls under my skin again.

Elouise claps her hands together and looks at me warmly. "Yeah, I *can* believe it," she says in a quiet voice, which I assume is meant for my ears. She nods to Cassandra. "You're a very lucky woman, Cassandra."

Cassandra links her arm in mine. "He's a'ight," she says in a joking tone.

I chuckle and nudge her with my shoulder.

Michael returns from down the hall, this time with two little boys. The older looking one wears a white tank top, denim shorts, and a pair of thick, horn-rimmed glasses, and couldn't be more than five. The younger-looking boy wears a pair of shorts and a T-shirt that says '#1 All Star' on the front. Clutched under one arm is a plush toy basketball.

The boys tilt their heads back, staring up at us adults curiously.

"Kevin, Junior—this is your uncle Adam," Elouise says to the boys. "Say hi."

Junior looks up at me and pushes his glasses up the bridge of his nose. He gapes. "Whoa! Uncle Adam's a giant!"

We all laugh, except my brother, who disappears down the same hallway again.

I kneel before the boys and extend my arms. "Is this better?"

Kevin and Junior grin and nod.

"Good. Now can I get a hug?"

Junior runs to my arms first, crashing into me hard.

"Oof!" The wind is almost knocked unexpectedly out of me.

Kevin follows and I embrace them both. Then I stand, carrying them up with me. The boys laugh and hold onto me tight.

"Whoa!" Kevin says. He clutches his basketball tightly under his arm.

Laughing, I turn to Cassandra with the two boys clinging onto me. "What do you think?"

"Your nephews are absolutely adorable," she says, laughing as well.

"You forgot one more," My brother says, returning to us carrying a younger, disgruntled-looking boy in his arms. "This is Dominick."

I look over to the boy, who wears a scowl. "Hey, Mr. Grumpypants," I say, smiling.

Dominick turns his head away and doesn't respond.

I kneel and set Kevin and Junior down. "What's up with your brother?" I ask them, but all they do is shrug.

"He's mad 'cause he can't play with his cars right now." My brother replies, handing Dominick off to me as I stand up. "This is your uncle Adam," he says to the boy. "You be nice."

"He's *always* grumpy when he can't play with his cars," Junior says.

"Oh yeah?" I say, holding Dominick in my arms. "Well maybe he won't be so grumpy today when we go to the big Space Needle. Maybe get some pizza afterward, eh?"

Dominick's eyes light up at the sound of that.

"Pizza!" Kevin and Junior say in unison, looking up at their brother and me.

Dominick wraps his little arms around my neck and gives me a hug. Just holding my nephews for the first time has sparked a strange feeling inside. Warm and happy. Calm.

Cassandra leans over my shoulder and admires Dominick. "He's precious," she whispers.

I smile. "Yeah." It's then I realize it's the first time I'm holding a kid like this. The first time I've had a kid cling to me—a stranger, a hoodlum, someone that no parent would want their kid to be around.

I look sideways at Cassandra, and my gaze drift down to her faint belly. Maybe being a dad wouldn't be so bad. Maybe everything will be all right. Maybe I *can* do this. I can't keep leaving Cassandra hanging and run away from this responsibility anymore. And I'll be damned if I ever become like the deadbeat father I barely knew.

The six of us pile into the station wagon, and my brother drives the thirty-minute trip up to Downtown Seattle. Excitement had overtaken the stress of all the possible family drama. The boys squirmed around in their seats restlessly, and I was eager to make the most out of today. I'd gone through hell these past few months, and I could use an emotional break.

Cassandra and I are in the backseat with Dominick, who's strapped in his car seat, while Kevin and Junior took the cargo seat. We're only five minutes into the trip when Dominick has already nodded off to sleep.

Despite the many times I'd been to Seattle, I'd never once visited the Space Needle, nor spent any time exploring Pike Place, so everything about this trip will be new to me. For Cassandra, on the other hand, this would be a homecoming.

"Uncle Adam! Look!" Kevin exclaims. He plasters his face against the side window and ogles the giant body of water that surrounds us as we drive across the Hadley Memorial Bridge.

I laugh and rest my arm on the back of the seat. "Careful, kid, you might fall in." I ruffle Kevin's hair, and the smile he gives me warms my heart in a way I hadn't ever felt before.

I glance at the rearview mirror and meet my brother's cold gaze.

He breaks the stare and returns his focus on the road.

"It's like riding on the George Washington Bridge," Junior says.

"Yeah, but this one's longer." Cassandra says with a chuckle. "And newer too. It was just built two years ago."

A 'Wow!' and 'Cool!' come from Kevin and Junior in unison. It sure doesn't take much to amaze them.

As I watch the two of them laugh, chatter, and try to get my attention for every little thing we pass, a small part of me swells with emotion. Those two were really close, just like Michael and I were once upon a time. As much as I wish I could see those days again, I know they'll likely never come back.

In roughly seven hours, we'd scoured much of Downtown Seattle, including visiting Pike Place, which Elouise found fascinating. The boys had a blast during the educational trip at the city center, where we'd spent much of the afternoon visiting the Children's Museum and Theatre, the Pacific Science Center, and lastly, the Space Needle.

We gather in the observation deck and admire the breathtaking view of city, as well as the surrounding Elliot Bay and

Lake Union. Staring down at the world below, it was easy to think about all the crazy shit that has gone on in my life. For all the pain I'd endured, I'd still managed to rise above it. And yet, there was so much further to go.

I snap a few photos of the view with my disposable camera that I'd picked up at Pike Place. It's time to make some new memories.

"Pretty, isn't it?" Cassandra says, wrapping her arm around my waist.

I smile. "Yeah. It's a different kind of vibe than New York City, but still pretty damn breathtaking."

She looks at me, her expression curious, yet mischievous. "I see that look in your eye. You've had that look all day today."

"What look?"

"You're thinking about something…" She sinks her teeth into her bottom lip, takes my hand and brings it to her midsection. "Considering something."

My fingers gently press against her, and I feel the back of my throat tighten. "I might've been thinking about it…" I mutter.

"And?" She takes both of my hands and spins me around to face her.

I stare into her eyes a moment, then swivel my gaze back to the observation window and sigh.

"I see the way you talk to your nephews. The way they cling to you," Cassandra continues. "They've only just met you today, and they already trust and look up to you like you're their superhero. It's hard to gain a kid's trust like that."

I blow a raspberry. "They only like me because we're family."

"You know that's bullshit."

I exhale a soft chuckle, then return my gaze to her. "Okay, they make me smile. I *might* be willing to give this dad thing a shot."

"I think you'll be a great father." She leans in and plants a soft kiss on my cheek.

My heart swells at her declaration.

"Whish! Whoom! I will destroy you both, and this tower will be mine!" Junior suddenly cries out.

I look over my shoulder just in time to see Junior chasing Kevin and Dominick around the observation deck.

"Quick, Mega-Morph D! Blast him with your Ultra Freeze Ray! I'll use my super speed!" Kevin says to Dominick.

I grin. They sure have a vivid imagination.

After taking a bunch of family pictures, we finally leave the Seattle Center, pile back into the station wagon, and drive around looking for a good place to eat. Cassandra suggests the University District, which has tons of eateries, so we head there.

"Mmm… University of Washington," Elouise mutters, reading a passing sign. "The campus looks beautiful." She turns and looks in the backseat. "That looks like a nice college campus you three could go to one day."

Kevin scrunches his nose. "I don't wanna go to college."

"Hey, you can do a lot of cool things if you go to college," I say.

Michael snorts and mutters under his breath, "As if your sorry ass would know…"

I glare at my brother, the urge to respond on the tip of my tongue, but I'm not about to lose my shit in front of the boys like that. *This is supposed to be a peaceful family outing,* I remind myself. Ignoring my brother, I ask Kevin, "Don't you want to be a doctor when you grow up?"

Kevin shakes his head. "Nope."

"Lawyer?"

"Nah."

"Okay. What *do* you wanna be?"

He looks thoughtful for a moment, and then his face lights up. "Fresco Davis!"

I arch an eyebrow. "Who, or what, is that?"

"He's a professional basketball player," Michael interjects. "Just a rookie, but he's Chicago's latest sensation. All the kids love him."

"Huh. Well, I never played basketball, but I *was* on the Freshman wrestling team back in high school," I shrug at Kevin.

"Yeah, until you decided to drop out," Michael mutters again under his breath, a cynical smirk hinting his lips.

I scowl. *Asshole.* Was he really starting this shit now with all these little jabs? I start to open my mouth—I guess the boys will have to see the ugly side of their uncle Adam now.

"By the way, Kevin," Michael continues before I have a chance to retort, "Fresco went to college first before he got picked up by the pro league, so remember that."

Kevin pouts.

I rub the top of Kevin's head, trying my best to ignore my brother's snarky comments. I told Elouise this would be a peaceful family trip, and I intended to keep it that way. "You can be anything you want to be, kid."

We park in an empty space along the curb and unload. The district is filled with shops and eateries on both sides of the street. Endless choices here, it seems. As we walk around and explore, trying to decide where to eat, I suddenly get a whiff of pizza nearby. I inhale and smile. That smell doesn't come from just any kind of pizza. *Fresh, brick-oven-baked bread.* I hadn't smelled anything that authentic since I'd left New York.

"Mmm… Let's get pizza," I announce.

"Pizza!" my nephews yell in unison.

I follow my nose and point across the street to a rustic green building with a lighted red-white-and-green pizza sign. Attached to the red-and-white awning is a sign that reads 'Loriano's Pizza.' Even the building's exterior sparks one of very few pleasant memories of my childhood back in New York. "Let's go there," I say.

Michael follows my gaze, sniffs once, and a small smile hints on his lips. "Oh man…"

I almost have to do a double take. *Holy shit, he's actually smiling?* It's amazing what smells can do to people—or maybe authentic, New-York-style pizza really is just that incredible. I decide to take this rare moment and run with it. "Remember when Grandma used to take us down to that pizza joint in the South Bronx on 152nd street?"

He chuckles. "Hell yeah, that pizza was the shit."

I check for traffic, and then we head across the street. I sweep my gaze left, and then right again, when a face in the crowd catches my attention. He looks familiar, but I can't place him. He walks alongside another man, talking energetically with a sour look on his face. *Where have I seen him? The crowd in front of them parts a bit, and I can see the familiar face's outfit—jeans and a white t-shirt, covered by a red puffy vest. A red bandana hangs and sways from his back pocket. One of the Red Raven punks from the night Jacob won the drift race. Un-fucking-believable.* I lower my head and quicken my pace toward Loriano's. *Please, God, don't let them recognize me. Not here. Not with my family.*

I open the door and try to herd the group in, feigning excitement at the chance for some authentic pizza. The strong, authentic aroma billows out, teasing my frazzled senses. Michael walks in first, and Elouise follows. She glances at me and smiles. I can almost hear her silent thoughts. She's probably amazed—and relieved—at my brother's good mood, also. I fake a smile back for her. *If only they knew what else was going on.*

The rest of group shuffles in, and I wait behind them as they decide where we'll sit. For now, it looks like we have the entire restaurant to ourselves. I try to casually keep my eye on the glass door behind us, waiting. The group decides to claim a large, six-seater table in the back, and heads that direction—just as the guy in the red puffy jacket passes by the storefront in my periphery. *Thank God.* I exhale with relief and run my hand over my face. *That was too much.*

Michael goes to the counter to order, while Elouise and Cassandra head to the ladies' room. That leaves me with temporary babysitting duty over the boys, who playfully poke at each other and laugh while I catch my breath. I smile at the small snippets of bittersweet memories of Michael and me when we were their age that are now overshadowing that almost-run-in with the punk outside. If only things had turned out differently, maybe I wouldn't have been a high-school dropout, turned street thug.

Michael returns with an armful of soda cans, and I help him dispense them around the table.

"Need some help with the food?" I ask, but he turns his back on me and returns to the counter.

I frown. Looks like he's moody again. *Well, that little bit of happiness didn't last long.* I think about our entire family day so far. The women and kids have been nothing short of excited, but Michael seems stuck in his own world.

Then, it hits me. *Of course.* Michael must be regretting this whole outing. The two of us were never that close. The handful of times we'd smiled and laughed had usually been short-lived. Sometimes I wonder if Michael wanted to do this in order to get some of his own childhood back. Maybe he thought if we all had fun today as a family, he could get some of those fond memories back.

I wish I can help him. I wish I can help *us*.

My thoughts return to the present, to my three nephews. Junior deliberately chugs about half his soda, then lets out a loud, obnoxious belch. Dominick and Kevin giggle hysterically.

"Damn!" I say, amazed that such a monstrous sound could come from a scrawny boy.

Junior beams proudly. "Betcha can't beat that, Unc," he says.

"Oh yeah?" I pop the top of my soda, about to show him how it's done, when I spot Elouise and Cassandra walk out of the bathroom. "Uh-oh. Here comes trouble," I mutter jokingly to the boys, making a small head gesture.

The kids go into another snicker-and-giggle fit.

"Well, aren't you all in a happy mood," Elouise says.

"Always." I hop up and pull out the two women's chairs, and they seat themselves. My brother returns with a massive pizza pie, and we all dig in. It's amazing having all of us here together as a family. I never thought I'd ever see something like this.

It's almost six o'clock in the evening when we're finally back on the road to Renton. All three of my nephews are conked out, exhausted after a long day. I smile, watching them sleep peacefully. For the first time in a long time, I actually feel happy to be around my flesh and blood.

CHAPTER 28

THE MONTHS FLY BY, AND I FEEL LIKE I'VE FINALLY GOTTEN settled into this new life as a businessman, uncle, and future father. Cassandra is very pregnant now—as in she is due in a couple of weeks. She'd insisted that we keep the baby's gender a surprise, but I didn't see what the big deal was. I would love our new son or daughter all the same.

Ever since Cassandra had accepted motherhood, she's exuded an aura of femininity that I never knew existed in her. And yet, she's still that no-nonsense, spunky gearhead who had stolen my heart last year. She doesn't let that big belly stop her, either. Not only has she been working part-time as a Marketing Assistant at Q&R Corporate over in Kent, but on nights and weekends, she helps me rebuild engines and keeps up with the books at Anderson Antique Auto.

As much as I try to make her take it easy in her condition, she doesn't want to hear it. She's the hardest working woman

I've ever met. And I never knew in a million years that this rough-and-tumble girl from the streets would have embraced parenthood as well as she has.

As for me, I've accepted my role as a father, but I'm still not as sure as she seems to be that I'll be a good parent.

Things have been surprisingly peaceful between Michael and me. Ever since that first family outing to Seattle, Michael seems to be a changed man. Maybe he's finally come around and accepted the fact that he couldn't get his childhood back. Or maybe he was just happy about his new masonry job. Whatever the reason, I can't complain. I'd gotten a chance to bond with my nephews more, and it was great to see Elouise's bright smile every time I came to visit. I'm sure she was over the moon that Michael and I had somehow managed to bury the hatchet—at least for now.

Anderson Antique Auto has been thriving too. There's been a surge of new clients, and it's been tough keeping up. I'd finally decided that I needed to hire help, as much as I didn't want to. After all, Grandpa ran this shop all on his own, and I wanted to continue his legacy—but I knew my limits. Between keeping up with office paperwork and the endless restoration jobs, it was getting overwhelming. So, just last month, I'd stuck a 'Help Wanted' sign out on the shop's front window. I was naïve to think that I would get a surge of job applications. Restoring antique cars was a bit of a learned skill, and I wasn't going to hire just anyone.

Now I know why I was Grandpa's only employee.

With all my attention on the business and family, I'd lost touch with the racing scene. It's been ages since I've seen the old crews, and I was especially glad that I hadn't run into the Red Ravens again. It's been peaceful, and relieving, that I didn't have to keep looking over my shoulder all the time for those Red Raven punks like I'd once did. Jacob must've still been holding the turf down, and for that, I was glad.

I roll out from under a baby-blue '57 Bel Air after spending half the day replacing the exhaust and shocks and wipe my oil-and-dirt-smeared hands on a towel. I swipe up my can of root beer from the tool bench, and as I guzzle what's left, I hear the little bell jingle on the front door. I glance toward the office through the open side door at the mailman, who drops off several envelopes on the front desk. He looks my way, waves, and leaves. I head into the office and can't help but sigh at the mess. The desk is covered with unfinished ledgers, unopened mail, and more. Cassandra did what she could when she was here, but it's become more and more obvious that I need a new full-time bookkeeper.

I do a quick sort of today's mail, and then return to the garage bay to finish my work. The Bel-Air needs to be out the door by the end of the day.

As I reach for my torque wrench, the bell on the front door jingles again. I sigh. *Another customer. I'll never get all this work done before six o'clock.* Tossing the wrench back onto the tool bench, I walk back into the office and plaster on a polite smile.

"Good afternoon. How can I help—" I halt in my tracks and gaze upon the last person I'd expected to see.

"Whoa, Adam?" Luke slides his sunglasses up on his head and looks at me wide-eyed.

My jaw drops. It's been over a year since I'd last seen him. He has a few new more tattoos on his forearms and around the sides of his neck, but the faint smears of pink and blue aerosol paint on his hands means that he still hasn't given up his graffiti obsession. He still looks like the same grungy, metalhead skater I remembered.

"Holy fucking shit. Luke?" I say breathlessly. Seeing my old friend makes my eyes burn, in a strange mix of happiness and cutting memories of that fateful night when the fire at the Shed tore us apart.

Luke quirks a crooked smile. "Damn, what's up, man? I didn't know you were still here."

"I never left." We do our special handshake that the crew used to do. It's bittersweet. "What are you doing here? I thought you left Tacoma."

He frowns slightly. "I did, but things didn't work out, so I came back…"

"What are you doing now?"

He shrugs. "Eh… Got tired of the squatter life, so I'm looking to make a li'l cash so I can get myself a decent pad. Y'know, boring adult stuff."

"Not racing anymore?"

"Had to sell the truck for some extra cash, so no."

"Damn…"

"Yeah… I miss racing, though."

I nod. Sometimes I still miss it too. As much as I'd tried to convince myself that I was over the racing game, that itch sometimes came. But thankfully, for my sanity' sake, I had too much work to deal with at the shop to seek to satisfy that urge.

Luke looks around. "You the only one working here today? Where's Gramps?"

"Yeah, just me today. And uhh… he passed away. I took over the shop."

His eyes widen. "Whoa, when did that happen?"

"Not long after the fire…"

"Holy shit. I'm sorry, man." He scowls, his eyes turning slightly glassy. He averts his gaze. "Your grandpa not long after… I still can't believe they're gone… It's been, what? Over a year?"

I exhale a deep sigh. "Just about…"

He looks distant a moment, then his eyes veer toward the open side door. "You still got Sasha?"

I nod slightly, relieved that he decided to change the subject. "Of course, man. She's safely tucked away in the back alley." I point my thumb over my shoulder. "I ain't giving her up for nothing."

His gaze flicks back to me, and he raises his eyebrows. "You still racing?"

"Nah. I got a lot going on. Haven't been out to the old strips or seen or heard from the crews in a while."

"Heh. I was out of the loop for a while, too, especially since I didn't have my ride anymore." He leans his back against the wall, crosses his arms, and lets out an airy laugh. "I went by the old airstrip in Fife a couple weeks ago to see if anything was going down. Sure enough, the same ol' suspects were out there in full force. Saw some newbie crews out there too. Dude! Since when did Jacob get back into drifting?"

I laugh. I still hadn't seen Jacob since he won his big drift race last year. It's good to know the bastard is still alive, living the fast life. "You missed a lot, man." I take the next couple minutes filling him in—the Red Ravens and Oculus X, Cass and me building the car, and Jacob's big win.

Luke's face turns pale when I finish. "Whoa… the Red Ravens and Oculus X were teamed up?"

I furrow my brow, hearing the fearful tone in his voice. "Yeah. Why? You've seen them recently?"

"Yeah… a couple months ago when I was down in Portland, I ran into one of the Red Ravens. They remembered me and started asking about you."

I arch an eyebrow. "About me? You sure?"

"Dude, I was about to get into it with him because he thought I was lying when I said I had no idea where you were."

"What was he asking you about me for?"

Luke shrugs. "Something about you owing their crew a ton of money or something."

I snort. "I don't owe them shit."

"Maybe they're still pissed about Sasha. They were talking about coming back."

"They're not welcome back here." It seems I was right about Jacob holding the turf down and running the Red Ravens out. *Good riddance.* "So, what brings you back here?" I ask Luke.

"Like I said, I'm looking to make some bread. I saw the Help Wanted sign out front, so…"

"You know anything about restoring antique cars?"

Luke scratches the back of his head. "Uh… no."

"Bookkeeping?"

"Of course, I still got my sketchbook, y'know."

I rub my forehead. "Oh, for fuck's sake. Look, man. I'm sorry, but I can't hire you."

"Why not? We're friends, right?"

"Yeah, we are, but I've also got a business to run. I need someone who can handle the books or help take some of the load of getting these cars restored."

"It can't be that hard, right? I mean, I practically rebuilt my truck from scratch. And I'm good with numbers."

"Building a truck from scratch is a far cry from restoring cars that are over fifty years old."

"I mean, maybe. But I can try. Give me a chance."

I sigh. I suppose I could give him a chance. Though I'm wary about trusting him with the books. One little mistake— one missed decimal point or comma—could potentially bankrupt this company. I sure as hell know Grandpa wouldn't have hired someone like Luke.

Then again, he'd hired me…

"I dunno, man…" I say.

Luke throws his hands up. "Aw, c'mon, Adam. I got a record. No one else around here is gonna hire me."

I frown. "You're a graffiti artist. What the hell can you—" I suddenly have an idea. *Holy shit. Of course!* "You still good at doing body paint?"

He blinks several times and looks at me like I'm from another planet. "You *do* remember my sweet-as-fuck chameleon paint job on my truck, right?"

"Yeah, that's why I want to make sure you still know your shit."

"An artist never forgets. So do I get the job or what?"

I rub my chin. "Yeah… I think I can get you set up with some jobs. I got at least five customers waiting to get their cars repainted. I've had to send them to a guy in Lakewood. It'd be nice to keep the cash flow here, y'know?"

"Yeah, I know." Luke grins. "Don't worry, man. I gotcha covered."

"All right, when Cassandra gets here, I'll have her update the books so—"

"Whoa, what?" Luke stares at me, wide-eyed. "She's here too?"

I stiffen. "Yeah. She's my girl. And future mother to my kid."

His mouth drops open. "H-Holy shit…"

"You missed a lot while you were gone. Is this still going to be a problem?"

He closes his mouth and shakes his head. "Naw, man. I… I'm just surprised. I thought she would've run back to Jacob or something. And now to hear she's knocked up…"

"Yeah, well, you know. Life happens. I don't want any shit between you two, all right?"

He holds his hands up in surrender. "Trust me, I'm over that shit."

I sure hope so. I don't need old baggage being dragged into the shop. Now, I only hope that Cassandra would be on board with it too.

I give Luke a quick tour around the place, now that he's my official-unofficial employee. I show him my current restoration project—the Bel-Air—resting on four jack stands. He has no idea how to mess with old cars like this, but I guess everyone has to start somewhere. It's reminiscent of the days Grandpa used to show me the ropes when I'd first started working for him. After a while, it all sort of grew on me. Who knows? Maybe Luke might find a new love too.

Cassandra came by the shop around four o'clock, while Luke and I had our heads stuck under the hood. I'd given him a crash course on the basics and pitfalls of doing a "level two"—showroom quality—restoration. Cassandra and Luke's initial meeting had gone just about as I'd expected—a bit of shock from both sides, followed by a spat of anger, and finally, reconciliation once they put the past behind them.

After a bit of paperwork, and Cassandra going over the numbers once, twice, and three times more, I cut Luke an advanced check so he could find himself a new pad tonight.

The three of us get the shop ready to close. As I'm pulling a tarp over the Bel-Air, Luke leans in close. "Wanna check out the races tonight?"

I give him a slight frown. Part of me wants to, if only to find out if the Red Ravens and Oculus X really *did* come back as Luke had alluded to earlier, but I doubt Cassandra would be cool with it. "I can't, man. I gotta keep an eye on Cassandra. Besides, like I said before, I'm done with racing."

"Dude, that woman is lugging heavy shit around the shop like it's nothing. I'm pretty sure she can take care of herself for a little while."

"She's gonna have a kid soon!"

"So you're saying the kid's coming in the next couple hours?"

"It's not due for another week or so, but still—"

"Another *week*? You're worried about nothing, then. C'mon. Let's go tonight. Besides, who said you had to race? I want to see the old guys again. They'd probably love to see you too."

I consider it a moment, then look toward the office at Cassandra filing the last few papers into the file cabinet. I had made a promise to slow down, especially with the baby coming soon. It wouldn't be fair to Cassandra if I got caught up in that world again.

"I'll let you know," I say to Luke. "Call me at the house later tonight." I scribble my phone number on the back of an Anderson Antique Auto business card.

Frowning, he swipes up the card. "Damn, you really have changed."

"Fatherhood can do that, I guess."

The three of us leave the shop, and I lock the door. It's almost eight o'clock as we stand outside, facing the not-so-busy-street.

Luke stuffs his hands in his pockets and rocks on his heels. "Mind if I come in a little late tomorrow? I'm wanna get an early start and talk to some landlords."

I snort out a laugh. "This is barely your first day, and you already want time off?" His face pales, and I chuckle and slap him on the back. "Kidding, man. Take as long as you need."

"Thanks!" His face brightens again, and he looks at Cassandra. "We still good, right?"

She crosses her arms, strikes him with cool look, then quirks a smile. "Yeah, we're good."

Luke turns, flips up the hood of his hoodie, and slinks down the street toward the north side of town. My mind is all sorts of jumbled. My feet want to go home, but my brain wants to stop and process all that happened today. Reuniting with my best friend and closing the book of our past life was enlightening, and yet, when Luke brought up the races, I realized part of me still didn't want to let go. I've tried hard to move on from that life, and yet every time I turn around there's something to pull me back in.

A soothing warmth touches my hand. "Ready?" Cassandra asks.

I shake out of my thoughts and nod to her. "Yeah, sure," I say.

A car's engine suddenly roars like thunder from across the street, and Cassandra and I flinch. A set of headlights flash on, and the engine gives another low, hefty growl.

Furrowing my brow, I look across the street at a mysterious black GTO that's parallel-parked. The windows are tinted, and I can't make out the driver. The car maneuvers its way out of the space, makes a U-turn, and heads north. The brake lights suddenly flash and the car creeps along at a snail's pace for a moment, then zooms off out of sight.

"Well, that was weird," Cassandra says, then tugs my arm and leads me around the building to the back alley, where our cars are parked.

"Yeah…" I say, distracted and unsure of myself once again. The sudden sound of that GTO's engine had roused those urges that had been asleep for so long—the urge to take Luke up on his offer.

CHAPTER 29

I WAS TOO CHICKENSHIT TO TELL CASSANDRA WHERE I WAS going, but that annoyed look in her eye when I'd walked out the door said everything. She was too smart to not know, especially when I had left at ten p.m.—the usual time. I'd picked up Luke, who was currently living at a motel, and we'd headed to the old airstrip in Fife.

I grip the steering wheel as we zoom through the back roads, a strange feeling unnerving me. I still can't shake off what Luke had mentioned earlier today about the Red Ravens looking for me. I'd been out of the racing game for months. There was no way they were still looking for revenge after their Oculus X brother lost—that was yesterday's news. *It had to be the missing brick they thought I stole...*

"I can't wait to see the look on Jacob's face when he sees you again," Luke says, breaking me out of my thoughts.

"Can't say I'm anxious to see him, but… I don't know. A lot's changed," I say flatly. Part of me felt like Jacob and I had buried the hatchet, and part of me was already anticipating another mess he'd want me to help bail him out of.

We turn down the familiar dirt road and are greeted by a sea of dressed up cars parked in front of the racing strip. A rowdy crowd watches two cars zoom down the 1320 strip. Nearby, a black sedan performs drifts and burnouts before a cheering audience. Even some of the sport bike crews are out here, popping wheelies and showing off.

It looks like Jacob had kept up his end of the bargain and brought all the communities together.

What a great sight.

Luke and I scope out the mixed-aged crowd. I spot some familiar faces among the adults, mainly some of the Burn Dawgs and the Chefs, the two big crews here tonight from what I can tell. They seem to be the ones keeping order around here as usual, while Jacob's crew runs the show.

I park Sasha away from the crowd. I don't want any attention on her tonight—or on myself. I get out the car, stuff my hands in my pockets and walk with Luke toward the drag-racing gathering.

We pass a group of barely legal teenagers hanging out around a tricked-out black-and-orange Camaro with a custom intake manifold and some sick-looking bladed rims. Both doors are wide open, and the bass-thumping tunes of KRS-One blare from a custom speaker system that's outlined with flashing neon lights.

Tires screech in the direction ahead of us, as a Mustang and Supra face off in a drag race. The crowd watches and cheers, holding up cans and bottles of beer.

Luke points out the nearby circle of drifting enthusiasts observing an E30 Bimmer doing donuts and burnouts. The smell of exhaust and burning rubber socks my senses, and a tingle runs up my spine. I still miss this life—carefree youth with no responsibilities—despite what I keep telling myself. But my life had changed faster than I could blink.

"Adam? Holy shit, you're back!"

I turn as Martin from the Burn Dawgs approaches me, firmly holding an excited Apollo's leash. We do our handshake, ending with a shoulder bump.

"I ain't seen you in a minute," Martin says. "What's happening, man?"

"I was in the neighborhood," I reply.

Martin nods to Luke. "Hey, man. You back now too?"

Luke returns the nod. "Yeah." He pauses, looks around, and his face turns a shade paler. "There ain't been no trouble around here tonight, has there?"

Martin cocks his head. "What kind of trouble?"

"The red kind."

Martin's expression hardens. "They know not to start shit again. They don't come out here, anyway. At least, not in force."

"I saw a couple of them a bit ago when I was in Portland. They were giving me a hard time."

"What did you do?" Martin asks, rolling his eyes.

Luke shakes his head. "Nothing, I swear!"

"Apparently they're looking for me," I interject.

As if sensing my annoyance, Apollo lets out a low growl. I look at the dog, but I don't try and calm him—tonight he doesn't seem very welcoming.

Luke grimaces at Apollo and slowly backs away. "Hey, uh, I'm gonna check out the races," he says to me, pointing his thumb toward the next drag race about to start.

Before Martin or I can say anything more, Luke zips off toward the crowd. Apollo barks after him, then looks up at Martin and wags his tail.

I haul my attention back to Martin. A strange feeling churns in my gut. "The Red Ravens and Oculus X haven't been back, have they?"

Martin flares his nostrils. "Not in Tacoma. And after his big win, Jacob gave us back our turf here in Fife. This is Burn Dawgz territory again, and everyone's welcome. Neutral grounds like it used to be. I've seen some Red Ravens and Oculus X guys I recognized come around here every so often, but they weren't wearin' colors. I think they've been humbled enough not to start any shit again."

"Tell that to Luke," I say.

"Yeah, well you two better watch yourselves. Seriously, man, they might not be hangin' around anymore, but you don't wanna get wrapped up in their bullshit."

"Believe me, I know. Hopefully they're not out here tonight," I mutter. I look around warily, but there are too many people out here wearing some kind of red for me to spot anyone who might run with them.

"Haven't seen any tonight… yet," Martin says. "Then again, I've been more interested in the drag races. By the way, are we gonna see Sasha in action again tonight, or what?"

"Nah, man," I say, relieved that he's changed the subject. "I'm just observing."

Martin arches an eyebrow. "You never 'just observe.' What's up with you?"

"Long story. But I'm glad you guys are keeping with the old traditions out here. I see some new crews too."

"Eh, a lot of 'em are into that drifting shit, but otherwise, they're cool. Hell, even Jacob's back to drifting."

I chuckle. "So I've heard."

A wave of rowdy cheers suddenly erupts from the drift crowd, and Martin sighs. "Well… better go keep these knuckleheads in line. Don't be a stranger, man. Everyone would love to see Sasha out here again."

"Yeah…" I watch Martin leave, tugging Apollo along. I look toward the drag-race crowd, but don't see Luke, so I decide to walk around. Flashy, souped-up cars are parked everywhere, and more than a few have their hoods popped. I wonder how many of these newbies use—or even know about—Q&R products these days? After seeing almost nothing but LeatherRock in the first several cars I pass, it seems like the answer is probably 'none.'

For the past year, LeatherRock has been under legal fire—especially after what happened at the Shed. Enough complaints had been made about the company, along with a surge of part recalls, that a class-action lawsuit had been started. Despite what had happened to my friends, the whole ordeal seemed to be swept under the rug by the company, even with the ongoing lawsuit. I couldn't join in because my friends weren't legally family, and I couldn't afford a lawyer on my own, so all I could do was helplessly watch LeatherRock literally get away with murder. How many more people had to die before that company was finally shut down?

And yet, even now, I see a bunch of LeatherRock loyalists out here showing off their faulty mods. They'll suck that company's dick till the end of time.

I stop in front of a red Fiero with a set of flashy silver rims with two-inch spikes capped on the lug nuts. I inhale the smell of new rubber, indicating this car got a set of brand-new tires recently. As I study the two-door hatchback, my heart suddenly drops. *Fuck...* I look around for any sign of Drew or the Red Ravens, and my hand moves instinctually to my jacket pocket. It's empty. *Of course, of all nights, I decided to leave my .45 at home.* It's been a year, but I remember this car all too well. *But where's that god-awful spoiler?*

"Sweet, ain't it?"

I spin at the sound of a voice behind me, ready to swing. I pull up short when I realize the person behind me isn't Drew, just some random guy I've never seen before. I try to nonchalantly run my hands through my hair, trying to disguise the fact that I almost decked him.

"Y-Yeah, man. That's a nice ride," I stammer in reply, trying to will away the adrenaline running through my veins now.

"You drift too, bro?" The stranger asks. He stands a good bit shorter than me, with dark hair that falls to his shoulders.

"No. No, I don't really race anymore." I give the guy a quick smile, do an about-face, and walk away. Luke's talk about the Red Ravens earlier must have gotten into my head worse than I thought. I almost knocked some poor guy out because his car looked like Drew's.

I stop and look around the racing strip, trying to get my mental bearings back. Luke and I were supposed to just come here and check out the races. Instead, I'm freaked out and paranoid about Drew and his posse showing up.

It's time to go. Where's Luke?

I search through the mob of people, trying to find a baseball cap and brown bomber jacket somewhere in the milling crowd. After a few minutes, I spot Luke in the ever-present gleam of headlights on the strip. He's walking toward the races though, like he was coming back from the entrance where we parked. I walk over to meet him.

"Hey man, I've been lookin' for you. Where were you at?" I ask.

"Uh, I had to take a piss," he offers up, nodding in the direction he came from.

"Whatever. You ready to go?"

"Sure, I guess. Something wrong?"

"Naw, I'm fine. Just gotta get back to Cassandra," I answer.

Luke chuckles and shakes his head, then joins me as we walk back to where Sasha is parked.

We're almost to the car when the loud roar of an engine kicking on thunders close by. Headlights shine in our direction. I can't make out the car with the light glaring in our eyes, but the rumble is familiar. The vehicle revs twice, then pulls out of where it was parked. I catch a glimpse of it as it turns right and peels out toward the main road. A GTO… black.

I blink. *Didn't I see that car earlier? Am I being followed?*

I shake the thoughts from my head. *No, it can't be.* The anxiety from thinking I ran into Drew must have still been messing with me. *All this paranoia sucks. I definitely need to get the hell out of here.*

"You okay, man?"

I shake out of my thoughts and shift my gaze to Luke. He regards me with a look of slight concern, his brow pinched.

"Yeah, uh… I thought I saw someone I knew," I respond in a wary tone. "Guess I'm just seeing things, or whatever. Anyway, let's get outta here."

Luke shrugs then hops into my car in silence.

I climb into the driver's seat and tear out of this place as fast as I can.

I drop Luke off at the motel and don't get home until after one in the morning. I take a quick shower and quietly slide into bed, careful to not wake Cassandra next to me. I stare up at the ceiling, unable to sleep. I can't get that GTO out of my mind. I've seen it twice now—with a car that hard to find, it had to be the same one. It probably means nothing. Or it might mean I'm still anxious as hell about my beef with the Red Ravens, and the drugs that got burned up in the Shed fire, despite what I've told myself. Apparently, Clayton never got a chance to follow through on his promise. And now his fucking corpse haunts me every time I think about the Red Ravens.

"So? Are you done?"

I blink out of my thoughts and look beside me at the sound of Cassandra's voice. "Huh?"

"Don't play dumb."

I fall silent a moment. "We've been over this already."

"Yeah, and you didn't sound too sure of yourself." She pauses, sits up in bed, and clicks on the light on the night table. I squint from the shock of light, but still notice that she's wearing one of my extra-large T-shirts—a white one that shows off the roundness of her belly, and her hard, perky nipples. *My Lord, she looks so sexy.*

"Is this how it's gonna be from now on? Now that Luke's working for you? You're gonna try and get a new crew together and make things like they used to be?" She purses her lips. "I thought you were done with all that now, Adam." She places her hand over her belly. "I thought you were going to settle down."

I haul away my lust and sigh. "I *am* stopping. I swear. It was just this once. A favor for a friend."

She rolls her eyes "Listen to yourself. You sound like a damn addict."

Addict. I cringe. "Look, it's not how it sounds, and you know it." I lean closer to her. "You're my number one priority right now." I kiss her gently on the lips.

"Am I?" She fights a small smile, and then reluctantly returns the kiss. "You better keep your promise and be the best damn father you can be."

I deepen the kiss, tasting her need, and a thought hits me. I *do* want to be the best damn father I can be for this baby, and for her. And I want to be more than that too—I want to be her husband. The idea scares me, and yet, in this moment I've never been more sure of anything in my life. "I'll be more than just a good father. I'll be a damn good husband, too, if you'll have me."

She stops kissing me for a moment and simply looks at me. "Husband?" she whispers.

Noting her initial shock, I kiss her again. "I… I don't have a ring, but…"

"That's okay. I don't need a ring to say 'I do.'"

I stop kissing her a moment and look at her wide-eyed. My heart pounds in my chest. "'You do'?"

She smiles. "Let's make it official before I have this baby."

"Yeah," I whisper, lowering my face to hers again. *Holy shit… She said yes!* Part of me is stunned by her words, and yet I couldn't be happier. Her declaration, her carrying my child… she's never looked more beautiful to me than she does right now. "But first, tonight, I want you to say 'I do' every time you cum."

She caresses my cheeks as she plants a deep, passionate kiss on my lips. My hands plunge beneath the T-shirt and explore the curves of her body. My dick throbs as I grope her breasts, which feel heavier, firmer, and fuller now.

She moans against my lips. "They hurt... so much."

I smile crookedly. "Yeah? Well, I'll make them feel better." I lift the shirt and toss it to the floor. "They look so gorgeous. I fucking love your tits." I admire them a moment longer, and then gently kiss her down her sternum. She squirms and exhales, letting out small whimpers. I press my tongue against one of her hard nipples while I twist and tease the other with my fingers.

"Ahh... y-you're making me numb..." she stammers.

Smiling, I lift up from her breasts and slide out of my sweatpants and boxers. I run my hands gently along her belly, admiring just how beautiful she is carrying my child inside her. I want to make her feel like the queen she really is tonight. I part her thighs and lift, wrapping her legs around my waist. I feel her body tense.

"Adam... the... the baby... early labor..."

I kiss her lips. "I'll be gentle." I press my hips against hers, my dick easing its way inside her slick pussy. Holy shit, it's magical. So tight, so wet. She's just as horny as I am.

Her body shudders, and she moans.

"Like how that feels?" I groan against her lips.

"Mm-hmm..." she whimpers in response, digging her nails into the back of my shoulders.

I push deeper, until my dick reaches her barrier, forbidding me to go further. Her walls pulsate eagerly around my throbbing dick. *So warm...* My midsection presses against her taut belly.

I kiss down her neck, my breathing becoming ragged. "Please, Adam. Please..."

I brace myself, then grind into her—gentle, yet firm—my ears relishing the sounds of her wet pussy smacking with each movement. I lift one of her legs slightly, the back of her thigh resting on my forearm, and I thrust into her faster. Her heavy tits bounce and jiggle in a hypnotic dance with each thrust.

"Suck them..." she whispers, as if she can read my mind.

Oh, hell yes...

I grab one of them with my free hand and give it a gentle massage. It's so hard, so heavy... so full. No wonder she's in pain.

She moans and looks up at me with need. "Please, Adam..."

I eagerly guide one of her luscious nipples into my mouth and gently suck. I flick at it with my tongue until I feel it enlarge a little and stiffen.

"Harder... Suck harder..." she pleads.

I moan at her erotic demands and obey. I suck her hard and fast, letting my tongue swirl around her nipple while I slowly slide in and out of her. A dollop of something warm and sweet graces the tip of my tongue. *Her milk... Ho-ly shit...*

I drive my steeled dick into her in a final, forceful thrust, and her body shudders. She cums hard, her walls squeezing my dick for dear life. A wave of chills surges through every nerve in my body. I cum into her—so hard, so raw—filling her up with my hot seed.

She throws her head back, open-mouthed, wailing "*I do!*" over and over.

"My wife…" I stammer out at the height of my climax, moving my hips against hers, trying to ease the spine-tingling sensation. I finally pull out, the evidence of our lovemaking dripping out of her.

I lay behind her, wrapping my arms around her, and gently caress her belly. I kiss the back of her neck and taste the tiny salty beads of her sweat as she savors the afterglow.

"My husband…" she whispers.

Hearing her affirmation, I smile broadly. Words can't describe the joy and happiness I feel to have my future wife and child here in my arms.

Chapter 30

Cassandra was glowing the next morning, and from the way she looked at me, I guess I was too. *My future wife.* We shared a brief meal and a kiss, and then she was off to work. Despite her practically ready to burst, she'd still never missed a day of work. I envied that woman in more ways than one.

Later that morning, Luke comes into work, all smiles. He'd finally gotten himself a new car, a white—or maybe it used to be red since the paint had long-since faded—'81 Challenger that he'd found in the Classifieds for only five hundred bucks. The car was in pretty bad shape, though, even for that small amount. Its sunbaked body was crumpled so badly, it looked like it'd barely survived an accident with a semi. But miraculously, the jalopy still ran.

Luke says he plans to restore the car one of these days. I sure hope so, because that thing is a constant eyesore next to Sasha.

As the day drew on, however, that good news turned into anxiety, as memories of last night's ordeal at the airstrip in Fife haunted my mind. *Am I going to see that GTO again today? Is someone following me?* My thoughts flow to the Red Ravens and the drugs I owed them—or at least the money for them. The bricks were all burned away with Clayton. The police report had mentioned remnants of heroin found in Clayton's destroyed car when they finally released it a few months after the incident. That must have been the brick Clayton promised me he'd deliver to Drew that night. Instead, Clayton got caught up in that damn race for some shitty LeatherRock parts that cost him his life.

My thoughts returning to the present, I realize I need to either pay off the Red Ravens or find a way to get them off my back for good. Paying them off would be too easy, though. They know who I am, and they would demand more than just money, no doubt. I'd have to do things the hard way. Just like back in New York, things *always* end up being done the hard way.

"Did you notice that Jacob and his crew weren't at the airstrip last night?"

I look up from my workbench, where I'm halfway finished with rebuilding a brake cylinder, and over to Luke. He has his head down, busily sanding the stripped '59 Corvette sitting on a raised dolly. This is his first paint project since he's started working full-time for me, and I know he won't disappoint.

Before Luke, I'd contracted all the paint jobs to a specialist in Lakewood, the same guy Grandpa had always used. While the guy did quality work, it was this company's biggest expense. Maybe that was why Grandpa didn't take on paint jobs too often. He'd sworn that guy was the best painter in Washington—he'd obviously never met Luke. And not only is Luke good, he's *fast*.

"No, I wasn't particularly looking for him," I finally answer Luke. "But now that you mention it…"

"I asked around while we were out there. Turns out, he's been keeping a low profile in the drag circles, and he's hanging out more with the drift crews, now."

"Good for him."

Luke stops sanding and looks up at me. "Really? Don't you realize this means he sold out? He and the Ninez probably ain't never gonna drag again. And we've still got some baggage to work out."

"Let it go, man. Things ain't the way they used to be. People change."

Luke resumes his sanding. "Says the guy who's about to be a father. What are you gonna do when the baby comes?"

I lower the spring inside the cylinder bore and pause. "What the hell kind of question is that?" I look toward my friend.

"A serious one, man. Are you even gonna have time to do shit at the shop?"

I purse my lips. I had never thought that being a parent might compromise my business. Maybe Luke was exaggerating. It's not like he's had any prior experience, anyway. "Yeah, I'll have time," I say nonchalantly, securing the cylinder's spring cups. "If I have to, I'll hire a third hand."

"You better. Unless you can replace a timing belt while changing a diaper." He snickers.

"You sound like you've done it before."

"*Hell* no. And I don't intend to, either. Don't need baby mama drama in my life."

I laugh. "Well, I'm sure it won't be *that* bad."

"Yeah, you keep telling yourself that."

I roll my eyes and continue my work.

The bells jingle on the front door. I look through the glass as Cassandra waddles into the office. Smiling, I set down my tools and wipe my hands on a towel. "Be right back," I tell Luke, heading to the side door into the office.

I meet Cassandra just as she plops down behind the desk. The bottom of her black Q&R shirt hikes up slightly, over her large, round belly. I plant a deep kiss on her lips. "Hey. How y'doin?"

She leans back in her chair, deflating with a huge sigh. "My feet hurt."

I quirk a smile. "Well, I'll massage them for you tonight. How's that?"

She seems to mirror my expression, but the smile doesn't quite meet her eyes. "Don't tease me."

I kiss her again. "It's a promise."

She pulls back from the kiss and presses her finger to my lips. "You have work to do, so go do it."

"Yes' ma'am." I do an about-face, leave out the side door again, and return to the garage. As I continue my work, it's hard for me to not think about Cassandra's expression. Something's on her mind, I can tell.

I hear the water running and dishes clinking from the kitchen as I finish putting the dining room table back in order.

I turn away and head to the kitchen, where Cassandra stands at the sink. She casts a brief glance at me, the returns to her work. There's a hint of worry on her face.

"Hey," Cassandra says absently.

I gently push her out of the way and take over doing the dishes. "What's wrong?" I ask her.

She pauses. "What do you mean?"

"Something's on your mind, I can tell. I saw it all over your face back at the shop." I stick a clean plate onto the drying rack.

"Nothing's wrong." She turns and begins heading out of the kitchen.

I shut off the water, reach out with a wet hand and grab her arm, stopping her. "Bullshit."

She looks back at me and frowns. "Look, I'm fine, all right?"

I sigh and gently release her arm. "Talk to me."

She pauses, still keeping her back to me. Then she inclines her head.

"Well?" I persist.

"I got a call earlier from a co-worker... Erica. She said she overheard the boss talking today about potentially moving me to less hours per week."

I raise my eyebrows. "Are they cutting your pay too?"

"I don't know. Probably. I'm sure I'll be in for a rude awakening, come next week."

"They can't do that. I mean, for fuck's sake. You're about to have a kid! How the fuck can those assholes cut your pay?"

She swallows. "Adam, I don't want to lose my job. I'm finally living my dream being at Q&R. I'd already talked everything over with my bosses, and it seemed like we were all on board with the situation and what would happen the next couple weeks. Apparently, I was wrong."

"They can't fire you. Do you think they're doing this because you're pregnant or... or the baby's about to be born? I mean, that's pretty messed up if that's the reason. Isn't that considered workplace discrimination? We could raise some legal hell if it is."

Cassandra spins around and shakes her head. "I don't think it's that, but I'll know for sure on next week, probably. I just... don't know what to do if I can't help bring bread to the table, y'know? I can't help our baby like I'd planned."

I blink. "What? Is that what you're afraid of? Well fuck that. I would no sooner see you quit that place than have them cut your hours and try to push you out. Stop worrying about money. You've done more than enough." I feel as though a dagger is being twisted in my heart. How can Q&R—our favorite company, and such a huge part of our racing lives—do this to her? "If it really comes down to it, why don't you stay here with the kid?"

Cassandra gives me a dubious look. "Adam, you should know by now that I'm a woman who likes to work. Being a homemaker was never my style, and it won't ever be. So don't think you're going to forbid me to work, because you're going to lose. Every. Single. Time."

Rolling my eyes, I sigh in defeat. "Fine, damn it. I'll stay out of your way. But I can't help it that I love you too much to let anyone treat you like shit. You are an amazing, hard-working woman, and deserve nothing but the best."

"Thank you, Adam. That means a lot," she says softly.

"I mean every word. I love you."

CHAPTER 31

The light sounds of brakes screeching outside draws my attention to the front door. I glance out the glass and notice a black delivery van parallel-parked in front of Cassandra's car, its emergency flashers blinking. The side of the van is branded with the Q&R logo. Looks like our morning delivery is here.

I frown. Normally, I'm excited to see the Q&R delivery van, but after what Cassandra told me last night, I'm furious. I'd been a Q&R loyal for as long as I could remember, but after Cassandra's revelation, I'm tempted to sever all ties with the company.

A young man wearing a black polo shirt retrieves a steel dolly from the back of the van. He loads two large wooden boxes on them, sets a clipboard on top, and then wheels the dolly toward the front door.

I purse my lips while I watch him approach, then begrudgingly open the door. "Mornin,' Collin," I mutter.

Collin grins, bright and cheery, as if he doesn't have a care in the world. *I wonder if he knows anything about Cassandra's work situation...*

"What's up, Adam?" Collin greets. He sets the boxes next to the desk and hands me the clipboard.

"Busy. Y'know how it is," I say, signing my name on the delivery papers.

"Hey, Collin," Cassandra says in a lackluster tone.

Collin raises his eyebrows. "Hey, Cass. You not coming in today?"

"I'll be in the office in about an hour." She gives him an uninspired smile and looks down to the Q&R polo covering her stomach.

Collin follows her gaze. "Congratulations again, by the way!" Still grinning, he pats me on the back.

I stiffen. "Thanks, man," I say in a low voice, and then thrust the signed clipboard back at him.

"You know," Collin says, looking back at Cassandra. "Hopefully you won't have to be out too long. It won't be the same around the office without you."

She shrugs. "Well... looks like you may be seeing less of me anyway."

"What? Why?"

"I heard that my days might be getting cut. That's never a good sign."

"Man! They can't do that," Collin says. "If anything, they need to give you a raise. Even being pregnant you're the hardest worker there and you know our products like nobody's business. Hell, you probably know 'em better than the damn CEO."

She lets out a hollow chuckle. "Tell that to my boss."

I ball my fists, unable to listen to any more of this shit. She doesn't deserve to get tossed away like this. If this was how they were going to treat her, she should just quit and find another company that appreciates her. But I can't make these choices for Cassandra. I understand her loyalty to the company and the brand, but I still can't stomach it all. Whatever her decision, though, I'll respect it.

"Thanks, Collin." I open the door to the garage and prepare to return to work on the engine rebuild of a '53 Corvette that I'm supposed to have finished by the end of the day.

The staticky sounds of R.E.M.'s latest hit from Luke's favorite radio station wails from the boombox sitting on the wall shelf. Luke is standing in front of a black 1949 Studebaker, meticulously painting a realistic image of red-and-yellow flames on its hood.

I approach the next bay where the Corvette sits covered in a protective cloth. A disassembled engine rests on a steel workbench next to the car.

As I move around, Luke doesn't seem to notice me. He's lost in his own artistic world—I guess that's how he makes his magic happen.

Collin suddenly whistles. "Holy shit! Whose car is that?"

I pause and look over my shoulder. I thought at first that he meant the Studebaker, the only car not covered, but I follow his gaze out the back window in the office to the alley. *Sasha. Shit.* "Mine."

"Wow. That's awesome. Can I get a closer look?"

No. So fuck off. I clench my jaw. The words are on the tip of my tongue, but then my rational side intervenes. It's not fair for me to take my anger out on Collin. He obviously had nothing to do with Cassandra's problem at Q&R.

I take a deep breath, slowly uncurl my fists, and nod to him. "Sure," I finally say.

Collin joins me in the garage, and we walk past Luke toward the steel door that leads to the back alley. Luke, still not acknowledging us, continues his detailed, flaming masterpiece, while he sings along to the lyrics of *Losing My Religion.*

In the alley, Collin admires Sasha from all angles, and then I pop the hood so he can take a peek at her goods.

"Oh shit! You're using the T-series intake system? That's gotta be one of the best systems they ever put out!" Collin says.

"Yep," I reply. "I only use top-of-the-line Q&R products in her. Nothing less."

Collin looks thoughtful for a moment. "Have you ever thought about having your car be a model for one of the Q&R magazines or something?"

I blink. The thought never occurred to me before, and once upon a time, I probably would've jumped on the opportunity. But not now. Not after the way the company's treating Cassandra. "Not really, no."

"I hear you can make *mad* money. And this car right here could be your ultimate cash cow. I'm telling you, man. I ain't never seen anything this sweet done with Q&R parts before. You could probably even get it into the Q&R Auto Museum. Oh, shit. If you got it there, you'd be set for life. Seriously. I hear they pay millions for some cars to be put in there."

I raise my eyebrows. *Millions?* Even still, it sounded like I would have to give Sasha up for good for her to end up in the museum. She carries memories though—good and bad—and I'm not sure I'm ready to part with her yet. But, sometimes, I wonder why I still continue to hold on to her. *You're done with that life, remember?* I remind myself, and also hear Cassandra's words, as well. "I dunno," I mutter.

"You should think about it, man," Collin says. "See ya around."

After he leaves the shop, I exhale a deep sigh and return to the garage, but suddenly find Luke standing there with his arms crossed and wearing a smile wider than the Cheshire Cat. I start. "What are you so happy about?"

"That deal."

I furrow my brow. "Wait, you heard us? I thought you were busy painting?"

"Your little meeting with Collin looked important. You never show off Sasha like that outside of a big racing event, so I had to eavesdrop. It's gold!"

"I don't follow…"

"Adam… it's the same thing that we talked about the other day. What *are* you gonna do with Sasha? She's built for racing, and you've made it pretty clear that you're not doing that no more. So why not bank on all those great years you've had with her?"

I swallow a lump in my throat. "You want me to just give her up?"

"I mean, if the price is right, why not? What does she really mean to you, huh? Are you just gonna let her sit?"

"She means a lot. She makes me think about Clay, Mariah, Gabe... our friends—our family. Sasha's been there through all that."

Luke's smile fades. "Yeah, I get it. I miss them too. Well, think of it this way. If Sasha gets put into the museum, then nobody else will be allowed to drive her. She'll be preserved forever, and you can see her whenever you want."

I half-smile at that idea. Nobody else *was* worthy enough to drive her. But then reality hits my mind like a brick wall. "No. I'm not giving Q&R shit. I don't care how much money they want to offer me. Nobody treats my wife like that."

Luke perks up. "Wife? Wait, you two are..."

Damn, I slipped. I sigh. "We're... engaged. Kind of. There's no date set yet. And I don't have a ring or anything, but..."

"Well, shit! When were you gonna tell me? I get to be your best man at the wedding, right?"

"Of course, but I really don't know any details yet. We may just go the courthouse route, who knows?"

"Fair enough. Okay, look. I know you're angry about Q&R right now, and you've every right to be. Maybe you can use Sasha as some sort of bargaining chip to get them to change their mind about dropping Cassandra's hours?"

I wrinkle my nose. "Hell, no. I'm not using Sasha as some bargaining tool. I might as well be begging for them to keep

Cassandra. I don't beg to nobody. *They* should be the ones begging Cassandra to stay. She's worth more to that company than they realize. If they're gonna treat her like that, then I'm not wasting my time with them, and neither should she."

Luke shrugs with a sigh. "Suit yourself. I'm just saying, man. I think you're sitting on a goldmine right now."

Maybe I am, but I just can't let go of her yet. Cassandra knows how much that car means to me—she would be furious if she found out I bargained Sasha just to sway her bosses to keep her hours. The money would be nice, but money wasn't the answer to all life's problems. I'd learned that the hard way many times.

My love for Cassandra is strong, and there's no amount of money in the world that will ever come between me and her. Trading Sasha for money and favors would be just like running those drugs to buy her Hemi. The guilt and shame of that was enough to dissuade me from ever considering something like that again.

And nobody, not even my best friend, Luke, is going to make me change my mind.

I had the '59 Corvette's engine almost put back together by the time Cassandra returned from work. Luke was almost done with his paint job too. As was usual the past few weeks, Cassandra waddled in and plopped down in the desk chair in the office. I watch her sigh from inside the garage—it doesn't look like she got good news at the office today. Catching

Luke's attention, I nod toward the office door, then head in that direction.

"So? What'd they say?" I ask her.

"Nothing. Maybe they haven't decided yet. Or maybe they're waiting until the end of the week... I don't know." She wipes her hands down her face, then rests them on her stomach. "Waiting for an answer like this is killing me."

"There's only a little bit more to do before Luke and I can close up. Then we can get out of here and you and I can go relax."

"Sounds wonderful," she says with a half-smile. I give her my own, then head back into the garage with Luke.

I'm back at the Corvette's open hood when I hear the muffled sounds of the front door creak open, followed by Cassandra's cheery greeting. Smiling to myself, I pick up my torque wrench and return to my work, letting Cassandra do her thing.

"Where is he?" says a man's voice.

I pause and furrow my brow.

"I told you I—hey!" Cassandra cries out.

Luke stops painting and looks up. I death-grip the wrench and scramble back to the side door. Slamming it open, I barrel into the room like a bull.

Cassandra cowers behind the desk, holding her shaky hands up in surrender. Two men wearing red stand before her, one aiming a gun.

My eyes widen. Suddenly, the world around me goes black. Rage bubbles inside me, and the urge to protect.

I have to protect my family.

The two men snap their gazes to me—my sudden entrance must have caught them by surprise. *One shot.* I lunge for the guy with the weapon and grab his wrist, pushing the gun away from where Cassandra is sitting. I'm ready to break his arm with the heavy wrench and toss his ass over in a breathtaking body slam. Suddenly, the other guy—the one wearing a backwards baseball cap—whips out his gun and presses its cold steel against my cheek.

"Let him go, or I'll blow your fucking brains out," he warns.

I halt, exhaling a slow, steady breath, as I look sidelong down the barrel of his Mag. I slowly release his friend's wrist.

"Adam?" Luke comes through side door, his expression curious. "Is everything all—shit!" He halts in his tracks.

"Don't even think about it, Luke," Baseball Cap Guy says, not turning to look at him. "Just go on back where you came."

Luke swallows. "C-C'mon Andy. Why you gotta do this?"

"Do as he says, Luke," I say. "And take Cassandra with you." I glare at Baseball Cap Guy—*Andy*—whom I assume is the leader of this duo. *Why does Luke know this clown's name?* "It's me you want, not her."

Andy scowls, looks thoughtful for a moment, then gives a small nod. "Fine, whatever. Your ass is ours now anyways."

I nod to Luke, silently letting him know that it's okay.

Luke quickly ushers Cassandra out of the side door and into the main garage.

"Adam!" Cassandra's yell is cut off as the door slams shut.

I exhale a deep breath once she's safely away. *Thank God...* I return my attention to the Red Ravens. "All right. Here I am. What are you gonna do?"

Andy smirks. "We're gonna give you one last chance to give us our five grand. Then we're gonna tear this place up and have a little fun with your girlfriend."

I grit my teeth. "If you touch her..."

Andy presses the gun against my cheek. "Pay up."

The cold steel sends a shiver down my spine. I swallow a lump in my throat. "I don't have that kind of money on me."

"Bullshit. Looks like there's a lot of money in this shop. Even better, there's a certain 300ZX named Sasha parked out back. She'd do real nice."

My heart drops to my gut. *Give up Sasha to these fuckers...* All those memories, the possibility of the museum, even... I said I wanted out of this life. I promised Cassandra and swore to settle down with her and the kid. Looks like the universe is forcing my hand. *But I don't want to see those memories end up in the hands of the very same people who destroyed my life, my friends, and ripped nearly everything I loved away from me.* I can always build another Sasha if I wanted. A bigger, better one. *It wouldn't be the same though...* It pains me to even think about it, but I have wife and child to protect.

I have to do it. For my family. I'm sorry, Clay... Rai... Gabe...

I take a deep breath. "Okay. I'll trade you Sasha," I say bitterly. "Take her and get the hell out of here. Leave me, my family, and my friends alone and never show your ugly fuck-ing faces around here again."

Andy's smile broadens. He finally lowers his gun and se-cures it at the back of his waistband. "Oh, you ain't giving her up that easy. You're gonna race for her. Drew wants to humble you."

"I don't drift, man. That's Jacob's bag," I say.

"You're gonna do it. Everyone knows about you, Adam. Everyone knows who the real king of the racing game in Ta-coma is, even if he's been hard to find lately—and it ain't Ja-cob, that's for sure. It's gonna be a big deal. And it'll be the last race of your career. You're going to let everyone know that while you surrender Sasha to us. Drew's gonna take your car, and your pride. And you just might get to keep your life."

I wrinkle my nose. "I'm not doing that shit."

"Yes, you will. And once Drew takes your car, Tacoma is going to belong to the Red Ravens."

"Didn't you learn your lesson from that spanking Jacob gave your boy?"

Andy chuckles. "Kaine was full of shit. Oculus X ain't fit to run a damn thing. But the Red Ravens are about to rise. Drew knows what he's doing, and he'll easily smoke Jacob just like he will you."

These motherfuckers... The more this guy talks, the angri-er I get. I'm still trying to process the fact that these guys found me, my business, and almost hurt Cassandra. Not only that, to hear that Drew would go so far as to betray his own allied crew to claim his turf made the Red Ravens even more dangerous. This is getting out of control. These guys need to be silenced. For good.

But how?

"I'm not agreeing to your terms, asshole," I spit.

Andy shrugs. "Yeah? Then I guess you won't mind us giving your shop a little TLC—Red Ravens style. I'm sure your girlfriend wouldn't either…" He casts a wicked smile. "She could use a little TLC too."

I clench and unclench my fists. I'm trapped like a rat by these fuckers, with nowhere to run. *I have no choice…* "Where and when?" I reluctantly concede.

"Where it all started: Fife Airstrip. Friday night. Eleven p.m."

I scrunch my nose. *Two days.* Two fucking days to get my shit together and to get Sasha dialed in. "I'll be there," I say.

The two men finally back away from me toward the front door. "Don't be late," Andy says, and then the two slip outside and out of sight.

I wait a few beats, then rush to the door. I peer out and try to locate their car. I suddenly hear the squealing of tires, and then spot a black car pull away from the curb from across the street. *That fucking GTO again. So, they* were *watching us.* I swivel the lock on the door shut and flip the 'Open' sign to 'Closed.' My mind is in no shape to deal with the business right now.

I race through the side door, and discover the garage is empty. "They're gone," I announce.

Luke and Cassandra slowly emerge from behind one of the unpainted cars that Luke was going to be working on.

I rush to Cassandra and hug her tight. "Are you okay?" I ask her. "Did they hurt you?" I check her from head to toe for injuries.

"I'm okay." She pulls away and looks at me with a frown. "Those were Red Ravens. What did they want with you?"

Luke regards me, pale-faced.

"Hey," I say to my friend. "Go ahead and get out of here. Shop's closed. There are some things I need to talk to Cassandra about. Don't worry, I'll pay you the missed time."

Luke shakes his head. "For once I'll say that I don't give a fuck about the money. I'm just glad you're okay."

I quirk a smile. "I'm fine, man. Glad you're okay too. And thank you… You saved Cassandra's and my unborn child's life back there. I owe you—big. Now get out of here. Don't go out the front. Take the fire exit." I point to the door at the back of the garage.

He hesitates, and then slowly takes his leave. "Okay. Later, man."

I wait until the fire door crashes shut, and then haul my attention back to Cassandra. She stares back at me with an expectant look in her eyes. I swallow a lump in my throat. After all this time, I've never told her about my secret dealings with the Red Ravens back then, when I was trying to help her afford that Hemi. I always deflected or blamed their interest on wanting Sasha. I can't believe my love for her has been the cause of all this mess. And now, after this, it's too much for me to bear, and it's high time I finally tell her the truth. Tell her *everything*.

With a deep sigh, I pull up a stray metal folding chair that was leaned against the wall and set it down in front of me. "Have a seat," I say to her.

Her nose wrinkles slightly as she gives me a funny look, and then she lowers herself on the seat.

I run my hands over my hair as I fish for the right words. "So, uh. Where do I even begin…"

"Just spit it out," she says.

The memories flood through my mind like a nightmare. "It's about your Hemi…"

She lifts an eyebrow. "What? What about it?"

At her command, I spit it out. The whole story—how I did it and why. I'd done it because I loved her so much—then and now.

But the shocked reaction on her face made it seem like she didn't quite agree with my reasoning.

Her face is red, her eyes wild with rage. "You… You did *what?*" She snaps, springing out of the chair. Her fists clench until her knuckles turn snow-white.

I deflate, slumping my shoulders. "I did it all for you. I knew how much you wanted that Hemi—more than any-thing in the world. I wanted to make your dream come true, even if it meant doing something I told myself I'd never do again."

She narrows her eyes, steps closer to me, and socks me hard against my cheek. My jaw cracks and I wince, my head snapping to the side. A burning sensation stings from my jaw, and I can taste iron—blood.

I deserve this, I know. I can't be upset with her. She has every right to be mad at me. I'm not sure how to respond—or if I even should—so I stare blankly at a spot on the garage's concrete floor.

"You've gotta be fucking kidding me, Adam," Cassandra says. "You kept that shit from me for this long?"

I sigh and close my eyes. "I didn't want to do it. I didn't know it would get out of control. I just… I was stupid…"

"'You're damn right, you were. You've been putting me and this kid at risk this whole time. What in the actual *fuck*, Adam!"

I stiffen. "I didn't mean for this to happen. It was never supposed to come to this. They crossed the line this time. No one threatens my family and gets away with it. I'll make things right. I'm gonna shut this shit down once and for all."

Her expression hardens. "Oh yeah? And what are you gonna do, huh? Cap 'em all? Get locked up for murder and never see your family again?"

I scowl. "No. I'll find a way to get these bastards off my back for good."

She purses her lips, then shoves me in the chest so hard the chair nearly tumbles backward. "Fuck this. I'm going home." She storms past me. "I can't even drive that fucking Hemi anymore. I'm going to get rid of it."

I swallow. The memories of seeing her face lighting up brighter than Christmas when she'd gotten that car are shattered like glass. "Don't. You wanted that car so bad. You've done so much to it."

"It doesn't mean shit now, Adam. It was bought with drug money. In case you forgot, you told me you gave all that up a long time ago. You wanted to distance yourself from that life as far as you could. *You* may go backwards, but *I* don't." She returns to the office and slams the door behind her so hard, the wall shelves shake.

I grimace. Her anger is justified, and it's her choice what she does with her car. This is all my fault, and it's up to me to make it right—for real, this time.

And I definitely won't be getting any sleep trying to get Sasha dialed in for Friday.

Chapter 32

In the morning, I get a special delivery of an old 1953 junk hot rod that I'm planning to restore for the classic car show coming up next month in Cottage Lake. It's the same one that Grandpa used to enter—and win—for the past seventeen years, as was evident from the gold trophies lining the high wall shelves around the shop. I feel obligated to carry on his legacy, and even more so to prove to myself that Grandpa didn't make a mistake in leaving his shop to me.

But I have to put that project aside for the moment and concentrate on my current problem. Once the daily shop work is done and five o'clock rolls around, Luke and I close up shop and stay afterhours in the garage working on Sasha. After Cassandra and I had rebuilt the Datsun, I had a good idea of what we'd need for Sasha, but it had taken us four weeks to put that together. Granted, we had started with just the shell, but now… *Two days.*

"I can't believe I'm about to say this, but…" Luke begins, assessing the amount of work that still needed to be done on Sasha. "I think we need to get Jacob in on this."

I frown. It's true, Luke and I won't be able to finish all the upgrades in so little time, and we were still missing parts. If anyone could help, and do it right, it'd be Jacob. I swallow my pride and say, "I think you're right."

Luke takes out his keys. "I'll go get him."

I purse my lips. It's probably for the best that Luke goes instead of me. I was better on the mechanics than Luke, and we needed every moment we had to get Sasha built right. I'm just not sure Jacob and his guys will listen to him. "Okay. If they give you any shit, tell Jacob to call the shop and talk to me directly. He owes me."

He nods and rushes out the back door. Once he's gone, I call Dave pray that I can get a conversion kit and as many parts as I can for Sasha's major upgrades tonight. It's a large order—and an *expensive* order. But no dollar amount will ever come between me and my family's well-being.

It's after four in the morning by the time Luke, Jacob, Preston, Bryce, and I finally finish.

With all hands on-deck, the time it had taken to acquire and install the conversion kit, tires, and other modifications was cut in half. Dave had most of the parts we needed on hand, and amazingly Jacob had been able to fill in the gaps with some of the spare parts the Ninez had. As Luke and I had worked alongside Jacob and his friends, I could sense that there was still a truce between us—and a bit of a mutual respect, at least, from Jacob. I'd explained my dilemma to him, and he was more than willing to help. After all, we shared a common enemy, and the debt that Jacob owed to me was as endless as the universe.

My eyes are heavy, and at this point, my feelings about going home are too muddled to make any sense. Part of me is afraid of facing Cassandra—if we were already married, she would've probably wanted a divorce by now for what I'm planning to do tomorrow. But mixed with the fear is guilt and regret for leaving her alone in her condition, and I couldn't just ignore her.

Jacob plops down in a metal folding chair and wipes his hands on a rag. "Finally. She's ready, man."

I look Sasha over a final time. She's been converted to a rear-wheel drive, has new steering, brakes, tires, and other mods. I hate that I had to do all this to her for one damn race—as well as the serious hole that's burned in my wallet—but this is a matter of saving my family.

"I still can't believe I'm doing this," I mutter, rubbing my hands over my hair.

"I'll tell ya what, man," Bryce says. "She's clean. We did a damn good job."

I wrinkle my nose. "She was never meant to drift."

"Well, now she is," Jacob says. "And you're gonna win, damn it."

"For fuck's sake, man. I don't even know *how* to drift. She might have the parts, but she doesn't have the driver… This is going to be a disaster."

"Remember that story I told you about when I first learned how to drift? It was a stupid dare. I sorta got thrown into the wolves' den. Who knew I'd end up liking it?"

I shake my head. "I'll never like it. None of you guys get it. I'm not racing anymore. Period. After this race, that's it. I'm done. And none of that changes the fact that I don't *fucking* drift."

Jacob shrugs. "Yeah, I get it. Look, don't sweat it. You already know how to drift. You watched me practice my ass off for my big race, remember?"

"Watching and doing are two different things, Jake."

"We got one day left. Let's meet at the industrial park later tonight. I'll get you ready for Friday."

I blink. "You can't possibly think I'm going to master drifting in a day!"

"You can, and you will. Trust me."

I purse my lips. *I can't believe I'm actually going to put my trust in him.*

"You got this, man," Bryce said, shaking his fist. "You *have* to win. Nobody wants the Red Ravens runnin' shit around here."

"All they want is Sasha," I say. "I was willing to give it to them, but they want to stretch this shit out."

"Of course. They want to humiliate you," Preston adds. "Your reputation precedes you."

Jacob quirks a small smile. "It's no secret you're the best driver in these parts. And most, if not all, of the crews are cool with you. And even if they weren't, they respected you. They'd listen. You're essentially the peacemaker. I don't think you realize how much you held together, man… So, of course the Red Ravens are going to try to take you down, break the crews apart, cause chaos—make their own rules. You're the last thing standing in their way."

I exhale a long breath, my nostrils flaring. *Why the hell does shit always have to fall on my shoulders?* I really want to go home and see Cassandra, even if she was most likely asleep and still angry at me. "All right. Fine," I say. "I guess I'll be cramming for this test."

That night after work, I'd spent hours at the industrial parking lot with Luke and Jacob, practicing. Jacob was right—drifting wasn't too hard to learn. I just needed to perfect my timing when I took the curves. Regardless, I'd still prefer drag racing over this. I don't know what people found so fascinating about drifting.

Finally, around three o'clock Friday morning, we call it quits. Returning home so early in the morning, I discover Cassandra fast asleep. I don't bother waking her. Ever since our argument the other day, we'd avoided each other. Cassandra is still pissed at me, and I want to give her space. Watching her sleeping peacefully eases my heart and reminds me why I'm going through all this trouble—she's worth everything.

"It'll all be over soon," I whisper to her as she sleeps, though in reality, it's probably more to myself.

Chapter 33

I tossed and turned for hours, and barely gotten any sleep. Cassandra was already gone by the time I had woken up that morning. The workday went by in a blur, and my mind wasn't at the shop—I couldn't concentrate with that damned race looming over my head.

After work, I popped over to Dim Sum Noodle House to think for a while and get some grub. I was starving all day, but I barely made a dent in my lo mein dinner. *Damned nerves...* At last, I gave up and trudged home.

Finally, it's ten thirty at night. *Time to head out.*

As I grab my keys, I hear the front door open. Cassandra waddles in, wearing her oversized Q&R work shirt. It's the first time in a few days that we'd finally bumped into each other like this. It makes me realize just how much I've missed her. I rush to the living room to greet her.

"Hey, baby," I say. "Long day at work?"

She regards me with an exhausted look in her eyes, and then tosses her keys and purse on the coffee table. She makes her way to the sofa, kicks off her shoes, and eases down with a huff. She spreads her thighs a little in order to compensate for her distended belly, which peeks out slightly beneath the oversized shirt. She looks like she's ready to pop at any minute, but here I am about to do some stupid race with a bunch of punks. I need to be here for her, damn it.

I grit my teeth. *But if I don't show up, the Red Ravens may try and come for her to get to me. I can't let that happen.* "Hey, uh… I need to step out for a bit. You need anything?" I ask her.

She sneers. "There's nothing I need from you."

I sigh. "Look. I swear, this is it. No more. I promise."

She sighs and closes her eyes, rubbing a hand over her belly. "Don't make promises you can't keep, Adam."

"When it comes to my family, and the people I love, I'm a man of my word. Just trust me, please. I'm doing this for us."

Scowling, she turns her head away. "Whatever. Go. Leave me the fuck alone."

I hesitate, then slowly back away from her. *'I love you,'* I want to say to her, but she's already had enough of me. I spin and walk out the front door. I should be here to take care of my family—I'm going to make this business quick.

This is what I get for caring too damn much…

My hands are numb from death-gripping the steering wheel the entire drive to Fife Airstrip. *Where it all began.* The entire area is covered in a sea of tricked-out cars, trucks, motorcycles, and Jeeps. It looks like all the crews—old and new—from Washington and beyond have converged on this one stretch of concrete.

My heartbeat stutters. *Are they all here for Drew or me?* I wonder, spotting many familiar faces as I drive slowly through the mass of cars and people. It's been a long time. I'm probably a forgotten rumor for some of them, despite what Jacob and the Red Ravens seem to think.

Crowds of people scour the area, checking out the cars, playing loud music, smoking weed, and shooting the shit. My headlights shine on a narrow path created by the parked cars, which leads me right to the airstrip's starting line. Spectators ogle my car and wave to me, but I don't acknowledge them.

Among the sea of vehicles, I spot the Ninez's cars parked in a tight group. I don't even know if Luke is here, and right now, I don't care.

The crowd parts for Sasha as I creep closer to the asphalt airstrip. The strip itself is lined with cars purposefully parked to create a winding path lit by hundreds of headlights. Some people sit on the hoods and roofs of the cars, eagerly waiting for the race to begin.

I observe the course and blink. *I have to drift through that?* It's nothing like what I'd practiced nonstop with Jacob all night last night and early this morning. My shitty timing the previous night has got me really worried, now.

I'm fucked…

I slow to a stop at the starting line. A wave of deafening cheers erupts all around me, and all eyes are on Sasha's return after a long hiatus.

Luke emerges from the crowd wearing an LA Kings hockey jersey and a backwards baseball cap. He rushes to the driver's side and raps on the window, a big smile on his face.

Sighing, I crank the window down.

"Man! Look at this crowd!" Luke exclaims.

"Yeah. The question is, whose side are they on?"

Luke gives me a pat on the shoulder and a thumbs up. "Doesn't matter. You know what's up. Smoke Drew's ass." He backs away and heads toward a group of people nearby— Jacob and his crew. He points me out to them, and they all look my way.

I lock eyes with Jacob a moment, and then return my focus to the racing course.

I spot a red Fiero from the corner of my eye driving up beside me, stopping on the line. I shift my gaze sideways. Drew eyes me from the driver's seat and smiles crookedly. He steps out and we're suddenly surrounded by the rest of his red-clad crew.

"Well, well. Adam Anderson…"

That familiar voice sends fire through my bones, and the anger I felt the other day at the auto shop comes roaring back through me. I get out of my car and confront him. "Drew…" I say through clenched teeth.

"Ready to pay up?"

"I don't owe you shit."

He steps closer. "You stole my stash. You didn't think I'd forget that, did you? You had more than enough time to come up with the money. And now… this time… the money ain't gonna cut it." His expression twists into a wicked sneer.

"So I hope you got bus fare, 'cause Sasha is about to be mine. Your reputation is about to be mine, Adam. Your *pride* is about to be mine."

I lift my chin and glare at him. *You ain't taking shit from me.* "What are the rules?"

"Be the first to make it to the end in one piece." Drew gives a clipped laugh, but there's no humor in it.

"That's it?"

"That's it."

I wrinkle my nose. "Sounds easy enough." *A little* too *easy…*

Drew chuckles. "Yeah? Show me, then. Make it to the end in one piece."

I nod once. "This bullshit ends tonight."

"Yeah. It does." Drew gets back in the Fiero. I jump into Sasha and stare straight ahead.

A Red Raven member holding a flashlight hops up on a wooden crate in front of me and Drew, situating himself as both of our cars roar to life.

Drew revs his engine a few times and nods to the flagger. I do the same. Sasha's engine growls.

Adrenaline rushes through my veins, different than the feeling I used to get when I raced. This feels like the same rush I got when Andy and his boy busted into the shop. The same rush as when they threatened Cassandra and our child. I grip the steering wheel and take a deep breath. The faint odor of gasoline and exhaust fill my nostrils. Memories of my friends Clay, Mariah, and Gabriel flash in my mind.

Memories of the look on Cassandra's face when Andy pulled his gun…

The Red Raven flagger flicks the flashlight on once.

Ready. I take another breath.

I stare at the winding path of cars parked ahead. I just have to cross the line first. Jacob had told me about the different types of drifting styles and warned me that Drew had a hard-on for Cat-and-Mouse—letting the other car take a small lead so he could take them out in the turn. That means this shit ain't gonna be easy. After witnessing what Kaine had almost done to Jacob during his race, I'm not going to let Drew do that same shit to me.

The flashlight flicks on again.

Go!

I floor the gas pedal and Sasha roars with the acceleration, the force pushing me deep into the driver's seat. *These Q&R upgrades were worth every penny.* I keep my gaze straight ahead, but I can still see Drew's car in my periphery, keeping a steady distance, but not quite trying to pass me… yet.

I reach the first curve and begin to ease on the brakes. When the needle drops two notches below sixty, I release the brake, whip the steering wheel toward the direction of the curve, and throttle into the drift. My heart sinks to my stomach as Sasha swings, tires squealing. White smoke kicks up around me, and I'm unable to see the path of cars—but somehow through all the noise I can hear the screaming crowd. From out of the smoke, like a looming shadow, Drew emerges. He's drifting straight for Sasha's backend, looking to knock me off the course.

"Shit!" I force the steering wheel as far as it can go, trying to use the sharp curve to my advantage and create some distance. Drew comes around hard and fast. Thankfully, another straightaway approaches in the nick of time. I whip the steering wheel the opposite way and steady the car once more, then floor the gas again to get as far ahead of him as possible. I run Sasha's engine hard, clawing for her top speed, but the short straightaways and sharp turns leave her handicapped. I seem to lose Drew for a moment, but in a blink he's back, trailing a bit beside me again, waiting for the next turn.

I growl. *So, he's gonna play that game, is he?*

Another turn is coming, this time to the right. I ease on the brakes again, preparing to slide into it, but this time I slow a little more to see if Drew is going to follow suit. It's a big risk, because he can either trap me or blaze ahead while I'm creeping around like a scrub.

To my surprise, he keeps up with my pace, sliding in even closer beside me this time. I sink my teeth in my bottom lip and try to ease through the curve, all the while attempting to dodge a dark-red SL-560 that's parked a few inches ahead of the aisle, its nose sticking out like a sore thumb.

Drew's car comes dangerously closer to mine until our doors are almost touching. I've steered as far as Sasha will go. Sucking in a breath, I steer toward the car sticking out ahead and brace for a painful impact.

Fuck. I'm trapped in this gauntlet, just like Kaine had done to Jacob. There's no way to escape without wrecking. *I promised Cass I'd make things right. If I lose Sasha now, will she and the baby still be safe?* Drew had betrayed his *allies*, so how could I trust that he would be true to his word about leaving me and my family alone?

No, damn it. I'm not giving up, no matter what.

The curve turns sharp. Drew oversteers for a second too long and eases away from my car as he tries to adjust. His brief stumble clears a small enough space for me to maneuver over and zoom past the hazard sticking out, avoiding a head-on collision. *Not done yet.* A high-pitched screeching sound of grating metal pierces my ears, and sparks shower against my door as I scrape the front bumper of the rogue car in passing.

Shit! Sasha's damaged, but I can't stop now.

Drew zooms ahead of me this time. Now I have to play catch-up with this son of a bitch.

I glare at his red taillights ahead. *What's his real game?* Either way, I can't let him win.

I flip on the nitrous switch under the steering wheel and give Sasha an extra burst of power for a split second. She catches up to Drew in no time. We reach another curve, but this time, I hug slightly further away from the inside so I can avoid being trapped. Drew seems to have caught on to me though, and he follows my movements, remaining just in front of me. He drifts around the curve with ease, the blur of headlights and the cheering crowd whipping past.

I attempt to cut past him on the other side and sandwich him into the barrier of cars. *Two can play at this game, bitch.* I push closer, slowly closing the gap.

Drew inches nears the wall of cars, and the side of his Fiero swipes a bumper, sending a few sparks showering against his window.

I exhale. The curve begins to straighten, and I punch the gas again, leaving Drew behind in the dust.

Looking ahead, I notice the end of the wall of cars just past the final curve, which is so sharp, it looks damn near like a ninety degree turn. The finish line is beyond. My heart pounds. I'm almost there. I'll be out of this nightmare soon. Cassandra will be safe. I'll have my life back again.

I begin to brace for the curve when a red blur speeds past me. It jumps ahead and veers right in my path. I brake slightly, then try to maneuver around him before he traps me again, but he matches my every move.

He slows down enough to sandwich me between the wall of cars, and then closes in on me fast as we approach the turn. There's a loud thump, and my body jostles.

I glance out the passenger's window. I can't see anything through the Fiero's dark-tinted glass, but I can only imagine the devious smile cut across Drew's face as he attempts to finish me off.

His car rams into mine. I smash into a bumper in the car-wall, and he pins me there and drags me along. A couple of cracks appear in my windshield from the impact. This is going south fast. All it would take is one car edged out a little further than the others to send me cartwheeling, or worse. *The only way out of this is forward...* Gritting my teeth, I grasp the steering wheel and bury my foot into the gas pedal. I flip the nitrous again and burn through all she's got left, trying to speed out of Drew's deathtrap before we enter that hellish curve.

Drew loses his hold on me, but he's still right on my tail as we both slide into the turn. He clips the side of my bumper, the force causing me to fishtail toward the opposite wall of cars. I quickly regain control and yank the wheel straight. Sasha's tires squeal, her back half whipping too far around from my oversteering. She smashes against the side of Drew's car.

"Shit!" I hiss, trying to keep my balance and control as Sasha ricochets off the Fiero. White smoke clouds my periphery from Sasha's burning tires as I desperately try to correct her out-of-control slide. The force of the collision sends Drew's car spinning wildly and veering right into a massive 4x4 truck with monster wheels. Sasha's backend slams into the push bar of an Impala in the wall, inexplicably setting her straight. The Fiero's tires screech, and it crashes head-on into the unmoving—and unscathed—truck, crunching the car like a sardine can.

I watch the disaster unfold in my rear-view mirror, then book it to the finish line. I zoom past the last cars in the wall, screech to a halt, and put the car in Park. For a moment, I just sit there staring straight ahead. My ears are ringing, and my heart can't stop pounding away from my blood-pumping adrenaline.

I... I won?

Leaning my head back on the headrest, I exhale a deep sigh and try to calm the anxious, shaky feeling in my body.

It's not until I hear the growing noise of the crowd behind me that I realize the race is officially over.

It's over.

In seconds, I'm swarmed by the cheering throng. They're smacking their palms on the windows and yelling their victory cries. I remain in the car. Normally, I would be furious that these fuckers are touching Sasha, but I'm too focused on the relief surging through my mind. It wasn't like they could do any worse damage than what Drew had done. I don't even want to think about how bad of shape she is in after that race.

She did good. And as of tonight, her racing days are over. *Going out with a bang...*

I search the crowd for Luke, but I don't see him. There are so many people out here, that at this point, I can't tell who's friend or foe.

"Cops! Cops!" someone suddenly yells.

Like cockroaches, the group abandons my car and scatter in all different directions.

I gasp. *Cops?* I look in my rearview mirror, but I don't see any flashing lights. The Burn Dawgs, who own this turf, most likely have a few hidden lookouts at the airstrip's main entrance.

Drew's car is still crunched against the monster truck's tire. He hasn't gotten out yet, and with the windows tinted it's impossible to tell if he's okay or not. *Don't wish harm on your enemies, or it'll bite you in the ass,* Grandpa used to always say to me when I was a kid. As much as he's made my life a living hell, a small part of me feels inclined to go make sure he's okay. But the scene at the shop from two days ago plays again in my mind, and it's quickly followed by everything the Red Ravens had done to me over the past year and half.

I make a U-turn and drive toward the collision, but not to help. Instead, I'm hoping to find some sign that this really *is* over. The Fiero's window is rolled down—and Drew is alive and well—but the steering column is pressed against his chest and the doors are caved-in. He's trapped inside. *Good.* He'll make a great present for the cops.

A burly guy wearing a green bandanna hops in the driver's seat of the truck and backs away, releasing Drew's crunched car. He speeds out of sight.

I look around to see if any of the Red Ravens come to Drew's rescue, but everyone is scattering to the exits. He's alone. *Everyone's abandoned him,* I muse. Loyalty is out the door now for these guys. Some 'crew' the Red Ravens had turned out to be.

I'm done with him too. *Done with this life.* And I need to leave now before the cops find me.

A set of headlights shine on me and grow larger as I start to pull away from Drew's crunched Fiero. Luke's shoddy Challenger pulls up beside me and we stop in unison. The car's driver's side window rolls down.

"Fuck yeah, man! I told you ya had this! The cops are almost here, though. Follow me. I know another way outta here." He speeds off before I can say anything more.

Behind me, far in the distance, I can make out faint red-and-blue flashing lights. Luke leads me through the forest on the outskirts of the airstrip on a faint dirt path that looks like it's been used occasionally by vehicles. The road is bumpy and just wide enough for our cars. I take a glimpse in my rearview mirror. The police lights and the airstrip are gone, hidden away by the dense forest. I'm not sure where we're going, so I keep my eyes locked on Luke's taillights.

Luke eventually makes a hard right, and soon, we emerge on smooth asphalt again. It's too dark to see anything; there are no streetlights on this road. I've lost my sense of direction, but Luke drives as if he knows exactly where he's going.

We drive for several minutes, then reach an intersection. We turn left, and soon, we're graced by streetlights and civilization. I begin to recognize some of the stores and landmarks in Fife and regain my sense of direction. I know we're far enough away from the airstrip that no one would think we'd have come from there.

Luke pulls into the back parking lot of a 24-hour diner. We park together and get out of our cars. I'm still shaking as my feet touch the graveled ground. I brace myself on Sasha for a moment, then notice a glaring scratch on the side of her door. I grimace. But then I see the rest of her and realize the scratch is the least of Sasha's problems. Her paint's fucked. Her whole body's fucked.

"That was wild, man," Luke says, grinning from ear to ear. "You were *amazing!* You got some serious fucking drifting skills, man!"

I scowl. "It was pure luck. I had no idea what he was gonna do, and I had no idea what the hell I was doing."

Luke shrugs. "The Ravens play for keeps. And you did what you were supposed to do—win."

"Yeah, I won. That means everyone needs to back off me. I'm done racing. I'm done with that life. I got family obligations now."

Luke's smile falters a little. "Yeah, yeah. I get it. Hopefully this is the last of bullshit like theirs in the community. The cops pretty much got the Red Ravens' leader. Maybe they'll trace him back to Oculus X too. With both of those motherfuckers gone, things might be a little quieter around the racing scene again, y'know?"

I shrug. "Maybe. But how long will that last before some other punk tries to take the reins?"

"Hopefully that'll never happen." Luke looks thoughtful for a moment. "I'm gonna have a little chat with Jacob. You may be done racing, but he's not, and he's got everyone's respect after that race with Kaine."

"If Jacob's gonna be the guy he wants everyone to think he is, then he needs to act like a damn leader. He needs to take a more active role in maintaining and policing the community so shit like this doesn't happen again. Fife is Burn Dawgs' territory. If he's smart, he'll hook up with Martin to keep the riff-raff and the guys who want to act like Drew and think they know their shit in line."

Luke raises his eyebrows at that. "You think Jacob would do that?"

That's one thing I'd noticed about Jacob the night he'd won his race with Kaine. He had been transformed into a new man, or maybe back into the one he used to be. The Jacob I used to know—the one I became friends with. The vibe I'd gotten from him was pure confidence—strength. It's interesting how much a man can change after they're put under pressure. Jacob had passed his test. Now, it was time for him to put it all into practice.

"Yeah, I think he would," I finally say with a slight, thoughtful nod.

Luke gives me a skeptical look and remains silent.

"I'm going home, now. I need to be with Cass."

"Yeah, man. Of course. See you around."

I hop back into my car and rush home. Back to my girlfriend, the mother of my child, and hopefully soon, my wife. The emotions of the night have my mind racing with all the sexy things I want to do to her—if she'll let me—when I get back.

When I finally get home, I notice all the lights are off. I don't care if she's asleep. I'll wake her up if I have to. Tell her how much I love her. Tell her I'm a new man now.

I get out of the car and head inside. I maneuver my way through the living room area, anxiously trying to think of the right words to say. A faint sound filters out from the master bedroom, and I pause. I listen again and can hear the distinct buzzing sound of a telephone off its receiver for too long. Then I hear small whimpering.

I rush into the bedroom, thinking we might've been robbed. I flip on the light, ready to kill the bastard who would dare break into this house. I squint a moment while my eyes adjust, and then I see everything clearly.

The phone has been knocked over from the night table, the receiver nesting in a mass of tangled curly wire.

And Cassandra is sprawled out on the floor next to the table, crying and breathing heavily—in labor.

Chapter 34

Time has frozen. I'm paralyzed, and not sure if what's in front of me is a dream, or reality. But the longer I stare at Cassandra writhing, groaning, and breathing hard, the more real everything gets.

I widen my eyes. *Holy shit. The baby's coming!*

"Cassandra!" I rush to her side and take her hand. I try to sit her up and lean her back against the side of the bed. "Say something, please!"

She opens her mouth as if she's about to speak, but only a loud groan escapes. Tears are streaming down her cheeks.

Fuck! What the hell do I do? I feel like such an idiot right now—why am I freezing? My eyes cut to the phone. *Oh yeah. Duh! The hospital.* I lunge for the receiver, and my shaky fingers dial 9… 1…

A loud scream pierces my ears before I can press the "1" button a final time. I drop the phone with a start and look at her. *Oh my God.* She looks like she's dying. She looks back at me, terrified, vulnerable. I rub her shoulders, and make sure she's not hurt.

"Tell me what to do," I whisper to her, trying to stay calm.

She shuts her eyes and lifts a shaky finger toward the discarded phone. Yes, of course. I need to focus and get the dispatcher on the phone quickly.

"Stay there, okay? I'm right here," I assure, grasping for the phone again. This time I manage to dial the three numbers in succession.

"9-1-1. What is your emergency?" A woman's voice answers in a calm tone.

"H-Hello?" I stammer. "I need an ambulance! M-My girlfriend's in labor!"

"Calm down, sir. Has her water broken?"

"Um…" I swivel my gaze to Cassandra.

It seems like an eternity of back-and-forth chatter between me and the emergency dispatcher, all while Cassandra grunts and writhes in the background. The more she explains, the more I realize that the baby will be here soon—and before the paramedics arrive. Miraculously, the dispatcher somehow manages to talk me through the entire process while the ambulance is on its way. But when I finally glance at the clock, only five minutes have passed.

And our new son is born.

I don't know how in the hell this dispatcher knew how to deliver a baby, or how to walk someone through it over the phone, but holy shit, that was some magic.

The ambulance soon arrives, and Cassandra is wheeled away on a stretcher holding our son to her chest. I follow right behind her, and plant myself outside the back of the vehicle with Cassandra and the responders. Staying silent, I watch the paramedics scramble with tubes and beeping machines that they hook up to Cassandra and the baby, who's wrapped in a towel.

Eventually, one of the paramedics circles to the back and tells me where they're heading, shuts the door, and then they speed away with their lights flashing and siren howling. I hop in Sasha and follow closely behind. My mind is blank right now. I feel so useless. I can't help Cassandra or my son, and I'm scared for them both. I've never experienced anything like this in my life. This kind of fear feels far worse than having a gun pulled on me, staring eye-to-eye down its cold, steel barrel.

Far worse than the threat Drew made about coming after my family—at least I could do something about that. This fear hit deep in my soul. I can't lose them.

Is God testing me right now? Some kind of sick trick? I've lived a shitty life as it is. Does He have to rub salt in those wounds? For fuck's sake. I promise on my own life that I will keep my nose clean from now on. No more racing, no more running drugs, no more reckless bullshit...

At last, we arrive at the hospital. I watch the paramedics scramble out of the back of the ambulance and wheel Cassandra and the baby inside as I try to find a parking spot for Sasha. By the time I've parked and made it to the emergency room entrance, they've already disappeared. I spot a set of double-doors labelled 'Maternity Ward,' and head in that direction. I ignore the stares of the patients and the staffs' piss-poor attempts at trying to stop me from passing through the doors and finding their room. These fuckers will have to kill me before I'm separated from my wife and child.

Finally, I'm stopped by a security guard who seems just as tall and twice as hefty as me. He grabs my arm and yanks me back away from the Maternity Ward's entrance doors like a ragdoll. He squeezes my arm, and I can quickly feel my fingers go numb. I grimace.

"Cassandra!" I yell, reaching for the doors.

"Hey! I said calm down!" the guard barks.

I take a few deep breaths. This guy has me good, and I can't escape. "Get your fucking hands off me! That's my girlfriend and son in there!" I say through gritted teeth.

He looks at me skeptically, then gestures to one of the nurses at the station. A woman clad in white and wearing a nametag that says 'Patricia' runs over to us. The guard holds me a few seconds longer before letting go.

"This guy is claiming he's with that woman that just got wheeled through there. You okay with him going through?" the guard asks.

The woman looks me up and down, and then swallows. "Ah... W-What is your name, sir?"

I growl. "It's Adam Anderson. Her name is Cassandra, she just had our baby, and I need to be with them. Now let me through, damn it!"

Her mouth opens and closes, as though she's flustered trying to find the right words. Finally, she nods to the guard.

"Let him through, Gary." She looks at me. "She's in room 7A."

7A. I etch the room number in my mind. "Thanks." I shoulder past the guard, sneering at him, and march through the double doors.

The air in the Maternity Ward is cold and crisp, and I can hear faint sounds of dozens of babies crying from some of the private rooms. Ignoring the stares and glances from several medical staff I pass by, I make my way to room 7A.

I quietly open the door and notice a few nurses and their assistants crowded around a bed. The lights are dimmed in an attempt to create a calm and cozy atmosphere—which would have worked if not for the insistent beeping of the machines sitting beside the bed. I slowly approach the group and peer at the bed.

Cassandra lays there, her eyes closed, while the baby is looked over in a pediatric bassinet. The baby wails, his little face redder than a strawberry. Several tubes, wires, and patches attached to both mother and baby are hooked up to strange machines that beep, whistle, and click. The setup reminds me of a mad scientist's experiment from those old, cheesy sci-fi flicks I've always liked.

I stay out of the way of the medical staff and helplessly watch them do their work. I try to calm my nerves. *These people do this sort of thing all day every day. Cassandra's in good hands,* I remind myself.

Several minutes later, Cassandra stirs and opens her eyes. The baby continues wailing his little lungs out. "How do you feel now, Mrs. Anderson?" one of the nurses asks. Her authoritative voice tells me that she's most likely the one in charge. "You were in shock there for a bit."

I perk up. *'Mrs.' Anderson?* Then, I realize I never gave the paramedics Cassandra's full name, only mine. Of course, they would assume she's my wife. *Soon it will actually be true.*

Cassandra regards the nurse with a slight raise of her eyebrow, as though she were equally surprised by the way the nurse addressed her. "Um. I'm okay. Thanks," she said.

The head nurse smiles, breaking the façade of her imposing demeanor, and carries our baby to Cassandra. "You have a beautiful baby boy here."

A faint smile parts Cassandra's lips, and she gently guides him to her breast. The crying immediately stops, and my ears are ringing from the sudden silence.

The staff finally acknowledge me. One of the assistants gathers a machine on wheels and rolls it out of the room.

The head nurse looks to me and smiles. "Congratulations, Mr. Anderson. He's a healthy boy."

I quirk a small smile. "Thanks."

"We'll give you some private time. The doctor will come by in about thirty minutes." The head nurse motions to the rest of her staff, and they quietly make their exit.

Once we are finally alone, I approach the bed. I stare blankly at Cassandra cradling our son in her arms, the emotions almost too much to process.

Cassandra looks back at me and smiles. "He's beautiful, isn't he?" she whispers.

I stare at the little baby, who continues suckling at her breast. My son. *Our* son. Is he really real? Am I actually a dad? "Y-Yeah… he's perfect," I murmur.

She looks thoughtful. "How about… Xavier?"

I blank out for a moment, and then shake myself back to the present. "Huh? Oh yeah. I like that name… His name is Xavier… If you like that name too."

"I like it," she says, looking back at the baby. "It sounds very… masculine." She winks.

I lean over and kiss her forehead. I can taste a hint of salty sweat from her skin. Seems like she'd had a rough couple of hours. "Are you sure you're okay?" I ask.

She closes her eyes a moment and exhales a deep sigh. "I think I lost a few years off my life after that ordeal, but I'll survive." She gently pulls Xavier from her breast. His eyes are shut, and he seems to be in a deep sleep.

"Well, what do you know, he ate himself to sleep." She chuckles softly.

"That's good, right?" I hold my hands out. "Can I?"

"Of course… 'Dad.'" Smiling coyly, she hands Xavier over to me.

I take him carefully into my arms. He's so tiny. Lighter than a feather. So delicate. In that moment, nothing else in the world matters. Is this how Michael and Elouise felt when they had their first child? If there was ever a time my brother had known what it meant to be truly happy, perhaps it was then.

CHAPTER 35

Three days later, I return to work. Cassandra was itching to go back to work already, too, despite the uncertainty around her job position at Q&R. She had even thought about bringing the kid along, but I had to put my foot down on that. I admire her hard-working ethic, but I care about her too much to let her go back to the job so soon—she hasn't even fully healed from the whole ordeal. Thankfully, she'd listened to me and gave her mind and body a break.

As much as I want to spend every moment with Cassandra and Xavier, I still have a business to run, and I'm afraid of what I'm going to discover since I'd put Luke in charge while I was away. He was no businessman—then again, neither was I.

I just hope the building is still standing, at least.

That goofball son of a bitch surprises the hell out of me when I enter the office and notice the entire place is still in tip-top shape. Aside from a quick phone call the day Xavier was born giving him a heads-up, I hadn't seen nor talked to him since that night of my drift race against Drew.

I ignore the pile of unopened mail that's stacked on the desk and head to the garage area. A Red Hot Chili Peppers song blares from the boombox, drowning out the sounds of light tinkering. Luke is in the first bay, his head hidden under the hood of the '53 hot rod that I plan to enter into the Cottage Lake Auto Show.

The second bay is currently empty, and I'm tempted to park Sasha there so I can work on her. I haven't had a chance to look at all the damage she'd taken from the race, let alone fix her. I'd been caught up in my new family and neglected her. But now that things are starting to get somewhat back to normal, I can work on restoring her back to her pristine glory. I might have sworn off racing, but there's no way in hell I'm gonna be seen another day with Sasha's body looking beat-up, bashed in, and scratched like she'd got run over by a semi-truck.

"Damn, Luke. Maybe you should be the boss around here instead of me," I say, approaching the hot rod.

Luke stops tinkering, pulls his head out from the hood, and grins at me. "Yo, Adam! You're back! Hope you don't mind me working on this. I know it's for your grandpa's car show and all, so I wanted to help out a little, since the event is coming up soon."

"Of course I don't mind. Seriously, man. I'm impressed. I can't believe you were able to run this place yourself."

Luke lets out an airy chuckle. "Yeah. I got lucky. There weren't many new customers that came around in the last few days, so I could just focus on finishing projects, and working on this new one."

I smile. "You really saved my ass. Thanks, man."

"Hey, that's what friends do." He sets down a crank wrench atop the rolling tool cabinet, swipes up a towel, and wipes his hands. "Congrats, by the way—er—I assume she had the baby, right?"

"Yeah." I beam. "A boy. Name's Xavier."

"Nice! So, when'll I finally meet him?"

I shrug. "I dunno. Soon." I glance at the empty bay again. "I need to fix Sasha."

He follows my gaze and frowns. "I thought you weren't racing no more?"

"I'm not. But I can't stand the way she looks."

"Yeah, I know how you feel. You should see what Cammy looks like now." His frown morphs back into a smile.

I quirk an eyebrow. "Cammy?"

"Yeah, my Challenger. Ain't nothing like what you re-member. The new rims and paint on her look *suh-weet.*"

I nod once. My gaze travels to the hot rod—I really should do some work. *I wonder how Cassandra and Xavier are doing?*

"Hey, you okay?" Luke asks, breaking me out of my thoughts.

"Uh, yeah… I, uh… should go through all that paperwork on the desk," I say absently.

His brow creases slightly. "Sure, man."

I turn and head back to the office. My mind is a jumble of thoughts. Between everything with my home-life, work-life, and trying to de-stress from life in general by giving Sasha a facelift, I wasn't sure what to deal with first.

After spending almost an hour sorting through some of the mail—more bills and junk—I eventually take out the Q&R catalog and begin perusing it for parts to get Sasha back into her original drag-racing shape—the way she was meant to be. I write down a small order that will breathe new life into her, but I still need to figure out how I'm going to fix her exterior…

I finish going through the rest of the mail, deal with some important paperwork, stuff envelopes, and get all the out-going mail ready for the mailman to pick up tomorrow. It's almost four o'clock in the afternoon by the time I finish catching up on the administrative stuff. I need to get going soon—my brother and his family are planning to come to the house in an hour to meet Xavier. My mind is exhausted, an-yways. Thank God Luke is here. I'll make sure he gets an ex-tra bonus in his paycheck for coming through when I needed it the most.

I poke my head in the garage. "Hey, Luke, I'm heading out now. Got some family shit to do. Call me if you need me. Don't forget to lock up."

Luke is at the workbench, where one of the hot rod's door panels sits, and steadily scrubs the rust-covered metal piece with sandpaper. "Got it, man," he says, not looking up from his work. "Oh, and hey, let me work on Sasha this weekend.

I'll get her bodywork done and deck 'er out with some new paint."

I raise my eyebrows. "Seriously?"

Luke finally looks at me, a mischievous glint in his eye, and gives me a thumbs up. "Sure. I'll get her looking as good as new again."

I tilt my chin up slightly. "Okay, what's the catch? You want a raise or something?"

"Nah. I just wanna keep my hands busy. I haven't been tagging as much anymore these days. I kinda lost the drive. I'd rather just keep it all in my black book now, anyway."

Damn. Luke no longer interested in vandalizing buildings? Now there's a switch. Maybe I really am dreaming. Or hell froze over. "Uh… okay. I guess if you really wanna work on her, I'll drop her off tomorrow morning."

"Cool… Later, man." Luke turns back to the door panel and continues his sanding.

I leave the shop. Before heading home, however, I make a quick stop at the jewelry store. I had been meaning to stop for months, but one thing kept leading to another and I always ended up forgetting. Today, however, is finally the day I remember.

By 4:25, I'm finally back home. As soon as I walk through the front door, I'm engulfed in the delectable aromas of cooked meat and vegetables.

Cassandra's lounging on the couch in a pair of short-shorts and a tank top watching *The Oprah Winfrey Show* while she breastfeeds Xavier.

I lean over and kiss her cheek. "Hey."

She glances at me, then returns her attention back to the television. "Is the place still standing?"

"Yeah, the son of a bitch kept things going."

She pauses a beat. "I want to go back to work, Adam."

I frown. "Don't start that again."

"Start what? I'm fine, Adam. I can work and still be a mother."

"And what about Xavier? You work all day and he'll never see his mother."

She turns and raises her eyebrows at me. "Q&R allows employees who are new parents to bring their newborns to work. There's even an on-site nursery there. Xavier won't be away from me that long."

I sigh. "Why can't you just stay home?"

Her expression hardens. "And what? Want me to go barefoot too? Make you a sandwich? For fuck's sake, Adam. Get with the times."

"You know that's not what I meant."

"When I said I wanted you to take care of me so that I could take care of our son, I didn't mean it like this. You work to provide for this house. I want to work to provide for our son's future."

"You're already planning for his future?"

"Yeah. I read about it in a parenting book. Anyway, I want Xavier to have a better life than you and I did."

I purse my lips. She already has it all figured out, it seems. I guess I better start reading that parenting book too.

"Not to mention," Cassandra continues, "while you're at work, he's not exactly seeing his father either, is he? You need to be taking care of him just as much as I am. You have an equal stake in this job too, you know. Why don't you bring him down to the shop sometime, huh?"

I blink. "What? The shop is dangerous for a kid. And loud."

She rolls her eyes. "Oh, for fuck's sake, Adam. It's not like he has to be under the hood with you, handing you a wrench…"

"Why are we even talking about this?" I ask.

Her stare turns hard, and her eyes become glassy. "Why? Because I want my son to know his father, since you and I barely knew ours."

Her reasoning stings. "I won't be anything like my father, Cass. Xavier is my world. He'll *always* know his father."

Her face contorts like she's about to cry, but she holds back her tears. "I hope so," she whispers, her gaze dropping to Xavier.

I sweep around the couch and sit with her. "I promise," I say, kissing her on the cheek.

Xavier stops feeding, and I take him from her. "Here. I'll get him cleaned up. Michael, Elouise, and the kids will be here in less than an hour. Why don't you get yourself ready?"

She groans. "Oh, shit. I forgot about the roast in the oven…"

"I'll check on that too. Now go." I cradle Xavier in my arms. His eyes open and close slowly, as if he's fighting the urge to sleep.

Cassandra looks at me carefully. "Are you sure you're okay with them coming over? I mean…"

I tighten my jaw. I don't mind Elouise and the kids, but I'm always wary about Michael. I hope that this new addition to the family might help bring us a little closer together like our trip to Seattle, or at least help him calm the fuck down.

"Yeah, I'm fine with it," I finally say. "He's still family. Xavier deserves to know his uncle."

"Okay…" Cassandra hesitates, then gets up from the couch and heads down the hallway to the master bedroom.

"All right, li'l man," I mutter to Xavier as I make my way to the kitchen. "Let's see what your mom's been cooking…"

I pace around the living room with Xavier asleep in my arms. At 5:10, the doorbell rings. Not a second goes by before three sets of excited knocks follow. I smile, knowing who those knocks belong to. I make my way to the door. "I got it," I call to Cassandra, who's in the kitchen finishing the dinner preparations.

I unlock the front door, and it immediately flings open. My three young nephews come barging in.

"Hi, Uncle Adam!" Kevin and Junior shout at the same time. Dominick, who still can barely talk in complete sentences, tries to imitate the same sing-song voices of his brothers' and mumbles something incoherent.

Cringing, I place a finger to my lips. "Shh! The baby is slee—" at that instant, Xavier starts bawling his little lungs out.

My nephews cower, hanging their heads as though they were guilty of a serious crime.

I let out a sigh and rub Xavier's back soothingly, but it does nothing to stop his insistent crying.

"Oh, what a handsome little man he is!" Elouise says, approaching me. She extends her arms out for him.

"Heh. Yeah. Sorry, he's so fussy." I surrender him.

As soon as she takes him, he immediately goes silent. *Wow, she's got the magic touch. Or maybe it's just a woman thing.* I guess having three boys of her own gave her plenty of practice.

While Elouise admires him, I glance at my brother, Michael, who stands by watching her. His face is blank, unreadable, and I can't tell whether or not he really wants to be here.

Elouise holds Xavier out for Michael. He stares at the baby with a certain coldness that I don't think I've ever seen from my brother. My heart pounds. I suddenly have these irrational thoughts of Michael intentionally hurting my son out of spite for me. Maybe he thinks me inviting him over here—to Grandpa's old house—was some sort of slight against him. I know he's probably still mad about Grandpa's will.

Michael hesitates, then takes the baby from her. He holds Xavier awkwardly in his arms as though he'd never held a baby in his life. After a few moments, Xavier stirs and starts crying again. My heart leaps to my throat. Those thoughts I had earlier return. *Is that bastard hurting my kid?* I take a step forward, balling my fists.

Michael glances at me, then quickly hands Xavier back to Elouise. "He likes you better," he says.

Elouise smiles, taking Xavier and cuddling him in her arms. His crying stops.

I exhale and unclench my fists. I remember Cassandra saying from one of the parenting books she'd read that babies could sense danger. Maybe Xavier is trying to tell us something that we adults can't see—or don't want to see.

I don't think that Michael is a bad person. Yes, he was bitter at the world because he felt like it always treated him like shit, but I think he really does try to do the right thing—fight the good fight. I wish Michael would open up a little more like he did when we all went to the Space Needle as a family.

Maybe he's just afraid to show compassion because he's afraid of being betrayed. I'd felt like that once. But then I met Cassandra, and she totally turned my life upside down.

I shift my gaze back to Elouise, who gently rocks the baby and whispers to him. As if Elouise has cast a sleeping spell on him, Xavier lets out small coos, his eyes grow heavy, and he falls back asleep.

Cassandra finally comes out of the kitchen, all smiles. "Hey, everyone! I hope you all are hungry."

Dinner is amazing. For someone I'd thought was only good at fixing cars, Cassandra is a world-class chef. There's so much food on the table, it looks like Thanksgiving, but somehow, we manage to eat everything. I think my three nephews had more food than all of us adults combined. How in the hell can those little runts eat so much?

We not only eat as a family, but we also chat as one too. Our conversations are civil and positive—it's surreal. We talk about plans for more family outings, places in Washington to visit, and more. We even *laugh* together.

After dinner, we return to the living room and talk some more while the boys take turns holding Xavier. Michael even smiles a few times. All of us act like a real, genuine family. It's something I've missed and longed for since I was a kid and our own parents walked out on Michael and me. It's important that our kids get to see what a real loving family looks like, and not grow up alone and afraid like Michael and I did. I hope this is the start of something amazing for all of us.

"Hey, I got something for you three." I nod to my nephews.

The boys perk up and scoot on the edge of their seats on the couch.

"Ooh! What'd'ya get, Uncle Adam?" Junior asks.

Grinning, I get up from my chair. "Be right back." I rush down to the basement and retrieve a box of some of Grandpa's old things I'd found while I was cleaning it out last Saturday. I thought it would be nice for the boys to keep a piece of their great-grandfather's legacy, even though they never got a chance to meet him in person.

I return to the living room with the box and set it before the boys. "Dig in."

The boys' eyes light up as if it's Christmas Day. They rummage through the box, chatting excitedly and going through each of the items while the adults watch. Even Michael smiles a little.

"This ball looks weird," Kevin says, holding up an old leather basketball that looks like it'd barely withstood the tests of time.

"That's what the basketballs used to look like back in the forties," I explain.

Kevin's eyes go wide. His jaw drops. "The forties! Whoa! That's like a hundred million years ago!"

The adults snicker. Michael presses his hand to his mouth as if he's trying to appear deep in thought about something, but I can tell that he's hiding a big smile.

"It belonged to your great-grandpa, so yeah, it's pretty old," I quip.

Kevin examines the ball some more. "What's this say?" He points to some writing on the ball.

I study the writing, which is actually a signature. My eyebrows raise slightly. "Sodaman Evans…?"

Michael matches my expression. "Sodaman? Wow. He was a famous basketball player for the New York Stellars back in the day. Didn't know Grandpa got his autograph."

Cassandra chuckles. "What kinda name is Sodaman?"

Michael shrugs. "No idea. That was just his nickname."

"Maybe he liked drinking soda?" I say jokingly.

"I like drinking soda," Junior jumps in. He reaches in the box and pulls out a metal, fifteen-pound dumbbell. He grins. "Oh, cool!"

"Be careful with that, Junior," I warn. "It might be a little heavy for you."

"Nah," Junior says, setting the dumbbell down and retrieving the other from the box. He holds the dumbbell with two hands, then attempts to do a bicep curl and grunts. He barely gets halfway before he starts to fall backward with it.

I rush behind him and catch him before he takes a painful landing, then snatch the dumbbell away. The thing feels lighter than paper. "Wait till you're a little older before you start messing with these, eh?" I say to the boy.

Junior pouts. "But I wanna keep 'em. I wanna get strong like a superhero."

"Listen to your uncle, boy," Michael warns in a stern tone, glaring at him.

I quirk a small smile at my brother, then turn back to Junior. "If you want to get strong like a superhero, then you have to do it safely. I'll show you how when you're a little older, and you'll be lifting them in no time."

Junior's pouty face fades, and he looks up at me with hope-filled eyes behind those thick glasses. "Promise?"

My smile broadens and I pat the boy on the shoulder. "Promise."

"Box!" Dominick discovers an old wooden box that says 'Erector' on it. "Box!" he chirps.

Junior opens it, revealing small metal tools, screws and bolts, and strange gadgets. "Wow! They had Erector sets when Grandpa was little?"

I laugh. "I guess they did, huh?"

"It brokened," Dominick says, taking out a metal hexagonal plate with holes in it.

"Naw, it's not broken. You gotta put it together," Junior explains. "It's like a puzzle."

Elouise wrinkles her nose. "Uh... Junior, I think Dominick might be a little too young for that."

I rub the back of my head. "Yeah, your mom is right. Make sure you're helping him with it okay?" I turn my attention to Elouise. "I figured the boys could play with it together—Dominick should be fine as long as his brothers are with him. I just wanted the boys to have something of their grandfather's."

"That was very thoughtful of you." Elouise smiles.

"I wanna fix!" Dominick whines.

I return my attention to the boys.

"You gotta follow the book," Junior explains to his little brother as he holds up a yellowed instruction book.

"I fix!" Dominick insists, then grabs a bolt from the box. He pokes the bolt through the hole of the hexagonal piece and turns it a few times. Afterward, he stops and stares at it a moment, his expression pensive.

I watch Dominick carefully. He was smart enough to put the bolt through the hole. I wonder if he'll figure out how to keep the bolt in place? He appears to be thinking hard on it. He's determined, all right.

Dominick studies the assortment of oddities in the toolbox again. Then he reaches in and grabs a nut. *Damn. Smart kid...* It's bigger than the one he needs for the bolt, though.

"Nut!" Dominick says, holding it up triumphantly. He puts it over the bolt and turns it a few times. After several moments, he frowns and takes the nut off. "Too big."

I smile slightly and watch as he goes through different nuts in the box until he finds the correct size. He screws it onto the bolt and holds up his metal piece triumphantly. "I fix! I fix!"

I raise my eyebrows at him, then look over to Elouise and Michael. "He's only three years old and he knows how to do that?"

"We got him one of those pretend plastic toolset toys for his birthday last year," Elouise says. "It's one of his favorite toys."

"He's really smart," I say.

Michael smiles smugly. "He gets the brains from me."

I snort. *Yeah right,* I want to say, but I bite my tongue. Michael is in a good mood, and I don't want to spoil that.

"Dominick likes fixing things. He *loves* puzzles and building blocks," Elouise says.

"Yeah, brain food, I get it," I say, then rub Dominick's head. "Maybe you'll be a scientist one day. Or maybe an architect. They get paid the big bucks, y'know."

Dominick gives me a funny look.

By nine p.m., Michael and his family leave. I let out a sigh as I watch the taillights of his blue Aries station wagon disappear down the street. What a day.

I step back inside, and Cassandra meets me at the door. "Xavier's asleep," she says with a genuine smile. "That was a nice night with your family."

"It was, wasn't it? Even Michael seemed to have a good time." I put my arms around her and look down into her eyes. The emotions of the night, the feeling of family and love, it all felt—perfect. Cassandra was perfect. "I love you."

She smiles and draws closer, kissing me deeply on the lips. I return the kiss with hungry, earnest need. I've always loved these silent times to ourselves, alone like this. And I better enjoy them while I can, with the baby here.

"You're an amazing mother, and an amazing woman. I love you. So much. And I'll keep saying that until death do us apart."

She chuckles. "You can't say that yet. We're not even officially married."

"Yeah?" I smirk. "Well, I guess we'll need to make it official, won't we?" I pull out a black velvet box from my back pocket with Christian's Jewelers etched in gold on the top and flip it open. Taking a knee, I present a glimmering platinum diamond ring to her.

CHAPTER 36

I HAVE NEVER BEEN MORE EXCITED ABOUT A MONDAY THAN today. Cassandra drives me to the auto shop at seven o'clock in the morning. After all this time, she still forbids me to drive her Hemi. Thankfully, she's finally gotten over being angry with me about buying it with drug money. I'm glad she'd changed her mind about getting rid of the car.

Cassandra parks along the curb, behind Luke's Challenger in front of the shop. I hop out, open the back door, and then unstrap Xavier and take him out of the car seat. Meanwhile, Cassandra retrieves the stroller from the trunk. I secure Xavier, and Cassandra wheels him through the front office door. My heart's racing in anticipation, like a kid eager to open his Christmas presents. After giving Cassandra a quick kiss on the lips, I leave her in the office with Xavier and race into the main garage.

As soon as I open the door, the strong smell of urethane and Turtle Wax socks my senses.

My heart stops. My eyes widen.

Luke is leaned over Sasha's hood, wiping her cherry-red paint in small, slow circles. The paint glistens and reflects every object in the garage like a brand-new mirror. Thin, white racing pinstripes accent the bottom sides of the car, near the front and back wheels. Her bumper and side-panel has been fixed, and I can't make out a single scratch on her. She looks even better than before. She's more than a new car, she's a new *treasure*.

"Ho-ly shit…" I say breathlessly, as I inch closer to the car.

Luke stops wiping, looks at me, and grins. "You like it?"

"You've outdone yourself, man. And you even fixed the bumper!"

"Psh. I needed something fun to do this weekend. The damage wasn't as bad as I thought. I mean, you were really tearing it up during that race."

I frown, the mention of the race drawing up memories I've been trying to forget. "Yeah…"

"Speaking of which," Luke continued. "Thought you might be curious about the latest news."

I swallow. *Not really… But… Were all our efforts worth something, or are things about to get worse?*

"What's going on?"

Luke's smile grows. "Jacob's taken charge now, and Martin's on board with it all. Everyone loves him. He's like a new man now. You'd totally not recognize him. Between Jacob, and the Red Ravens and Oculus X getting driven out of town, the streets have been pretty quiet. There's something going on pretty much every night at all the hotspots—drag and drifting. All the old crews are back together again too. Everyone's racing for the fun of it, just like it used to be."

My frown slowly fades, though the mention of 'all the old crews' gives me pause. *Not* all *the old crews...* "Good to hear. So, the Red Ravens are gone for good?"

"The cops busted Drew that night at the airstrip. Surprise, surprise—he had a warrant. He ended up snitching on the rest of his crew and Oculus X. Ya know, his 'allies.' Wasn't long before all those bastards were picked up."

"Wow, a douche *and* a snitch? Damn."

Luke snickers. "Yeah, but that shit's over now. No drama since."

It does make me feel a little better now that everyone's moving on from me and my glory days with Sasha. This is Jacob's world now. He belongs in it more than I ever did.

I'd raced because I didn't know who the fuck I was. The adrenaline rush allowed me to forget about my own demons. But all that running got me nowhere fast. Those demons knocked the shit out of me—almost made me lose the most important things in my life—but I fought back hard. I came out with a few bruises, but at least I won.

Now I understand what Grandpa meant.

Luke looks beyond me toward the office door. "Cass here? Oh! Did you bring the kid too? I wanna see him."

"Yeah, they're both in there. Cass is about to head off to work with him in a few."

We return to the office. Cassandra is sitting at the desk, sorting through some unopened mail. Xavier is still in his stroller with his head lolled to the side, fast asleep.

"Hey, Cass. Welcome back, and congrats!" Luke greets, waving.

She looks up and nods. "Hey! Thanks. And thanks for taking care of things around here."

"No prob." He looks over at Xavier and his smile broadens. "Wow, is that him?"

Her face softens. "Yeah. His name is Xavier."

Luke walks over and kneels before the stroller, admiring him. "Handsome little man."

I'm half-tempted to tell Luke that Cassandra and I are also engaged, but I'm waiting to see if he even notices her big fat ring first. So far, he's totally oblivious.

Luke gives Xavier another big grin, and then turns his attention back to Cassandra. "Hey, you gotta come check out Sasha!"

Around eight thirty p.m., I return home with a bag of Chinese takeout. I check the wall-mounted mailbox next to the front door. Today's mail is still inside; I guess Cassandra forgot to get it when she got home earlier. I spot the Q&R logo on one of the envelopes and frown. *Must be the pink slip inside...*

I walk inside and discover Cassandra conked out on the couch amid a mass of papers and ledgers from Anderson Antique Auto. Staticky silence plays from the baby monitor. A ballpoint pen dangles from her fingers. I drop off the food and mail in the kitchen and return to her. Smiling, I remove the pen from her hand and kiss her on the forehead. She doesn't stir a bit. Her face is flushed, like she's run a marathon. I've never met a more hard-working woman. In addition to being a mother, and her job at Q&R, she has never stopped being my bookkeeper. *Talk about having a long day.* I pick her up and carry her to bed.

Once I've tucked her in, I peer into the bassinet next to the bed. Xavier sleeps soundly. *My little man.* I give him a kiss atop his bald head, and smile. Every time I look at him, I still can't believe he's my son. Is this what being a father feels like? I can totally get used to this.

I return to the kitchen, about to indulge in my lo mein dinner, when I notice the answering machine's message count is flashing a red '2'. I play the messages back while I set Cassandra's takeout portion in the refrigerator.

"Hey, Adam," Elouise's voice filters from the speaker.

I yank open the utensils drawer to grab a fork, and I halt.

"I just wanted to call and say thank you for inviting us over last Friday." She pauses a moment. "I don't know what happened, but Michael's been a new man and a perfect husband. He's been so happy, and so am I. Maybe it was meeting Xavier for the first time. I don't know. I just know that I have my husband back, because of you. That's all I ever wanted. Thank you again, Adam. Talk soon."

I hit Pause on the answering machine and stare blankly at it. *What was she thanking me for?* I didn't do anything. But I'm glad to hear that my brother seems to have changed his ways. Maybe all he needed was to get out of his old life in New York and live someplace new and different.

Still, I'm glad he's better, and that Elouise is happy. I decide to call her back.

"Hello?" she answers on the second ring.

I smile at the sound of her voice. "Hey. I got your message."

"Oh! Thanks for returning my call."

"I'm glad to hear he's starting to turn things around. I hope this means things will get better for you and the boys."

"Oh, Adam. I had no idea what was going on with him. He was in such a good mood all day today. Then, earlier during dinner, he makes this big announcement about his promotion at the masonry company. He absolutely loves his job. I've never seen him so happy like this before."

My smile falters a little. "So, it had nothing to do with Friday, then, huh?"

She goes silent a moment. "I... I don't know. Maybe it had some part in it. I want to believe it did."

"Well, the main thing is that he's happy. That's all that matters, right?" I say.

"Yes. I would give the phone to him so he can tell you himself, but he's in the shower right now."

"That's okay." I'm a bit relieved that I can't talk to him right now, anyway. I'm afraid him hearing my voice will spoil his happy mood.

"It's all because of you, by the way," Elouise continues in a soft tone. "You're the one who told him about the job—you didn't have to do that... Without you, he would have never had that job in the first place. Now he's quickly moving up the ranks. If it weren't for you, we'd still be back in New York, probably living on the streets."

I swallow the lump in my throat at her last statement, then remember that day I gave Michael the telephone number to Henge Masonry, all because I heard an advertisement for it on the radio. Who would've thought that would lead to something more?

"Hey, you're family," I say. "I'll always help whenever I can. That's what family does. I worry about my brother, but I also worry about you and the boys, too."

"Oh, the boys love you, Adam." She chuckles. "They can't stop talking about you. Whenever we go out, they always ask if they can come see you."

"Yeah? Well, you should bring 'em over sometime. I don't mind."

"Oh, no. Not while you and Cassandra have your hands full with a newborn. You two must be exhausted every day. The boys will wear you out faster than you can blink."

I laugh. "Well, I guess you're right. But I do want to see them again sometime. Maybe on a Saturday? We can make it another family thing."

"That sounds wonderful. I'd love that, and the boys would, too."

We talk a little while longer, then hang up. I run my hand over my face, thinking about our conversation. Maybe everything really *is* cool with Michael. Maybe I can finally lower my wall with him and talk to him again without the fear of starting an argument.

I chow down on my dinner while I listen to the second message. "Hi, Cassandra. This is Holly from Q&R Human Resources. You should've received your letter in the mail today. If you haven't, please give me a call as soon as you can."

I stop chewing and stare at the answering machine. *Letter...* I forcefully swallow my food and swivel my gaze to the stack of envelopes, particularly the one with the Q&R logo. It's addressed to Cassandra. I purse my lips. I don't want to wake her up, but I also want to know what those bastards at Q&R had to say about her in that letter. *Fuck it. I'll deal with her beating my ass for opening her mail.* I swipe up the envelope and tear it open.

There isn't a pink slip inside. Instead, it's several crisp, folded white papers with Q&R letterhead. My hands shake as I read the letter addressed to Cassandra:

Dear Ms. Williams,

We are pleased and honored to inform you that you have been promoted from Sales Associate I to Senior Product and Sales Representative in Q&R Ltd. We congratulate you for your achievement and recognize your hard work and dedication in our company. With this promotion comes new assigned roles and responsibilities that we are confident you will meet and exceed.

The details of your new salary structure, compensation, perks, and benefits are enclosed. For any further questions or concerns, please contact the Human Resources department.

Congratulations, again, on your progress, and we look forward to seeing your future endeavors and accomplishments for our company.

Sincerely,
Holly Tribble
HR Manager
Q&R, Ltd.

I read and re-read the letter. *P-Promotion?* I rub my eyes, just to see if they are deceiving me, but the letter is as real as it gets. My mouth drops open. The letter falls from my fingers and flutters to the table.

I feel like the biggest ass for thinking Q&R didn't value Cassandra.

Story of my life.

CHAPTER 37

CASSANDRA WAS SPEECHLESS WHEN SHE FINALLY READ THE promotion letter the next morning. She'd worked herself so hard the day before and was so stressed about her job that she didn't even bother checking the mail then. But her promotion was well-deserved, and I couldn't be prouder of her.

I'd decided to let her enjoy some time alone to bask in her achievements, while I took Xavier off her hands and brought him to the shop. I still thought it was a crazy idea to babysit a newborn at a noisy, dangerous auto shop, but she was right—I've got a role to play too. And she deserved some R&R.

So here I am, doing just that, while I rebuild an engine on a lime-green '57 Cadillac. Luke is in the other bay, repairing the shocks and rotating the tires on a black '68 Mustang. We had to rearrange the garage a bit to make room for the '53 hot rod that Luke and I had been working on. The restoration was coming along nicely, but once again we had to put the project on hold while we took care of customers' cars.

Despite all the shop noise, Xavier is fast asleep in his pop-up playpen next to the office door, where it was safe and free of any stray car parts or other hazards. The office door is propped open so I can keep an eye out for visitors.

"Dude," Luke says, not looking up from his work, "I still can't believe you brought him here. Alone. Without Cass. I mean…"

"Hey, I'm trying to be a good dad here," I say. "She's been taking care of him a lot more than I have. It's about time I gave her a break. Besides, she got a job promotion recently—she deserves it."

"No shit? Wow, Q&R must really love her."

"Yep. She's at the office now. I'm sure we'll hear all the details soon enough."

"That's great, man. So, does this mean you've got no beef with Q&R anymore?"

I make a sour face. "For now, I don't."

"Does this *also* mean you're gonna accept Collin's suggestion and let Q&R take Sasha off your hands?"

"Ehh… I still want to read the fine print, first. I'm not handing her over to just anyone."

"Q&R ain't just 'anyone.'"

He's right, of course, but I'd been shitted on most of my life, taken advantage of by people I trusted, and even used to the point that I'd endangered the people I loved. I promised myself I wouldn't make those mistakes again. I'd lived too long—and seen and experienced too much—to take shit like this lightly. At this point, Sasha wasn't just a car. She was a part of me.

Lunchtime rolls around and Xavier awakens for his next feeding. Cassandra had left me with everything I could possibly need for him and more in his baby bag, from bottles, to diapers, to wipes. She'd packed ten full bottles, and he'd already gone through three of them this morning. While I enjoy my meager lunch of peanut butter crackers and a can of Coke, I feed Xavier his fourth bottle, which he downs in record time.

Ten minutes before closing time, the sounds of the outside traffic filters into the garage as the office's front door opens. I lift my head from under the hood of the Cadillac and look toward the office. A man in a suit is standing there, looking around curiously. I shut the hood, grab a rag from atop the rolling toolbox and hustle toward the office as I wipe my hands. I glance at Xavier in his playpen before I head inside the office. He's fast asleep.

"Welcome to Anderson Antique Auto, sir. How can I help you?" I ask the suited man. He's tall, slightly older, clean-shaven, and judging by the looks of that leather briefcase he carries, he's most likely dripping with money. Probably a potential new client. Guys with a lot of bread loved to splurge it on classic cars.

The man's piercing, icy-blues stare me down. "Adam Anderson?"

I furrow my brow. "Yes…" I say warily.

His stern expression softens, and then he grins, extending his hand. "Ed Danosky. Acquisitions Manager of the Q&R National Automotive Museum in Bellingham."

I blink. *Acquisitions Manager* "Uh, h-hi," I mutter, slowly shaking his hand. "What can I do for you, sir?"

"Well, Mr. Anderson, I've been down in this area for a few days, and was advised by one of the employees at Q&R's main office that I needed to come to this shop right away to meet a potential business partner."

I get a sinking feeling in my gut. "As in, you want me to hand over my Q&R-dialed-in car?" I say flatly.

Ed laughs. "Absolutely not. I would never ask you to 'hand over' anything. I must say, though, word travels fast around headquarters. There're rumors about an amazing car built almost entirely of Q&R parts. I would love to see this gem."

I give him another once-over. "You got a card?"

"Absolutely." He fishes a business card out of his breast pocket and hands it to me.

I scan the card. *Seems legit. Address, telephone number, photo, official Q&R logo...* I pocket the card and gesture with my head for him to follow. "This way."

I take him through the garage and out the back door to the back alley where Sasha is parked.

"There she is," I say with a small hand gesture. "Her name's Sasha."

Ed's eyes go wide. "She is *amazing*, Mr. Anderson. Absolutely stunning!"

"Thanks," I say.

He walks around the car, studying it like a scientist.

While he's checking it out, the back door slowly opens and Luke peeks out. He regards me with raised eyebrows. "Everything all right, man?"

"Yeah, it's fine," I assure. "Keep an eye on Xavier, will you?"

"Sure thing." He disappears back inside.

I open Sasha's doors and pop the hood so Ed can take a closer look. I'm surprisingly feeling a little excited, but I'm also anxious. All that work I put into Sasha. All those years. I love her. But there has to come a time for me to finally let go of her. Let go of the past. Maybe today will be that time.

I'm a dad now, after all, I remind myself.

Ed peeks under the hood, then looks back up at me, his face awe-struck. "This is incredible. And you built all this yourself?"

"Most of it, yeah. My buddy Luke gave her the new paint job. Q&R brand, of course. Cherry Candy Red, color 1108."

He grins. "Impressive. I see you are truly a loyal ambassador to the brand."

"I trust no one else, sir. Q&R is top-of-the-line for all things aftermarket and custom."

"And what are your future plans for Sasha?"

I shrug. "I don't know yet. She's been good to me all these years. For now, she's just sitting pretty."

"Have you ever thought about her sitting pretty in a museum where thousands of people can admire her?"

I purse my lips. *And there it is. The offer.* "Not really, no."

"Have you ever been to the Q&R museum, Mr. Anderson?"

"No."

"Well, I encourage you to take a trip up to Bellingham sometime and see it."

"Okay. Maybe I will. But what good would Sasha be in a museum?"

"She could be our flagship example car of Q&R excellence," Ed explains. "The gold standard. She shows off many of the possibilities that our products offer. She would be displayed front and center at our museum. I've never seen a car almost *completely* customized with so many of our offered products like this before.

"I truly believe that Sasha would be an inspiration to car enthusiasts all around the world, Mr. Anderson. We showcase some of the greatest and most famous race cars, and other vehicles, from all over the world that use our products. As I mentioned before, the museum gets thousands of visitors a day—including celebrities.

"Furthermore, every time a new piece is added to the museum, we get national news coverage on all the major networks. The Q&R museum has been a popular destination for car enthusiasts around the world for the past twenty-two years."

Twenty-two years… Twenty years after the Q&R company first started, I muse. The idea of Sasha having so much prestige sounds tempting, but I still need to stay vigilant. *What's the catch?* "Okay, Ed," I finally say. "If I do decide to hand Sasha over, what'll be the terms?"

"Well, for starters, you will always remain the original owner of the car and will be credited as such. You are just giving us your permission to display Sasha. We'll create a special display for her that will track each visitor that comes to view it. Being a showcase car, for the first three months, you will earn a one percent commission per visitor, per month."

I nod. It all sounds good so far, and if what he says is true about the museum getting thousands of visitors a day, I could certainly see this being a lucrative business opportunity. "Go on…"

His smile broadens. "Of course, Mr. Anderson. I am prepared to also offer you a one hundred and thirty thousand dollar advance payment for Sasha to be placed permanently in our museum."

My mouth opens slightly. *O-One hundred and thirty thousand dollars plus commissions just for Sasha to sit there and look pretty? Hell* fucking *yes!* I gather my composure and try to maintain a straight face. "That all sounds nice, Mr. Danosky. But I *would* like to see all this in writing, first."

His smile morphs to amusement. "Of course, Mr. Anderson. I wouldn't expect any less from a successful businessman like yourself. I came prepared to make this offer, of course." He opens his fancy leather briefcase, takes out a manila envelope from it, and hands it to me.

I open the envelope and peek at the contract inside. Nothing immediate sticks out to me, but I plan to go over it with a fine-tooth comb before I decide to sign my dear Sasha away. "I need some time to look at this fully before I consider your offer, if that's acceptable." I say.

His cheery expression falters a moment, and then he nods curtly. "Of course, Mr. Anderson. Please take as long as you need."

He's not rushing me. Well, that's a good sign. I scramble to try and remember all the things Grandpa had told me to look out for to determine whether a deal was legit or bogus. "Thanks," I say.

Ed turns and heads for the door back into the shop. "Well, then, I guess we're done here. I do hope you consider my offer. You have my card. I look forward to hearing from you soon."

I follow him back inside and see him to the main exit. After he leaves, I return to the garage and exhale a huge sigh.

"So? Did you do it?" Luke asks. "Did you sell off Sasha?"

I shake my head. "Nah. He did offer a hundred and thirty grand for her, though."

Luke marches over to me, staring wide-eyed as if I'm from another planet. "What in the actual *fuck*, man! Are you crazy? A hundred and thirty grand? How the hell can you refuse that?"

I quirk a smile. "Relax, Luke. I know what I'm doing. I gotta make him sweat a little. That's what businesspeople do." *At least, that's what Grandpa used to do whenever he wanted to get his way.*

He shakes his head. "I still can't believe you, man. I swear, you're either the smartest man in the world, or the stupidest."

I snort a laugh. "I really do need time to think, though. I want to read the contract and make sure I'm not getting screwed over. I want to make sure Sasha's going to a good home and not just sold off to the next highest bidder." *And I need to come to terms with actually letting her go.*

"Okay, I get it. That's smart. Still, though… A hundred and thirty *grand*, man!"

I pat him on the shoulder. "I got this. Now let's close up shop."

Luke rolls his eyes. "Whatever, man." He does an about-face, grabs the push broom in the corner and begins sweeping the shop floor.

Xavier suddenly starts crying. I perk up and haul my attention to the playpen. I recognize those cries. He's hungry… again. I pick him up and take him in the office.

I grab bottle #5 from the mini fridge against the wall behind the desk and warm it up in the microwave sitting atop the fridge. I give Xavier the bottle and watch him go to town on it. *How in the hell does a kid this small eat so much?*

The office phone rings, and I hesitate. I glance at the desk clock—one minute left before the shop officially closes. There's always that one customer who sneaks a call in before then. Sighing, I do a one-handed balancing act with Xavier and the bottle, and then reach for the receiver with my other hand. "Anderson Antique Auto. Adam speaking," I answer.

"Adam, it's me," Cassandra answers, her voice sounding unsure.

I smile at the sound of her voice, despite her hesitant tone. "Hey, babe. What's up?"

"Let's get married. Right now."

It takes me a moment to comprehend that. Then, I do a double take. "W-what?"

"You heard me. I want to be your wife—officially."

I swallow a lump in my throat. Surely, my ears are deceiving me. *Like... right now?* I wonder, as I try to understand her words.

Xavier starts crying again. I look down and notice he's finished his bottle. Those aren't hungry cries, but he's irritable. *Probably from wolfing down that bottle.* "Uh..." I try to answer Cassandra while I hold Xavier over my shoulder. His little belly is bloated and tight.

"So, are we getting married or what?" Cassandra persists.

I gently pat and rub Xavier's back while I try and focus on her question. "Uh, s-sure. What suddenly brought this on?"

"We've only been together a little over a year, and yet so many great things have happened in my life. I want nothing more than to be your wife, Adam. Till death do us part."

I smile slightly. "Okay. So... we're doing the courthouse, then?"

"Yeah. I don't need some fancy, expensive wedding just to say, 'I do.' I love you, Adam.'"

My smile broadens. "I love you too."

"Let's do it. Adam. Right now. Today."

I can't help but laugh. "The courthouse is closed now, but we can do it first thing tomorrow morning, okay?"

There's a brief pause. "Okay. I had told my job I was getting married soon, and they're letting me take that day off. So, I guess it's tomorrow, then, huh?"

"I guess it is."

"I love you, Adam."

"Love you, too, Cass." I hang up the phone and stare at it a moment. My heart swells. She must've had a *really good* day today. That promotion must have been even better than what the letter had said. *I'm so proud of her.* And I sure as fuck can't wait to marry her tomorrow.

Xavier suddenly lets out a loud burp, and I haul my attention back to him. He seems content now, so I return him to his playpen in the garage and then help Luke clean up.

"Hey, Luke. We're gonna open the shop a little late tomorrow," I say, putting stray tools back in their respective places in the rolling toolbox.

Luke wraps a long extension cord of a caged work light and hangs it on the wall with the others. "We are? Why? What's going on?"

I smile at him. "Cassandra and I are getting married, and I need you there as a witness and my best man."

Chapter 38

The next morning, Cassandra and I got married. It was short, sweet, and official. Luke was there as both a witness and "best man," and Cassandra had found a notary in the courthouse to be our second required witness. By nine-thirty, Cassandra and I were out of the courthouse as official newlyweds.

Cassandra had wanted to be with Xavier during her day off work, so I took them both back home before I headed to the shop. Then I'd called Ed Danosky and told him my decision.

Just before lunchtime, Ed had stopped by. I'd already had the contract signed and ready for him. I'd gone over it the night before—Ed was legit, as was the contract. Sasha would be in great hands. Between the marriage and letting Sasha go, it felt like I had officially closed the door on my old life. I didn't need Sasha to hold on to all those memories, and if I ever *did* feel nostalgic, I knew exactly where to find her.

It's one o'clock, and Luke and I are back to work on the '53 hot rod for the classic car show coming up in a week.

The office door opens, and an older man walks in. He wears a navy-blue polo shirt and khaki pants. It's Mark Thatcher, one of Grandpa's close friends, and his partner for the annual car show since the beginning. He was devastated when I had told him the news of Grandpa's passing. But he was more than willing to partner with me and continue their tradition of competing in the Cottage Lake Auto Show, as if Grandpa had never left. This '53 hot rod was more for him than me.

Ever since Grandpa had opened the shop in Washington, he and Mark had had a long winning streak at this particular show. The winnings consisted of a big trophy and a ton of money—Grandpa never cared about the money, so he took the trophy instead.

I'd never known about Grandpa's relationship with Mark until only a few months ago when Mark had come by the shop. It was as if Grandpa had been hiding him from me. The two of them were good friends, like brothers. Kind of like me and Luke.

I smile and wave to Mark from the garage. "Hey, come on in."

Mark grins and joins us. He slowly walks around the car, admiring the work Luke and I have done so far. She's looking good, but there's still a lot more to do before the show. Together, Luke and I make a great team to carry on Grandpa's legacy.

"It's coming along nicely," Mark says.

"It'll be a winner for sure, once I apply the paint," Luke says, giving him a thumbs up.

"I'm still waiting on a couple of parts to arrive in the mail so I can finish putting together the manifold," I explain to Mark. "But she'll definitely be ready well before the show. I'll make sure of that."

Mark nods. "You've got that same spark of determination that James had. I don't doubt you one bit. I just wanted to stop by and let you know that I got all the registration and logistics done. She's officially entered. I'll drive her up there the night before, so no worries on that end. You're going to come to the show too, right?"

I rub the back of my head. I'd never been interested in classic car shows, and any time Grandpa had gone to them I was always out street racing with my friends. "Uh, I'll try and get out there, if I can get away from the shop."

"I hope so. Your grandfather really loved it," Mark says wistfully. His eyes dull a moment, and then he turns to the exit. "I'll leave you both to it, then. I'll be in touch again soon."

I watch him leave, and I get a guilty feeling in my gut. I *have* to win this for Grandpa. I'll put every ounce of my effort into this project.

For him.

Around 3:15, the office phone rings. I abandon the hot rod and rush out the garage to answer it.

"Hey, Adam…" Elouise says in a lackluster tone.

Smiling, I relax in the desk chair. "Hey. How's your day going?"

She sighs. "Not so good. Junior broke his glasses while he was sparring in Tae Kwon Do class yesterday, so I'm on my way to the optometrist to get him some new ones."

"Oh, man. That's gotta be, what? The fifth pair this month?"

"Tell me about it. I keep telling him to be careful, but he doesn't listen. He's been getting really aggressive lately too."

I frown. I was aggressive at his age, but the situation was different. Unlike me, Junior had a home and a family that loved him. What could possibly be triggering his aggression?

"But…" Elouise continues. "What I really called about is that… I… I don't think we'll be coming to visit this weekend…"

"What? Why not?" And here I was hoping to see them all again, especially Dominick. I had plans to bring him to the shop so he could see all the 'cool tools.' That boy would probably feel like he was at Disneyland.

"It's Michael. He's… irritable again," Elouise mutters.

I deflate with a sigh. "What happened now?"

"I don't know. He won't talk about it. I suspect it's something with his job. I really wish he would talk to me. He just keeps it all to himself. And he's been snapping at the boys too…"

I clench my jaw. I guess that explains where Junior's aggression was coming from. *Damn it, Michael.* "Look. If you ever just ever need to get away for a while, you know you can always come stay at the house."

"Thank you, Adam. But I need to be here for my husband. He's troubled, and the last thing he needs is to be alone. I need to be a good wife to him. I love him."

Her words sting a little. She loved her husband unconditionally, despite the fact that he treated her like shit sometimes. "Yeah," I say in a choked-up voice. *He doesn't even realize how damn good of a wife he's got.* "Hang in there, okay? Call me whenever you want."

"Thank you. I will."

We hang up, and I exhale a deep sigh. It bums me out that I won't be able to see my nephews this weekend, just because Michael decided to be a fucking ass again.

Being unable to rescue my brother from his demons leaves me feeling helpless…

I trudge through the front door at six-thirty in the evening. I'm immediately engulfed in the mouthwatering aroma of chili as soon as I enter the house. I beam. Cassandra's chili is always out of this world.

"Damn, smells good in here," I say, following my nose to the kitchen where my beautiful wife stands at the stove.

She holds Xavier in one arm while she uses her other hand to stir the pot of chili with a wooden spoon. She looks over her shoulder at me, smiling.

I lean in and kiss her cheek. "Enjoy your day off today?" I ask.

Her smile widens. "It was the best." She shakes the excess chili from the spoon and covers the pot.

I kiss Xavier atop his head. He squirms and fusses. "What? You're not happy to see your ol' man?" I pout.

Cassandra chuckles. "I bet you're hungry," she murmurs to the kid, carrying him off to the kitchen table.

"Of course he is," I say, rolling my eyes. "He's *always* hungry. Seriously, I don't know where the hell he gets that appetite."

"His father, naturally," she quips.

"Hell no. I don't eat *that* much," I protest.

"Have you seen our grocery bill lately?"

I grumble under my breath.

She gives me an amused smile, then lifts one half of her shirt and brings Xavier to her breast. His fussiness comes to a halt. *Ain't nothing better than that magical titty-milk.*

Meanwhile, I fill a big bowl to the brim with Cassandra's awesome chili.

"Hey, baby," she says as I sit down across from her. "I have some news."

I stiffen, noting the slightly troubled look on her face. "Good news, I hope?"

"I don't know what you'd call it." Her gaze flicks back to Xavier.

"Well tell me what it is, and I'll decide." I begin chowing down on her delicious chili. *Holy fucking shit* it's an orgasm on my taste buds.

She goes silent. "It's about that promotion…"

"What about it?"

"Well…" She swallows.

"Well?" I repeat, my mouth full. I've cleaned this bowl of every incredible drop in record time.

Cassandra looks back at me, her gaze rigid. "This new job entails travel—lots of it. For the first five years or so, it'll be based in and around the Seattle area. Afterwards, my travels will get a little further. National. Eventually, if things go well… I'll be traveling globally, which means I won't be home every day of the week."

I swallow the last bit of chili as I take a moment to think on her words. "It sounds like you'll be away from us a lot…"

"Not until I reach my ten-year mark in the position. I'll be promoted to International Liaison then, in which case I'd be traveling to other countries."

"How long would you stay in these countries?"

"Not long. A few days at most, maybe. I would only be travelling to the satellite headquarters in each of the five countries they operate in."

A small tightness forms in my throat. Ten years was a long time before she would be travelling internationally, but it would come faster than I could blink. "What does this mean for our family? For Xavier? Is he going to grow up barely knowing his mother?"

She shakes her head. "Of course not. I'll be there for him. Always. I negotiated with my boss to only send me on these global trips no more than three days a week. He seemed fine with it. Granted, he gets to pick which days I travel, but I was willing to accept that in order to be able to be with my family more."

I frown, noting the hint of certainty in her voice. *Does she want to be away from her family?* "You make it sound like the decision is already made. Have you stopped to wonder how I might feel about you being away for so long?"

"Yes, which is why we're sitting down here talking about it. I don't want to be away from my family any longer than I have to be, but I also want to pull my weight around here—as your wife, and Xavier's mother. I'm not doing this job for me, Adam. I'm doing it for our son. I'm going to fund his college… Make sure he's well-off by the time he's our age. I want to make sure he doesn't grow up hard like we were forced to do."

I exhale a deep sigh. I can't fault her for trying to be a good mother. All I can do at his point is nod. "Okay. I'll support whatever you do. But come back to me, please."

She smiles at me. "You never have to ask, Adam. I'm yours forever." She looks back at Xavier. He's gorged himself, and now he's fast asleep.

The kid may be full, but I'm sure as hell not. I get up from the table and help myself to another filled-to-the-brim bowl of that addicting chili. As I sit, Cassandra bursts into giggles.

"What's so funny?" I ask.

"Like father, like son."

Chapter 39

Two weeks pass. Cassandra has been getting used to her new position. I can't say I was thrilled about it, knowing she would eventually be traveling out of the country on these business trips. But this job was something she had always wanted, and I was happy to see her finally achieving her dream. For now, I've made it a point to spend as much time with her as I could, spoiling her like the queen she is.

As an incentive for accepting her new position, she was given her own company car—a brand-new, black '91 S-Class Mercedes, decked out with Q&R's logo and blue-and-purple racing stripes along the sides of the car. It was fucking sweet.

Cassandra was a superwoman: being a wife, mother, and career woman. She had her shit together. Compared to over a year ago when I'd first met her, she was an entirely new person.

And so was I, thanks to her.

It's Friday morning, and Luke and I are working on restoring a customer's pink '57 Bel-Air convertible. I'm rebuilding the engine while Luke does the paint job.

Light glints off the brand-new gold trophy displayed with the others on the high shelf. I smile, remembering that great day at the Cottage Lake Auto Show last week, and the look on Mark's face when the judge announced our hot rod as the winner. Mark was moved to tears, and I almost was too. Grandpa wasn't there, but I felt his presence. I was glad I hadn't failed him.

I'm babysitting Xavier again today. I'd been bringing him to the shop a lot more this week, now that Cassandra had started her frequent travels in and around King County.

I'm going to have to look for another bookkeeper *real* soon. The paperwork is getting out of control. I miss Cassandra's organization skills.

The office phone rings. I throw down the lubricant-smeared towel and rush out of the garage to answer it.

"Hi, baby," Cassandra's voice filters through the earpiece.

Hearing her voice always soothes me, no matter how stressful my day's been. "Hey, how's work going?"

"Fucking amazing. I'm in Bellingham right now. And guess what I saw?"

"Surprise me."

She snorts. "Duh! Sasha! I'm at the Q&R museum!"

I clench my jaw. Ever since I'd watched Sasha get towed off last week, I was trying my damndest to finally get over her. I thought it would be easier when I signed the paperwork, and, for the first couple of days, it was. But now, after a week, I felt like losing her really *was* like losing a piece of my identity. Nothing had felt the same since. Not only that, it left me without a car, and I had to rely on Luke to bring me to work every morning. It was pathetic. I'd shopped around for another car, but nothing felt right. Nothing felt quite like Sasha. She was perfect in every way. *And now, she's gone.*

"What does Sasha look like now?" I dare to ask, my heart aching as I think about what Ed Danosky has probably done to her. *Maybe re-upholstered her seats, changed her tires, stripped out her nitrous system…*

"She looks the same. Nothing on her has been touched. Holy shit, Adam. You have *got* to take a trip up here sometime and see this place for yourself. I can't even begin to explain how epic it is. There's this *huge* enclosed courtyard inside the museum. And situated right in the middle is a roped-off display with Sasha.

"At the right time of the day, when the sun shines down on her from the skylight, it lights up her gorgeous paint and all of her Q&R innards. It looks like some kind of heavenly light from above. It's beautiful, Adam. I think I finally understand why you were so attached to her. She really is beautiful to look at. I took lots of pictures. I'll get them developed before I head home tonight."

My cheeks hurt from smiling so hard, as I feed off Cassandra's excitement and enthusiasm. Sounds like Ed preserved Sasha as I'd hoped. I'm glad that car has a new purpose now. "That's great. I can't wait to see the pictures. And I'll definitely have to take a trip up there at some point."

"We'll go together. We'll make it our long-awaited honeymoon."

I grin, thinking about all the times she and I spent alone together.

On Sasha's hood.

Fucking like rabbits.

"I can't wait."

Friday night, Cassandra and I lounge on the living room couch with the television on. Xavier is in his pop-up playpen next to the couch, cooing while he gums a stuffed, plush race car toy. The cheesy, old black-and-white sci-fi flick on television provides background noise while I busily sift through the endless glossy photos of every detail, angle, and inch of Sasha on display at the Q&R museum. I can't stop smiling. Sasha isn't just some random display piece. She is *the* face of Q&R!

"I've seen it, and I still can't believe it," I say, going through the photos for the tenth time.

Cassandra chuckles. "Believe it. Maybe now you can finally let go of her, knowing she's gone to a much better place."

"Yeah…" I sigh. *Damn it. Why does she always have to be right?*

"I love my job, Adam. I love my family… I love… I love my *life*. I never thought I would ever say that."

I look up at her and grin. "I love you too." I emphasize the point by stealing a kiss. A deep, passionate kiss on her beautiful lips.

I feel her smile, and then she slowly pulls away. "Adam, I really am grateful that you've been so supportive of my choice."

"Hey, you more than deserve this. I'm happy for you. I hope—no—I *know* you will go far."

She lets out a hollow laugh. Then her face turns a little more serious. "You think one day I might move up to an executive position there?"

"Hell, at the rate you're going, I wouldn't be surprised if they made you president of the company."

She purses her lips and tilts her head. "Is that what you want?"

I shake my head. "It's not about what I want. This is your choice. Your dream. What do you want?"

She goes silent a moment, and looks toward the playpen. Then, she picks up Xavier and cradles him in her arms. "I want to be with you and Xavier."

"And knowing you, you'll find a way to make it happen and still do all the amazing things that you already do." I lean in and steal another kiss. "Babe, you're destined for greatness, and you deserve only the best." I shut off the television and set the remote on the coffee table. I rest my head on her shoulder and gently stroke the fine hairs on Xavier's head while I stare at him adoringly. He looks back at me with his big brown eyes.

Sasha and I had a good run. We made a lot of great memories. But those memories will never compare to the new ones I'm making now with my beautiful wife and son.

About the Author

Marie Long is a novelist who enjoys the snowy weather, the mountains, and a cup of hot white chocolate. She's an avid supporter of literacy movements like We Need Diverse Books (WNDB) and National Novel Writing Month (NaNoWriMo). To learn more about her, visit her website: www.marielongauthor.com.